The Loving Cup

WINSTON GRAHAM was born in Lancashire, but when he left school his parents moved to Cornwall, where he lived for thirty years. His novels have varied from taut suspense novels of today to works of historical fiction, and have been translated into twelve languages. He is particularly well known for the Poldark books, of which the first seven were made into the celebrated television series of twenty-nine instalments by the BBC. Of his other books six have become feature films for the big screen, most notably *Marnie*, which was directed by Alfred Hitchcock. His latest television production, a six-part serial of *The Forgotten Story*, received a silver medal at the New York Film Festival. Winston Graham is a Fellow of the Royal Society of Literature, and was made an OBE in 1983.

Charles Vivian Raffe POLDARK (1667-1708)
m. Anna Maria Trenwith (of Trenwith) (1680-1758)

Agatha Mary (1697-1795)   Claude Henry (1698-1748)   Mary Ellen } died
                            m. Matilda Ellen Peter (1699-1756)   Robert   } young

Maria (1717-79)   Charles William (1719-86)   Joshua (1724-83)
m. Alfred Rupert Johns (1719-81)   m. Verity Michell (1740-73)   m. Grace Vennor (1740-70)

Rev. William Alfred Johns (1744-)
m. Dorothy Grenville

many children

                            Charles } died
                            Claude   } young
                            Robert   }

            Francis (1760-92)
            m. Elizabeth Chynoweth (1764-99)

Verity (1758-)   Claude Anthony   Ross Vennor (1760-)
m. Andrew Blamey (1748-)   (1764-71)   m. Demelza Carne (1770-)

Andrew (1793-)   Geoffrey Charles   Julia   Jeremy   Clowance   Isabella-Rose   Henry
                  (1784-)   (1788-90) (1791-) (1794-)   (1802-)   (1812-)
                  m. Amadora de
                  Bertendona

- -

Tom CARNE (1740-94)   Luke WARLEGGAN (1715-1800)
m. Demelza Lyon (1752-77)   m. Bethia Kemp (1716-44)

                                 Nicholas [of Cardew] (1735-1805)
Demelza (1770-)   m. Mary Lashbrook (1732-)
Luke (1771-)
Samuel (1772-)   Cary Warleggan
William (1773-)   (1740-)
John (1774-)   George (1759-)
Robert (1775-)   m. (1) Elizabeth Poldark (née Chynoweth)
Drake (1776-)   (1764-99)
                                     (2) Harriet Carter
                                 Valentine (1794-)
                                 Ursula (1799-)

WINSTON GRAHAM

The Loving Cup

A Novel of Cornwall
1813-1815

FONTANA/Collins

First published by William Collins Sons & Co. Ltd 1984
First issued in Fontana Paperbacks 1985

Made and printed in Great Britain by
William Collins Sons and Co. Ltd, Glasgow

TO MAX, DOMINIC AND ANTHEA

Book One

Chapter One

I

On an evening in late June 1813, His Majesty's Packet Ship *Queen Charlotte*, Captain Kirkness, master, slid into Falmouth harbour, the long hull scarcely disturbing the water, the evening sun making angular haloes about her lower topsails as they were lifted and furled. She did not immediately make for her anchorage in St Just Pool but stood off at the entrance to Penryn Creek and lowered her jolly boat to transmit passengers and mail ashore at the nearest point to the land. As she came in she had passed and exchanged greetings with one of her sister ships, *Queen Adelaide*, which was leaving as usual on the Friday evening tide on passage to Lisbon. *Charlotte* reported an eventless voyage and wished the same to *Adelaide*. In these days when Biscay was infested with French and American privateers, it was not just a conventional interchange.

Of the six passengers, two climbed down into a smaller boat, which would take them direct to Flushing across the creek. Captain Kirkness, who also lived in Flushing, like many of the other Packet captains, sent word with the travellers to tell his wife he would be home in a couple of hours.

The last of their luggage was settled into the stern, and the sailor began to row them towards the sheltered brick and slate-hung village which unlike Falmouth faced the declining sun. As the boat was rowed over the glassy water it left little spreading goose feathers of motion in its wake. The passengers were a man and a woman. The man, tall and thin and quite young, was wearing the uniform of an officer of the line: it was anything but a parade uniform, being stained and worn, with faded lapels and a repaired sleeve. His blue eyes showed up vividly against his sunburnt face; a thin moustache above a tight mouth, a dent in his lower jaw; as he helped his companion down into the boat it seemed he could not open his right hand to its fullest extent.

The woman was small both in build and in stature, though it was his height which emphasized this. She was wearing a grey travelling cloak of which the hood had fallen back; she had no need of the hood for warmth, and the breeze blew her black hair about her face in graceful wisps. She was good-looking rather than pretty with a rather long pear-pointed face and brilliant young eyes which took in everything about them. As they were rowed ashore the officer was pointing out one landmark after another. He spoke in broken Spanish.

The tide was slip-slopping gently against the quay as the sailor came in and loosed and re-looped another rowing boat so that they could run in alongside the weedy steps. The young officer pointed out to the girl that as the tide was falling the lowest two out of the water would be slippery. She nodded. He added something else, also in Spanish. She laughed and replied in English: 'I remember.'

Presently they were both on the quay with their luggage, and she was standing looking about, one hand to her hair; he tipped the sailor. There were lobster pots on the quay, a few coiled ropes, a seagull padding in their direction hoping for fish, an upturned cart, two boys of about twelve staring.

'Byertiful,' said the girl.

'Beautiful,' said the young man smiling at her.

'Ber-youtiful,' said the girl, smiling back.

'Stay here with the cases, my little, just two minutes while I . . . But perhaps these lads . . . Hey, my son, which is Captain Blamey's house? Know you that?'

The boys stood staring, overcome by the responsibility of

speaking to strangers; but just then a small man in a blue jersey and tattered serge trousers insinuated himself from behind a drapery of nets.

'Cap'n Blamey, sur? Yes, *sur*. Fifth 'ouse on left, 'e be, sur. You be goin' thur? I doubt 'e's 'ome. But Mrs is. I see Mrs go in scarce 'alf an hour gone. Carry your bags, shall I?'

A dozen people were in the street they turned into; horses clattered over cobbles; a girl was selling fish; two puppies rolled in the gutter. The packet had not of course come in unobserved; she had been spotted from Falmouth when miles out at sea, watched all the way in. The only surprise to the watchers was that two of her passengers should choose to land at Flushing instead of at Falmouth. They must have been cleared through Customs and Quarantine while still on board.

A green front door almost as square as tall, with a brass knocker and a glass fanlight; a climbing rose, hipped after its flowering season. Then a fluffy-haired girl in a pink lace cap and apron.

'Mrs Blamey? Yes, sur, who sh'll I say 'ave called?'

'Captain and Mrs Poldark,' said the young man. 'Captain and Mrs Poldark junior.'

As they were ushered into the low hall a white-haired fresh-complexioned woman was coming down the pitch-pine staircase. She stopped and stared and gave a whoop of joy.

'Geoffrey *Charles*! I – never expected! Tell me I'm not *dreaming*!'

He was up three steps to embrace her. 'Aunt Verity! I believe this is part of a special dream we have all had . . . You look *well*!'

'How did you? – But this – this is Amadora. My dear . . . What joy this gives me! Welcome, welcome!'

Amadora was similarly embraced, smiling briefly, but did not kiss the lady back, being unsure of the etiquette of the meeting.

Talking, chattering, laughing, the two Poldarks led the Spanish girl into the parlour, and conversation was continuous between them, each wishing to ask as many questions and to make as many answers in the shortest possible time. They had come home unexpectedly, Geoffrey Charles explained, so there was no time to write and give due notice. The battle of Vittoria, when Napoleon's armies had finally been flung out of Spain, had been about to begin when, annoyingly, he had been wounded yet again: in the chest this time, and not serious, but a fever had set in and he had been laid low all through the stirring events of that glorious victory. Then the surgeon had made matters worse by saying no more active service for at least three months; so, as soon as the injured man was fit to travel, he had returned to Ciudad Rodrigo to rejoin his wife, and as soon as she was ready to leave they had taken the packet from Lisbon. They planned to spend six weeks in Cornwall, perhaps more – it depended how the war progressed – but it seemed the perfect opportunity to show Amadora something of England and at the same time to allow his relatives to meet his wife.

Seeing the girl smiling much but saying nothing, Verity said: 'Does Amadora speak English?'

'She understands *everything*,' said Geoffrey Charles, 'so have a care you do not praise her too highly. And she speaks to *me*. Indeed we made a pact that as soon as she stepped on English soil she would speak only English to me. Did we not, *querida mía*? She is a thought bashful in expressing herself freely to a stranger. Something ties the tongue. But she learned the basic elements at school, and has had a good deal of practice in the six months since we were wed!'

'Except you will be away so long,' said Amadora.

'You see? When I speak Portuguese or Spanish I hesitate and worry about my tenses. But she does not and so becomes ever more fluent.'

'Tenses?' said Amadora. 'Who is she?'

'No rival, my loved one. Is she not beautiful, Verity? I cannot imagine why she ever consented to be my wife, but so it is, and I have to show her to you first of all.'

'So you must stay tonight at least. Stay just as long as ever you wish. Young Andrew is at sea. My Andrew will be home

8

within the hour and will be delighted.' Verity hesitated. 'Of course . . .'

Geoffrey Charles fingered the crevice in his jaw. 'Of course my own home is only twenty miles away, and my foster home a bare six. Therefore it is more fitting . . .' He stopped and smiled. '. . . that we should stay with you. What would I find at Cardew? Is Valentine? . . . He won't be home from Cambridge yet, will he? And I have little fancy for my step-father. Do you know his new wife?'

'I met her once, quite by accident. She is very distinguished looking.'

Patty brought in canary wine, and a glass was poured for each of them.

'You will be tired, my dear,' said Verity to Amadora. 'You would like to go to your room?'

'No,' said Amadora. 'Not tired. Not so. Have you wish private conversations?'

'Not at all, my little,' said Geoffrey Charles, putting an arm round her. 'Taste this. You will find it good. But not so good as your father's port. That was – *délicieux* . . . No, we are not fatigued, Verity. It is splendid just to talk. What time do you sup?'

'Oh, about nine. Or it will be so tonight. You asked after your step-father's marriage.'

'Casually. I fear I am not emotionally involved. I suppose I wish George no great ill. He was faithful to my mother's memory for twelve years, which is more than can be said of many a worthier man. In some way I was never able to understand, they were – fond of each other. I was never able to comprehend it, I suppose, because I so greatly disliked George. He did not fit into my father's place. He had no breeding, no instinct of gentility. Money to him has always been the right hand and the left hand of behaviour. I can only be sorry for this – this daughter of a duke if she has allowed herself to become imprisoned in the same cage my mother found herself in.'

Verity sipped her glass. 'I do not at all know how it has been with them. When Valentine returns you must ask him.

Though I do not think Valentine has any great affection for his father.'

'Ho-hum.' Geoffrey Charles moved from the stool on which Amadora had been sitting, and stretched up to his full height. 'Well, before we pass to more pleasant subjects I will tell you what I propose. Tomorrow we shall ride over to Cardew in the forenoon and present ourselves to Sir George and Lady Harriet – and if we are invited we shall take a glass of something with them. Then I shall ask for the keys to Trenwith. It is my house and –'

'Geoffrey Charles, I think I should warn you –'

'I know it has been greatly neglected. Ross told me so when we met before the Battle of Bussaco. The two Harry brothers and the wife they have in common have charge of it, and nothing has been done by way of salvage or repair. So I am prepared for an ill-kept and unattended and partly unfurnished house. What is more, I have prepared Amadora for it. She tells me, bless her, that she is looking forward to this. Whether she understands the extent of disrepair, or whether I do, remains to be seen. But tomorrow afternoon, brooking no further delay, we shall ride over there and discover it for ourselves.'

II

Andrew Blamey, now in his late sixties, was slower in speech and in movement than Geoffrey Charles remembered him; but warm in welcome and in pressure on them to stay as long as they possibly could. Over supper they all talked much, all except Amadora, whose eyes went from face to face, following or trying to follow the conversation. Verity could well understand her fascination for Geoffrey Charles. She was so young and fresh; her skin peach-fine, her expressions mobile and fleeting; her face never in repose; her hair, un-luxuriant by some standards, curled and wisped about her forehead and face. But not only was she sensitive, she was touchy; the colour could mount quickly to her face at a temporary misunderstanding.

'And Ross and Demelza? You say they are well. I was astonished to hear of little Henry. No one told me of it until it was all over. That will delight them. The new mine, you say . . .'

'It is really the old mine you knew as a child, Wheal Leisure, but reopened under Jeremy's promptings and supervision. Only last October did there come a good find. Until then it had been losing money. I believe some old workings were discovered which dated back to medieval times.'

'We are talking of Jeremy Poldark, my love,' Geoffrey Charles told Amadora. 'As you know, he is my cousin, Ross and Demelza's eldest child. Jeremy is twenty-two, Clowance is nineteen; then there is Isabella-Rose, who is about eleven, and now, quite by surprise, Henry, who is only half a year old.'

'Understood,' said Amadora. 'But Valentine. Which is Valentine?'

'Ah, he is my half-brother. We had the same mother, but my father was Francis Poldark, who was killed in a mine, and Valentine's father is Sir George Warleggan whom you will meet tomorrow.'

'Yes, yes, I recall. You shall have told me this in the voyage.'

'Tenses again. Leave out shall have and you make the perfect sentence.'

She ate like a bird, Verity thought: only half the cod was gone, the veal steak with mushroom sauce was being toyed with. No baby coming yet, it seemed. She must be coaxed to eat more. And Geoffrey Charles's fascination for *her*? Not quite so easy to discern. Barely twenty-nine yet, he looked at least thirty-five, with a lean face like his cousin Ross, the thin line of moustache paralleling the thin hard line of the mouth; eyes that had seen ferocious carnage, *bitter* campaigning; in the constant company of men; the hand that would not properly open, the crevice in the jawbone, the strong yellow teeth, that air of self-possession than can only come to a man who has lived with death and seen it all and come to a confidence in his own sheer physical ability to survive.

And yet with it all a lightness of heart. A marvellous lightness of heart, considering; bred out of who knew what sense of camaraderie, sense of purpose, sense of celebration of the mere miraculous fact of being alive? Perhaps that was what most appealed to Amadora. Or did she also, as one of a proud and martial race, deeply admire those qualities which Verity had listed as likely to put off an elegant and fastidious girl? Certainly, at this present, they were deeply in love with each other. Verity's heart went out to them. Might it last.

'What?' she said, coming out of a reverie.

'I was saying, so Clowance is not wed. It is difficult at a distance, reading a few crackling letters while the guns are sounding, to judge for oneself, but the impression I had was that her engagement to marry Stephen Something . . . ah, Stephen Carrington – that this engagement was not greatly to the family's liking.'

Verity took a sip of wine. 'Neither Ross nor Demelza objected in so many words – they adhere to this unfashionable belief that children should choose for themselves – and, save for money or position, there was little to object to. His intentions seemed to be honourable, and if there were whispers about him . . . Well, as you say, they became engaged. Clowance herself broke it off. No one quite knows why. Now he has left the district. Clowance more recently has been receiving the attentions of a young man called Tom Guildford, a friend of Valentine's.'

Geoffrey Charles shook his head. 'Never heard of him. Eligible?'

'Oh, I believe so.'

'Except that he be a friend of Valentine's,' said Captain Blamey.

Geoffrey Charles looked at the older man's grim face. 'It is so long since I saw my half-brother that I did not know of this fearsome reputation. He was always, of course, a bit of a spark.'

'Perhaps I should not have said that –'

Verity said: 'I'm afraid your uncle does not take greatly to Valentine – in part because he has become a close friend of our own son and we think he – no doubt light-heartedly – runs young Andrew into unnecessary debts and other extravagances. But we cannot and must not make such sweeping judgements. Tom Guildford is a nephew of Lord Devoran and his parents are pleasantly monied without being very rich. He is about twenty-four, personable, reading for the Bar.'

A rare silence fell. 'And what are your plans?' Andrew Blamey asked. 'Yours and Amadora's. I hope you are going to settle here when the war is over.'

'When. Ah, when. You know I have no money, Uncle, not a bean except an allowance from Step-father George, and my pay, which, to make life endurable, does need a constant supplement. I gamble: with dice, on horses, on donkeys, with cards; and because I am wiser and older and cleverer than most of those I play with, I generally win. Enough, at least, to survive. But now I have married a de Bertendona. Does that mean anything to you?'

'I fear not.'

'Amadora, I am about to tell them of your family. Will you permit me?'

'If you shall have the wish.'

'I shall have the wish. The de Bertendonas are an old Spanish family – impoverished, they say, by the war, but still the possessors of estates. Amadora's great – five or six times great grandfather – commanded the vessel that brought Philip the Second, King of Spain, to marry Queen Mary of England in – when was it? I don't know, about 1554. *His* son commanded a squadron of the famous Armada, and indeed commanded squadrons in each of the succeeding armadas. Each following son has been a distinguished hidalgo. Amadora's father is a member of the Cortes and a poet. I have married *well*, uncle. Can you doubt it? But had Amadora been a serving wench in a tavern I should still consider I had married well. So much do I love and esteem her . . .'

'Steam,' said Amadora, pushing her hair back. 'That is new word. How shall I steam?'

'*Esteem*,' said Geoffrey Charles. 'Love, care for, venerate, cherish, admire – that's as far as I can go! But as to the future, who can see it? If the war ends, then we shall return, with perhaps enough money to put Trenwith to rights and to set us up as landed gentry of a very small but comfortable type.'

'It may not be so long,' said Captain Blamey. 'Napoleon is reeling.'

'Well . . . There is this truce he has agreed to on the eastern front. Of course it has come about because of his defeats in Russia and in Poland – but also because of Wellington's successes. He has sent Soult, I gather, to try to repair the defeats in the Pyrenees. He must not be underestimated. There are decisive battles still to come.'

Amadora put her hand on her husband's arm. 'Talk not of battles now.'

He put his other hand over hers. 'It is a new thing for me. Always before I had nothing but myself to lose. Now I have all the world to lose. Pray the Lord such good fortune does not turn me into a coward.'

'Coward?' said Amadora. 'Who is this coward? But we shall talk nothing of battles now. What is fated will happen.'

Chapter Two

I

Jeremy Poldark had been to St Ann's on business and cut across the cliffs on the way home. Skirting the workings at Wheal Spinster, which was a Warleggan mine, and observing the now silent engine house of Wheal Plenty – also a Warleggan mine but closed by them last year – he circled Trevaunance Cove and took the cliff path for Trenwith. It was not uncommon for him to walk these days. Journeys on foot took longer and gave him more time for thought. The more tired he was at night, the more prospect there was of sleep.

A young man to whom life had offered few complexities until he met Cuby Trevanion, nothing had ever seemed quite simple since. He had struggled with protest, impulses in his own blood that he could not rationalize, followed by actions that he could hardly condone yet saw with an instinctive fatalism as part of a pattern of revolt that he could not alter. Even now he had not yet come to live with it.

As he climbed one of the stiles he saw a handsome grey horse cropping the grass near a hedge which separated one field from the next. The horse was saddled and the reins hung loosely about his neck as he quietly tore at the grass. It was a side saddle. Jeremy jumped down and walked towards him. The horse gave no sign of knowing that he was being approached.

'Hey-ho,' Jeremy said soothingly. 'Come, come, what is this? I don't know you, my beauty. Have you been straying a little and lost your way?'

The horse shook his head, making the bridle rattle, and showed a white eyeball. Jeremy, who knew a good deal about animals, saw how taut the muscles were.

Bees were humming in the hedge. No other sound.

'Where's your mistress, eh? Has she gone to pick flowers? Should you not be tethered, my beauty? *Tck, tck – Tck, tck . . .*'

He put a gentle hand forward to stroke the horse's neck and instantly there was a galvanic movement: everything shook and jerked and rattled and after a few moments the horse resumed his cropping twenty yards away. A flying hoof had just missed Jeremy's face.

'Like that, is it? Well, well, old boy. What a fuss to make! A little show of temper? Too much corn I suspicion.' Jeremy looked round. The sun was two hands' breadth from the sea. Crows were circling the high sky.

'Hello, there, is anyone about?'

A group of cows raised their heads and watched him with bovine disinterest from the other side of the field. Probably, since there was no one at Trenwith, the horse had come from Place House. Jeremy thought now he had seen him before, but not recently.

A distant cry. He scrambled over a hedge, which was tall and riotous with foxgloves. At the other side of the next field a young woman was half-sitting, half-lying on the grass. She was in grey, with a grey tricorn hat near-by. As he trotted towards her he saw it was Mrs Selina Pope.

She also recognized him as he came up and gave him a painful smile.

'Jeremy . . .'

'Mrs Pope. You've come a cropper?'

''Fraid so. It's my ankle. I fell awkwardly.'

Her blonde hair, dressed in a chignon, had partly fallen loose, and two locks hung across her shoulder.

He knelt beside her. 'This one?'

'Yes.'

'Have you been lying here long?'

'Twenty minutes. Perhaps half an hour. I don't know.'

'It was lucky I was passing. Otherwise you might have been here a long time.'

'Yes. Yes, I might. Until some alarm was raised.'

'Are you hurt otherwise, do you suppose?'

'My shoulder.' She felt it.

'Bad?'

'No, I think not.'

'I think we should take this boot off.'

'Could you not get help from Place House?'

'Of course. But it would be better to relieve the ankle before it swells.'

She pulled her skirt up a few inches. 'I believe it is already swollen.'

A calf-length boot of fine grey kid with six buttons down the side. He began slowly to undo these, taking care not to put any strain on the leg inside.

After Sir John Trevaunance died in 1808, his heir and brother Unwin had sold Place House to a Mr Clement Pope, reputedly a rich merchant who had come from America bringing with him a very pretty blonde second wife, called Selina, and two daughters in their late teens by his first wife. Mr Pope, an unamiable character of sixty with a long thin neck, had a fastidious manner and a voice like an unoiled hinge. His ambition had been to launch himself and his family into Cornish society, particularly to obtain good marriages for his daughters, but this attempt had not been successful. It was largely his own fault, for he had an unequalled blend of austerity and unction which offended those he most wished to impress and which made old Sir Hugh Bodrugan say he was 'like a damned draper'.

The Poldarks had met the family on a number of occasions and were on moderately friendly terms, chiefly with the daughters, Letitia and Maud, because they were of an age with Clowance. Horrie Treneglos had for a while flirted outrageously with Letitia, who was a plain girl; but was now more seriously pursuing Angela Nankivell of Lambourne. Jeremy quite liked the pretty Maud, but had cheerfully avoided any commitment. As for the step-mother . . .

As for the step-mother, she looked about twenty-six . . .

'I tried to catch your horse, Mrs Pope. He was having no truck with me at all. Generally I can manage horses. He seemed a thought wild.'

'Amboy is my husband's horse. But Mr Pope has not been

well enough to take him out, so I thought to exercise him.'

'You would have been wiser to have left it to a groom.'

'Oh, I have been on him often before,' she said stiffly.

'How is Mr Pope?'

'Not at all himself. It seems that exercise or undue excitement brings on these gouty pains.'

'Dr Enys is your doctor, I suppose.'

'Yes. Of late.'

'I'm sure you could find no better.'

'So I have been told.' She was still a little on her dignity.

The last button undone, Jeremy saw that the ankle was indeed swollen. He took the heel of the boot and applied slight pressure. She winced.

'I can't stand that.'

'I should cut it off for you. That is if you do not mind the damage to the boot.'

'No. Oh, no. But . . .'

He looked at her. She had always been 'Mrs Pope' to him, he 'Jeremy' to her. It marked the difference in their status, in the relationship of a young man towards a married woman who acted *in loco parentis* towards two girls he was supposed to admire. It need not mean that their relationship had to remain on that level, though it had never occurred to him before that it should ever be otherwise.

She said: 'Can you not go and fetch help?'

'That of course I'll do. But your foot would be more comfortable if I cut the boot away first.' He fished in his pocket and took out his folding knife. The blade, he knew, was sharp for he had honed it yesterday.

He unfolded the knife and slid it between her leg and the material of the boot. She watched him with interest.

The knife cut through the kid without even tearing her stocking. When he had eased off the boot she said: 'Thank you, Jeremy.'

'A pleasure.'

She lowered her eyes. 'Yes, my foot *is* swollen.'

'If you will take your stocking off, I'll bind it with a cold cloth. I passed a ditch with water in it on the other side of this field.'

'Where is the cloth to come from?'

'My kerchief will do.'

'Can you not catch Amboy?'

'I don't think there is the least chance. He's out to enjoy himself. In any case you could not ride him home.'

'Well . . .'

'Why did you call him Amboy?'

'Why not?'

'It is an unusual name.'

'It was where we lived in America. Just south of New York.'

Jeremy squatted a moment longer beside her. The sun was setting into summer mists. A shoal of gnats glinted as they hovered among the foxgloves.

'I never thought to ask. Are you American, then?'

'My mother was. But no. Not really. It happened that I was born in Essex.'

He got up. 'I'll go and soak this kerchief. If you could take your stocking off while I'm away.'

He walked across to the ditch which contained just enough drainage water from yesterday's rain. He tore the kerchief down the middle and soaked half of it. When he went back he found she had obeyed him. He grinned at her in a friendly, youthful fashion to take the charge out of the situation and bound the linen round her naked foot and ankle. As it happened he had never seen a woman with painted toe-nails before. At first he had thought it was blood. The look of them fascinated him.

She said: 'It *was* fortunate you were passing.'

'So shines a good deed in a naughty world.'

'What is that?'

'That? I don't know. I believe I learned it at school.'

'Were you coming back from St Ann's?'

'Yes. I had been consulting with the captain of Wheal Kitty.'

'You are very clever, I'm told – passing brilliant in designing engines.'

'I am not an inventor, Mrs Pope. I work on other people's ideas and sometimes I hope to improve on them a little.'

'That is all any inventor does, Jeremy. Each one takes a little step forward building upon the last.'

He smiled. 'That's a kind way to regard it.'

'And right.'

'Partly right. But the true inventors are those who make the big steps, where no one has quite thought to step before . . . Do you have a pin?'

She hesitated, then took out a short pin with a silver head from the lapel of her jacket.

'Thank you.' He slid it through the end of the bandage to hold it in place.

Amboy was still peacefully tearing at the grass quite nearby.

'Do you think you can catch him?'

'No. Not without help. Or not till he's cold and tired.'

'Well, perhaps you would be good enough to fetch help.'

He straightened up. 'It is not quite how a surgeon would have done it, but it should hold. I'll carry you home.'

She looked up at him, sandy lashes narrowed over wisteria blue eyes. 'It is more than a mile,' she said coldly. 'Pray don't consider it. Let them know at Place House.'

'Which will take best part of forty minutes there and back. And the sun is going down. I don't think Mr Pope would approve of my leaving you here alone.'

He picked up her stocking, rolled it and slipped it in his pocket. Then he picked up her hat and her boot.

'We'd better save this,' he said. 'No doubt it can be stitched up. If you could hold it for me.'

A few wisps of cloud overhead were aflame like fragments of burnt paper blown up from a fire. A cow, deprived of its calf, was roaring in the fields sloping down to Trenwith.

'I am not *light*,' she said.

'You must be,' he replied, and bent to take her round the waist and under the knees.

At the last moment she put her arm round his neck and straightened her uninjured leg so that he did not have too much difficulty in lifting her. He gave a slight grunt and she was up.

'Damn it,' he said, 'I had forgot your crop. Wait, I think I can bend –'

'*Leave* it,' she said. 'It can be recovered later.'

The procession began. After making the proposal he had thought of the hedges between there and Trevaunance Cove and speculated how he might negotiate them; but as it turned out all the hedges, in the way she directed him, had openings to give access from one field to the next, and there was only one stile and one gate. The latter he was able to open without setting her down; the former he lifted her over and she perched on one leg until he was able to follow.

Although she was in fact a bit heavier than he expected, Jeremy did not find it an unpleasant journey. They talked little on the way, but she did say stiffly: 'Pray rest if you are tired.'

'No, thank you.'

'You must be very strong.'

'Not really.'

'Well, not at all the effete young gentleman.'

'I work about the farm. And of course at the mine. And other ways . . .' He frowned, eyes briefly shadowed.

'Other ways?'

'My parents have always taught their children it is proper to soil their hands.'

'Very good advice. Perhaps it should have been given me.'

'Oh, that's different.'

'With a woman? Maybe. But I do not suppose Clowance bothers, does she?'

'Bothers?'

'About soiling her hands.'

'No. I don't believe she does.'

'What has happened to that very good-looking sailor with whom she was so friendly?'

'Stephen Carrington? He went away.'

She noticed the change in his tone. 'For ever?'

'It would be better.'

'Why?'

'I don't think they were suited.'

'That I can well understand. It would be such a poor match.'

'It was not what I meant. Unless you use the word match in a wider sense.'

She smiled. 'You are very wise for one so young, Jeremy.'

'Is twenty-two young?'

'It seems so.' She was going to add 'to me', but did not.

He took another grip of her. Every now and then he had to do this, for she tended to slip.

The sun had been gone down well before they came within sight of Place House. Swallows were wheeling. A long twilight was yawning up the sky.

'This will do,' she said. 'I am most grateful to you. See, the bank here will do for me to sit while you go for help.'

'What help is necessary now?'

'If my husband is looking out, as he may well be, he might become unduly alarmed, think I am serious hurt.'

'We shall soon be able to reassure him.'

'And jealous,' she said lightly. 'My husband, because I am so much younger than he, is jealous of all men.'

'Oh,' said Jeremy, 'that I can understand.'

'Thank you.'

He set her down on a piece of greensward between two rocky outcrops.

'Thank you,' she said again.

'And what would you like me to do now, Mrs Pope?'

'If my husband does not see you, then the best way will be to go round to the stables. Music Thomas will still be there. Ask him to come. I believe I can lean on his arm.'

'Why not have two men and sit in a chair?'

'We have no other men about the house, Jeremy. Mr Pope will not have them.'

'Indeed.'

'Tell one of the maids. If possible tell my personal maid, Katie Carter. Ask her to inform Mr Pope, but on no account to alarm him. He must not be subjected to shocks.'

He took the stocking out of his pocket and put it beside the boot. 'I shall be back in three or four minutes.' He turned to go.

'Jeremy.'

'Yes?'

She stared at him with eyes like a cat's, more open with the coming of dark.

'Believe me, you have been most obliging.'

II

Music Thomas was the youngest of the three brothers Thomas who lived next door to Jud and Prudie Paynter; he sang alto in the choir, walked on his toes, and was not the brightest of men. He worked at Place House as a stable-boy, and in the light of the startling information Mrs Pope had just given Jeremy, it occurred to Jeremy to suppose it was Music's apparent disabilities which made him employable by Mr Pope.

That the strange, now sickly, Robespierre-like figure of Mr Clement Pope should insist on presiding over an entirely female household, like some sultan jealous of his harem, gave Jeremy a disagreeable *frisson*. It lifted a curtain on life. There had been rumours from the first that Mr Pope kept a cane for his daughters, which was *not* used on their hands, and that even now when one was twenty years of age and the other twenty-one, the sanction at least still existed. What of Selina, his wife? It had been said that she came of a poor family, her father an army surgeon who had died young. She had married for money, and so far as one could tell had kept her part of the bargain. That Mr Pope doted on her was plain to see whenever they appeared in company together. Was *she* subject to the same discipline? It seemed unlikely, since any pretty woman with an old husband has ways of making her pleasure or displeasure felt. But it was clear that Mr Pope was insanely jealous. A friendly neighbour, nine or ten years her junior, must not be seen carrying her into the house after a mishap on a horse. And the only man employable, within permissible touching distance of her, must be one whose manhood was in considerable doubt – and even he did not sleep in.

23

Jeremy was lucky enough to find Music at the first call, and Music who, unknown to Mr Pope, was betraying all the conventional signs of being normal by having fallen hopelessly in love with Katie Carter, was delighted to be given the excuse to seek his beloved out and pass on the message that Mrs Pope had sent. Then he accompanied Jeremy, with his lolloping twine-toed walk, to succour his mistress.

Unknown also to Jeremy, indeed unknown to anyone but the surgeon, Music Thomas had been several times to see Dr Enys on the subject of his own disabilities. Though he could only with great difficulty tell the time, and never knew what a month was, he was quite capable of living a fairly normal life, if other people would allow him. Unfortunately he was the butt of small boys, who whistled and gestured after him, and he was aware that he didn't really 'count' where women were concerned and that particularly he didn't count where Katie Carter was concerned, that clumsy, black-haired, long-faced girl on whom his mind and his heart had settled fond hopes. He meant nothing to her; he was a joke, a chorister with the wrong voice, a young stupid who was always making mistakes and getting into scrapes, some of them true, some of them apocryphal, invented by witty, scabrous tongues. ''Eard the latest 'bout Music, 'ave ee?' In order to impress Katie, in order to be thought a serious young man worthy of being her suitor, he wanted to shed this reputation, this sort of false renown.

It was this tall gangling stable boy who helped Mrs Pope home; and Jeremy went on his way.

He took the cliff pathway, skirting Trenwith land – a dangerous route in the twilight for one who did not know the way, for the fences put up long ago by the Warleggans had rotted or been stolen for firewood, and here and there the cliff had fallen, taking part of the path with it. Little detours to skirt the sudden precipices were easy to miss in the dusk. But he knew his way all too well. It was a way he had walked so often this year.

Down into the depths of Sawle village, with a few sickly lanterns and candles gleaming here and there; broken and boarded windows, half doors patched with driftwood; the stink of stale fish and sewage and the skeletal clang and clatter of the stamps. Poverty clung round the Guernseys like sediment at the bottom of a pond; there had been no change, no improvement since Jeremy was a boy; but as one climbed the cobbled rutted way up to Stippy-Stappy Lane, so the small respectabilities grew, past the Carters' shop and up the hill towards Sawle Church. Then past the church with its inebriate spire and through Grambler village, which was just a row of cottages on either side of a miry lane, put up when Grambler mine was working, but now, though all inhabited, mainly in a high state of disrepair. The Coads lived here, and the Rowes, the Bottrells, the Prouts, the Billingses, the Thomases, and next to the Thomases, last cottage in the village, the semi-hovel where Jud and Prudie eked out their last days.

There was a light in their cottage, and Jeremy stepped delicately past, not at all anxious to be recognized and called in, when a hand touched his arm.

'Well, me old lad. Well met, eh?'

Even in the dark the tawny hair showed; anyway no one could mistake the voice.

'Stephen! For God's sake! What are you doing here?'

Teeth showed in the dark. 'The bad penny, eh? Or should it be the bad guinea?'

'You never wrote. I didn't know what to expect –'

'You must have expected me back soon or late. And I was never one much for the letter.'

'When did you come?'

'Landed at Padstow yesterday. Borrowed a nag from there.'

Belatedly they shook hands. Old friends, old comrades, old companions in crime.

'Anything happened here?' Stephen Carrington asked.

'No. Not in that way.'

'No questions asked?'

'Why should there be?'

'How's Paul?'

'Well enough.'

'Being careful, is he?'

'Yes. I think so.'

From the Paynters' cottage came the crash and rattle of pans and Jud's complaining voice.

'Are you walking home?'

'Yes.'

'I'll come a way with you.'

They went off, tramping together in the dark.

Jeremy said: 'Did you find your privateer?'

'There were two or three propositions I carefully considered.'

'But?'

'They weren't right. And the money wasn't really enough.'

Jeremy did not speak.

'Have you taken any of it yourself yet?'

'No.'

'You're a fool, old son. We agreed to split by a third.'

'I'll take it in due course.'

'Oh, yes. I know — I know. We were all in a bit of a stank to begin with. But by now things must have quieted down.'

The sky was lightening where a moon was due to rise.

'How is Clowance?'

'Well.'

'Is she wed yet?'

'No.'

'That fellow Guildford will be no good to her. She'll wipe her feet on him. She needs a firm hand.'

'Such as yours?'

'Oh, well, let's not go into that yet a while.'

'Where are you staying?'

'With Ned and Emma Hartnell. They have agreed to put me up for a few days.'

'Is that all you are staying?'

'Not in Cornwall. I've new ideas for Cornwall. But mebbe it will not be in this district.'

'Privateering?'

'No. Pilchards.'

'What?'

'I'll tell ye about it sometime.'

Jeremy laughed humourlessly. 'It's a far cry from fighting the French at sea to catching fish on the Cornish coast.'

'Mebbe you think so. But one could be as profitable as the other. And not without risk neither.'

'You rouse my curiosity, Stephen.'

'Hold hard for a few days and I may satisfy it.'

As they neared the old trees around Wheal Maiden the moon was just glimmering over the top of the sandhills. A geometry of bats were drawing their eccentric triangles against the sky.

There was a light in the Meeting House. 'Your uncle still belongs to that lot, I suppose?'

'Oh, yes. The leader of it. You'll never separate him from his religion. He's a rare good man.'

Stephen grunted. 'And how's Wheal Leisure?'

'Production up. Some of those medieval galleries have been interesting; and we've profitably explored the north sett. You have money due from the last dividend.'

'How much?'

'Sixty pounds.'

Stephen grunted again.

'It's more than a 50% return on your investment,' Jeremy said sharply.

'Oh, aye. I don't complain. Far from it, me old lad. It will all help in this new project I have. I wish twas ten times as much!'

'I am sure no one would object; but at least the mine is paying, and it has only been in operation fifteen months.'

'And Ben Carter?' Stephen said.

'What about him?'

'He's back as underground captain, I suppose?'

'Yes.'

'He would be, so soon as I was out of the way.' Stephen stopped. 'This is as far as I shall come, Jeremy.'

Jeremy said: 'I should ask you in but Clowance is home, and it would not be fair to her just for me to turn up with you.'

Stephen said: 'D'ye know, but for Ben Carter I'd be married to Clowance now. D'ye realize that?'

'I suppose so.'

'No suppose so about it. If he hadn't picked that quarrel . . .'

'Come, Stephen, you don't expect me to believe it was that way round.'

'Well . . . whichever way round it was, *he* was the one who came between us. Faults I have a-plenty, but harbouring old grievances I never thought was a failing of mine. All the same, I'll kill him one day. That's a promise.'

'We'd lose a good underground captain,' Jeremy said, trying to lighten the tone.

'Oh, yes. Oh, yes.' Stephen stirred the ground with his foot. 'You can joke. But let me ask you this. Suppose you'd ever been betrothed to marry your Cuby – or whatever she is called. Suppose the wedding day had been set. Suppose someone came between you and her. However the quarrel happened, supposing one man came between you. How would you feel about him?'

Jeremy looked into his own life.

'Well?' said Stephen, peering into his face.

'Yes,' said Jeremy, not wanting to be drawn about his own affairs. 'But you've got to remember Ben Carter will never be your rival. He could never marry Clowance. Clowance is just fond of him. If you'd had any sense you'd never have flared up the way you did. I know it's easy to talk –'

'Yes, it's easy to talk. But when you're in love you're easily jealous, and things come out. You say things . . . But, Holy Mary, I said but little! She took it all as if twas mortal hurt . . .'

'We've talked of this too often,' said Jeremy wearily. 'Clowance has strong, deep loyalties. Anyway, the quarrel happened. As I've said to you before, it has always seemed to me – a sign of a deeper complaint. Things must have been going wrong between you before, though maybe you did not notice it. And she hasn't come round. I think you'd best forget her.'

'Some chance.'

'Oh, I know.'

The two young men stood silently for a few moments longer, each considering his own ill-treatment at the hands of fate.

Stephen said: 'Well, I'd best be going.'

'I'll see you sometime.'

'Is the – stuff where it was?'

'Yes.'

'We can meet at the Gatehouse, then. Tomorrow about noon?'

'I can't. I'm to go with my family to St Day Show Fair. I have not been very sociable of late, and I especially promised my mother I should go.'

Stephen thought this out. 'Very well. So be it. Perhaps tis better this way. I'll meet you at the end of the month. Saturday week at noon at the Gatehouse, eh?'

'Agreed.'

'By then I shall know for certain whether me present idea for – for a new type of investment will look promising enough to follow. Maybe I shall interest you.'

'Maybe.'

Stephen Carrington said impatiently: 'You cannot keep your share of the stuff lying there for ever.'

'Why not?'

'All the risks we took: were they for nothing?'

Jeremy smiled into the dark. 'On the whole I believe for nothing worth while, Stephen. But I admit it is a personal view come to after the event. Do not let it depress you.'

Chapter Three

I

Both Sir George and Lady Harriet Warleggan were home when the young Poldarks called on the Saturday forenoon.

It was a disagreeable day. Seeing the pellucid sunset of last night and the clear moon that rode through the hours of darkness, it would have been a perceptive sailor or shepherd who could have foreseen the grey dawn, the steady south-westerly wind and the intermittent rain that came with it.

In fact Lady Harriet was in one of her customary places – the stables – when a maid arrived to tell her of the visit, and she tramped through the kitchens, kicked off her muddy boots, and, accompanied by her two great hounds, came in stockinged feet into the larger withdrawing room where George, himself disturbed from an interview with Tankard about the rotten borough of St Michael, was sitting opposite the two young people, sipping sherry and looking cold and unwelcoming.

It was not really surprising, for Geoffrey Charles accepted his allowance of £500 a year without a sign of gratitude or obligation, and never wrote. The only correspondence which took place was with Valentine.

But the arrival of a step-step-mother, as it were, did help to break the ice. So did the dogs, which, though well behaved, were so enormous that they provided light relief and a topic for conversation.

Harriet had a talent for taking a situation as it came without regard to history, ancient or modern. She neither knew nor cared what other people were feeling, and every circumstance was treated strictly on its merits. Also, having discovered the nationality of the little dark girl, she immediately began to chat to her in broken Spanish. It seemed that when she was seven years of age she had spent a year in

Madrid, in the home of a grandee who was connected by marriage to the Osbornes. Amadora was enchanted, and soon lost that element of defensive shyness with which she was accustomed to greet new situations or Geoffrey Charles's old friends.

George said evenly: 'I have no keys. They are with the Harrys. All you have to do is go over and call at the lodge. They will give them to you at once. You will find the place neglected. The Harrys were always rogues.'

'I wonder you kept them on.'

George shrugged.

'After your mother died I could find little interest in the place.'

And little interest in preserving it for Francis's son, thought Geoffrey Charles. 'I have not seen my home since Grandfather died, which must be seven years, or nearly so. Is it still furnished?'

'Partly. Many of the new pieces I had taken there were later brought here. You'll observe that bureau. Such original furniture as was not disposed of remains. Is that a permanent injury to your hand?'

Geoffrey Charles looked down. 'Who knows? It only happened in April of last year. So it may yet improve. But in fact, excepting that I find it impossible to open the fingers wide, it is little inconvenience. The trigger finger is not impaired.'

George eyed his step-son. It was difficult to relate this tall thin tight-faced man with the genteel, delicate, over-plump, over-mothered boy he had disciplined so many years ago. In the early days George had *tried*. Indeed, before he married Elizabeth, before even Francis died, he had tried hard to please the boy, bought him presents, attempted to please the mother by pleasing the child. Even after their marriage he had done his very best with Geoffrey Charles, wanting to befriend him, until the quarrel over Drake Carne, Demelza Poldark's brother, had written off any friendship between them for ever.

Now at this meeting after so long a gap, the less said the better. They had nothing more in common, except the old

elvan and granite house of Trenwith. The one important
interest they had once deeply shared had died nearly fourteen years ago, leaving a five-day-old baby behind.

George said: 'Well, the war has taken a favourable turn at
last. Your Wellington should feel better pleased with himself now.'

'I believe he is. Though he is never one for self-
satisfaction. Is the Armistice still in operation?'

'Yes. And will be I suspect so long as it suits Napoleon to
rebuild his armies after last winter's defeat in Russia.'

Geoffrey Charles said: 'For almost two weeks now I have
been without up-to-date news. If the Armistice continues
with Austria and the rest, it means that Wellington's
Peninsular Army is the only one at present in the field
against France.'

'Exactly what many people are thinking. As you say,
there is little cause for self-satisfaction.'

Silence fell between the men while the women chatted on.
Even in this brief interchange there was something in
George's turn of phrase or tone of voice that rubbed Geoffrey Charles the wrong way. George had always been a critic
of Wellington; Wellington had very briefly occupied one of
George's parliamentary seats and had left it without a thank
you; George never forgot slights; Geoffrey Charles knew all
this and knew also that George had always criticized the
decision to send British troops to Portugal and Spain.

'Well,' he said, uncrossing his long thin legs, 'I think we
should go. It will take us a couple of hours, I suppose . . .
Amadora . . .'

'Go?' said Lady Harriet. 'Before you have been dined? I'll
not bear it. Otherwise I shall suppose you have no fancy for
your new step-mother.'

'Oh, far from it, ma'am! The contrary! But when we
reach our house we shall have much to do before dark –'

'So you shall go with candles. I cannot conject what
Amadora's mother would think if she learned that we had
turned her away.' Harriet got up. 'Down, you blasted
brutes; there is no occasion for excitement!' She glanced at
her husband, who was trying not to glower. 'Dinner shall be

early to accommodate them. But for half an hour first, Captain and Mrs Geoffrey Charles, you shall see my livestock.'

II

They dined with a modest lack of disaccord. Geoffrey Charles thought that on the whole his step-father had done well for himself, though he could not see Lady Harriet fitting into the compatible but slightly subordinate role his own mother had filled. There would be ructions in plenty here. She was an attractive woman, more beautiful than pretty but not quite either. And young. Only a few years, he'd swear, older than himself. She had an eye for a young man, he could tell that. Would George be able to satisfy her, to keep her, to prevent her from straying? If she felt like it, there would surely be no stopping her. George looked older; lines were indented in his cheeks, his hair iron-grey, thinning.

Present at the table too was Ursula, now a strapping girl of nearly fourteen, with a fat neck and thighs so sturdy that they made bulges in her skirts; but none of it flabby, all hard flesh, ready to stand her in good stead in life. Geoffrey Charles could scarcely believe that his own slender, delicate, patrician mother had borne her. And a girl of few words, curtsying awkwardly to Amadora, allowing her cheek to be brushed by Geoffrey Charles, but firmly intent on the main purpose of the hour: food.

Valentine, George explained, was not yet come from Cambridge. He was expected next Wednesday, if he could be bothered to take the coach and did not squander his money in London. He had not been home at Easter at all, having spent the vacation with Lord Ridley, a new friend of his – said George smugly – in Norfolk. So his last visit was Christmas. When, Harriet volunteered, he had turned the house upside down. Then they had all been quite mad with delight at the news of Napoleon's retreat from Moscow.

'Which should have ended in his fall,' said Geoffrey Charles. 'But he hypnotizes the French. They worship him –

so when he calls for more cadres to fill his decimated regiments, they come in their thousands: old men; boys of sixteen.'

'Not always willingly, I'm told,' said Harriet. 'They have no choice. The *levée en masse* in France is complete.'

'Nothing of which detracts from Napoleon's greatness,' said George. 'He bestrides the world like no other man. Our own politicians, our own generals, the petty kings and emperors who oppose him, are pigmies by comparison.'

'Perhaps you'd be surprised,' Geoffrey Charles said, 'at the admiration and respect he inspires in the soldiers who oppose him – *our* soldiers particularly. But that does not – or should not – remove the necessity to bring him down. While he exists as Emperor of France there can be no peace, no security, no hope of a lasting settlement that will leave other nations free.'

'I believe his Russian defeat has been a salutary lesson to him,' said George. 'He will be more amenable now. If Castlereagh has his wits about him we can achieve a peace with honour without the necessity of more fighting.'

'Do you intend to return to your regiment soon?' Harriet asked.

'As soon as possible,' said Geoffrey Charles, with a tight little smile. 'If you have been so long on the hunt you want to be in at the kill.'

After a pause: 'And Amadora?'

'Will come back to Spain with me. But all that is weeks ahead.'

'Those are miserable poor old hacks you are riding. Do their knees not knock together as they carry you? . . . Let me lend you something with better blood. As you observe, we are not lacking. Are we, George?'

'No,' said George.

'Thank you, ma'am; you're very kind. We hired them from the Greenbank stables. But I am sure we can manage . . .'

'Why should you? A man shall take them back tomorrow. You may borrow two better mounts for the duration of your stay.'

'T'ank you,' said Amadora, beaming. 'We have in Spain also good horses too.'

'I *know*. Don't I know! Anyway, my nags are eating their heads off at this time of year. It would be an obligement if you took 'em off my hands.'

'Sawle Church and churchyard,' said George, 'is in a very bad state. You would think that Ross Poldark would make some effort to support it, financially and otherwise; but no. It is not a question of Christian doctrine, it is a question of social obligation. When I was at Trenwith – and indeed when your father was at Trenwith – we accepted a trust, a responsibility. No longer so. When I was last over there your mother's grave was vastly overgrown and –'

'And my father's?'

The question was sharp. When a woman marries twice and then dies, shall she be buried with her first husband, even though her second husband pays for and supervises the funeral? It was a sore point with Geoffrey Charles that his father had been buried in the family vault, his mother given quite a separate entombment thirty yards away.

George, choosing not to pick up the challenge, said: 'And your father's, of course. I could wish that you might settle at Trenwith, so that there was again a patron to oversee the benefice. At present the Nampara Poldarks totally neglect it. And Odgers – their nominee, incidentally – is now so far gone in senility that by rights he should be removed.'

'As bad as that?'

'I'm told when he goes up for his sermon now his wife ties one of his legs to the pulpit so that he can't wander away until he has read his piece.'

'Reminds me of my bachelor uncle,' said Harriet. 'When he went to church he always took his tame jackal to sit beside him in his pew and wake him when the sermon was over. Misfortunately the jackal would go to sleep too and its snore was much to be wondered at. Sometimes the preacher could scarcely go on.'

'I did not know you could tame a jackal,' said Geoffrey Charles.

'Tame pretty near anything if you have the patience. I once had a bear cub but he died ... My cousin owns a snake.' She lifted a dark eyebrow at George and gave her low husky laugh. 'So you see, George, how much more trying my little friends might be.'

'I am well used to your little friends by now,' said George. 'Mrs Poldark, will you take tea?'

It was a sign for them to move, and after refusing further refreshment they took leave of George, who pleaded pressure of work, and followed Harriet, Ursula, and the two hounds back to the stables. There Harriet insisted on lending Geoffrey Charles a horse called Bargrave – 'we bought him in a sale; your cousin Ross bid against us, but we got him; he has good quarters and makes nothing of these muddy lanes' – and a pale sorrel mare of much slighter build for Amadora – 'you'll find Glow hasn't quite the stamina but she is fleet over short distances and has the gentlest mouth.'

The rain had almost ceased as they rode away; it was a barely visible dampness just freckling their faces. Amadora laughed at the pleasure of it, and indeed at the pleasure of the morning's visit. They chatted in Spanish all the way down the drive and she said: 'I do not see Sir George as such a wicked man.'

Geoffrey Charles said: 'In his life I know him to have done a number of wicked things; things I find it difficult not to recall when I meet him; but I have no means of assessing evil and no special wish to judge him. He is older – for one thing ... Also ... the causes – at least some of the causes – are no longer there. It really all centred round my mother.'

'How is that?'

'Oh, *mon Dieu*, how can one say it all in a few breaths? Ross Poldark, my cousin – the other Captain Poldark, whom you may meet tomorrow – although happily married to his wife, Demelza, loved my mother first.'

'A triangle *eterno* – perhaps?'

'More of a quadrangle, if you gather my drift.'

They clopped on for a few moments in silence. They were now descending the hill towards the main turnpike road.

36

'Ross and George had been at loggerheads for some time: over a copper-smelting scheme, over matters relating to my father, over charges of riot and assault which nearly brought Ross to the gallows . . . My mother's marriage to George caused the already deep division to become an abyss.'

The track was again narrow and they went temporarily in single file.

Amadora said: 'England is so *green*. I have never seen so much green. It is so rich, so lush, so *exuberante*.'

'Wait till you cross the spine. On the other coast – my coast – it is quite different.'

They reached the turnpike road, but instead of turning right or left upon it, Geoffrey Charles led the way up the opposite hill. It was a steep and awkward climb by the narrowest of tracks much overgrown with fern and bramble. In twenty minutes they had reached the top and reined in breathless, looking back the way they had come.

'So *green*,' said Amadora again.

'In a moment we shall join the track to Redruth, which at least is well worn. Then we shall fork right for St Day. But this is the worst of the route. Are you tired, my little?'

'*Tired?*' she said. 'What is tired?'

They went on.

'And?' said Amadora.

'And?'

'Did not all this you have talked about occur when you were most young?'

'Yes. Oh yes. Too young to understand at the time. But I have learned of it since – picked up a pretty fact here and there . . .'

'Your governess, you told me – Malvena – there was much trouble over her?'

'Morwenna. That was later, when I was ten . . .' He flexed his injured hand. 'She and I became great friends. That did not matter, but one day we met Drake Carne – Demelza's brother – and he and Morwenna became great friends; more than friends. They came to love each other deeply. The only let was that Drake did not come of the same class as

37

Morwenna – and, being related to a Poldark made him specially hated by George. George arranged an imposed marriage for Morwenna, to an odious clergyman called Osborne Whitworth.' Geoffrey Charles gave an angry shrug of the shoulders. 'All that time . . . it is best forgotten. But when I remember it . . .'

Amadora took a firmer grip of her reins. 'But you have told me that now – that some years ago this Drake and this Morwenna became married. How is that?'

'Whitworth – the parson – was killed by footpads, or fell from his horse with some sort of a stroke. Anyway he died. And after a while Drake and Morwenna married. At the time I was fifteen and away at school. Of course he wrote to me. So did Morwenna. But even so one had to read between the lines, to learn more of the truth from other people.'

'What is that truth?'

'Soon after they were married a small boat building yard that Ross owns in Looe lost its manager when a man called Blewitt – who was part owner with Ross, and part manager – died. Ross offered the position to Drake, who took it, and they moved there in the following December. They have one daughter, thanks be . . . Now do you see what I mean? All the foliage is going.'

They had broken through the rough tangled trees and come to moorland, with goats pasturing, a water wheel turning in a stream and activating noisy iron rods, a few hovels on the sky-line, mules with panniers being driven along a cross lane. A strong wind blew the clouds low.

'Ah,' said Amadora, 'it is a little more like Spain.'

'But without the sun.'

'Without the sun. But you do see it *a veces*? There is sun last night.'

They jogged on.

Geoffrey Charles said: 'The Reverend Osborne Whitworth had been so grossly offensive to his wife that Morwenna swore when he died that she could never marry again – not even Drake. The physical act of love had been turned for her into something obscene. It was only after much persuasion, and after he had undertaken not to expect her to become his wife in a physical sense, that she eventually consented. Yet – a year and a half after their move to Looe a daughter was born . . . I was anxious when I went to see them . . . Do you follow me, or do I speak too fast?'

'No, I follow.'

'I found them both very happy with each other and devoted to their child. Morwenna – Drake said – was still subject to nightmares, and after such a nightmare she was out of sorts for a week or more and could not bear that he should touch her. But the nightmares were becoming less frequent; and anyway, always, Drake said, there now were the times in between.'

Pigs were rooting outside a thatched cottage which leaned drunkenly towards a triangular field in which a woman and three children worked.

'That is byertiful,' said Amadora.

Geoffrey Charles laughed. 'It depends how you look at it. You see there were two cottages, but the other has fallen down. Do you understand the word picturesque?'

'Of course. *Pintoresco*. But byertiful too.'

The woman and the children had stopped work at the sound of voices and stared curiously. Geoffrey Charles raised a hand but none of them waved back.

Now they were entering a most desolate scene, in which there was no trace of vegetation left: all was given up to mining. The few cottages were squalid; naked or semi-naked children played among the attle thrown up from the excavations; green pools of slime let off an odour that was partly diluted by the smell of sulphur and smoke drifting before the breeze. Miners and muleteers in smock frocks moved about; thin and pale-faced older children were at work on the dressing floors, stirring the tin round and round in the water with their bare feet. It seemed that everybody was digging the ground, or had already dug it. There were oval pits, part full of water. In excavations only big enough and deep enough to hold a coffin a spade or two appeared and disappeared, and sometimes a felt hat was to be seen. There were seven or eight mine chimneys smoking, and as many dead, some of them already in ruin.

'What is those things?' Amadora asked, pointing to the circular thatched huts which were dotted about.

'They are whyms.'

'Wims? What is wims?'

'Whyms. They each cover a windlass, which lowers a bucket down that particular shaft. The bucket can bring up either water or ore.'

Amadora reined in to stare at one of these huts, and at the two mules which moved in constant slow motion round and round the building, pulling a bar. An impish child sat on one mule driving them on with a stick. He made an obscene gesture at the well-dressed people staring at him.

They rode on.

'Take heart,' said Geoffrey Charles, seeing his wife's face; 'it is not all like this.'

'It shall be going to clear – see,' said the girl. 'Over there.'

Like a sliding cover the cloud bank was slipping up from the horizon, revealing a sliver of bright light.

'We must see them soon,' Geoffrey Charles said.

'Who?'

'Drake and Morwenna. I must write to ask them to Trenwith. Or we could ride over and see them.'

'How far is it?'

'Thirty miles. Maybe less. But we should have to spend the night.'

They descended a valley, where trees suddenly grew again in green bird-haunted clumps, passed a fine house, only just removed from the attle and the waste.

'Thomas Wilson lives there,' said Geoffrey Charles. 'He is the mineral lord for this area, and so takes a dish from what is raised on those mines you have just passed.'

'Dish? *Plato*? Again strange. Dish is what you eat off, no?'

'A dish is what you eat off. But in this country there is another meaning to it. It means a share. A portion. The mineral lord takes a fraction – perhaps one ninth – of the value of the ore raised.'

'So he is rich?'

'If the mines prosper, yes.'

'But there is no such dish at your house – Trenwith?'

'At one time there was. The Poldarks owned a large share of the mine too — it was called Grambler — but twenty-odd years ago it failed; and so we have been poor ever since.'

'But can you not begin other mines, like your cousin, the Captain Ross Poldark? Does he not open one mine upon another?'

'He has only tried three, and has been lucky with two of them. Unhappily on Trenwith land we have only Grambler, which would cost a fortune to unwater — that is to drain. For it was always a wet mine and needed pumping at an early level. No one has been successful with any new working in the vicinity; though one or two attempts have been made. My father attempted by gambling to recoup his losses and so to prospect for new lodes; but alas this only led him further into debt.'

'*Qué lástima!* Well, well, who knows? Perhaps we shall try again when this war will be over.'

The moorland now was not so desolate; they dipped into valleys through narrow tracks and between high hedges whose brambles and thorns plucked at their hats and cloaks.

'We are skirting Killewarren,' said Geoffrey Charles. 'Where the Enyses live. He is a doctor, a surgeon, greatly respected and liked. It is said, such is his repute, that he was called to London to see the old King when he first lost his reason.'

'I am in difficult,' said Amadora. 'How to remember these names.'

'Don't try. They will come to you quick enough when you meet them.'

'The King he lose his reason?'

'Oh, yes. And that was years ago. He is still alive, but sadly lacking.'

'Then how shall this fat man be King?'

'He is not. He is Prince Regent, and will remain so until his father dies. But he is king in all but name.'

'Sadly lacking,' said Amadora. 'That is new. Sadly lacking. I like. It has a pretty sound.'

'*You* have a pretty sound, *mi boniato*.'

'When you call me that I know you shall be a tease.'

Geoffrey Charles laughed and tried to pat her hand, but her mare lurched away from him. He said in Spanish: 'I can only tell you, my little, what joy it gives me to see you riding with me in my own country, in my own county, towards my own home.'

III

Geoffrey Charles avoided the well known landmarks, coming in by the cross-roads at Bargus and so missing Sawle Church. It pleased his fancy that no one who knew him should see him arrive, though he did not deceive himself that it would remain a secret for long.

He made no attempt to call at the lodge, in the expectation that the place would not be locked – it never had been in the old days. When they came in sight of the house Amadora gave a little gasp of pleasure.

'*Qué hermoso!* You did not tell me so much! *Qué magnífico! Y gracioso!*'

'Wait,' said Geoffrey Charles. 'It is still lovely from a distance, but . . .'

They reined up outside the front door, and he helped her to dismount, holding her a long time in his arms before he let her down. By now the sky had lifted its lid but the sun was not yet out and the front of the house was in shadow. He turned the ring of the door and pushed. The door groaned open upon the small and unimpressive entrance hall. He strode through it and opened the right hand door which led to the great hall. This room, with its minstrel gallery and its enormous table, was illuminated by the one window in which it was said there were 576 separate panes of glass. The time to see the room at its best was when the sun was slanting in, but even now the effect was highly impressive. Geoffrey Charles hoped she did not hear the rustling and scampering at the end of the room as she threw herself into his arms with delight.

Hand in hand they explored their home. Geoffrey de

Trenwith, who had designed it, or at least superintended its building, had directed his money and his craftsmen towards the several splendid reception rooms; of the fifteen bedrooms most were dark-panelled and poky, and even the four best were not large by modern standards. The living Geoffrey showed his new wife the little turret room up the stairs which had been his when he was a boy, and was delighted to find a number of his own childish sketches still on the walls. The bed was covered with a dust-sheet which was drawn up and wrinkled as if someone had quite recently left an impression on the bed; there were blankets on the floor, one of them badly gnawed; the light slanted through half drawn curtains.

They went to Aunt Agatha's old room and found it in even poorer shape than the rest of the house. Two pictures on the walls had their glass smashed, and one frame sagged. A part of the dressing table was broken and the thing stood bent-legged, like a soldier on a crutch. The wardrobe door swung open on one hinge. An empty bird cage hung by the window, its bars glinting in the sun, and inside a tiny frail-boned skeleton lay aslant gathering dust.

There was a tomb-like smell to the whole house.

'Let us go on,' said Geoffrey Charles sharply, his arm about Amadora. 'I do not think this is a happy room.'

Nor was his mother's, for again part of the curtain and carpet was gnawed away, and mice droppings were everywhere; moths had holed the pretty pink bedspread; beside the bed were an hourglass, a bottle containing furry liquid, a spoon . . .

His step-father's room was cleaner, looked better cared for, but Geoffrey Charles would not stop there. He led the way to the room which most recently had been used by his grandparents, Jonathan and Joan Chynoweth, for it was perhaps the sunniest, with blue damask curtains over lace, a flowery wallpaper above the half panels, pink and yellow silk curtains decorating the fourposter bed. That the bed needed drying out, that the moths here again were in the curtains, that there were sinister rustlings in the wainscot, were matters to be taken in one's stride.

'Let's go down,' he said, after he had thumped open two windows. 'We'll sleep here. I'll light a fire here after I've lit the one in the kitchen. Then I shall go and find those two knaves who pretend to look after this property. They can come and stable our horses and rub them down, but I don't want them putting their ugly faces in this house – our house – tonight. If they saw unexplained lights it might disturb their drunken stupor, and cause them to come stumbling up here at the wrong time.'

'Wrong time?' said Amadora.

'Wrong time.' They went down the dark stairs arm in arm, jogging slightly to keep in step. He led the way through to the kitchen.

Three steps led down to a flagged floor become uneven with time and now silk-threaded with snail-trails. The fireplace was black and cold and rusty. A great kettle was still suspended above it on a hook. By the back door was a wooden pump with a bucket under it. The bucket had split. Cobwebs festooned the shelves and there was a smell of decayed food. The place was dark from its single dirty window, and Geoffrey Charles went across and flung open the half door. Light flooded in.

'That's better. We cannot hope to clear much tonight, but a fire will make a big difference. And some fresh air . . .'

Amadora glanced at him sidelong. 'Do you wish I shall cook?'

'We've got the chicken, butter, eggs Verity gave us. Bread. Cheese. *Can* you?'

'It was part of my training. But I do not know if I shall be cooking to please the English officer.'

'Anything you do will please the English officer so long as you do it yourself, so long as we are alone.'

'It shall be our first meal ever alone.'

'. . . I think there will be some wine left in the cellar; there's some plates in here – they'll need washing – knives and forks too; candles. We will dine at that great table, you at one end and I at the other! Amid all the squalor of this neglected house! What a glorious thought!'

'So far apart . . .'

'Yes, for otherwise the food you prepared would not get eaten. Afterwards, in our bedroom upstairs . . .' He turned her towards him and kissed her forehead and then her lips.

'Husband.'

'Yes, my little,' he said, 'it shall be all that and more.'

Chapter Four

I

Jeremy found the letter waiting for him when he returned
with his family from St Day Show Fair. It had been a
pleasant day, which would have been more pleasant if he
had not caught sight of Cuby Trevanion in the distance with
her brother.

As always, despite the distress in the county as a whole,
these fairs drew the crowds, and although many looked
ill-clad and undernourished there was money about. People
were bidding for cattle, buying trinkets, patronizing the
booths, eating and drinking the buns and milk. The beer and
gin tents – run by the local inns – were well filled, and before
the day was far advanced men were sprawled in corners
insensible to anything more the fair had to offer.

The Poldarks had taken a large surplus of piglets to sell,
and baskets of soft fruits. Raspberries had been planted for
the first time only four years ago, but the canes, aided by
good top-dressings of rotted pig manure, were rampant in
the sandy soil. The half brothers, Dick and Cal Trevail had
taken the produce in two dog carts, and they brought back a
variety of things Demelza needed or thought she needed or
just fancied the look of. Apart from the youngest child,
Henry, it had been the complete family; and nowadays,
with Ross often away or one or other of the elder children
on pursuits of their own, it didn't happen too often that they
all went out together. She never lost her pleasure in riding
beside Ross and watching the three horses on ahead. What
marvellous, beautiful, intelligent and charming children
they were! She supposed most parents felt the same but it
didn't deflect her from her full sense of pride. Jeremy, at
twenty-two, tall and thin and attractive with his high colour
and blue grey eyes: gifted in unusual ways, comical of

46

speech, usually hiding his deepest and most complex impulses behind a curtain of flippancy, devoted to animals and painting, and apparently entirely artistic, if one did not know of his passion for machinery. Clowance, soon to be nineteen, sturdily slender, blonde as a Scandinavian, always frank, incapable it seemed of dissimulation or feminine wiles, pretty enough to cause men's eyes to follow her, a tomboy but warm and impulsive and generous. Little Isabella-Rose, now eleven, dark as her sister was fair, with the darkest of brown eyes, slender, vivacious, always thumping on the piano, always dancing as she walked, with a powerful but unmusical young voice; she was never still, seldom silent. Men would start looking at her *very* soon.

They were all hers, that was what Demelza at times found so overpowering. Hers and Ross's, products of their blood, their union, their love. All seed, all flowering differently, all adorning the family and the home. And at home a *fourth* – another boy, Henry – or Harry as he was already being called – little more than seven months old, gurgling cheerfully, jolly as a sprig, who with luck would grow up to complete a quartet of disparate yet related human beings carrying on the blood and the name. It was the strangest miracle.

No one pretended that there had not been problems already with the two eldest, no one denied the likelihood of many more with all of them: that was part of the challenge and the stress and the stimulus of life.

When Jeremy got upstairs he impatiently broke the seal of his letter and frowned at the handwriting. It was new to him. He carried it to the window and read it in the fading light.

Dear Sir,
   Over the last few months I have heard from my friends that you are developing or attempting to develop a steam carriage for use on our common roads. This is a subject which has fascinated me all my life, and I would be greatly obligated to you to be told something of the progress of your experiments. I have

met Mr Trevithick on two occasions and am fascinated by his mechanical and scientific genius.

I am a doctor by profession, being junior partner to Dr Avery of Wadebridge – from which town I write, and alas admit it to be in an area remote from the centres of experiment. However, I have an uncle who is Vicar of St Erth, and several times I have been able to visit him, and also have been privileged to meet Mr Davies Giddy and Mr Henry Andrew Vivian of Camborne, who first told me about you.

I should be especially interested to learn in what way you intend to combat wheel spin, also whether you have ever considered the proposition that the bursting of boilers is not always occasioned by the pressure of steam but can come about through the decomposition of the waters? Is it not possible that hydrogen combined with nitrogen and oxygen may form an explosive compound?

These and many other matters I would welcome your views on, and if your machine is sufficiently advanced that it may be seen I should esteem it an honour to be shewn it.

If you should be so willing, and consider a preliminary meeting appropriate, I could come to Truro any Wednesday, preferably in the forenoon, and we could talk over the matter. Although Mr Trevithick now says not, I believe there are enormous commercial possibilities in this development – and not so far ahead. Steam carriages are the national conveyances of the future.

I have the honour to be, Sir, your obedient servant,
G. Garner

Jeremy turned the letter over, and if he had known how to smile sardonically he would have done so. Mr Garner, whoever he was – Doctor Garner – was a little out of date. Jeremy's attempt to build a new steam carriage had ended more than a year ago when Trevithick had come upon him unexpectedly in Harvey's Foundry, had examined the carriage that was being built, and had pronounced it unworkable: *far* too heavy, with a boiler of obsolete dimensions. Of course Trevithick had tried to soften the blow, but, remembering his remarks later, one could see that he really thought the machine was a young man's folly, with no prospect of success whatsoever.

Sometimes the thought of constructing a horseless carriage, the ambition to try again, still disturbed Jeremy in the night, the argument being, as Stephen had once put it, that Mr Trevithick's disapproval need not mean the automatic end of the idea; or as Cuby had said at their one happy meeting of last year, that it was not the way of a true inventor to give up after a first set-back.

All the same, Dr Garner was too late: the events in January of this year still stood abrasively across Jeremy's mind. There were a number of things he could still do with his life, but the patient, slow-evolving world of engineering and invention did not seem to be one of them.

So a brief reply to Dr Garner politely choking him off.

In the chest under the window were all the papers Jeremy had accumulated during the years when his passion for steam had had to be purely theoretical: the newspapers, the magazines of his boyhood, the sketches and drawings of the later period, together with calculations and estimates he had jotted down when first visiting Hayle and discovering the boiler for himself. After his meeting with Trevithick last spring he had thrust his later sketches on top of the rest and shut the lid. Except for taking out occasional things he needed from day to day, he had not used the chest. Now he lifted the lid again and fumbled about among the fish hooks, the crayons, the half-finished sketches, the old newspapers, and came out with a cutting from the *Sherborne Mercury* of early 1803. It was the first cutting he had clipped out to keep for himself.

In addition to the many attempts that have been made to construct carriages to run without horses, a method has lately been tried at the hamlet of Camborne in Cornwall which seems to promise success. A carriage has been constructed by a Mr Trevithick, containing a small steam engine, the force of which was found sufficient, upon trial, to impel the carriage, containing several persons amounting to a total weight of 30 cwt, against a hill of considerable steepness, at the rate of four miles an hour; and upon a level road at eight or nine miles an hour.

Just that. Just that; nothing more; no attempt to speculate or to elaborate; an item of news, of no greater importance, it seemed, than the one following, which reported a tithe feast in Probus.

Jeremy smoothed out the newspaper, which was already yellowed with age, put it on the dressing table, fished in the chest again. A half dozen cuttings were in his hand. One was a flippant announcement from the *London Observer* of 17 July, 1808.

The most astonishing machine ever invented is a steam engine with four wheels so constructed that she will with ease and without other aid, gallop from 15 to 20 miles an hour in any circle. She weighs 8 tons and is matched at the next Newmarket meeting against three horses to run 24 hours, starting at the same time. She is now in training on Lady Southampton's estate adjoining the New Road near Bedford Nursery, St Pancras. We understand she will be exposed for public inspection from Tuesday next.

And on to the end of it Jeremy had pinned one of the highly coloured admission cards they had all bought – he and his father and his mother – admission cards to go into the compound on that early autumn day of the same year. Printed in pink, it showed a drawing of the engine, called *Catch Me Who Can*, and was headed 'TREVITHICK's Portable Steam Engine. Mechanical Power Subduing Animal Speed.'

It had not lasted, that wonderful experiment. The engine had performed well but the rails had frequently given way. The number of people willing to pay a shilling admission, with the opportunity of a ride if they felt like risking it, had not been enough to defray expenses. The exhibition had closed. The moving steam engine, whether on rails or on road, was a freak, a sideshow without practical applications. It had best be forgot. Trevithick, from that day on, had decided to forget it.

So who was this man writing from Wadebridge? Some amiable crank. Someone who had convinced himself that if you refined and heated tin long enough it would turn to gold, or thought that if you fixed bamboo-framed wings to your back you could fly. Cornwall was full of dotty inventors.

Jeremy read the letter again. 'Combat wheel-spin?' It was perhaps not an irrational question, for many believed that insufficient traction could be obtained by wheels being forced round by pistons. The horse was the obvious example. Wheels were too smooth. But how out of date was this man? Did he not read the technical papers? Was it even necessary to reply, or did one just ignore the letter?

He was saved the decision by the sound of footsteps on the stairs. A tap on the door. Unusual.

'Come in.'

His father entered, stooping in the doorway. Ross's gaunt face had an inscrutable but pleasant expression. He didn't often come up here.

'Did you not hear the commotion?'

'No. Bella? But she always makes a noise.'

'It seems we are waiting for you.'

'Supper? Good.'

'No, not supper . . . Don't you need a light?'

'I was just going to make one.'

Ross said: 'This damned door is too low. Do you not often scrape your head?'

'Not often now, father. I've grown used to it.'

'When we put you up here you were hardly five feet tall. An extra foot or so makes a difference. Something should be done. Perhaps we could raise it. Cut a piece of the wood out.'

There were shouts from downstairs.

'And what,' Jeremy asked, 'have you come to tell me?'

'Geoffrey Charles is back.'

'*What!* Here? When did he –'

'At Trenwith. They arrived last evening, it seems.'

'They?'

'Yes, he's brought his young Spanish bride.'

'Good God! After all this time! Wonderful! And what –'

'We left too early this morning to hear of it. Jane has just told us. She heard it from Ern Lobb, who heard it from someone else, I forget who. They've gone into the house and are living there, it seems, all on their own, except for the tender care of Liza Harry.'

'They haven't been over here today while we were out?'

'No. I imagine it is a pretty mess at Trenwith and they want a day or two to sort things out.'

'But that's where we can help them!'

'Of course.'

'Papa, Papa,' came the husky young contralto of Isabella-Rose. 'Are you coming?'

Ross looked at Jeremy and smiled. 'You see?'

'You mean – you're going over tonight?'

'Against my better judgement. I put it to your mother and to Clowance that for four people to come beating at your door at half an hour after nine o'clock at night, clamouring to be let in, is the sort of welcome that Geoffrey Charles no doubt could survive. But if his wife is of a nervous disposition it could well prejudice her against the family for ever. No use. They didn't heed me.'

'What did Mama say?'

'Never mind. The question is, do you wish to eat supper on your own, which would give pleasure to Jane, who will feel hurt if everything she has prepared has to stand and go cold for hours? Or do you feel that, having waited so long for Geoffrey Charles, even one day lost will make a difference?'

'I'm coming with you,' said Jeremy. 'But chiefly to see his Spanish girl.'

After Ross had left the room to precede him down the stairs Jeremy paused and picked up a silver stock-pin which had arrived by messenger a couple of days ago. Though it did not really suit his present attire he fancied it and thrust it into the lapel of his jacket.

Music Thomas had brought it. Inside the parcel was a small printed card which read: *From Mrs Clement Pope, Place House, Trevaunance, Cornwall.*

Chapter Five

I

The following week Ross and Demelza were supping with Dwight and Caroline Enys at Killewarren.

Ross said: 'You haven't seen them yet?'

'No,' said Dwight. 'Caroline was for calling, but I thought they were better to have a few days on their own to settle down.'

'Settle down!' Demelza said. 'The house is in a rare jakes! We have been over every day – Jeremy and Clowance and I – doing our most. And Geoffrey Charles has hired three women from the village. And there are five men trying to mend the chimneys and repair the leaks in the roof. And the Harrys have been given a month's notice to leave. I thought poor Amadora would be overwhelmed.'

'A pretty name,' said Caroline. 'A pretty creature?'

'You must ask Ross,' said Demelza; 'he was much taken with her.'

'I have always liked little dark girls,' Ross said. 'You must know that.'

'I'm not little,' said Demelza.

'Well, you were when I first saw you.'

'Sorry if I have overgrown my strength.'

'Oh, I like tall dark girls as well,' said Ross. 'Also tall redheads with beautiful eyes.'

'After these little flippances,' said Caroline, 'perhaps you would consent to describe her to us.'

Ross grunted. 'She's small and dark – with a proud little face – half scared – prickly, half ready to fight – half wishing to be warm and loving.'

'That's three halves,' said Caroline. 'But I believe I take your meaning.'

Dwight said: 'And what of Morwenna and Drake, who had such a friendship with him?'

'They are coming next week. Geoffrey Charles wrote at once, but Drake had just received an order for a new schooner, and, Drake like, does not feel he should leave until the keel is laid.'

'She's a Catholic, I suppose?' said Caroline suddenly.

'Amadora? Must be.' Ross accepted another slice of strawberry pie. 'A pity.'

'I thought you were rather in favour of Catholics?'

'I'm not in favour of Catholicism. I'm in favour of people being able to worship how they will, without penalty — which they can't do yet in England.'

'Nor the Wesleyans.'

'Nor the Wesleyans indeed. What I dislike most is religious exclusivism, from whatever direction it comes.'

'The two sects we've just mentioned are notably among the most exclusive. The Wesleyans believe that only the saved will see Christ. The Catholics don't believe we are members of Christ's church at all!'

'I know. It's a bigoted world.'

'From which we're not free either,' said Dwight. 'Those anti-Catholic meetings all over the country last year! After all, for the last two and a half centuries most of our own countrymen have been taught that Rome is the Scarlet Woman, etcetera.'

'Surely,' said Demelza, 'if two people love each other, that will be most important. Where there is real love, there can be give and take.'

Ross said: 'Well, it depends on the strength of the love and the strength of the religious conviction. Doesn't it? In two or three years when children start coming and the love is not quite so warm . . .'

'Ross, no doubt, judges from his own experience,' said Demelza, scowling at him.

'It's because my own experience is so rare that I cannot judge from it,' said Ross. 'Look around you. Present company naturally excepted.'

Caroline said: 'But does anyone know yet whether the young couple intend to settle here?'

'Geoffrey Charles is returning to join his regiment in a couple of months. She will go back with him. But how they will feel when the war is over . . .'

Demelza said: 'How they feel when the war is over will much depend upon how they feel at the end of this visit. And how *she* feels will much influence how *he* feels. Isn't that so? And how she feels, who knows? may be just a small matter influenced by how nice we are to her.'

Caroline patted her hand. 'Put very well, my dear. I shall go and wait on her tomorrow and offer her . . . what can I offer her that she hasn't already got?'

'Can you speak Spanish?'

'Enough to know that the Italian for *butter* means *donkey* in Spanish. No more.'

'Apparently Harriet Warleggan can. They struck up a sharp friendship that cannot be welcome to either of their husbands.'

The meal came to its end with nuts and grapes and raisins – and of course port. Demelza sipped her port and stretched her legs. Still lacking a little of the vitality she had had before baby Henry was conceived, she was nevertheless zestful enough for most occasions; and of all the meals of her life these were the ones she enjoyed most. (Saving the noisy family meals, which were a thing apart.) To sup at Killewarren with her oldest and dearest friends, in Ross's company, was better even than when they came to her. There was no niggling anxiety as to whether the veal would be properly done or whether the poached peaches would be served half cold. Caroline always seemed able to employ better and more efficient servants. Demelza admitted that she was not a very good manager herself. She had never quite got into the way of being angry with servants if they didn't do what they were told. (Ross could do it in a second; but it was not Ross's business.) This was the luxury of enjoying an excellent meal and wines without a thought to the kitchen.

'Please?' she said, having not heard a question.

'Dreaming again,' said Caroline. 'I was telling Ross that I might be losing Dwight sometime soon.'

'Very unlikely,' said Dwight. 'Caroline is romancing.'

'Far from it! I know from his manner.'

Dwight said: 'What Caroline is trying to tell you in her roundabout way is that I have recently received a letter from Sir Humphry Davy. You remember him, Ross: you met him at the Duchess of Gordon's party.'

'Yes, of course. And since somewhere, I can't recollect where.'

'*Sir* Humphry?' said Demelza.

'He was knighted last year. And is recently married.'

'To a widow,' Ross added. 'Does she not also have money?'

'A considerable fortune. But I believe they are truly in love.'

'Money doesn't prevent that,' said Ross.

'No, but it can give rise to unworthy gossip . . . They were here in Cornwall in May, visiting his parents in Penzance. George Warleggan and Harriet invited them to spend a night at Cardew. We were asked to sup there.'

'Well, I suppose Davy is now the foremost scientist in England.'

Dwight took a nut and cracked it, but did not put the kernel in his mouth.

'When I met Davy at Cardew he told me of an invitation he had received from France. He has kept in touch with most of the leading French scientists through these latest years of the war. Scientists of note like Ampère, Guy-Lussac, Laplace. Early last year Napoleon himself heard of Davy's discoveries and achievements, and at once offered Davy unconditional permission to visit Paris and to travel through France and anywhere else in Europe he chose. It is a notable recognition of his achievements. And I think also a notable testimony to Buonaparte's breadth of vision that in the middle of so bitter a war he should make such an offer to a national of his bitterest enemy.'

'And Davy? He did not accept the invitation?'

'Not then. But it was an open invitation, and he thinks of accepting it this autumn.'

Demelza took a sip of port, but no one spoke.

Then Ross said: 'It's a different situation now for Napoleon. Then he was riding high, true master of Europe. Now

57

he's between two fires. I should ask for a further assurance if I were Davy.'

'I don't believe Napoleon would go back on his word.'

'Don't forget the end of the Treaty of Amiens,' Caroline said. 'Ten thousand British tourists interned as prisoners of war. Yourself and Ross escaping back across the Channel by the skin of your teeth. And me alone in this house carrying Sophie!'

'And this letter you have had from Sir Humphry?' said Demelza, seeing already how the land lay.

Dwight smiled. 'He has been told he may take his wife, a couple of servants, one or two friends of like mind.'

'Such as who?'

'What?'

'Such as what friends?'

'Oh . . . a chemist, a scientist perhaps, not more than two or three. As you will have guessed by now, he has asked me if I would like to be one of them. He suggests that as a medical man I could be of value to them, travelling as they are as a small group in a foreign and hostile country.'

Ross glanced at Caroline, who was frowning with concentration at a black grape.

'A dilemma.'

'The letter only reached me yesterday. It is a delectable thought to be able to meet all those French scientists on their own ground. Even to see Paris again, right in the depths of the war . . . But I believe Humphry Davy intends to go on to Italy after his stay in Paris; he has some plans to visit the Auvergne and even go as far as Naples, which would mean his being away at least a year. And that would not be feasible – or tolerable – for me.'

Caroline said: 'I wonder what the French authorities would feel about it if Sir Humphry brought with him an escaped and unransomed prisoner of war!'

'I doubt, my dear, if they would be likely to discover it after eighteen years.'

'Caroline has a long memory,' said Demelza. 'We both have! And little wonder.'

There was a tap at the door and Myners came in. 'Dr Enys, sir. Mr Pope is sick again. A messenger has just come from Place House. It is Music Thomas, who says it is urgent, but of course . . .'

The implication was that Music Thomas was not the most reliable of informants.

Dwight said: 'Tell Tresidder. Ask him to saddle Parsee. And tell Thomas to go back and say I am coming at once.'

'Very good, sir.'

When they were alone Caroline said: 'D'you know it is just about a year ago, isn't it, that this happened before? You were supping with us, and someone came from Place House asking for Dwight. We must be careful not to allow this to become a habit.'

'Do you see much of them – socially, I mean?' Ross asked.

'Our girls are too young for theirs; and I confess he rather gives me the creeps. She's well enough – if she would only stop worrying as to whether she ought to be condescending or be condescended to.'

Dwight said: 'I have visited him monthly since last year. They live in a social strait-jacket. And not only social. It is a queer household.'

'Did you hear about Jeremy?' Demelza asked. 'Mrs Pope fell off her horse, and Jeremy found her and helped her home.'

'When was this?'

'Only last week. She sent him a silver stock-pin. Jeremy is quite taken with it.'

'He might well have been taken with her too,' said Ross. He added: 'Do you know anything more of the mine Unwin is supposed to be opening on Mr Pope's doorstep?'

'I believe it is hanging fire,' Dwight said. 'Isn't that so, Caroline? You heard something from Harriet Warleggan.'

Caroline yawned. 'A story that it was to be delayed. To do with copper prices. Chenhalls of course is the moving figure. But Unwin has certainly not been down of late.'

Dwight got up, patted Ross on the shoulder, kissed Demelza on the cheek, put fingers over his wife's long fingers. 'Well, I suppose we must not keep the old gentleman waiting. Last time, my dear, I think you offered me a brandy before I left.'

'What a memory,' said Caroline.

II

Place House was square and solid, put up about a hundred years ago by masons who had used local stone and had no time for fripperies; but the second owner, having been to London and seen the work of Inigo Jones, had added a Palladian front to give a touch of elegance and distinction. In essence it was a roomy, but in its exposed position a draughty, house, built of elvan and heavy slate; the elegance had never quite come off; the pillars had stood the weather less well than the rest of the stone. There was no garden at the front to speak of: just a terrace with a balustrade looking down the combe towards the sea.

When Dwight arrived the interior seemed to be fluttering with newly-lighted candles. Katie Carter let him in. Her manner was as agitated as the candles, her hair untidy, spraying out tonight from under her cap like seaweed. Almost as she let him in she began to explain breathlessly that she had been the first to answer Mrs Pope's urgent call and had run up the stairs and found her trying to bring the Master round. Nowadays, Katie said, he had a light supper in bed; so he must have been took queer soon after eating it and wandered out upon the landing and fallen down in the open door of one of the other bedrooms, where the Mistress had found him. She, Katie, and the Mistress had managed to carry him back to his own room and lift him onto the bed.

It was not usual or proper for a parlourmaid to say so much to a surgeon in a hoarse whisper as she led him up the fine polished staircase, spilling commas of candlegrease as she went, but Ben Carter's sister was one of the village family and took such liberties without knowing she was taking them. Taller than Ben and just as dark in that Cornish way which had given rise mistakenly to stories of shipwrecked sailors from the Armada – though not perhaps mistakenly to a later dash of Spanish blood – she was as unlike Ben in most ways as she could be. She was altogether a big girl, clumsy, nervous, and her nervousness made her morose. Her feet were too big, and she often seemed to fall over them. Yet taken in hand, Dwight thought, she need not have been ill looking: she had escaped the pox, her skin was clear; her eyes, under lashes so black they might have been kohled, were large and full.

Mrs Pope was waiting for him at the door of the bedroom; they shook hands gravely and he went to the patient. At first Dwight thought he was dead. His face was the colour of the sheet, his body was cold and there was no perceptible pulse. The pupils were dilated and turned up, the tongue was just showing between the decayed teeth. Dwight took a hand mirror and held it to the man's bluish lips. After a few seconds the mirror became discoloured.

Dwight said: 'Warming pans, if you please.' He rummaged in his bag and took out a bottle of ethyl oxide, spilled a few drops on a pad and held it to Mr Pope's nose. Over his shoulder he said: 'He has clearly had a severe spasm and has not come out of it yet. Has he been taking some exceptional exercise or been involved in emotional strain?'

'Not at all,' Mrs Pope said. 'He retired at seven. This has been his habit since you first saw him. In that sense he has been a very good patient. I – er – took my supper downstairs and as usual his was sent up. Apparently he ate it. When I have finished my own meal I always come up to make sure that he is comfortable and wants for nothing. I found him like this, where he had fallen, on the threshold of his bedroom. We lifted him onto the bed and sent Thomas in haste to fetch you. I – feared him dead.'

Dwight put a few drops of laudanum in a spoon, dipped his fingers in it and dabbed it on the old man's lips and tongue. 'The bell pull is by his bed. He had no need to get up.'

'None.' She shivered as if cold, pulled her green Chinese-silk morning gown more closely about her. Sometimes her long fair hair was elaborately built up, but this evening it was twisted into a casual pile and pinned in place by an ebony-coloured Spanish comb. 'He never leaves his room after retiring, Dr Enys. At least I have never known it before. But since he was not bedridden I suppose he could do so if he chose.'

'Are his children here?'

'No. They are spending the night with the Teagues.'

'I think they should be summoned.'

'Tonight? They will be returning in the morning.'

'Well, it is for you to choose, Mrs Pope. But when a man is in such a condition as this – which is virtually syncope . . .'

'Does that mean? . . .' Mrs Pope said. 'Does that mean he is going to die?'

'We cannot tell. But it has certainly been a very close call.'

Mrs Pope began to cry. At least she took out a handkerchief and dabbed her nose, and gave an occasional trembling sigh. Dwight held the mirror up again, and thought the misting came a little more quickly. Presently Katie Carter and another woman came in, each carrying a warming pan.

'*Quiet,* Kate,' said Mrs Pope reprovingly, as the pan clattered.

'Sorry, mum. I was in *some* 'aste . . .'

The warming pans were slid under the sheets at the feet of Mr Clement Pope. Dwight took out a jar and put a leech on each of the man's wrists. Unlike most of his profession, he was disenchanted with the practice of bleeding, but this was a case where it might ease the pressure of blood to the heart.

Mrs Pope said to the other servant: 'Pray see that Miss Pope and Miss Maud are sent for immediately.'

' 'S, mum.'

The women went out. It occurred to Dwight to wonder whether Mrs Selina Pope always supped in this elegant deshabille. It was not his business to inquire. It was not even his business to ask whether Mr Clement Pope had altogether obeyed his instructions to lead a quiet, regular and celibate life.

'You will stay, Dr Enys?' Mrs Pope said, looking at him from under damp lashes.

'For the time, certainly. Until he regains consciousness or – there is some other change.'

'Can I – get you something to drink? The maids will . . .'

'No, thank you.'

Time passes quickly or slowly when waiting, according to how occupied or pre-occupied the mind is that waits; so Dwight never knew, perhaps Selina Pope never knew, how long they sat there, Dwight on a chair by the bed, Mrs Pope on an early Georgian window seat upholstered in yellow silk.

Dwight thought of his own two daughters, growing away now. Sophie eleven, Meliora nearly ten. Four years after the tragedy of Sarah's death Caroline had found herself pregnant again and had produced these two girls in quite rapid succession. As if to redress the balance after the frailties of their first child, these two had ailed little and given small cause for anxiety even when they caught the childish diseases. Both thin to the point of being bony, they were bundles of vigour and energy, only exceeded in this by Bella Poldark. Sophie was *going* to be pretty but her looks were taking a long time to develop; Meliora didn't have the features and her mouth was too big, but she would easily make up for this lack by sheer charm of manner. Both were fair but neither, surprisingly, a redhead.

Dwight had wondered once whether to ask Sir Humphry Davy if he might bring his wife at least as far as Paris; but he knew without asking that she would not leave the children for longer than a month at the most. The idea of meeting the French scientists filled him with excitement; but he knew already that he had no alternative but to refuse.

All this time there had been virtually no change in the patient; Dwight had removed the leeches and occasionally added a drop more ether to the pad he held under the sick man's nose; Selina had crossed and uncrossed her elegant legs a number of times and had lifted her arms to bind in a thick strand of yellow hair. So perhaps it was an hour – during which there had been virtually no conversation between them – before Mr Pope spoke.

Yes, Mr Pope spoke, breaking a silence which for him had endured ever since he fell down with his heart attack.

Quite gradually, and unnoticed by them both he regained

consciousness. His eyes fluttered, staring first up at the ceiling, and then, gaining a degree of focus, at the figure of his wife, silhouetted in graceful green against the darker curtain. He licked his lips and spoke.

'Whore,' he said quite distinctly and with some feeling. And then again: 'Whore.' After which he died.

Chapter Six

I

Mr Pope's funeral took place at midnight on the 14th August. He had decreed the time in his Will, made soon after he returned to England, on learning of the vast expense to which many widows were driven when their rich husbands died and it was expected that half the county should be invited to the exequies. A careful man in all things, he was careful not to embarrass his widow by leaving her a choice. Not, of course, that he had supposed he or she would be in such a situation for a very long time to come. People seldom do suppose such dire things, especially perhaps those of middle age returning to England to retire in comfort with daughters still to marry off and pretty young second wives to hold to their bosoms. Whether or not he had changed his opinion in the last few months one could not tell, at least he had not changed his Will.

Whether indeed those strange last words to come from his lips referred to anyone or anything in particular it was also difficult to tell. Dwight discreetly ignored them; he also ignored the hot flush on Selina's face at the time. Eminently correct and in his most detached medical manner, Dwight did all that was required of him – including mixing a soothing draught for Selina, and for both the girls to see them through the night when they returned. Only when he was leaving and once again was being escorted to the front door by Katie Carter, did he ask a question of an unusually silent and tearful parlourmaid who seemed reluctant to let him go.

'Your master is dead, Katie. Nothing more could have been done to save him by you or by anyone else . . . You did say, didn't you, that you found Mr Pope outside his bedroom door?'

'No, sur. Oh, no sur. Twas outside of the bedroom door next but one to 'is own. The blue bedroom they d'call it. There he was when I run up, lying flat on 'is face and Mrs kneeling beside of him.'

'Ah, yes, I see. Well, thank you, Katie.'

She hung at the front door, eyes aslant at another servant who was going past. 'Twasn't my fault, sur. Y'know, sur. Twasn't my fault at all!'

'Fault? How could it be, Katie?'

'Seeing what I seen, Dr Enys. I mean to say, was it now?'

'Of course not,' Dwight said soothingly. But it was simply not in human nature, however constrained by medical etiquette, for him not to go on: 'I'm a little unsure as to what you mean by this, Katie.'

'Oh, sur –' she began, and then Music Thomas came forward with his horse and the chance of further confidences was past.

II

On the morning after Mr Pope's death Music, who had lingered by the still room door where he really had no business, in the hope of seeing Katie again, was rewarded by her sudden appearance in search of a jar of preserves. She still looked distressed by the night's events and was too impatient to speak to him; though she was aware that the sudden emergency of Mr Pope's heart stroke had temporarily brought them to a more confidential association than they had ever had before.

None of the Thomas brothers was married. John, by far the eldest, had a woman friend called 'Winky' Mitchell who had a nervous twitch to one of her eyes, and a deaf husband who never rose from his bed; John Thomas visited her every night he was home from the sea. Art, only a year older than Music, was often linked with his younger brother by name – Art and Music seemed to go together – but he was much different in appearance and temperament; indeed he was capable of calculations quite outside his brother's comprehension and was at present courting Edie Permewan, a widow old enough to be his mother, in the hope of coming in for the tanner's business left to her by her husband.

Music, generally speaking, worked to short-term ends: he did not go much further at the moment than the hope that Katie should smile at him – or hold him in sufficient esteem to consider him worth speaking to.

'Reckon twill be different wi'out the Master,' he said for the third time, hoping that water would wear away stone.

It did. 'You've no manner of business in 'ere, Music Thomas,' said Katie severely, 'and if the Master were 'live ye'd not come lousterin' in like this!'

'I aren't lousterin',' said Music. ''Twas just I was round in 'ere, see, and . . .' He paused, not able to confess the unconfessable by blurting out that his only real purpose was to see her. 'What you said to me last night . . .'

Katie found the jar she was seeking. She wiped it round with her sleeve to take the dust off the top, and almost dropped it.

She glared at him. 'There see what you near made me do! Go on now – off with ee.'

He stepped aside to let her out of the room and glimpsed Ethel, the head parlourmaid at the end of the passage.

Disapproval shining in every pore Ethel said: 'Katie, you're wanted in the music room. Mistress wants you. What be you doin' 'ere, Thomas? Tis no place for you to be, mourning house or no.'

They hurried off in opposite directions. Katie thought: from Music to music room; what can she want? not to talk about last night, I 'ope, for I couldn't bear it. My dear life, I reely couldn't! What will she *say*?

The small room that had once been Sir John's study had been turned into a music room for the two girls, but neither was present, only Mrs Pope.

Black suited her. It was only a makeshift attire but the simple frock with the black hair veil was more becoming than the widow's weeds now in process of being made. Even the severity of the hair style did not detract from her good looks. Only the expression of her face did that. Katie supposed it was grief; at least she hoped it was grief.

They had not seen each other since the night before. Katie had busied herself downstairs, as much as possible out of sight.

It was an odd subject for the first day of bereavement, but Mrs Pope opened the conversation by saying that Miss Maud's pianoforte was not being kept clean. The keys were sticking and were turning yellow. Naturally, she said, there would be no playing of the instrument while mourning was being observed; but it was *essential* that the keys should be cleaned weekly with milk and *not* neglected by careless, heedless and untidy servants. Miss Maud had complained about it only yesterday.

It was the beginning of a series of stern complaints about the quality of work in the house. Katie said, yes 'm, and no mum, and well, mum, I 'ave tried but they do say as . . . and then kept her head down hoping that in time the bombardment would expend itself. She had always admired her mistress and envied her her feminine allure – the graceful chatelaine with the keys at her waist, keeping a gentle eye on the good order of the house – and what did it matter etc. etc. . . . Harshness had been left to Mr Pope; it was his prerogative; Katie sincerely hoped Mrs Pope was not going to adopt this role as her own with Mr Pope hardly yet cold upstairs. It sometimes happened.

Perhaps with Mrs Pope it was just the shock, the grief. She'd get over it, be her own easy self again. Or perhaps it wasn't grief. Perhaps it was anger over last night. Katie could see that she was the object of her mistress's annoyance. Perhaps it was better this way, just to be scolded, if only it could be left at that.

Presently Mrs Pope did stop. She looked at the harp and sat on a low stool and let her fingers tremble on the strings, but so lightly that no one outside the room could have heard.

'Kate,' she said, 'you were first on the scene last night when Mr Pope had his heart attack, were you not?'

Oh, Holy Moses, here it came! 'Yes 'm.'

'I was grateful for your help. My dear husband was struck so suddenly that I almost fainted at the sight of him lying there so still on the floor.'

'Yes 'm. Twas some awful shock, you.'

'It may be,' said Mrs Pope, looking feline, 'that in the confusion of that time you imagine you saw things which did not in fact exist.'

Katie stared and sniffed, resisting a desire to wipe her nose with the back of her hand. 'I don't rightly know, mum. I don't know nothin' 'bout that.'

Selina Pope gravely acknowledged this confession of confusion with a slow nod. 'Exactly. At times like that one often fancies one sees things . . .'

Katie said: 'Well, mum, all I d'know I seen was –'

'*Enough,*' Mrs Pope said. 'Whatever you *think* you saw is quite beside the point. As I have *told* you, in moments of *shock* and *stress* one fancies one sees all sorts of imaginary things which just do not exist in the world of reality at all.'

'Do you, mum? I dunno, mum. Tedn for the likes of me –'

'What I am concerned to know is whether you have passed on these fancies of yours to anyone else.'

Katie stared. 'Please?'

Mrs Pope repeated her question.

Katie tried to push some loose strands of hair under her cap. 'Fancies? Fancies, mum? Oh, no mum. I 'aven't mentioned no fancies.' She tried again.

'Leave your cap alone.'

'Yes 'm. Last night, just as he were leaving Dr Enys were saying –'

'What? What about Dr Enys?'

'About it being an 'eart attack and 'e couldn't think why Mr Pope 'd been mazing 'bout the landing like that.'

'And what did you say?'

'Didn't say nothing, mum. Tweren't for me to say nothing, was it.'

Mrs Pope allowed her fingers to produce the faintest ripple of sound. She knew these Cornish girls, who would lie themselves out of anything. But Kate was a simple girl – not

69

simple in the sense of being half witted, but credulous, uneducated, gullible. She seemed to have hardly any friends. A little dissimulation, a little feminine subtlety would have helped her a lot. It seemed improbable that she was employing any subterfuge now.

'Kate, do you remember breaking that Japanese teapot last year?'

'Oh, yes 'm. Don't I just!'

'Mr Pope was very angry, very distressed at the loss. And do you remember those two gold-rimmed Staffordshire plates you broke in January?'

Kate hung her head. 'Yes 'm.'

'When that happened Mr Pope was for discharging you: he felt all our fine china was in danger.'

'You stopped it all out of my wages, 'm. Twill take till November to pay 'n off, you.'

'That may be. But I assume you would wish to stay on as parlourmaid.'

'Oh, yes 'm! Don't rightly know what I could do, where I should go, if you sent me away!'

'Well . . . now that I am a widow I may well be reducing the number of servants I employ. It is early days yet, but one will soon have to begin to think of these things. I may have no alternative but to live in a more restricted style.'

Mrs Pope stopped and allowed that much to sink in. This was a horribly embarrassing interview, but so far she felt it had gone well.

'Whatever happened upstairs last night,' she said, resolving to be a little more frank, 'whatever happened, or whatever you may think happened, was witnessed and imagined only by you. No one else, Kate. No one else at all. Do you understand?'

'Oh, yes 'm!'

'Naturally, I wish anything that happened between my husband and me to be kept private. I do not wish the old women of the village to be rabid with ill-informed gossip. So if such gossip should begin, who would be responsible?'

'Please?' Katie frowned at this difficult problem of ethics and logic.

'Who would be *responsible*?' Selina said, losing patience. 'Why *you*, of course! Who else? Only *you*.'

'But, mum, I never uttered a word! Tedn me! I d'say nothing! Twas some other gullymouth as 'as been geeking around, I tell ee. Why, 'ow could it be me –'

'I didn't *say* it was you! I didn't say *anyone* had so far been guilty of spreading tales! What I am trying to *tell* you is that if any such tales *did* spread they could only come from you because only you *know*.' Mrs Pope hastily corrected herself. 'Because only you can *wrongly interpret* what happened last night. No one else can, for no one else was there. Don't you see that? So if lying rumours and tittle-tattle get around I shall know such lying rumours come from *you*, shall I not?'

Katie's eyes had filled with tears. 'I 'aven't said nothin', mum. I swear to God I 'aven't said nothin' to a living soul. I don't disknowledge I were there, but I never spoke to a living soul bout 'n.'

'Nor will speak?'

'Please?'

'So you promise you will not speak?'

'Oh, yes. Tedn nothing to do wi' me. Tedn nothing 'tall!' (My dear life, she thought, I must tell Music Thomas t'keep 'is big trap shut!)

Mrs Pope got up from the harp, came slowly over to her parlourmaid. 'There, there, dry your tears . . . I only wished to make it all very plain to you. I *want* you to stay on here as parlourmaid. Although you are sometimes clumsy and careless I believe you have the makings of a good servant, and I wish to retain you. But you do understand, don't you, Kate, that it will depend on whether disagreeable rumours spread about the village.'

'Oh, yes 'm.' Katie blinked. And then, to get it quite clear in her own mind, she said: 'You mean – you mean I mustn't ever speak about Mr . . . about the young man who was upstairs wi' you last night?'

Half an hour later Music Thomas was grooming Amboy, who was restless and temperamental for lack of exercise – practically nobody but Music could get near him – when Katie Carter appeared in the stables. Music nearly dropped his brush.

'Katie,' he said, 'well now!' and grinned feebly.

'Music,' she said. 'I want a word with ee.'

This was so much more than she had ever wanted before that he was lost in wonder. He just stared at her admiringly.

Presently, while Katie was trying to decide how to start, it dawned upon her at last that this *was* a look of admiration, of physical admiration, he was giving her. It had never occurred to her before. True, he had made several approaches of a raw kind. True, after the debacle of the Truro races, he had come to her home – apparently to say he was sorry – but she had not taken this in the least seriously. After abusing him – with good reason – at the races, she had laughed at his later attempts to make up. Music, everyone knew, was not the type to be interested in *girls*. Indeed he was probably not the type to be interested in anything of that sort. He was a fool. A good-natured, amiable, ambling fool, to whom women meant nothing and could mean nothing – because he was a nothing himself. She didn't *dislike* him. He was well-meaning, willing, friendly: there was nothing to dislike about him. But . . . It did occur to her now that if somehow, somewhere in his make-up there was a gleam of normality, and that that gleam was temporarily focused upon her, it might be put to good account.

'I suppose you d'know,' she said, 'how bad you been doing your duties in the stables these last few months, like, eh?'

'What?' He stared at her, still amiably, but surprised at the turn of events.

Katie's eyes roamed around. 'Yes. Look at these 'ere stables. They'm clobbed wi' dirt and dust. See that wall. See that brush. And even the 'orses. Neglecting the 'orses too. Never brushing of 'em down proper. Amboy, Halter,

Kingfisher, Gauntlet ... them others; can't recall their names. Mistress was saying 'ow bad you saw to 'em. Master was displeased too afore he died.'

'Oh? Eh? I dunno what you d'mean! Me? I d'work 'ard all the time I'm 'ere. Katie, I –'

'What?'

'Katie, I . . .' He swallowed. 'It pleasures me a deal to see ee and take this talk. Reelly –'

'Tis for a purpose, boy. You mind last night?'

'Last night? Don't I just. Why –'

'You mind me calling for you, saying quick, quick, do ee go fetch Dr Enys just so fast as ever you can ride, for the Master's strick down! You mind that?'

A half smile crossed Music's face but was quickly gone because of the look on Katie's. 'Ais, you. I never seen ee in such a fetching. My dear life, I says, Katie's in a fetching. An' then you says –'

'Music,' Katie said. 'Last night was last night, see? and mebbe in the excitement ye thought, ye imagined what didn't exist, see?'

Music stared at her with his mouth open. 'Nay –'

'Like supposin' I said things I didn't say. Whatever *you* thought *you* 'eard me say, well, twasn't so, see? Twas the *shock* and the *stress*, and all that. Imagery things that didn't exist in the world of *reality*.' Katie paused for breath. She thought she was doing rather well so far. 'Fancies, see?' she said. 'Twas all fancies.'

Silence fell. Amboy shuffled back against his stall, rubbing his rump against the wooden side.

A slow smile of admiration spread across Music's face. 'My dear-r,' he said; 'don't ee go *on*!'

''Ere, are ee listening to what I *say*?'

'Ais. Tis some proper. I'd dearly like to hark to ee all day.'

'But understand, do ee? If we speaks o' what I seen it could cause a rabid of *ill-informed gossip*, see. 'Mong the old women of the village.'

'What's that? Ill-in-what?'

Katie thrust her face forward at him. 'I tell ee this, Music Thomas, if – if *lying rumours* and *tittle-tattle* d'get about,

73

twill be you and me as'll suffer! Do you want to be turned out from your job?'

She was trying to make as ugly a face as possible, but he saw only beauty. However, the thought of being turned away from here, of not getting his mid-day meal, and especially of not being able to see her, sobered him down.

'What's to do, Katie? Tell me what's to do.'

'That's what I just been *doing*!' she exclaimed in vexation. 'Don't ee ever breathe a word 'bout what I told you last night. Understand that, do ee? Got that in yer wooden noddle?'

'What? What you told me last night? 'Bout the – 'bout the young man – *'im, you* know – upstairs wi' she? Ais. I follow ee.'

'So we got to be close about 'n. Else *she'll* give us the discharge. Mind, I never mentioned no names, so ye can say no more 'n you was told, an' that you must forget.'

Music scratched among his untidy hair. This visit of Katie's was the best thing that had happened to him for many a long day – since maybe that day he'd sung the hymn solo in church when all the others were sick with summer cholera. So he wanted to prolong it. It occurred to him too that he might turn it to more permanent account.

'Reckon,' he said cunningly, 'reckon, Katie, we should talk more o' this by and by. Eh? You come see me now an' 'gain, just to make sure nobody's said nothing, eh?'

'You great lootal!' Katie said. 'There's only you and me knows! So tis for we to be close and no other.'

'But I *do* know who twas,' said Music, taking something from his hair and squeezing it between his fingers. 'I do know all the same!'

'Gis along! I never said a word o' that!'

'Nay, nor ye didn't. But I *seen* 'im. I seen 'im mount 'is 'orse. When I were going fetch surgeon. He got 'is 'orse tethered by the old smelting wall. I seen 'im mount 'is 'orse and ride away.'

Chapter Seven

I

The meeting between the three young men did not take
place on the date or at the place arranged: Stephen had sent
word that he would be delayed, and had suggested another
venue, which was probably more appropriate for what they
had to consider – if a little more suggestive of conspiracy if
anyone saw them.

Between Nampara and Trenwith, on the high cliffs not
far from Seal Hole Cave, there was a sharp V-shaped
declivity in the land, as if nature had intended another inlet
and then changed its mind. Sixty-odd feet above the sea the
declivity ended in a grassy plateau with the ruins of a long
dead mine-working, and a shaft, man-made, driven directly down to the sea. This shaft was about eight feet in
diameter, about twenty feet from the cliff edge and surrounded by a low stone wall.

A few years ago when Charlie Kellow was more nimble
and more adventurous, and when Paul was still in his early
teens, they had made a wooden ladder and nailed it to the
side of this shaft so that they could gain access to the
splendid little natural harbour created by the rock forma-
tion below. Here they had moored and kept their boat, a
thirty-year-old lugger of solid but antique construction, and
from there had occasionally sailed to Ireland or to France to
bring home contraband spirits or silks. Two years ago,
however, a fanatic storm had damaged the lugger so badly
that they had made no attempt to repair it, and it remained a
hulk wedged between rocks not reached by normal tides.
Since then no one had used the place, though it was still
known locally as Kellow's Ladder, and always would be.

About half way down the shaft the old miners had driven
another shaft, this horizontally, in search of minerals, but

after about twenty feet had given up. It was a rough scarred opening from the perpendicular shaft, much picked over at the entrance so that the entrance was quite broad and tall, but a little way in it became the conventional four feet by four feet tunnel by which miners hacked their way in search of gain. It was in this tunnel that, after some discussion, the three young men had decided to cache their spoils. In the time that they had used the cove below, no one else had ever come here – the place appeared to have an unsavoury reputation with the villagers – so there seemed little likelihood of anyone doing so now. Even if they did, the chances of their breaking off half way and entering this tunnel, and then turning over some evil-smelling sacks at the very back of it, was remote. At least it had been agreed that nowhere could the stuff be hidden with less risk of discovery.

They assembled just before dawn, when streaks of light discoloured the east and the wind had dropped. A disparate trio. Stephen with his lion head, cleft chin, wide cheek bones and handsome good looks, rough spoken, open handed, a man to whom action followed impulse, and reflection was more properly to be indulged in only if for some reason action failed; Paul Kellow, slender and dark and as good looking as a stiletto, quietly sure of his importance in the world, a man with few doubts about his own judgement or his own ultimate success; Jeremy Poldark, tall and thin and a little stooping, the only one with genuine brain but at the moment grown errant and unstable, flawed by circumstances that another less feeling man would have taken in his stride.

They went down; and, since recently the ladder had become shaky and some of the rungs unreliable, each man allowed the other to get off at the bottom before he put his foot to the top; they assembled again in the entrance to the cave, then Jeremy lit a couple of candles and stooped his way to the very back where he pulled away a dirty sheet of tarpaulin. Under it were three cleaner sacks, small flour sacks in the first place, each marked in ink with an initial. He brought them towards the entrance to the cave.

'All's well. Nobody's touched them.'

After a minute Stephen went to the sack marked 'S' and put his hand in, drew out a few bank notes, some coin, a couple of documents, a ring. He knelt staring at these, ran them through his fingers assaying what he had left. Presently Paul followed suit. Jeremy did not move but stood in the entrance to the cave watching them.

Stephen looked up. 'How much of yours is gone, Jeremy?'

'None yet. I told you.'

'So when are you going to use it?'

'Soon enough.'

'If they found out, you'd swing just the same whether you'd spent it or not.'

'I know that.'

Day was coming now, though in the shaft it would never be anything but half light. Jeremy took a piece of newspaper out of his pocket, unfolded it and began peering at it.

'What's that?'

'You've seen it before.'

'The account? Holy Mary, ye should never've kept it. Supposing someone found it!'

'It would mean nothing to them. And no one ever searches my room.'

In spite of being preoccupied with what was in the sacks they both eventually stood up and began to look over Jeremy's shoulder.

First there was the news item which read:

Daring Robbery on Stage Coach.
Last week the *Self-Defence* stage coach, one of the four coaches owned by Messrs Fagg, Whitmarsh, Fromont, Weakley & Co., which ply between Plymouth and Falmouth, was the subject of a daring robbery. Between the time of its leaving Plymouth on the morning of Monday last, the 25th ult. and its arriving in Truro in the afternoon, a breach had been forced between the interior of the coach and the strong box under the driver's seat; and the contents of the strong box removed. Attempts are now being made to trace the passengers who travelled inside the coach during the

journey: a Reverend and Mrs Arthur May; Lieutenant Morgan Lean of the Royal Navy; Mr Arthur Williams Rose, Mr Ord Cadbury and Mr Anthony Trevail.

On the front page of the same newspaper was an advertisement:

> One thousand Pounds Reward.
> Stolen from the *Self-Defence* Stage Coach on Monday, the 25th day of January. The contents of two strong boxes, the property of Messrs Warleggan and Willyams, bankers, of Plymouth and Truro.
> Among the property lost are Bank of England Notes of £40, £20 and £10, to the total value of approximately £2,600. All are numbered and dated, and a selection of these numbers is given below. Bank Post Bills payable at Warleggan & Willyams Bank, all at £15 to a total value of about £700. Together with other Bank and Local Notes valued at £850. A bag with 900 Spanish dollars. Another bag containing 360 guineas. Some foreign gold coin. A few small heirlooms, silver and items of jewellery, documents.
> A reward of £400 will be offered for information leading to a conviction of the thieves, a further £600 is promised for a recovery of the property stolen.
> Then followed the numbers.

Meeting in those cold mid-January days when snow had frequently blown in the wind, the three young men had pored over this advertisement. At first it had appeared that none of the Bank of England notes was usable, since they were all numbered and dated; then Paul had pointed out a tactical mistake Warleggan's Bank had made. No doubt the notes *were* all numbered and dated, but if the bank had a record of them all, why did they list only a selection at the bottom of the advertisement? It seemed certain they were listing the only ones they possessed. Seven were listed. These clearly could not be safely used. The others, Paul argued, could.

The Post Bills payable to Warleggan's Bank were

altogether more risky, since evidence of identity would probably have to be given before they could be encashed. After much argument, chiefly with Stephen who wanted to carry them to Bristol to see if he could change them there, Jeremy had burned them; also the seven listed bank notes. It had been agony for them all to see the notes blacken and twist and disappear in flame; but Jeremy had argued that unless the step were taken at once someone – one or other of them – would later be tempted to try to cash one; and that might bring all their other careful precautions tumbling down.

Everything else, as he pointed out, was negotiable and untraceable: guineas, Spanish dollars, gold coin, jewellery and the rest; and these should be divided as equally as possible into three parts at once and hidden away in separate sacks so that there should be no arguments later.

And so it was done.

Of this division Stephen had taken nearly all his share before he left for Bristol, Paul rather more than half his.

Stephen said to Jeremy: 'I thought it was all on account of a needy purpose you had to make a start at becoming rich! It was to be a beginning, ye said. Well, money will not multiply if it be buried in the earth. Indeed, it is quite likely to rot – the paper part of it. The bags are not damp proof.'

Jeremy's expression did not change. 'Let us say, Stephen, that once our pleasant adventure was over there was a little sour taste in my mouth, left as an aftermath. It has not yet quite gone. When it has gone I shall consider how best to spend the money.'

Paul said: 'Well, I don't think my father could believe his ears when I told him I could find the money to discharge some of his most pressing bills. At first he was suspicious, could not believe I had won it at the cockpit. I said to him: "My dear father, how do you think I have come by it, *stolen* it?" He soon accepted my explanation, as who wouldn't in his situation? There is an old proverb about a gift horse. Gradually I have become his blessed son. Of course I have been careful to release only by little and by little. Now when I go to Truro or Redruth he counsels me anxiously lest I wager more money and *lose* it.' Paul's lips creased. 'At least, unlike you, my two fellow miscreants, I believe I have done something worthwhile with my money. As a result of it the coaching company of Kellow, Clotworthy, Jones & Co. continues to function, and now, as things are picking up, only at a *slight* loss. Additionally my father is out and about his business and not languishing in a debtor's prison. My mother and my sister have not been turned out of their home and their belongings sold for anything they could fetch. The House of Kellow continues on its ordinary and, I hope, ordained way. So give or take a few days of shaking knees and watery bowels both before and after the escapade, I am very glad I indulged in it.'

Stephen said: 'Does your mother and Daisy swallow this story about the cockpit?'

'They know nothing of it. I swore my father to secrecy because my mother is over-religious and strongly disapproves of gaming. I do not think they have even asked. They never knew the depths of our predicament and so do not know the measure of their escape.'

Jeremy looked across at the other side of the perpendicular shaft. Earth had lodged in one or two crevices and tiny ferns were growing, and further up, nearer the light, a few tufts of sea pink had flowered. He folded up the newspaper cutting and put it back in his pocket.

'Did you have any difficulty in Bristol, Stephen?'

'Difficulty?'

'In changing the notes. I assume you changed the notes there.'

'No trouble at all; though I confess I had qualms about the two forty pound bills; but they went through without question.' He thrust a half-dozen Bank of England notes into his wallet. 'I wish I'd taken them all now.'

'And the jewellery?'

'Well I only took the ring. I sold the diamonds out of it. Got £70. Twas probably not full value.'

'Less than half I'd guess,' said Jeremy.

Stephen was staring at him. 'That's a handsome stock-pin you're wearing. It was not part of the booty, was it?'

'Not part of this booty,' said Jeremy obliquely.

'Come on, then, what is this you're concealing from us?'

'Nothing at all. At least nothing to do with anyone but myself.' Jeremy picked up his own bag and shook it thoughtfully. 'But I am much in favour of losing these recognizable pieces. You have two, haven't you, Paul?'

'The signet ring, which is worth little. And this brooch.'

'If I were you I'd prise the ruby out and throw the brooch into the sea.'

'It might be worth a little melted down.'

'Safer to let it go.'

'What has happened to that cup?' Stephen asked.

'What cup?'

'You know – the little one. The loving cup, or whatever it is.'

'It's back among the sacks, I suppose. We never actually decided whose share it belonged to.'

''Tis not worth much, is it?'

'No.'

'What did you do with your money in Bristol?' Paul asked. 'Jeremy tells me you didn't buy into a privateer?'

'No, there was naught I liked the look of. Another time it might've been different. But there was one or two men I wanted to avoid – hard lads I had had words with before . . . And more than words.' Stephen felt his chin. 'I need a shave. No, Paul, if ye are that interested I brought nearly all me money back again – but all in new money. I think maybe I shall invest it here.'

'Are you thinking that a privateer out of Falmouth would be more to your taste?'

Stephen looked at Jeremy and half grinned. 'Not exactly, like. I have a mind to invest in the pilchard fishing. Or in a roundabout way, like, that's what it'll amount to. And no one can say – not even the Poldark family can say there is aught illegal in that.'

'Well, tell us all about it,' said Paul. 'It is clear that you are dying to.'

'I don't think it matters what my family thinks,' Jeremy said, 'if you –'

'It still matters to him what Clowance thinks,' said Paul. 'Eh? . . . Well, I'll say in front of her brother that she's a handsome girl and a good catch. I'd try the water myself if she gave me half a hope of finding it tepid. If you marry Daisy, Jeremy, we could maybe have a double relationship.'

Jeremy's face was quite expressionless. 'What is this scheme you have, Stephen?'

Stephen was sorting through a few documents left in his bag. He looked up. 'Earlier this summer I was in St Ives – fishermen there – we were talking this way and that: d'ye know what they got for their pilchards last year? I'll tell you. Fifteen shillings a hogshead. As one of them said: it did not pay for the salt and the nets. And that in a sore year – when food was bitter scarce all over the county. But d'ye know what some others got? I'll give you a guess. They got 190/– a hogshead – more than a dozen times as much. Same quality fish caught in the same type of boats.'

Paul said: 'This is a riddle?'

'No. Just that some were more enterprising than others. They sold 'em in their natural markets.'

'Spain?' said Jeremy.

'Italy in this case.'

'What d'you mean – they ran the blockade?'

'Just that. The French can't patrol all the ports they own, any more than we can patrol all the high seas.'

Jeremy fingered his bag but again did not untie the cord. He was still reluctant to handle the money, to touch it.

'Was it one of the export firms – like Fox's of Falmouth – who broke the blockade?'

'Nay. As well you might guess. Too scared for their vessels. Nay, twas little men – in their own boats – taking a three month trip and coming home with gold in their pockets – chiefly from St Ives and – they said – Mevagissey and Fowey. Not a dozen in all. But not one was stopped.'

'And you propose?'

'To do it on a bigger scale this year. Likely it will be the same conditions – a glut of fish; no one to buy 'em – farmers taking 'em at knock-down prices and using them for manure in their fields. I reckon I can just about afford to furnish out a couple of vessels, make 'em suitable for such cargo, buy the pilchards after curing, pay over the market price to get the best, send the vessels out, maybe go with one of 'em; make a handsome profit that way.'

Paul was listening with his head on one side as if to hear something more behind the words.

'Are you serious?'

'No one's forcing ye to believe me.'

'And what have you done about it so far?'

'Nothing. Yet.'

'And when shall you start?'

'I shall be at St Ives on Tuesday week bidding for the *Chasse Marée*.'

'What's that in Heaven's name?'

'A French prize. She's not big, but big enough – about 80 ton. Fir built. Equipped in every way. She's called a fishing boat – and been used as one, ye can see – but her lines are clean. No doubt she's been used for deep sea work – with the speed to bring her catch in while tis still fresh. But I can see marks on her decks where guns have been fitted. I reckon she's been used for a little privateering now and then. She'll suit for the work I want.'

'What will she take?'

'What, carry?'

'Yes.'

'Well, it will need a little more careful working out than I have yet been able to do; but I would suspect two hundred and twenty-five to two hundred and fifty hogsheads. In that neighbourhood.'

'Um.' Paul nodded his head. 'If you make a gross profit of £8 a hogshead . . . You've your crews to pay and feed – but still . . . It looks handsome enough. What do you think, Jeremy?'

'I think it is likely to take more than three months to sail, say, to Genoa and back. And shall you expect to come home in ballast?'

'I had thought to bring back salt and wine.'

'Both contraband,' said Paul. 'You said you were turning over a new leaf.'

'So I am, so I am. No one in Cornwall even pretends to disapprove of contraband, as you call it. Even Captain Poldark, even Dr Enys, they were both engaged in it once upon a time.'

Paul laughed. 'Well, yes, I suppose it is "turning over a new leaf" for a man wanted for two hanging offences.'

Stephen said harshly: 'Never forget, Paul, that you're wanted for one of 'em, and maybe the first one as well. Accessory's the word they use!'

'Now, now,' Jeremy said quietly. 'Remember: "when thieves fall out . . ."'

After a moment Paul said: 'Oh, we're not falling out that bad. A little jesting, eh? I'm grateful to Stephen for what he did in Plymouth Dock. Else I might be a pressed man in the navy.'

Jeremy took a candle and went to put his sack back under the tarpaulin at the distant end of the shaft. He returned with a small metal cup. It had been in one of the bags they had taken from the strong boxes and was of silver, but tiny, little more than three inches broad, with its two handles, by two and a half inches high. Engraved round the rim were the words: *Amor gignit amorem.*

'And what shall we do with this?'

There was a pause.

'Melt it down,' said Paul.

'It is so light,' Jeremy said, 'it would hardly pay for the firing.'

'Throw it in the sea,' said Stephen.

'It would seem a pity. But I expect you're right.'

Stephen said. 'You're not *touching* your share, Jeremy. I can see that.'

'Have no fear. I will in due course.'

'Come in as my partner. I'm having a fishing vessel built too. A small drifter type of about sixty ton. I put the order in last week. This war cannot last for ever; nor can the conditions we can make use of this year. I say, make the most of 'em. Then when it's over, trading by sea won't end. It will *expand*. Folk who've two or three vessels in commission can use *those* conditions too. And legitimate if need be. If I buy the *Chasse Marée* I shall be stretched tight for money. Yours would come in very handy. We could start an exporting line: Carrington and Poldark. Carrington & Co. if you don't fancy it being publicly known. Why not sail to Italy with me this autumn? It will be an adventure, more surely than just going to the Scillies.'

'I'll think on it,' said Jeremy.

II

Later the same day Geoffrey Charles was walking beside the old pond of Trenwith when he saw a small procession wending its way up the weed-grown drive. In the lead by a few paces on an elderly mare was a thin dark man; behind him on two ponies a dark woman in a long grey linen riding cloak and a girl of about twelve, hair in pig-tails, bare legs showing under a dimity skirt.

Geoffrey Charles had been linking his wife, but he lifted both hands to squint into the sun – then he let out a whoop.

'My love, forgive me, it is Drake!'

He leapt across a narrow angle of the pool, splashed through a few feet of shallow mud and ran towards the convoy. As he neared it, the dark man saw him, called to his ladies and slid out of the saddle.

The men met equidistant from their respective wives. They stopped a few feet apart, then grasped hands. After a moment Geoffrey Charles took the other by the biceps, laughed, and kissed him on both cheeks.

'Drake, Drake, Drake, Drake, Drake!' he said, his voice breaking and tears in his eyes. 'So-o . . . After all these years! I can scarcely believe it!'

'Geoffrey Charles! I can scarce believe it neither! Indeed I can hardly think tis you, though, you're looking brave an' happy. My dear, you sent for me!'

'Indeed.' They broke from their affectionate clasp and Geoffrey Charles took a dozen giant strides to help the lady as she dismounted. 'Morwenna. *Ma foi! Ma petite!*' He took her in his arms and gave her a smacking kiss which knocked her glasses askew. 'And how is my governess? Blooming, it seems! What pleasure to see you again! And Loveday . . .' He went to the second pony and kissed the girl as he lifted her down. 'My dear, you have grown so much – grown so much!'

Drake Carne said: 'In wisdom and in stature and in God's esteem.' But he said it with a little smile that took the starch out of it.

'You still pursue that outlandish Methodism?'

'After a fashion. But we take in small doses – not like Sam.'

'All things should be taken in small doses,' said Geoffrey Charles, 'except friendship and love. Come, Amadora, don't hang back, come and meet my dear friends. Drake, Morwenna, this is my wife, my dearly loved and honoured wife, whom I have brought to Cornwall specially to meet you.'

They shook hands, Drake bowing over the hand, Loveday dropping a curtsy. All was conversation, laughter, chatter as they walked the horses slowly towards the front door. Drake had put on weight; one could not see the bones of his shoulder blades through his jacket any more; his hair had thinned but was still raven black; his face had more colour, but perhaps that was just the zest of the arrival. Morwenna seemed unchanged; short-sighted, shy, withdrawn, just as he remembered her seven years ago when he called in at Looe, just as he remembered her when she first came as his governess nineteen years ago. Loveday had the fine skin and dark hair of both her parents, but was of an age when child charm had gone and the looks of adolescence were yet a little way off.

At the front door Geoffrey Charles produced a whistle. Its shrilling brought a young man trotting round from the back, who raised his eyebrows and grinned at Drake.

'Well, I'll be darned,' said Drake. ''Tis young Tredinnick! But gracious knows whether tis Jack or Paul.'

'Jack, sur. Paul's still wi' your brother, sur.'

'I do not have servants as such,' Geoffrey Charles explained, 'as yet; I have helpers to whom I pay what they consider a reasonable fee. Jack is here to help.'

'Aye, sur; that we all do, sur. Glad to see ee, Mr Carne. An' Mrs Carne too. And Miss Carne, I s'pose.'

'Please to come in,' said Amadora, to Morwenna. 'Geoffrey Charles have so often spoke. This is the way. But you have known this house. You shall remember it well.'

'I am so happy for you, Mrs Poldark,' Morwenna said. 'For you both.' She looked round the small entrance hall as she entered it. She gave a little shiver.

'You feel cold? When you shall have ridden so far?'

'No, no. Far from cold,' said Morwenna. 'Very far from cold.'

III

They ate together in the winter parlour, which the young Poldarks were at present using as a dining room; the first night in the great hall had been for fun, for love, for excitement, for the sexual challenge; after that, when they came down to earth, it was too big for two.

Everyone on best behaviour, everyone so obviously wanting to do and say the right thing, Geoffrey Charles more hearty than natural, Morwenna, never a conversationalist, making a tremendous effort to join in, only Loveday excusably silent. Morwenna had wanted to get up and help Maud Tredinnick, Jack's wife, who waited at table; Amadora concerned for the cooking of the food, which was being done by Ann Bottrell, Ned Bottrell's wife from Grambler; but to each stirring at the table Geoffrey Charles was adamant. They should sit and wait properly and it should be done. And it was done. And the wine going down with the food was gradually relaxing nerves, easing tensions, making the genuine goodwill flow more naturally.

'We shall give a big party,' Geoffrey Charles said. 'A very big party. I had thought at first it should be a housewarming, when everyone should come to welcome us home. Until we saw 'the home'. Then it became quite clear that if

87

we did not wish to run the risk of some guest disappearing through the floorboards or a nervous lady finding a rat anxious to share her fruit syllabub, we should have to wait. So now it may become a house-cooling party – held perhaps a week before we leave. Or a middle-of-the-stay party when we have not grown tired of you all or outlasted our welcome. How long can you remain, Drake?'

'Here? Oh, I dunno. Did you wish for us to stay very long?'

'So long as you can. So long as you are happy here. You know how much I would have liked you both – you all – to make this your permanent home, to have cared for it while we were away, to have shared it with us when we eventually return for good. That is all now a cloud-cuckoo dream, I suppose? You are firmly rooted in Looe? . . .'

Drake looked at Morwenna, who did not speak.

'At present we live in Looe, Geoffrey Charles. It has become our home . . . But that does not mean we cannot see much of you, or of Trenwith, if that be your wish. It is a long trip; we left at four this morning; but if Captain Poldark do approve – I mean the other Captain Poldark – then it should not be impossible to have one home and one – one second home, where you and Mrs Poldark will ever be.'

'Of course.' Geoffrey Charles, since he could not reach Drake across the table, patted Morwenna's hand. 'It is understood. It has always been a dream of mine . . . you know that . . . You will stay now?'

Morwenna smiled at him. 'Just as long as you want – as long as you both want.'

'We should have been here the sooner,' said Drake, 'did we not have this sudden order for a new mackerel driver, which come in almost the same day as the letter from you telling us of the great news that you were home. This have delayed me, as twas a rush order, and the young man ordering her wishes for to see her launched in less than two month, which will be a test an' a trial. But I stayed to see the templates completed an' the frames marked and sawn. There's two-three weeks' work now before they shall think of needing me.'

'Well, let us enjoy these two or three weeks to begin,' said Geoffrey Charles. He smiled and ran a finger along the thin line of his moustache. 'It's strange: when I knew you last you were becoming an expert wheelwright. Now that has changed and instead you are a builder of boats.'

'Thanks to the other Cap'n Poldark – Ross. D'ye know after all this time tis quite an effort on my part to call him Ross.'

'Then we're in the same case, for although he is really my second cousin I have always called him Uncle, and it needs an effort every time I open my mouth to him to correct myself!'

'So I think I must tell 'im about the new boat I'm having built for this young man. Was not Clowance engaged to marry a young man called Stephen Carrington? This man is called Stephen Carrington who have come to me in Looe to order the new vessel. I wonder if tis one and the same?'

Chapter Eight

I

Returning from another equally early foray the following morning, Jeremy found his mother already abroad. As he crossed the plank bridge to the house she was coming out of the front door with a bucket of water.

The light had flooded the land long before the sun was up, and the sea, where wisps of mist clung to it, looked like milk in a pan being heated to make cream. The wind would come later, but at the moment there was none.

'You're up early, my lover,' she said.

'The same might be said of you, mother. Are you watering your flowers?'

'No.' She looked into the bucket. 'While it is dewy is the time to catch the snails. If you drop them into salt they die quite easy.'

'Is Father up?'

'Oh, yes. In the yard. We're starting the Long Field today.'

'Ah. A good crop?' That he should have to ask, he thought.

'It is a trifle thin the higher you go, but all the lower part is handsome.'

'So another pair of hands would not come amiss?'

'I don't need to answer that.'

'Well, first I'll go up and take a look at Leisure, see all is well there. What time do we break our fast?'

'In half an hour.'

'Then let me try my hand at some slug-murder. I see you have gloves. I don't mind snails, but slugs are uneasy in the fingers.'

'You take the snails, then.'

'I can't see any!'

'You will if you look.'

Mother and son crouched first about the hollyhocks. Jeremy, peering like a short-sighted man, felt something crunch under his foot in the long grass and discovered he had caught his first snail. They laughed at this.

'The only way I can see 'em is by treading on 'em!' Jeremy said.

'I'll get you your grandfather's spectacles,' Demelza said.

'Didn't know he ever had a pair.'

'They're in the long drawer in the parlour, right at the back. I tried them last year when my eyes were funny when Harry was coming, but they didn't help.'

'I didn't know your eyes were funny, as well as everything else.'

'Well, they aren't now,' said Demelza disgustedly unpeeling a yellow and brown slug from the side of a loose stone. 'And what d'you *mean*, as well as everything else!'

'Well, you were really quite ill, Mama, even though you may become indignant at the idea now.'

'I suspect I found my family too much for me!'

'Most particularly the one that was just arriving, no doubt. How is he?'

'Fretful in the night. But he's forgotten it now.'

They went on undisturbed for a few minutes. Then they moved over to the pansies. Jeremy said: 'I had a letter a couple of weeks ago from some man interested in steam cars – a doctor somebody. Difficult to tell if he's just a crank. He suggested we should meet in Truro one Wednesday. I haven't replied.'

'Why not?'

'I can't make up my mind.'

'Is there anything to lose?'

Jeremy laughed. 'An afternoon. To tell the truth I cannot work up a great deal of interest in the subject these days.'

Demelza sat on her haunches and looked at him. 'Or any other subject?'

'True enough, I suppose.'

'What happened last Christmas?'

'Christmas?'

'About then. About the time Harry was born.'

He turned the flower of a pansy. 'Something has eaten this one.'

'A caterpillar, it look more like . . . Yes, there it is. Such a little one, too.'

He said: 'You see too much, Mother.'

'It isn't only caterpillars.'

'I know.'

'But will not tell?'

'Cannot tell. Don't let it worry you.'

'It does. When my eldest son suddenly seems to – to go adrift. Is it still to do with Cuby?'

He flushed. 'Earlier, yes. I became very disgusted with the way my life was leading, and out of the disgust grew – other things. Now . . . I think I am just going through a bad patch. Give me a little time.'

'You don't even care so much for Wheal Leisure now, do you.'

'Not as much as I did.' He changed his tone. 'But don't ee fetch on so. Tis no more 'n a touch of the spiritual mulligrubs.' He patted her on the bottom. 'All will be well.'

'Not that way.'

'Well, look what you were like when you were carrying Harry! We've just spoken of it.'

'But you're not carrying Harry, my lover. What *are* you carrying?'

There was a plop as he at last found a snail and dropped it in the water.

He said: 'Even in spite of everything, I can talk to you better than anyone else. I wonder why.'

'I can't think.'

'Wasn't Father lucky!'

'Oh, ho, *thank* you. But for long he part-yearned for someone else.'

'I know. Very stupid of him.'

'Oh, she was nice. Nicer than in those days I ever cared to think.'

'Well, I suppose . . .'

'Yes, it's all over. The heartache and the happiness . . .'

'Oh, Mother, don't say *that*!'

She examined another stone, but it was clean. 'I don't mean it *that* much, that way. Perhaps what I was really trying to say was that . . .'

'That all things pass? Yes. But don't you need *too* much detachment – an unhealthy detachment – to come to that conclusion? Looking down from above at the poor little creatures wriggling, and thinking, "I'm no longer one of them!" Or looking back from a distance and thinking, "I *was* one of them!"'

Demelza peered into the bucket. 'There are one or two creatures wriggling in there that I don't like the look of . . . Jeremy, why don't you reply to that doctor Somebody and see what he has to say? At the worst, as you point out, it's a wasted afternoon.'

'I might *suffer*,' he said. 'Maybe he's a crank and thinks pistons grow in the centre of flowers.'

'Don't they?'

'They probably would for you. Is it time for breakfast yet?'

'The slugs think so.'

'All right. All right. I'll stay a bit longer.'

II

It was a close stuffy day on the Wednesday, with occasional damp flurries scarcely wetting the cobbles in Truro. The town was crowded for the market: cows and sheep filled the streets, lowing and bleating. Herdsmen gossiped at corners; drovers poked at their flocks; beggars standing in the gutters, beside or almost in the rivulets, had hardly room to plead their poverty. The Red Lion was full of noisy drinkers.

News from Europe had just come in – that Wellington, after his great victory at Vittoria, was on the move again, was investing San Sebastian for the second time and was likely to take it by storm. His troops were poised all along the Pyrenees, ready to invade France. Ross remembered the day when George Canning in the House had predicted that there would come a time when a British army would look down into France from the Pyrenees. He had been greeted with derisive laughter from many members then. Well, it had taken almost five years.

But Wellington was still biding his time. Napoleon, recovering rapidly from his disasters of the winter and with an army of which the leading sixteen battalions were raw youths, had scored a resounding victory over Blücher and the Germans at Lützen in May and followed it with another at Bautzen, this latter too costly in arms and men but of vital importance to the strategy of keeping the Allies on the defensive; then, still faced by the gathering forces of his enemies and the uncertainty of his friends, he had agreed to the armistice of Poischwitz, which lasted precariously from June 4th until August 10th. During the negotiations Napoleon had spent his time in Dresden, arguing terms but manifestly preparing for a renewal of the war. As soon as the armistice ended he flung an army at Blücher hoping to take him by surprise. There were rumours of another battle of Dresden, the outcome still unsure.

Gossip in the town was of a shipwreck in the fog off the Lizard: a tin-ship moving up channel, five men missing; of a musical festival to be held at the Assembly Rooms next Tuesday at which the principal draw was to be the renowned Madame Catalini; of a Society for the Prosecution of Thieves just formed in Truro under the patronage of Mr Paul, the mayor; of the bad harvest, of the wicked poor price of tin.

Jeremy went into the second room and spoke to the tapster, who knew him.

The tapster wiped the back of his hand across his mouth. 'Oh, aye, sur, Mr Poldark. How's the Cap'n and his lady? Well, I 'ope. Seldom see 'em in here nowadays. Dr Garner? Surely, if I recollect, tis 'im over there, sur. Dr Garner over there, sur. Him in the yellow jacket, see? Just getting up now, sur, and coming this way.'

Coming this way, pushing his way through the crowd of drinkers, was a medium-sized but sturdy youth, dark haired, full lipped, heavy lidded. Jeremy looked beyond him but saw no one else.

'Poldark,' said the young man, smiling and holding out his hand. 'Very civil of you to come.'

Jeremy stared, had his hand taken, but in his surprise hardly returned the grasp.

'Garner?' he said. 'Dr Garner?'

'Well, in a manner of speaking, yes.'

'But . . . you're not Garner. You're – Gurney!'

'True. True. Can't deny it. Wouldn't wish to really. Well . . .' The young man had flushed under Jeremy's un-compromising stare. 'It is all of four years since we met, and I thought . . .' He hesitated. 'Well, I was two forms below you, wasn't I. Under Hogg. Remember old Hogg? Knew his stuff, d'ye know. Not a bad teacher of his own subjects.'

'But why Garner?' Jeremy demanded.

'Allow me to order you a drink. The ale is fair here. I've downed a pint while waiting. Can I –'

'Why Garner?' Jeremy insisted.

'Well, to tell the truth, I thought you might not come if I said I was Gurney! Thought you might remember me as a fifteen-year-old and say to yourself, God's my life, why should I talk to *him*?'

This was so exactly what Jeremy would have thought that he half smiled and then did not smile. He remembered Gurney at the Truro Grammar School, a bright, pert boy two years his junior, but rather a thorn in the side of some of the older boys because of his quick wits and argumentative, combative character. Thomas Hogg, the headmaster, had made a favourite of him, which had not endeared him to his fellows, but Gurney had usually managed to slide out of any collective bullying. In fact Jeremy had not particularly liked him, if only because he often tried to be too smart; and indeed if the letter he had received had been honestly signed he would have replied to it quite differently, or not replied to it at all.

Having failed to find a waiter, Gurney had fought his way to the bar and was returning with two brimming glasses.

'There's two seats over there. I put a stick across 'em. What d'you think? – they say Austria's declared war on France. At last. Think you it will make much difference?'

'I doubt if you can rely on any of them very far. If Napoleon arrives suddenly at the gates of Vienna, they'll be suing for peace again in a trice.'

Gurney laughed as they sat down. 'Here's good fortune!' They drank.

'You have not joined the colours yet?'

'No. Not yet.'

'Nor I ever,' said Gurney. 'There are plenty who can fire a gun – few who can invent one. Tell me, Poldark, what started you on this experiment with the steam coach, and how far have you progressed?'

Over the drink Jeremy told him, though briefly, still too irritated to go into details.

'Andrew Vivian told me part of this – as much as he knew. I've seen Trevithick twice – I told you in my letter. He's as discouraging as you say – but is he necessarily right? I would not dare to question the great man in matters of steam engineering – but only in applying those matters. After all, he has not made any great practical success of his own life, has he.'

As they talked Jeremy allowed himself to speak more freely. It seemed that all the rest that Gurney had told him in his letter was true. Though barely twenty he had been admitted to a junior medical partnership by Dr Avery of Wadebridge, who was at present in ill-health. Because of this ill-health Gurney seemed to have assumed responsibility for half the practice. Jeremy wondered how much physical book learning he could possibly have had time for in so short a life, what practical experience he could have had. If you were ill, would you welcome a *boy* taking your pulse, bleeding you, prescribing some drug or herbal remedy to stop the pain, even with sager advice in the background?

And a boy moreover fairly bubbling with other thoughts. Did he tell his patients about Trevithick and his own absorption in the problems of steam? If one could judge from what he let fall inadvertently, the patients – even the older patients – seemed willing to transfer their allegiance and to trust his judgement.

In a sense his vitality hypnotized Jeremy – or at least fascinated him. In no time they were arguing. Gurney's conviction was that the wheels of an engine could never be relied on to provide enough traction on the roads. As they received the power, Gurney argued, the wheels would begin to spin round, sending up clouds of sparks while the carriage remained immovable. Jeremy cited the carriages of 1801 and 1808, which had proceeded without difficulty and had found traction enough. Gurney referred to another experiment of Trevithick's when the engine had reached the bottom of a hill, had stopped and, on being re-started, had spun its wheels round and round without ever making a move to go up the hill again.

His idea therefore was that any successful and *reliable* carriage of the future must be impelled in the first stages by legs which, coming into operation at the same time as the wheels, helped the carriage to push itself into motion. He was quite prepared to accept the fact that, once the carriage was moving, the legs could be retracted and the wheels left to do the rest. But to start, or on hills, the extra leverage would be necessary.

The stimulus of discussion, of argument, began to light lamps in Jeremy which had been dimmed for a year. Indeed he never had had another young man of like mind to talk with like this. Dwight Enys had lent him books. He had read everything he was able to get hold of. He had corresponded with a number of the authors. He had met Trevithick, in a technical sense, only once. All through the period when he had been taking secret trips to the Harvey works at Hayle, his only confederate had been Ben Carter, who understood little beyond a few of the practicalities, and Paul Kellow, who had a sharp intelligence but no flighting imagination to go with it.

This man had too much. In spite of Jeremy's initial prejudice, in spite of all the killing pessimisms which had surrounded him this year, he was caught up in his old interest. They talked for two hours over beer and rabbit pies. Gurney started up, saying he must go.

'It is as if we have only just begun, Poldark. We must meet like this again – and soon. And since you are a freer agent than I, why do you not come next time to Wadebridge? Then all the time I have spent riding forth and back today could be spent in fruitful discussion.'

Jeremy hesitated.

Gurney said: 'Of course it would be better to meet at Hayle; but it is too distant for me at present while Dr Avery is so unwell. In the meantime . . . But this machine you have built . . .'

'What were you going to say?'

'Well, whatever is at Hayle – what you have built at Hayle is useless, if Trevithick is to be believed – and I would accept his view unhesitatingly in such a matter: sorry, Poldark, if I appear blunt, but was that not very much what you said yourself? Until we have a suitable boiler . . . Did he say he had drawn a sketch for you of a suitable boiler?'

'As a crude pencil sketch. It implants the idea, gives one a basic design.'

'Well, why do you not bring it to Wadebridge one day next week? Spend the night! My landlady has a room, I believe. Or you could share mine.'

'I'll come over for the day,' Jeremy said. 'Next Wednesday, if that's your best day.'

'Bring everything you can. And I'll show you some experiments I have been conducting on sea sand. I was born by the sea, d'ye know. I believe the lime content of sea sand has yet to be fully appreciated.'

Jeremy rode home, his mind active in directions it had not been for some time. Gurney – *Goldsworthy* was his odd Christian name – Goldsworthy Gurney had greatly changed since they had last seen each other: for only just twenty his maturity of mind was startling. Was he at heart a crank, or likely to develop into one? He had some wild ideas; this talk of sea sand; numerous other side thoughts he had let drop; how practical would he or could he ever become? Yet there was a basic sense in what he said. A partnership between them might provide something jointly that each individually lacked.

And while there had been no mention of finance today, Jeremy had the impression that Gurney came of a genteel and monied family. Unlike Paul and Ben, this young man might be able to contribute towards the building of an engine. A partnership would mean half each. The only money Jeremy had, except for the dividends just beginning to be paid by Wheal Leisure, reposed in the sack hidden in the shaft at Kellow's Ladder. Would he feel justified? Surely if there was any purpose to which he could put his share of the money they had stolen, this should be the one.

Chapter Nine

I

Stephen Carrington, on his way back from St Ives, dropped in at the Fox and Grapes to rest his horse and to take a bite of food. The clouds were shredded with a wan light as sunset approached. The inn, being on the coaching road, was more dependent on passing travellers than on the sparse and needy population surrounding Chacewater and St Day. This evening it was quiet, and Stephen went into the dining room, hardly noticing the dark young man in the expensive grey riding suit who was talking to the one pretty barmaid.

Stephen was tired but jubilant, and he ordered curlew pie, expecting it to be old and unsavoury but not really much caring. When, however, the young man came into the dining room, bending his head to avoid the rafters, and walked towards his table, Stephen was immediately on edge and on his guard. The one thing he had come to fear in Cornwall was an unwelcome recognition.

'Good evening to you,' said the young man. 'Are you not Stephen Carrington?'

Stephen stared at the narrow face, the sparkling dark eyes, a shade too close together, the aristocratic nose, the smile.

'Of course,' he said. 'You're – er –'

'Valentine Warleggan. We met at Nampara last year, when that girl died. And then later at Truro races.'

'Of course,' said Stephen again, but cautiously. The name alone was dangerous.

Valentine said: 'The brandy here is not insupportable. Would you care to share this bottle?'

'Thank ye.' There wasn't much else to say. So far as he knew, Stephen could perceive no pitfalls in this meeting.

Valentine pulled a chair out and sat down. It was clear that this was not the first drink he had had. 'Just been in your district paying calls. It is your district still, I conceit?'

Stephen said: 'I have been in Bristol for a while, but I believe shall make me permanent home in Cornwall from now on.'

Valentine called for a second glass, and when it came he bobbled some brandy into it and pushed it across the table. 'Try that. Tell me what you think of it.'

'Um . . . Very good.'

'Last time we met you were engaged to my pretty cousin. Then you were no longer engaged. What went amiss? I quizzed Clowance but she was not forthcoming.'

'Tis a private matter,' said Stephen.

'Naturally.'

Silence fell.

Stephen said: 'Her parents were at her all the time to break it off. She's very much under their thumb, y' know.'

'I would not have thought that. Of all the girls I know I would have given Clowance the most credit for having a mind of her own.'

A worm of dislike for this young man turned in Stephen. 'Well, it happened.'

The pie was brought. He cut into it, considering the smell of the steam that came out. Valentine's eyes were following the girl who had brought it in.

'Attractive little creature. Pretty, don't you think.'

Stephen grunted. She was quite good looking, true, but he personally would not have given her a second glance.

'Girls of that sort are generally very simple,' said Valentine, musing over the rim of his glass. 'And easy got . . . Easy rid of too. Go a little higher in the scale and they become tenacious. There was a pretty little thing in my first term at St John's. But by God she was a clinger. Once she had obtained a footing inside my door she took a great dislike to the outside of it, and I had the utmost difficulty in uncolonizing her.'

The pie was eatable. And the brandy warming. Stephen's spirits rose again. He said: 'Of course I have not given up Clowance.'

'Not? Well, perseverance has its merits. Though, as I have said, Clowance has a mind of her own.'

'Is he *your* friend, this man Tom Guildford?'

'I introduced 'em. In all innocence, needless to say.'

'If he wants her, why is he not down here now?'

'His mother is gravely ill. I was the bearer of his messages. No doubt he has written too.'

'I suppose he has money.'

'His family are comfortably circumstanced.'

'That makes a difference, don't it. Never mind, maybe I'll have money before very long. I've just bought a ship.'

Valentine took his eyes reluctantly off the barmaid. 'Women fascinate me,' he said. 'Hypnotize me. They have this secret that I have to discover. That it is always the same secret does not seem to matter – until I have discovered it. When it is gone, then my interest has gone. Very sad. Many of 'em say I am unsatisfactory. That is, when I have given 'em marching orders they say this; not before!'

'And are you?'

'Unsatisfactory? Damn me, not at all, I assure you! It is not the act they complain of, but they appear to want something more afterwards. A relationship, so I might describe it. I am not at all interested in a relationship. I only want to rob them of their secret. Perhaps I am like a thief, always wishing to break into a safe.'

Stephen winced. 'Come, come, drink your brandy.'

'Or a bee, wishing to steal their honey. I have no lasting interest in the safe, in the flower. The pleasure is in the theft . . .'

'I know what you mean,' said Stephen, and continued with his pie. A second glass of brandy went down.

'So you are not so very poor,' said Valentine.

'What?'

'Buying a ship. You are not so very poor.'

'My uncle died in Bristol. I heard he was ill, but it was too late. He left me a small amount.'

'What is your vessel?'

'A French prize. I shall fit her out for local trading. And I have another building.'

'Where?'

'Looe.'

'What yard?'

'Blewett & Carne.'

'Is that not the Carne who is Ross Poldark's brother-in-law?'

'Yes. No harm in that, is there?'

'Nay, nay. So soon you will become a man of substance.'

'It is a long way off. But it is a beginning.'

The pie was done. Stephen picked his teeth.

Valentine said: 'You should meet my father. He is a great one for enterprising young men. Unfortunately he does not consider I am enterprising in the right direction!'

'Your father's too big a man for the likes of me.'

'Yes, maybe. Who knows? He told me last week whom I was to marry . . .' Valentine slopped a little brandy on the table.

Stephen stared at him. 'Does it please ye?'

'It pleases me that no instant marriage is suggested – not even a public betrothal. There is still some dotting of the "i"s and crossing of the "t"s to be completed.'

Stephen still stared. 'D'ye mean a marriage contract?'

'I believe you could call it that.'

'Riches marries riches, eh? It was always so. A man without name or money is always lost.'

'Does not follow, my friend, does not follow.'

'Who is the fortunate girl?'

Valentine spilled more of the brandy on the table. 'Have you heard the news from Europe? No sooner do we have cause to rejoice than the Little Corporal pulls some magic out of his bag. After putting Blücher to flight he has, they say, devastated Schwarzenburg at Dresden. The Allies lost 25,000 men taken prisoner, 30 guns, any number of flags. You cannot keep the man down.'

'That is what I am counting on,' said Stephen.

'What?'

'The war, I think, is not over yet. It will suit me book if it lasts another year or two.'

'You haven't told me what your book is.'

'Oh, this and that about the sea.'

'What's your vessel called?'

'The *Chasse Marée*. Know you what it means?'

'Damn me, I'm far from sure. Does it mean a Fish Cart?'

'A man at St Ives said twas just the French name for a lugger. I shall keep her name for the time being in case we find ourselves in French waters.'

'Privateering, I see?'

'Not so. Or it does not have to go that way.'

'Fighting the French.' Valentine leaned an elbow on the table. 'My half brother feels deep about it all. Rot me if I can understand why. I've just been visiting them – them among others. He's brought himself home a delightful little wife. *Spanish*. Can't you *tell*? Her dignity – quite fascinating! Well, by God, he has diced with death for the last six or seven years. Now he has wed a girl with money enough to live on comfortable. They're working day and night on that derelict old mansion of theirs to bring it back to life again . . . where I was born . . . where my mother lived so long . . . a house I would have been glad to inherit . . .' Valentine sighed and brought his glance back from the barmaid. 'Yet all Geoffrey Charles thinks about – I mean as an immediate future – when they have put their house to rights and given it a proper house-warming – is to go back to rejoin Wellington and fight the French! It defeats me . . . I should say *enough*: we have only one life; let others carry on. How shall you equate glory if it brings with it death or disembowelment? How shall it weigh against the possession of a woman – her naked shoulder, her breasts? . . . No wonder Napoleon is a poor lover. He must be thinking of battle flags all the time.'

Stephen fumbled in his purse and found a coin to pay for the meal.

Valentine said suddenly: 'Do you play Faro?'

'What?'

'Faro, the card game.'

'I have. It is a while ago.'

'Being unlucky in love, you must be lucky at cards.'

Stephen stared at him. 'I am, often as not.'

'Come and see me at Cardew, then. We often have little gaming parties.'

'Your stakes will be too high.'

'We play more for fun than gain.'

'Is that so?'

'I might also introduce you to one or two wenches who would take your mind off your long-lost love.'

'At Cardew?'

'No, for that pleasure we should have to go out again.' Valentine grinned. 'What of next Monday?'

Stephen thought round it. It was not an idle invitation, then. He was not sure he altogether trusted this young man. It was an odd sort of invitation, out of the blue. But Valentine had a reputation for gregariousness, for being eccentric. People had spoken of him in this way. Would he be shying at bogles if he refused? If sincerely meant, this invitation might lead to more promising things. And was there really any risk, apart from the risk he always ran in Cornwall, of a sudden recognition? And every month that passed, that risk was reduced.

'Thanks,' he said. 'What time?'

'About five. Are you your own master now? Have you given up the milling work?'

'Yes, from the beginning of this year.'

'When your uncle died?'

'That's right,' said Stephen. 'When me uncle died.'

II

The following afternoon three people were riding on Hendrawna Beach: Clowance Poldark on Nero, Geoffrey Charles Poldark on Bargrave, Amadora Poldark on Glow. They had been as far as the Dark Cliffs; Clowance had shown them the Holy Well; now they were half way home.

Geoffrey Charles shouted: 'This is one thing we lack at Trenwith.'

'Well, it's near enough. You can ride over any time without consulting me.'

'When does hunting start?'

'Oh, not for a month yet.'

'D'you know, though I followed the hunt as a child, I never can remember when it begins.'

'Why d'you ask?'

'Well, Harriet – Lady Harriet – loaned us these horses for the duration of our stay. But she is likely to want them back when the season opens.'

Clowance shouted: 'I do not think you need be anxious. She has a large enough stable.' She drew rein slightly to allow Amadora to catch up with them. She said to her: 'I have scarcely met Lady Harriet – Sir George's new wife, so I have not really got to know her. Do you like her?'

'*Ya lo creo!* She shall be very kind, very generous.'

Geoffrey Charles laughed. 'I think we both like her – Amadora especially because she speaks Spanish. But then Amadora even likes Step-father George!'

'Why shall I not? He has done no harm to me.'

Clowance said: 'Perhaps you feel the appeal of his wickedness. All nice girls, they say, are attracted by wicked men.' She spoke with a certain inner feeling.

Amadora looked puzzled, and Geoffrey Charles shouted a Spanish translation.

'Ah, so. But yet I do not see him as wicked – not yet. What Geoffrey Charles has to say to me about him – that is another matter.'

'When I met him,' Clowance said, 'I felt rather sorry for him.'

Geoffrey Charles said: 'You have never been under his thumb, as I was as a child. That makes a difference to one's feelings, I assure you.'

The horses had fallen to a walk. All of them were tired after a long gallop in the yielding sand. Their shadows moved with them, a pace or two ahead. The chimney of Wheal Leisure smoked lazily on the cliff. There was another smaller trail of smoke rising from what looked like a bonfire nearer Nampara. The sea was rumbling, far out. A flock of starlings fluttered against the sky.

Geoffrey Charles said: 'Well, then, we shall be able to

keep our horses until we return to Spain. That cannot be far off.'

'Oh, no!' said Clowance. 'You are hardly here! Amadora, you must persuade him otherwise!'

The Spanish girl lifted one gloved hand from her reins. 'Can I persuade him? I do not know. *Should* I? He is a soldier.'

Geoffrey Charles said: 'We shall give our party on Saturday sennight. After that, I think we should soon go. There is much happening. There is much to do.'

After a minute Clowance said: 'You remind me of my father.'

'That I look on as a high compliment. Where is he?'

'Papa? He went in to Redruth this morning. He should be back almost any time. You will sup with us?'

'Thank you, but Drake and Morwenna were coming to Nampara and should be there by now. We cannot –'

'Then you shall all surely stay. If my mother has not driven them to a promise by now I shall be surprised.' Clowance screwed up her eyes. '*Is* that a bonfire? Just in front of our garden . . . Oh, it might be . . .' She turned in her saddle to Amadora. 'Today they have been finishing cutting the harvest. It must be the same in your country. I believe they have finished now, and are drinking some of our ale. They will sit a while and maybe sing a little before night falls and they go home.'

As the three riders approached they saw a group of farm workers sitting on the rough ground that separated the garden of Nampara and the stile from the first sand; it was a rank barren piece with thistles and tree mallows and tufts of marram grass. Driftwood, come in with recent tides, had been pushed into a rough pile in the centre, with gorse used to fire it. Clowance could see her mother there and one or two of the indoor servants.

'Let us go this way,' she said to the others, turning her horse inland where the Wheal Leisure cliffs gave way to low sand dunes. She knew that if three people on horses arrived on the scene of the bonfire the workers would stand up and become self-conscious, and much of the fun would go out of it. She and the others, having dismounted at the house, could stroll into the group if they so chose, and no one would be disconcerted.

III

They had grown oats in the Long Field this year. Ross had decided that one smaller field of wheat near Reath Cottage would be sufficient, together with what he had over from last harvest. Demelza had asked for a single row of potatoes along the edge of the Long Field when it was ploughed, and they had cropped well and been drawn at the end of last month. Now the last sheaf of oats was reaped and tied and must dry off for a few days before it was gathered. As usual half a dozen extra hands had been brought in to help with the reaping, and these, with the regular workers on the farm, made up a group of sixteen, who sat around the bonfire and drank the small beer that Demelza had sent – and later taken – out to them. There was no tradition of lighting a bonfire, but the driftwood was there for the taking and it looked more friendly to squat around a flame even on a sunny afternoon. And, as everyone knew, although all the workers were men, women would come over from Mellin Cottages or even one or two from the house to gape and listen and giggle and chat.

'We're some late this year,' said Cal Trevail to Art Thomas, who was one of the casual helpers. 'Michaelmas but two weeks off and not all the fields in.'

'Tis like it all round,' said Art, sipping his ale and wiping his mouth on the back of his hand. 'Pilchards in J'ly, then naught for we since – St Ives 'ave 'ad 'em all on this coast. Reckon they catch 'em afore ever they get this far.'

'Else you'd not be 'ere, I s'pose?' said Moses Vigus, sidling up and squatting close behind them.

'No, I'd not, you can rest on that. But you grow tired o' waiting for the huer. Village 'll suffer if we don't get a shoal soon.'

'I 'spose Brother's there?'

'Which brother?'

'John, o'course.'

'Oh, 'e's out most days.'

'What's this I 'ear 'bout your other brother, eh? 'Bout Music. There's whisperings 'bout Mrs Pope. Music told ee any stories, 'ave ee?'

'Music be very tight-mouth these days.'

Cal Trevail said: 'I only heard tell something was amiss when the old man died. Thank ee, Ena, that's uncommon kind of ee.'

Ena Daniel was filling the mugs again. Cal Trevail smiled at her uncertainly through his hair; she bridled and turned away.

'Got an eye for she, 'ave ee?' whispered Moses Vigus, who never missed a thing. 'She'd suit you, Cal. Fit ee like a glove, she would. 'Andy size; not too broad in the beam. Been aboard yet? Get her forced put, then she cann't refuse ee.'

Cal allowed a wry grin to cross his face, then wiped it off with the back of his hand. 'Maybe so, maybe not.'

'Lot of this shilly-shallying,' said Moses. 'What *'bout* Music, Art?' he persisted. ''Eard tell strange stories 'bout he. They say he have a fancy for Katie Carter. How 'bout that! Dedn know *he* were fanciful for women – nor fanciful for nothing except screeching tenor in the choir. Tell us, Art, do he 'ave what most men 'ave?'

There was a cackle of laughter.

Art took a good gulp of ale. 'Moses, me old dear, your 'quiring for this, that and the other. Rumour about Mrs Pope. Rumour about Katie. Rumour about Music. Why don't ee ask that man over there? Mebbe he'd knaw more of everything you're 'quiring of. Eh? Do ee go'n ask him, me old dear.'

They looked up and saw Ben Carter, who had walked from Wheal Leisure and had stopped a few moments to talk to Mrs Zacky Martin, no doubt to ask after the health of his grandfather.

'What's it to do with he?' said Cal.

'Well, just as I be Music's brother, so he be Katie's

brother. Edn that so? And if thur be rumour 'bout Mrs Pope, or if there be rumours 'bout Katie or Music, then Ben be the man to ask! Just go ask 'im, now! See what he d'say.'

Ben was a slightly built man, quiet spoken and reserved. But as underground captain at Wheal Leisure he had gathered a new prestige; also his fight with Stephen Carrington had lost nothing with the telling. So, as he was generally known to be sharp tempered, men did not approach him with impertinent questions.

Just then Clowance came out, and any suggestion of a frown on Ben's brow instantly cleared. He was introduced to Geoffrey Charles, whom he scarcely knew, and to Amadora. They stood on the edge of the seated group, talking and drinking ale with the rest.

Ben said to Clowance: 'I come to see Jeremy, as he didn't walk up this morning. It was not of importance but I thought the whym engine had need of his looking at.'

'He has gone to Wadebridge, Ben. He left early this morning.'

'It is not important. She – the engine – she's not quite right, Peter reckon, but he don't fancy to stop her without Jeremy's permission.'

Geoffrey Charles said: 'D'you know, my knowledge of mining is of the most minimal. Of course I was only four when the great Grambler shut down, and a little over eight when my father died. Since then I have not had much opportunity . . . Jeremy has promised to take me down Leisure sometime. I must remind him.'

'Any time you d'wish, sir,' said Ben. 'It would be my privilege. Don't often get chances to take an army cap'n down – an officer of the 43rd Monmouthshires at that!'

It was a longer speech than Ben was normally given to. Geoffrey Charles laughed. 'I did not know my history was so well known.'

'Cap'n Poldark – the other cap'n, that is to say – sometimes mention it. Besides, who wouldn't be proud of fighten as you've been fighten – all through the Peninsula: under Moore, under Wellington.'

Mrs Zacky, who was standing near, said: 'Welcome to Nampara, ma'am. Welcome from us all.'

There were murmurs of agreement. Amadora found the Cornish dialect impossible to understand, but she received the message. 'Thank you,' she said. 'I shall be happy to be here.'

'Comen to live permanent at Trenwith, are ee, Cap'n?' asked Beth Daniel.

'Who knows? After the war.'

'Open Grambler 'gain, sur,' someone shouted.

'Didn' oughter ever've been shut reely,' said Moses Vigus in an aside.

Geoffrey Charles, who had the ears of a dog-fox, said sharply. 'Who are you? Do I know you?'

'Oh, tak' no notice of 'e, sur,' said Mrs Zacky. 'That's Moses Vigus. No one takes the least bit of notice of 'e.'

There was laughter.

'His father was Nick,' said Ben Carter, with some malevolence.

'Oh, I think I do have some recollections. Was Nick not very bald?'

'*Very* bald,' said Beth Daniel, with satisfaction.

'And a mischief maker,' said someone in the circle, and there was another laugh.

'More than a mischief maker,' said Ben, whose father had been led by Nick into ruin.

'There's nicer men than 'e 'round here, Cap'n Geoffrey Charles,' said an oldish man coming up just then. 'Paul Daniel. Recollect me, do ee, sur?'

'Of course, of course, and very good to see you.'

While this conversation was going on Demelza and Drake sat alone in the parlour except for young Henry Poldark who drowsed lightly sucking his thumb and occasionally stirring a fat leg. Isabella-Rose, having found a new cousin scarcely a year older than herself, had at once commandeered her. She had taken Loveday's hand and led her down to the cave to show her Jeremy's boat and some shells they had found when last out in it. Morwenna had said she would go with them to see they did not get into trouble.

'Why did you call him Henry?' Drake asked, staring down at his tiny nephew.

'We tried all the names we could think of,' said Demelza. 'All the family tried. It was quite different from the other children: we knew as soon as ever they were born. Not Henry. We almost called him Claude.'

'Why?'

'It was Ross's brother's name – who died young. And Ross's grandfather too.'

'And who was Henry?'

'Ross's grandfather too.'

They both laughed.

'Claude Henry,' Demelza explained unnecessarily.

'I thought I heard Clowance call him Harry.'

'So you would. Henry. Harry. Hal. That's what they called the Henrys who were kings.'

'And he has another name?'

'Vennor. I don't suppose he will wish to be called that, but it all depends how he feels when he grows up.'

Drake rubbed his hair beside his ear and frowned.

'I'm going grey, Demelza, have you noticed?'

'So am I.'

They both laughed again. 'But yours don't show.'

'I take care it doesn't show. It is easier for a woman. It is not considered vanity to touch up one's hair.'

'Vanity of vanities, as Sam would say.' Drake sighed. 'But it is good to be here again. This is the room where you taught me to read and write. Remember?'

'Just!'

'And once did you not say twould be better if I stopped trying to see Morwenna?'

'It's mean of you to recall that,' said Demelza. 'I was trying to save you trouble and injury from the Warleggans.'

'I know, m'dear. It seemed right for you to do so at the time. But in the end – the Good Lord be praised . . .'

'Sam warned you as well.'

'I know, I know.' Drake smiled and looked around. 'You've changed some things. New curtains again. That cupboard has gone.'

'The one I hid myself in once from Father. We kept it for years for old times' remembrance, but in the end I said to Ross it just has to go.'

'And Garrick?'

'Oh, that was *awful*, Drake. But that's *years* ago – did I never write and tell you? . . . We knew he was very old and not well, but maybe I was thoughtful for other things. One morning I was in here adding up my accounts. You know I really have no head for figures. *In* he came, lolloping as usual – I half expected him to overset some table. But he put his great paw on my arm, and then his head, and I cried, "Oh Garrick, don't do that!" for he would have made my pen hand all drunken. So he stopped and lay down, and I went on adding up my figures. And when they were done, I put down my pen and looked at him – and he was just lying there . . .'

'Ah . . . Too bad.'

'It *was* too bad,' said Demelza indistinctly; 'it was too bad that the last words he ever heard from me were a reprimand, as if he was not wanted . . .'

'I think he would know better'n that.'

There was a tap on the door.

'Beg pardon,' said Jane Gimlett. 'Ena d'want to know if we should open another cask of ale.'

'Yes,' said Demelza.

'Thank ee, ma'am.' She went out.

'And you,' said Demelza. 'How are you, Drake, really, truly? It has been good to be over there?'

'In Looe? Good in most ways. Though I miss you and Sam – and the north coast. Nothing in the south be quite so vigorous, like.'

'Would you ever come back?'

'Geoffrey Charles would like it – would like us to stay now when they d'leave – caretakers, like. His steward, he calls it. It was always what he planned when he was a boy. Of course he says he would not, could not expect us to leave Looe right away. He have offered generous money; it seems that Amadora have money, so he can afford it . . . Of course it is not all money, for we are comfortable enough in Looe.

But I see Geoffrey Charles's feeling: he have already spent so much on this house and now it may be a year before he returns; he will not wish it to go to ruin again while he is away.'

'How does Morwenna feel?'

'She have mixed thoughts about Trenwith.' Drake hurried on as Demelza was going to speak. 'Oh, she is glad to see Geoffrey Charles, and glad to see him wed to such a good and fine-spirited young woman. We are all well together – and I b'lieve we would remain so. But as you know, Morwenna's marriage to Whitworth left deep scars. It took long to heal them, and I b'lieve the skin over them is still tender. You sort of wonder if it would be right or wise to have her living here – 'specially after the others have gone.'

Demelza said: 'But Morwenna is happy with you now?'

The old smile came and went on his face. 'I b'lieve she've been very happy.'

'You and her?'

He stared down at Henry again. 'I wonder if it is in your memory to mind what I once said to you – can't remember just when. It was when I were young and romantic. I said that Morwenna was my night and my day.'

'Yes,' said Demelza.

'Well, it is just the same now.'

Henry grunted and his eyelashes fluttered. Demelza tucked him in.

'And for her, Drake,' she persisted.

'Yes, and for her, I b'lieve, I truly b'lieve.'

Another silence. 'We have only the one child,' said Drake, 'but it is not for lack of the loving.'

Demelza looked out at the bright day. She said: 'That's all I wanted to know.'

Chapter Ten

Goldsworthy Gurney had a cottage with a landlady to look after him at Egloshayle, a village about a mile from Wadebridge but on the other bank of the River Camel. Gurney was a busy man, for Dr Avery was now laid up and unable to attend to his patients. Jeremy rode to Padstow where he had never been before, and took tea with Goldsworthy's parents at Trevorgus.

In the morning and evening he talked and argued with Gurney, who had turned a spare bedroom into a sort of laboratory which was crammed with papers, junk, half-completed experiments, drawings and designs and scribbled speculations. It was hard to keep Gurney on one track for long: with the least encouragement his mind would scuttle off down a side turning.

From considering the question of working a locomotive by ammoniacal gas he would slip away into a discussion with himself as to the value of sea sand as a manure for the fields; and thence suddenly charge Jeremy to note the phenomenon that if you removed a hundred cart-loads of sand from the sea shore, it would *all* be replaced by tomorrow's tide; but if you did *not* cart *any* away, no extra sand would be deposited! Then back he would come to the theory that a carriage could be constructed with wheels connected by a swinging frame to the crank shaft of a steam engine so that they might rise and fall as required to accommodate themselves to the inequalities of the road surface.

Or did Jeremy know anything about the contrapuntal music of Palestrina. Or the organ fugues of J. S. Bach? When there was time Gurney hoped to build himself an organ, but the rooms in this cottage were so small. Jeremy told him about Ben Carter, who had built his own organ in the loft of his father's cottage, but Gurney was not interested in that.

They discussed Trevithick's sketch for the sort of boiler

he would design if again attempting a horseless carriage. It was a primitive scrawl, and to anyone not educated in the work the lower half of the sketch looked like an ungifted child's drawing of a thin cow with three udders, the upper half like a number of bolsters one on top of the other. To help, Trevithick had scribbed over the top half, 'horizontal tubes here' and 'perpendicular tube 8'6'' and '13 inches in the neck' and 'flue place' and 'fire door' and the like.

At the back of all the fluctuating discussions Jeremy detected a solid business instinct in his companion which looked further than his own. Whatever Gurney intended to collaborate in, he intended that it be turned to profitable use. Jeremy was concerned to take one step at a time, and to him the boiler was of absolute and paramount importance. Richard Trevithick with his inspired shorthand had almost designed it for them, but who was to make it, and if it could be made what would it cost?

Just before Jeremy left, Gurney began to talk about the passengers and how they might be attracted to the coach, how best they could be reassured that travelling in it was not dangerous. And what width of tyres to give the better grip, the quieter ride? How many wheels to the carriage, four or eight? What of the idea of two four-wheeled carriages, one drawing the other and thus separating the engine from the passengers and reducing the heat and smell to the traveller and the risk of hurt from an escape of steam? Would they be heavier, harder to control, especially going downhill? And could the levers or legs which were to be designed to provide extra traction also be used in an emergency as extra brakes?

As he rode home Jeremy felt a little as if he were already in such a coach and rolling inexorably downhill. Gurney did advance at a great rate. Last evening they had discussed finance, and Gurney had offered to put up a thousand pounds if Jeremy would do the same. Jeremy had provisionally agreed. But he had made it provisional. Perhaps it was he, he thought, who was sidestepping like a nervous horse at the incline, not Goldsworthy being too impetuous. What was holding him back?

On his journey home he took the main turnpike road to

Truro, for his mother had asked him if he could find some more music for Isabella-Rose.

The young Bella was shooting up now, with legs already nearly as long as her mother's, and she seemed to want to do nothing but dance and sing. Black ringlets bobbing, bright eyes glowing with enthusiasm, she would kick and spring and sing at the top of her voice with the slightest encouragement, and often without it. She also wanted to play the piano. Demelza had done all she could to encourage her to play in a proper way, to study black blobs arranged at varying heights between parallel lines, *notes*, she explained, which if carefully transposed to the fingers would create far more beautiful sounds and melodies than any vague strumming on one's own. If she would sit down for an hour with Mrs Kemp, Mrs Kemp would give her some lovely exercises to do, and then teach her the marvellous mysteries of scales and keys and tones and semi-tones. It was a most wonderful world to unlock, she explained to her daughter; she only wished – she only so much wished – she had had time when young to learn properly herself.

'But you play *lovely*, Mama! I just want to play just like you – only *louder*!'

'But you don't need to play louder, my lover. Anyway, when you learn to play properly you will see little letters beside the lines saying "f" which means loud or "p" which means soft.'

'You don't spell loud with an "f"!'

'No, but it stands for – what is it? – forty, which is French or Italian for loud.'

Demelza felt hypocritical trying to persuade Bella to subjugate her bubbling love of music in order to study it in an orthodox way. She herself had begun to strum, first on the old spinet, then on a harp, before she began to take lessons from Mrs Kemp. The lessons hadn't really gone too well. She had come to have a nice, warm, confident touch on the things she knew. When some new tune caught on in the countryside she could harmonize a simple accompaniment if anyone wanted to sing. She was happy at the piano, loved just the sound of chords, sometimes when alone would play her scales, moving from one key to another and finding as much pleasure in the climbing notes as in playing any sonata. But the sonatas themselves were generally too difficult. She wished there were not two hands to play at the same time and that they were not scored differently, so that 'a' in the left hand was not the same note on the music sheet as 'a' in the right hand. In the early years of their marriage and then at intervals since she had really tried to master this drawback in her talents, and Ross, strangely enough, never seemed to mind her trying when he was in the room even when she played a wrong chord.

But it hadn't worked. She had progressed as far as agreeable competence, and beyond that the door was closed. So, as she said to Ross, she felt on false ground trying to persuade Bella. Perhaps Bella would be happier and remain happier just strumming on the piano for pleasure.

'But there's no comparison!' Ross said.

'Not yet.'

'There's no comparison at all between the noises you got out of the spinet and the harp when you were about seventeen and –'

'Well, she's only *eleven* yet!'

'Yes, but she *thumps*! She hits the piano like a bal maiden spalling ore! –'

'Oh, no!' said Demelza, laughing.

'I don't know how she finds the strength in her fingers. And she doesn't sing, she *shouts*!'

'She enjoys it.'

'Oh, it may be, it may be. But who else does? I shall buy her another piano and put it somewhere out in the stables. But no, that would be bad for the animals!'

So Demelza had persisted in her blandishments to persuade Isabella-Rose into orthodoxy, and Isabella-Rose had been equally firm in being unwilling or unable to bring herself to read music.

Yet Demelza was surprised to discover that the little girl was not without her admirers. During a visit by Geoffrey Charles and Amadora, Bella was heard in the distance, and a few days later, when making plans for his party at

Trenwith, Geoffrey Charles had suggested that at the party Bella might be persuaded to sing.

'But she can't sing *in tune*!' said Demelza, astonished.

'Does it matter? She is so young and has such infectious glee. Everyone I believe will be enchanted.'

Amadora said: 'Do you think she shall be persuaded? Might she perhaps be too – what is the word? –'

'Shy,' said Geoffrey Charles.

'Perhaps she may be,' said Demelza hopefully; 'I'll ask her;' fearing the answer.

'Oh, Mama, would that not be *glorious*!' said Isabella-Rose. 'Cousin Geoffrey Charles is the sweetest of men, I'll be sworn, and also his dear Spanish lady too. But what am I to *sing*? What *could* I sing? Would Papa permit it, for I know I try him to distraction? What can be done, and in so short a time?'

Demelza said: 'There are many simple ditties that you know . . . Or perhaps something fresh could be bought for you. It does not take long to learn a song – if it is suitable. You could do it in two weeks.'

So as Jeremy was leaving for Wadebridge Isabella-Rose wound her arms fiercely round his neck and said: 'Get me something from Miss Seen, Jo-jo, get me something *nice*.'

There was no such thing as a music shop in Truro, but a Miss Amelia Heard did business in an upstairs room above a saddler's in Duke Street, near the church. It was mainly the sale of hymn books, psalters, and sheet music for choirs; but Miss Heard was not above stocking copies of the latest popular ditty, always provided that the words accorded with her sense of propriety. She was a stout little body with stays that creaked and rimless spectacles too big for her face, that made her look like a white owl. When Jeremy visited as a boy with his mother he at once called the lady Miss Seen-but-not, and this had abbreviated itself among the Poldark children to Miss Seen, and one had to be careful to remember not to call her that to her face.

When Jeremy, having left his horse at a tethering post outside the Red Lion, and walked to the saddler's, climbed the dusty wooden staircase and pushed open the reluctant door, which always opened as if something were pushing against it from the inside, he found that Miss Heard already had a customer. It was Cuby Trevanion.

She was in a walnut brown velvet riding habit, with cream lace at the throat and a darker brown hat. Sometimes, Jeremy thought, she did not seem to know what colours suited her; but this colour suited her; so did the sudden flush coming into her cheeks at the sight of him.

They murmured each other's name in greeting, made some sort of small conversation which neither was the least interested in. In their last two encounters Jeremy had been politely formal, trying to hide the raging bitterness which had driven him to such despair.

Well, it seemed that he had hidden his bitterness successfully, that she had assumed his cold formality was adopted for the occasions and had perceived nothing deeper in it. Now it was as if nothing had happened between them this year and she was continuing the cheerful truce of last September. She was smiling up at him and telling him that she had come into Truro with Clemency and was trying to buy some new music for Joanna Bird, who was staying with them – 'you remember her, she is abed with some summer indisposition and we thought to cure her by tempting her down to the music room.'

Jeremy stumbled over his replies, lost as ever merely in looking at her. He explained his own mission, about the coming party at Trenwith, about the difficulty of finding music for his unmusical sister. Cuby was amused by the idea. Had she not seen Isabella-Rose last year, that charming little girl with the dark ringlets, who walked in such a lilting way?

'That's exactly right,' said Jeremy. 'That's – how one could describe her.'

Abruptly they remembered the fat little woman who was waiting on the other side of the counter. She had been watching them, listening to the exchange and summing up their manner and their glances. Now, apologizing together, they bent over the various pieces of music she was offering. Cuby advised Jeremy as to what might be most suitable to a little girl singing at her first party, and Jeremy edited and revised this advice in his better knowledge of his sister. They talked a lot of bright brittle talk which was at least partly designed for their only listener, but it did not deceive their only listener at all. Eventually Cuby bought three new pieces for Joanna and Jeremy about a dozen for Bella. He chose them in a haze and hoped one or two might be approved of.

Beaming at them both, Miss Heard accepted their money and rolled up their purchases in thin tissue, tying each roll with pink string as if it were a lawyer's brief. Together, or as near together as possible, they went down the creaking flight of stairs.

Jeremy said: 'Can you take tea with me? The Red Lion has a quiet room and it is only a few paces away.'

'Jeremy, I would like to, but Clemency and the groom will be waiting. Heavens, is it that time? I must hasten!'

'Let Clemency come too. You know what friends we are.'

A shadow crossed Cuby's face. 'Clemency always speaks highly of you ... She is, you know, an altogether nicer person than I ...'

'But it is you I want,' said Jeremy.

A man in a faded uniform was standing in the gutter begging. He had only one leg.

Cuby said: 'Augustus is returning from London next week.'

'It is you I want,' said Jeremy.

'You must not say that. It was not in our agreement last September.'

'Where is Clemency?'

'At Pearce's. She will be tired of waiting.'

'I will walk you there.'

They crossed the newly-laid Boscawen Street by the Coinage Hall. A carriage was forcing its way over the cobbles and through the refuse. A fish jouster was shouting his wares. A group of soldiers and sailors were arguing on the corner, becoming contentious and noisy.

Jeremy took Cuby's arm. There was a terrible contagion in the touch.

He said sharply: 'Why do you not come to this party at Trenwith?'

'What? How could I?'

'How could you not? If I ask Geoffrey Charles he will invite you. You and Clemency and Joanna – and Augustus, if need be.'

'Oh, . . . I don't think . . .'

'You have never been to the north coast. You said so. And when my mother invited you to stay at Nampara, your mother refused!'

'You know the reason.'

'Well, it need not obtain so far as Trenwith is concerned. It will be a big party which many of the county will attend. There is little or no risk for you – risk as your mother and brother see it.'

'Is not your cousin – your second cousin or whatever he may be – is he not also called Poldark?'

'Yes, indeed. It is where we all come from, Trenwith.'

'Then I fear my brother will think it is some sort of a contrivance arranged so that you and I may meet.'

'So it is. I hope. But Geoffrey Charles is something of a war hero. And a married man. And married to a Spaniard. Many will come just to see them before they return. It is patriotic to do so. Why should not you?'

They had turned into Lower Lemon Street. Pearce's Hotel was on the corner by the new bridge.

'But we do not know them.'

'Quite unimportant.'

'Will you come in now and meet Clemency?'

'With pleasure. But first . . .'

'Yes.' She detached her hand from his arm as they reached the door of the hotel. 'Dear Jeremy, I do not know how it will be.'

'Well, let us try.'

She stared at some goats being driven down the street. 'Where would we lie? It would not be possible for us to –'

'There will be room at Trenwith – or should be. If not there, then Nampara . . . No, that would not do, would it. Place House. Mrs Pope will put you up.'

'Mrs Pope?'

'Yes, she is a new friend of mine. A widow with two grown step-daughters. They have a fair house only a couple of miles from Trenwith. She would be greatly flattered to house the Trevanions.'

Cuby's face was heavy with concentration. Then she glinted up at him, her eyes again alight. 'Very well. I'll try.'

'Promise.'

'First send the invitation!'

'Oh, that is not an obstacle, I assure you. It is your end where the obstacle lies!'

She took his hand in a brief clasp and then released it. 'I'll try. I'll get Augustus and Clemency to help me.'

They went into the hotel together.

Chapter Eleven

I

The next day Jeremy and Clowance rode over to Trenwith, and they and Geoffrey Charles and Amadora took a walk along the cliffs. Jeremy and Clowance had bathed in the morning, which was sunny and breathlessly still with an enormous incoming tide; by the afternoon as the tide receded one could see piles of seaweed and driftwood along the high watermark and dozens of people sifting it over for anything of value. The afternoon was still quiet but the September sun was streaky.

'Rain and wind tomorrow,' said Jeremy.

The path along the edge of the cliff being narrow, the quartet split up, Jeremy and Geoffrey Charles going ahead, the girls fifty yards in the rear, Clowance generally holding them up by picking wild flowers and offering them for Amadora to look at.

'This path was out of bounds when I was a child,' said Geoffrey Charles. 'Even Morwenna was not allowed to bring me here.'

'I suppose all mothers are the same,' said Jeremy.

'Sometimes it is good to be nervous,' said Geoffrey Charles. 'Amadora is not nervous enough. At least for herself.'

'You are determined to go back to Spain right after the party?'

'Determined? I suppose that is as good a word as any. I feel it my duty. And in a sense I look forward – after so many years of being pounded by the enemy I want to be in it when we at last are doing the pounding.'

'Do you think the war will be over soon?'

'There are so many fronts now . . . You see the Americans have had a success on Lake Erie. I suspect they will re-take

Detroit soon. They can get reinforcements so much more quickly.'

'So if there is peace in Europe there may be war in America for some years yet?'

'I confess I should not feel eager to return if I were returning to fight in Canada. Buonaparte is *my* enemy.'

Not to be outdone by Clowance, Jeremy stopped and picked a stalk of pink willow herb which was blooming by the path. He sniffed at it but there was no scent.

'Will you do me a favour, Geoffrey Charles?'

'Name it.'

Jeremy named it.

'Give me their full names and the address when we get home,' said his cousin. 'I'll send the letter tomorrow.'

'Thank you.'

'It may not be possible to put them up in Trenwith. You know our bedrooms. But I think as you say, Mrs Pope . . .'

'Have you met the Popes yet?'

'Last week. She called on Amadora. A pretty woman.'

'Distinctly so,' said Jeremy.

Behind them Amadora said: 'This bathing that you shall do today. Do you engage in it in all your clothes?'

'Oh, no. Mama has made a light costume which we have all copied. Have you seen the Greeks – pictures of the Greeks? They wore a sort of short thin tunic without sleeves. That, of course, was for men, and that was for daily wear, not for bathing. We use something like it for bathing. It is not at all what would be favoured in Brighton or Penzance but it serves.'

'But does it not display – all of the legs?'

'Yes. But who is to see?'

'Oh. I do not think I could do that! With you it shall be just your family. I am not one of your family.'

'Yes you are!'

Amadora said rather stiffly: 'Not in that way. I cannot undress myself in the front of Jeremy.'

'We'll go on our own sometime – right at the end of the beach.'

'Maybe. When the sea grows more warm. I used my hand in it last week and it was like the *ice*!'

'But this is September, Amadora. This is the warmest it ever gets!'

'Mother of God, I shall not bear that! I could die of chill.'

'And this,' said Clowance, stooping, 'is samphire. We use it in making pickles. Taste it, the leaves are quite nice.'

Amadora tasted, made a little moue, dropped the leaf. 'I think in Spain we have something of the sort. Clowance . . .'

'Yes?'

'We are the most near of an age, is that not so? There is one thing that shall be worrying me, as you will suppose it is worrying everyone. I have not spoken to your mother though she has been the most kind of all. It shall be worrying me always if I come to live in England.'

'That is? . . .'

'My religion.'

Clowance crumpled the other leaves and sniffed them.

Amadora said: 'I am from a convent, you will understand. In our convent we are taught that those who are not belonging to the Catholic faith are heretics. Must be shunned, avoided, shall be treated as evil people – the anti-Christ. I am taught that heretics cannot even be good-looking, for they have their wickedness written on their faces. This is how I am taught – until I meet the English – and Geoffrey Charles. Then I cannot believe that any more. *Afortunadamente*, my father, he is a very wise man, very *tolerante* – I am sorry, in embarrassment I lose my English . . .'

'Don't hurry . . . Yes, we're coming!' Clowance called to the young men.

'My mother, she is very unforgiving – and also my brother – my elder brother, Martin – he looks the dagger at me, as if I shall be casting myself into the pit. And as for Father Antonio – you need not ask! . . .' The girl sighed. 'Yet our love is such we ride over these obstacles – and it will continue so. I know it here.' She touched her heart.

'Isn't that really what matters?' Clowance said.

'Of course. Of course. *Por supuesto*. But now I am here I

say to myself: "But to them *I* am the heretic, the evil one, the anti-Christ. Those who are not having our love to sustain them, how shall they think other?"'

'Has anyone given you to think so?'

'Twice or thrice there is the look *de reojo* from this one and that. And since we have come here Geoffrey Charles has not ever been once to confession – never has he seen the priest, never to the church. It gives me to worry.'

'Because he has not been following *his* religion?'

'Yes.'

Clowance said: 'Have you spoken to Geoffrey Charles about this?'

'No, no, no. I could not. How shall I as his wife presume to question him on such matters?'

'My dear.' Clowance patted her hand. 'I do not think Geoffrey Charles feels his religious ties as deeply as you do. I do not think it has upset him deeply that he has not been to church because he cannot take you. And in our church there is no such thing as confession.'

'Not?'

'Not. The way we believe, it is not necessary to have a priest between ourselves and God. If – if we have anything to confess, we confess it direct to Him.'

'And who absolves you? Is that the word?'

'God does. Who better?'

'Ah,' said Amadora, mystified, and they walked on.

Jeremy said: 'There are a lot of things I want to ask you, Geoffrey Charles.'

'Such as?'

'How much would it cost me to buy a commission in the Army?'

Geoffrey Charles looked at his cousin. They were both tall thin men, Geoffrey Charles only the taller by being more erect.

'Does that mean you wish to go?'

'I have thought of it. Your advice on all fronts would be helpful.'

'Have you discussed this with your parents?'

'Not in detail. They know I might so decide.'

'And approve?'

'No. But they will not stand in my way.'

They strolled on a few yards. 'May I ask what your general reasons are, Jeremy? Do you wish to fight the French? Or have you some desire to get away from your home? Or do you like the idea of travel and living a rough life and finding adventure?'

'Mainly the second. I wish to get away.'

'From your parents? That surprises me. When I joined the army it was originally from the same motive, but I was getting away from my mother's death and from a step-father whom I hated!'

'Not from my parents.' Jeremy kicked at a stone. 'Can we just say that I have a girl in my blood, and she is privately engaged to marry someone else –'

'*This* girl? This one you have asked me to ask?'

'Yes.'

'And – that has hit you so badly?'

'I have tried to live with it. I have failed. To an outsider it will seem stupid but –'

'Not necessarily. But what do you want from me?'

'Details. Advice if you care to offer it.'

'About the army? Willingly if I know the answers.'

'For one thing,' Jeremy said, 'I imagine if I went to my father and told him I had to go, he would buy me a commission. But I don't wish him to be put to expense. As it happens I have come by some money in a rather peculiar way, and it seems to me it would be suitable if I spent it or part of it in such a manner.'

'Where does that lead down there?' Geoffrey Charles asked. 'I don't remember it.'

'A place we've called Kellow's Ladder. Paul Kellow, whom you've met – he and his father put a ladder down an old mineshaft and gained access to a pretty little sheltered beach. But the ladder is broken now – no one goes down.'

'What a view from here,' said Geoffrey Charles. 'Those

waves.' He took a deep breath. 'It's good to be home. I hadn't realized how good.'

'I remember hearing my father say once that to him one of the most important things in life was contrast. Maybe I shall come to appreciate this more when I have seen less of it.'

'But I thought one of your great interests is in the development of steam.'

'So it is.'

'You'd see nothing of that in the army. Technically they have only just learned to boil a kettle.'

Jeremy laughed, but it was not a very humorous sound. 'I suppose I'm on a tightrope – don't know which way to jump.'

'Well, I may tell you one thing,' said Geoffrey Charles. 'You need not pay anything to get a commission. Of course you may buy an ensigncy in a crack regiment and pay through the nose for it: the Foot Guards, the Welsh Fusiliers; the Life Guards most of all. But if you merely want a commission as such, and are prepared to take the regiment you are assigned to, I assure you there is no trouble at all; you must be able to read and write, and have a letter of recommendation from someone holding the rank of major or more. Then you will be in. Three or four months' training and you will be allowed to kill with the best.'

'I thought –'

'A great many people think. But we are at war – constantly expanding our regiments and constantly suffering casualties. Where are the rich men's sons who wish to pay and fill these vacancies? They don't exist. I was told last year that the demand for new officers in Wellington's Army alone is about a thousand a year. Probably half of those are to replace men killed or dying from disease. A fair number resign and a few are cashiered. The rest will be for new units just being formed.'

'I see. Then –'

'Of course you will need money to live on. The pay for an ensign is about 6/– a day, and from that there are deductions. You'll need at least £150 a year to live decently. Then you'll have to buy your uniform, your sword, your compass, your spy glass; best too to have a horse, even in the infantry. Probably an outlay near on £200. So you see it would not be difficult to spend some of your own money in any case.'

They went on.

Clowance said: 'Has Geoffrey Charles not spoken to you about your religion?'

'Yes, yes. He has spoke to my father. They were of accord.'

'Did he not tell you that you can practise your own religion in England just as in Spain? There are Catholic churches here in Cornwall. I – I'm afraid I don't know where they are, but I am sure there are some.'

'Yes, yes, my father says I shall be finding them. But – we have been so busy – it has been *malísimo* – I have done nothing. It is very guilty of me. I think soon we shall be home.'

'In England,' said Clowance, 'we would not call that a serious sin. Except perhaps among a few.' She thought of Sam. 'You used the word *tolerante* just now. Is that not what we should all try to be? And are we not friends – the Spanish and the English? Do we not fight for the same cause?'

'Yes, yes,' said Amadora. 'You comfort me, Clowance. It is good for me to find here such a kind *prima*.'

'*Prima*?'

'I do not know what the English word shall be. *Pariente*. I shall call Geoffrey Charles.'

Clowance coo-eed, but when the men turned back she said: 'This is Kellow's Ladder. Has Geoffrey Charles ever seen it? Can we not go down?'

'*No*,' said Jeremy. 'It is dangerous. I tried last month, and the rungs were insecure.'

'It was well enough last year,' said Clowance.

'Well, it is not well enough now, for I almost fell.'

'Oh, surely we can be careful. It is such an elegant little cove.'

'*No*,' said Jeremy. 'The ladder is quite unsafe . . . Look, let us turn back here and cut across the fields. Isn't it time for tea? Let us ask Amadora for some Spanish tea.'

II

They took tea in the summer parlour. It was a pleasant room, clean now, with a few pieces of velvet, cut down from the curtains in two of the bedrooms and draped over damp-stained chair-backs and moth-eaten seats. A lazy wind, the first of the day, stirred the tendrils of ivy growing over the windows; two chaffinches argued and chirruped outside. Drake and Morwenna had gone to see Sam and his wife; it did not appear to be creating too much embarrassment that Drake at one stage of his life had promised himself in marriage to Sam's wife. Rosina had been the injured party, but it was all so long ago, or she was sufficiently imbued with Sam's teaching of Christian forgiveness that she let it pass her by.

Later, while Amadora and Clowance chatted, Geoffrey Charles took Jeremy out and they examined the great table in the hall. Since being placed there three hundred years ago it had resisted all attempts at removal – even George Warleggan's attempts – but Geoffrey Charles was determined that it must come up for their party. He could not bear the thought of sawing off the central legs, which were of the finest and most imperishable oak; instead the flags of the floor must be dug up, the legs uprooted and the entire table either carried outside, or, if there was no way of getting it through the door, then it must be laid alongside one wall to take up the least possible space. It was the only room in the house big enough for a proper dance, and it was overlooked by the minstrel gallery. So for this occasion it had to be so used. Geoffrey Charles remembered an evening during his step-father's day when they had danced *round* the table; but it just would not do.

Jeremy said: 'What are the officers mainly like in the army? Mostly from the great schools, I suppose?'

'Not at all. I think I have only met six or seven I knew from my time at Harrow. And not so many titled as you would suppose from reading the newspapers, where of course they always attract the news. The vast majority of the officers are grammar school boys or the like. Such that is as I know and have casually learned from! One does not make it a major topic of conversation . . . You see here – these flags – I think they will lever up. If they crack it would not be difficult to replace them.'

'The table could stand on its end,' said Jeremy. 'The room is high enough and it would be less in the way. I can tell without your trying that you'll never get it through the door because of the other door beyond. You'd have to take the window out.'

Geoffrey Charles eyed him. 'Far be it from me, cousin, to deter you from joining the army if you feel you cannot bear to continue to live in Cornwall. But I assure you it is a dangerous and dirty life. Men are dying or being maimed all the time. And you are killing other men – or trying to – all the time. And it is constantly boring as well as dangerous. A fresh young man came out the week of our little fracas at Vittoria; he was attached to the 43rd. Called Thompson. Smartly turned out, good uniform, mighty keen to get into action. Son of a farmer, as it happens. He'd built up little affectations to make him seem more genteel than he was. Wanted to transfer to the cavalry as soon as he could. Was telling me of his amorous adventures in Portsmouth the night before he sailed. Next morning he went out – nothing had really begun – just a little sporadic firing. Stray bullet – couldn't have been aimed. It killed him just the same.'

'I'm under no illusions,' said Jeremy. 'I don't believe I am essentially soldier material . . . But were you?'

Geoffrey Charles smiled, his tight mouth a little tighter. 'No. But I believe I went in with greater reason. I understand you designed the new engine for Wheal Leisure, that you are highly gifted to take advantage of this new era of steam, that you have been working on a horseless carriage. As I said just now, the army will not help you in this pursuit. It seems a pity to set that all aside.'

A long pause followed. They heard laughter.

Jeremy said: 'I'm glad Clowance and Amadora get on so excellently well together.'

'Indeed.'

'What sort of an orchestra shall you hire?'

'There is one, they say, in Truro; plays at the Assembly Balls. But I shall make sure that they are not too staid. In the army I have become used to many jigs and country dances.'

After a moment Jeremy said: 'There is another reason which prompts me to go.'

'May I hear it?'

'If we are somewhere private. This room is a little large for confidences.'

'Will the garden do?'

'If there are no gardeners about.'

'None comes today until six, when they finish their other work.'

So they went into the garden, and Jeremy told him.

III

They walked beside the pool and Geoffrey Charles said: 'My God! I don't believe you! I *can't* believe you!'

'No?'

'Well . . . *No!*'

'I assure you that's what happened.'

'Just as you have said?'

'Just as I have said.'

'It's – out of all reason!'

'Possibly.'

'Well, *why*? What reason could you have had?'

'The obvious one. I wanted money.'

'And you got some?'

'Yes, quite a lot.'

'And – and how have you used it?'

'So far I have not.'

Geoffrey Charles thrust his hands deep into the pockets of his jacket. 'You are telling me the truth?'

'Why should I not? It is not a thing one admits to lightly.'

'Jeremy, you must have been *mad*!'

'A little, no doubt.'

'And the others too.'

'I cannot answer for them.'

'Were they similarly – bereft?'

'Geoffrey Charles, tell me, if you love Amadora as I love this girl, and you knew she was to marry another man only because he had sufficient money, which you had not, how would you feel? Just tell me that!'

'I should feel – if it is the way you describe it – that the girl is worthless.'

'But would it stop you loving her?'

'God knows! God Almighty knows! My dear cousin, how can anyone know what another feels? I am sorry if I called you mad. And yet . . .'

'A little mad,' said Jeremy. 'I accept that. For I know that what I stole could never be enough to win the girl from the man she is promised to. That is my chief madness. Even if we were lucky with the amount we got – as we were – I would have had to take a further risk by putting it to immediate use – indeed gambling with it in some way – for it to produce the sort of sum I needed. Instead of which – once done – once accomplished – I found the – the protest over-sufficient of itself. For the time being. So far I have done nothing with the money at all!'

'But the others have?'

'The others have. Cautiously. They no more wish to suffer the consequences than I do.'

'That's the great danger now. These are local young men?'

'I cannot tell you that.'

Geoffrey Charles grunted. 'But the risk of recognition . . .'

'We were all disguised after a fashion.'

'But how did you *do* it? You say it was in no way a – a stand and deliver?'

'The coaches only seat four inside. We booked our seats and booked the fourth for a fictitious man, who of course did not turn up. Once inside we drew up the blinds and cut through the back of the coach into the safe box under the coachman's seat. It nearly all went to plan.'

'Nearly all?'

'Well, there was one hitch that almost ruined it. A fat elderly lawyer called Rose insisted on taking the empty place inside from Liskeard to Dobwalls. However hard we tried to put him off, he would sit there; so for that length of time we were held up – part done but the work hidden – until he left.'

'I wonder you kept your nerve. And it was all your plan, you say?'

'Months before, my – er – one of the others brought in a London newspaper telling of a robbery on a Brighton coach. No one could imagine how it could have been done. I worked out one way in which it could be done.'

'Well, my God! . . .' Geoffrey Charles blew out a breath. 'This takes the biscuit! I have never . . . And whose money was it you stole? Did that ever come out?'

'Oh, yes, we knew that from the beginning. It all belonged to Warleggan's Bank.'

'War . . .' Geoffrey Charles stared at his cousin. 'It belonged to – to my step-father?'

'Yes.'

There was a pause and then Geoffrey Charles let out a great explosive shout of laughter. Startled birds rose from the other side of the pond.

'You stole it from – from Step-father George? From Smelter George? But how *appropriate* – how singularly, excellently, divinely funny! Do you not see it as funny, Jeremy?'

They had stopped and were standing facing each other.

'Not funny.' Jeremy was wooden faced. 'Maybe appropriate.'

Geoffrey Charles took out a handkerchief and blew his nose and wiped his eyes. 'I'm sorry. I should not have been – amused. It is no matter for amusement. *A Dieu ne plaise*! But I have to confess I am relieved that no widows or orphans are suffering for your crime!'

He took Jeremy's arm and they walked on.

Geoffrey Charles said: 'This is the place where Drake planted the frogs night after night, just to annoy my step-father. I laughed hysterically then. But it nearly cost Drake his life. So in a sense, though in many ways vastly different, there is a similarly personal note in my amusement. And this might have cost you *your* life! Still might.' The grip on the arm tightened. '*Why have you told me this?*'

Jeremy shrugged. 'It seemed – necessary.'

'Like the robbery?'

'No. I think a better reason.'

'Confession being good for the . . .'

'Maybe. Certainly I would never have spoken to anyone else. When I came this afternoon I had no intention of saying anything even to you!'

'You have told *no one* else?'

'Of course not.'

'Well, I counsel you to Trappist silence. I am embarrassed in a sense that you have asked me to share this secret with you. Of course you can rest assured your confidence will never be abused . . . But do you see this act – you clearly do – as another reason for getting away? Is it because of some-thing in yourself or because of the risk of discovery?'

'Something in myself, I suppose. Not the latter. I think now we are reasonably safe.'

'You will never be reasonably safe, Jeremy – not at least while the money is unspent – not for years. But the fact that you have spent nothing of it and now wish – or are considering – joining the army suggests to me that you are looking on this crime as something that needs to be expiated.'

'I wouldn't go so far as that.' Jeremy did not like the question. It was too close to the truth, yet in some way departed from it. He couldn't *simplify* his feelings to that extent. He did not feel exactly remorseful for what he had done; he didn't actually regret having done it. It was not expiation he needed so much as escape – escape from the circumstances which had provoked it – to be no longer surrounded, *stifled* by them. For a while in astonishment and self-disgust he had no longer had any desire for Cuby at all. That had not lasted; the action, the crime had killed feeling, killed sensation; but after a while the insensibility had worn off. His latest meeting with her in the music shop, and his contriving a future meeting at the Trenwith party was totally in accord with his old behaviour, as if the robbery had never taken place, as if he were still the stupid gangling boy, following her, hoping for the kind word, the light flirtation, and knowing all along its utter uselessness. It was in his acute consciousness of this return to an old situation, and his vehement rejection of it, which had prompted everything he had said to Geoffrey Charles today.

'You will not mind using this – your share of the money – in buying a commission or in the ordinary expenses of a military life?'

'No.'

'But don't wish to use it in furthering your experiments in steam?'

'That may be.' Jeremy said something of his meetings with Goldsworthy Gurney. 'It is a choice I must make within the next few weeks.'

They had strolled out into the fields and towards the wood where Geoffrey Charles as a young boy had first met Drake. In the distance Will Nanfan was seeing to his sheep. They waved.

Geoffrey Charles said: 'Well, since you have told me all this, I imagine you may be soliciting my advice.'

'I have said so.'

'Not that you are likely to take it. From talks in camp and mess, I generally assume if someone asks my advice he really wants support for the thing he has already decided to do.'

Jeremy half smiled. 'That may be. I don't know. I don't *promise* to follow your advice but I should greatly value it.'

'There has been no shadow of suspicion so far – cast upon any of the three of you?'

'No.'

'Then I think I should stay and face it out. This is a prime paradox! For isn't going to fight a little like running away? These problems you are facing are really within yourself.

Are they not? How you came to do what you did will still be an issue even if you are fighting on the Pyrenees. When the war is over . . .'

Geoffrey Charles paused and looked towards the main gate. Three people were coming through it. When they saw the two young men they waved and broke into a run, which clearly became a race.

'Let me know your choice. I would wish to know.'

'Of course.'

Drake was winning the race, with Loveday running clutching at her skirts just behind. Morwenna, who tripped quickly rather than ran, brought up the rear. As they came on, Geoffrey Charles wondered if he had given Jeremy the right advice. His cousin did not seem the stuff of which soldiers were made. If he had the sort of sensitivity of feeling which had driven him into the mess he was now in, how would he adapt to a world in which death was the daily possibility, one's friends were mutilated and one's feelings ever blunted by the harsh realities of camp life and of war? And yet, as Jeremy had pointed out, had *he* not himself entered the army as a raw youth who until then had lived a privileged and cushioned life? It was too far back for him even to recognize himself as the youngster who had loved Drake and been under the too gentle control of Morwenna as his governess. It belonged to another life, another person.

Now, just now, after so many years of strife and comradeship and inner loneliness, he had found Amadora . . . But Jeremy had lost his love. This girl must be *seen*, a girl on whom Jeremy so doted that, when he saw himself likely to be deprived of her, he lost his judgement, his caution . . . Did not one still have some belief in the Commandments? Thou shalt not steal. Thou shalt not covet . . . Thou shalt not kill . . . Who did *not* break these Commandments?

'D'you know,' said Drake breathlessly. 'I met Ellery. Peter Ellery! Y'know, we went on that venture together to France to rescue Dr Enys. We was always some close. After all these years – he'd hardly changed at all.'

'Nor have you, Drake,' said Geoffrey Charles.

Cuby Trevanion was the name. She must be quite an exceptional girl. Geoffrey Charles very much hoped she would come to the party.

Chapter Twelve

I

Michaelmas Fair was on the 29th. On the twenty-eighth Art Thomas turned his ankle in a rabbit hole and by the following morning could barely hobble. John, the elder brother, would not have any truck with such trade and never went near a fair or a fete, so Art said: 'Music, you be goin'. Aunt Edie have need of some potion for her blains. She d'say thur be an old woman d'ave a stall there – called Widow Crow. She have this potion that Edie say she need, so you can get it for she, stead of me. Eh?'

'Eh?' said Music. 'Eh?'

'You 'urd.' His brother repeated what he had said.

Music went on whittling at his stick. One of his five cats, the one called Ginger, came over and sniffed at the shavings but quickly lost interest and strolled away. 'Don't 'ave no dealings wi' witches,' Music was presently heard to mutter.

'Witches? Widow Crow ain't no witch, I tell ee, else Edie would never venture near her. She'm just a skirt old woman as knows 'ow to mix the potions. Why ye mind when Wallace Bartle 'ad that wambling of the innards; he took her potions, and was brave in no time. And Nigel Ellery's son – she cured he of the hooting cough. And –'

'There ain't no such thing as witches,' said John grumpily, who was not in one of his best moods because of the failure of the pilchards to arrive off the coast. 'Nor skirt ole women neither. They'm all pomsters, every last one of 'em.'

'Don't know as I be gwain,' said Music. ''Tes a long way to troach.'

'Giss on. Ye know ye never miss'n. If any soul be goin' fair or feast day, tis you, Music.' Art contemplated his brother. In spite of his amiable nature, Music was prone to occasional obstinacies, and Art did not want one to develop now. For two years Art had been courting the fat little Edie and her fat little tannery business, and he found it a constant strain sitting with her when juicy girls of his own age were to be had for the asking. Little errands such as this one were an easy way of obliging her. 'Tes only for the blains. Ye smooth it on and it cools 'em, stops the springeing.'

'Don't know as I be gwain,' said Music.

'Damnation cats,' said John, aiming a kick at one of them. 'Always under your feet – worsen children. Git rid of 'em, I say.'

'She'm a good ole woman, Widow Crow,' said Art. 'She've this stall nigh by the knife grinder; never misses. I expect ye've seen her many time there yerself, Music.'

'Don't know's I 'ave,' said Music.

'Girls go to 'er too. They say she've a fine line in love potions. Failing powers, bleeding ulcers, overlooked babies, wildfire, warts.'

'Just an old pomster,' growled John.

Music finished his whittling. With a long thin hand he began to brush the shavings together.

'They got a lunatic this time,' said Art. 'In a cage. Chained by the neck. I'd 've dearly liked to see her; they say she's violent. Tis a penny to go in. Penny back if you get'n to shake hands.'

'Didn't oughter be allowed,' said John.

'And a bull,' said Art, watching his brother. 'Yer was always one for the baiting, Music.'

'Never was,' said Music. But the idea of the lunatic appealed to him.

'And they do say Black Fred'll be there. We seen 'im five years gone at Summercourt. You mind 'im, John? He swallowed a live mouse on a string and then after ye've counted ten he d'pull 'n of it up again still alive and kicking. You didn't go that year, Music; you was 'ome wi' measles. Ye'd like to see that, Music, wouldn't ee.'

'Aw, leave'm bide, Art, do ee,' said John.

Music got up and threw the shavings of wood into the kindling box. The chickens scattered at the noise.

'The potion's sixpence,' said Art. 'Edie say tis very small

in bottle but it cool her blains wonderful. I reckon I'd pay ee twopence for your trouble.'

'Don't know as I be gwain,' said Music.

II

Yet he did go, and beheld all the wonders of the fair. The lunatic was disappointing – first because it was a man (and sometimes the women were scanty dressed) and second because he simply sat in a corner of his cage, and would not move even when poked with a stick. Black Fred disappointed too because the mouse was half dead and scarcely wriggled at all. But there were other things to entertain, and Music mooched about until it was almost nightfall before he approached Widow Crow. He had passed her booth half a dozen times but always there was someone at it, buying something or talking to the widow, and he was always sensitive at the thought of being laughed at. But the last time she was alone – indeed beginning to pack up and thrust her tins and bottles into an old sack to throw over her shoulders and carry home.

She was a thin tall sallow woman with locks like black horse-hair that fell to her shoulders, and big bony hands with enlarged knuckles and black-rimmed nails. She wore an old muslin blouse decorated with jet beads, a tattered black jacket and a long dusty grey fustian skirt. She was quick enough to sum Music up, and tried to put him at his ease, telling him she could see a fine healthy young fellow like him would never never suffer from the chilblains so he must be buying her special potion for someone else – a mother? an aunt? a sister? Music explained that it was for his brother's girl and then stuttered with nervy laughter at the thought of calling old Edie a girl.

'Got a girl of your own, have you?' asked Widow Crow.

Music went red. 'Sort of.'

'How sort of, my dear? You in love with she?'

'Sort of.'

The widow took a small stone bottle from her bag and put

it on the trestle. 'This be for your brother's girl, see. That'll be sevenpence.'

'Brother told me sixpence.'

'Sevenpence, my dear.'

With great cunning Music said: 'Tes a small little bottle for sevenpence, you.'

'D'you know what it cost me to make?'

'Brother told me sixpence.'

Widow Crow put the bottle back in her bag. 'It is sevenpence or nothing, my dear.'

Music hesitated. 'Sevenpence then.'

'D'you know what be in it?' the widow said in a low voice. 'Shall I tell you?'

'I don't mind,' said Music bravely.

'Frogs.'

'Frogs?'

'Yes. Frogs are red blooded creatures like you and me. But *cold*. See that, my dear? Cold. Cold to cool the blains. It is all in here. Frog spittle, frog sperm, frog juice, frog's eggs. And resin and balsam to bind. Lay it *cool* upon the blains and they'll disappear – just like magic. You see!'

Music fumbled in the front pocket of his breeches and gradually took out seven pennies. The widow's sharp eyes caught the glint of silver.

She counted the pennies as they were reluctantly passed over. 'You got a girl, you say, my dear? Only sort of? That what you say?'

Music grunted and took the bottle of lotion.

'You in love, you say? That right, my dear? But the young leddy? Mebbe she's not in love with you, eh?'

Music grunted again and put the bottle in his pocket. A few people were lighting lanterns, but much of the fair was about to close.

'Not in love with you?' said Widow Crow. 'A fine handsome, handsome fellow? Not in love with you, eh?'

'Mebbe. Mebbe not.'

'Like a love potion?'

'What?'

'A love potion.'

Music began to sweat. They seemed to be alone. People passed by, but now no one came to this stall. Perhaps it was unhallowed after dark.

'Not sure's I do,' he said.

Widow Crow took out a second bottle, even smaller than the first. 'It will cost you ninepence, my dear.'

'Coh!'

'It would be a shilling to most, but only ninepence to you, my dear, as a special favour. I've taken a fancy to you. Why, you'll never know all that's in this little bottle, but I can tell you plain that what's in it cost me eightpence ha'penny, so there's no profit in it for me to sell it so cheap. But I like the looks of you. A fine handsome feller any maid would be right to fancy.'

'Not sure's I do,' said Music.

'*Any* maid,' said Widow Crow, putting her fingers in front of one ear and pushing her lank hair away. 'But maids are hard to please. Some maids have fancy notions. Some maids are fickle. Some maids are as changeable as the weather. That's when you need a love potion, my dear.'

Music thought of Katie, her tall clumsy figure shambling about the house, her big black eyes, her hair, the colour of this woman's but shining with a lusty life of its own.

Widow Crow turned the small bottle round and looked at it lovingly. 'Ninepence,' she said. 'Just the one draught. Get her to drink it. That be all you have to do. It has no taste. The hearts of apple birds and grey birds be in it – and the horse-adder and wort. Just the one draught. Give it to 'er any way that comes along – in ale – in tea – in spirits – in water – or better still get her to drink it off sheer and plain. Sheer and plain. Then be sure to be beside her as the draught goes down; for so soon as ever it d'go down, then her eyes will light upon you, and she will love you till her dying day.'

A flurry of rain fell on Music's heated face. It was going to be a long, wet walk home. He did not consider it.

'Eightpence?' he said.

'Ninepence.'

'Ah,' he said, and began to fumble in his front pocket for the extra money.

On his last visit to Nampara Geoffrey Charles had asked Demelza if he might borrow a few extra servants for the party.

'Mrs Pope offered, so I expect we shall have three of hers as well. And I might ask Mrs Enys for two or three. It is better to have too many than too few.'

'Clowance and I will come ourselves if you want us,' said Demelza. 'I mean earlier on, to help with the cooking and the arrangements.'

'That's kind of you. But two cooks are coming the night before from Truro. I might yet send you a plaintive message saying "Help! help!" but if possible I wish you – I wish you all – to be guests – to enjoy it without the responsibility of being accountable for anything.'

'And Amadora?'

'She declares she is terrified, but I believe in her bones she is relishing the challenge.'

'I know how she feels.'

Geoffrey Charles got up. 'There is one other point I want your help on – your advice at least. I expect you know what I am going to say.'

'No?'

'It is the question of my step-father – whether I should invite him . . .'

Demelza hesitated. 'It is your party.'

'Had we come direct here without any contact, I should never consider inviting him. He's no friend of mine, as you well know. But we called on him; I thought it might even be legally necessary to tell him I was entering into my possessions, so to speak. When we met, after so long a time, I liked him no better than I had done before; but his new wife insisted – I'm sure against his wishes – that we stay to dinner, and then pressed the loan of two excellent horses on us, which we still have, outside at this moment and must keep, she says, until we return to Spain. So even if one wished to exclude him – as I certainly would wish – it is a little affrontful to her if we do not send an invitation. On the other hand,' Geoffrey Charles hastened on as Demelza was about to speak, 'the last thing I wish is to embarrass Cousin Ross. I know how he feels — what they feel for each other — and if Ross would consider the evening in any way marred by Sir George's presence, no invitation shall be sent.'

Demelza said: 'Why don't you ask Ross?'

'I had thought *you* might do so. I think he would express himself more frankly to you.'

Demelza laughed. 'That is so.'

An hour or so later Ross said: 'How many are coming to the party?'

'About eighty invited. Some will not come or not be able to come.'

'Then tell Geoffrey Charles to do as he pleases. We are all mellowing a little with age, and if I saw George coming my way I could very easily dodge.'

'Perhaps *he* will refuse,' said Demelza.

'Let's hope so.'

'I confess I would quite like to meet his new wife. But the house cannot hold very happy memories for him.'

'It's curious for how many people ...' Ross said and stopped.

'What were you going to say?'

'It's curious for how many people that house does *not* hold happy memories.'

Demelza was silent for a few minutes, wishing she could disagree. 'Well, now is the time for it to change.'

The following forenoon George received his invitation and took it to Harriet, who was with her hounds.

She said: 'Will it mean staying the night?'

'It's fifteen miles odd, and mainly rough tracks.'

'I imagine we can stay with Caroline.'

He said: 'You do not ask me if I wish to go.'

'He's your step-son. It has been your house. Why should you not wish to go?'

'I think you are being disingenuous, Harriet.'

She was wearing an open blouse which, in George's opinion, showed too much of her throat and breast for the good of Collins and Smallwood, who were working quietly nearby. Her hair was blue-black like a raven, glossy and strong; her gloves were filthy; so was the hem of her skirt; there was a smudge of dirt on one of her high cheek-bones.

She said: 'When you married me, George, you began a new life. As I did. We cannot spend all our time recollecting the old ones.'

The dogs were coughing and yapping all around her, and he hoped the servants did not hear this. They certainly did not hear his response, for he did not make one, but it would have been to the effect that neither was it necessary to spend all one's time looking after one's confounded animals and doing many of the rough jobs when there were ample well-paid servants waiting to perform them.

Nor, he would have liked to add, did one need parties like last night's – Valentine's, of course, in the first place but one in which she enthusiastically joined. Sitting up until the small hours playing Faro for high stakes. That new friend of Valentine's had come, the fellow who had once been affianced to Clowance Poldark; well dressed but with a poor accent; leonine head; (built like a blacksmith, someone had remarked, making George wince); Harriet had seemed to take a fancy to him, which was more than George could say; flashy somehow; he'd lost; serve him right. Another one who'd lost was that Blamey lad, Verity's son; who had looked pretty green about it; maybe he couldn't afford it; damn fools, playing for money, gambling; who on earth ever made a fortune gambling? Making money at gambling was like seeing ghosts: you never met someone who'd seen a ghost, only someone who knew someone who'd seen a ghost. You only met people who *knew* people who'd made a fortune at White's. Or on the racecourse. Like that fool John Trevanion. It was why George had delayed implementing the contract, why he had delayed until last month telling Valentine of his presumptive plans. Last year Trevanion had received a subsidy to carry him on until the marriage bond was tied, but, against all the assurances he had given, he had been off racing his horses, at Exeter and at Epsom, had come a cropper. So now he was a suppliant once more, greatly regretful of his own behaviour. When the Devil was broke, the Devil a saint would be. This marital bond that was to be tied: the deed must be foolproof, so that none of the money that went with Valentine on his marriage to Cuby could possibly be appropriated by Cuby's spendthrift brother.

Harriet was examining a puppy. She said: 'I see that Valentine and Ursula are also invited. I am sure Valentine will go. But Ursula – what shall you do about her?'

'Leave her behind.'

'Was she not born there?'

'She is not yet fourteen. Her time will come.'

'She is already very wilful.'

'No more so than her step-mother.'

The two kennelmen had moved away. Harriet's eyes flashed, but then she gave her deep sardonic chuckle. 'As you knew well enough when you married me. You knew it *all*. I was badly broken in by Toby. You can't teach an old horse new tricks. I know you had ambitions to try!'

George was restive, looked it. 'I don't think these equestrian metaphors are especially appropriate. Nor flattering to you. I certainly wish you would be more guided by me – at least in your social preferences.'

'Go on, boy, go on!' said Harriet, releasing the puppy. She took off a glove and scratched inelegantly under her arm. 'Pray what's wrong now?'

The hounds were all yelping and crying again, like a noisy group at a party.

In irritation George raised his voice: 'You cannot say I have not been generous in meeting your many and different requirements. Money has been available to you *always*, even when you have been at your most extravagant. You never seem to have any idea about money except to spend it.'

'What other use has it?' she replied contemptuously.

'I cannot believe you are so foolish as to mean that! Without the power and position that money brings – money well managed –'

'Oh, I know, I know, I know. So I am extravagant. It is nothing *fresh*. You knew it before we married. We were both marrying for the second time, and it is not to be supposed that we could change our lives and characters to suit the other.'

George took a deep breath. 'At least I think you owe it to me not to spend the whole summer in the stables as well as the whole winter hunting. And I think you owe it to me not to encourage my son and his friends to waste their nights in drinking and gaming!'

By having to speak loudly to each other the interchange had become even more emphatic than was intended by either party. Yet after he had finished George felt the flush of annoyance following, justifying and corroborating what he felt and what he had said. He stood there angrily among the dogs, then turned away.

As he got to the door she said: 'George!'

He half stopped.

She said: 'Does it not occur to you that it is better to see Valentine gambling and drinking in his own house than for it to happen outside, where he would certainly go if he were driven? And does it not occur to you that I spend no more time with my horses and dogs than you do with your ledgers and balances – and if you rode more with me you would see more of me, which would be agreeable for me and much healthier and more invigorating for you?'

He hesitated, not sure how to take it, frowning at the cynicism of her expression. 'That is all very well, but –'

'But what?'

'There is such a thing as permitting gaming and another in revelling in it oneself and openly encouraging it!'

'To tell the truth, George, I enjoy it. I am not one of your Methodies. And no amount of wishing can change *that*.'

There was a silence between them, though no lack of noise around.

She said: 'When is the invitation?'

'What?'

'The invitation to Trenwith.'

'The ninth.'

'I think I have a frock. It would be a mistake to wear too grand a one for a "family" occasion.'

'I agree.'

'But perhaps a new piece of jewellery.'

'You have plenty of jewellery.'

'A few old heirlooms. I think perhaps pearl earrings? We have ten days. I will look about.'

'There is an acute lack of liquidity in our banking position at the moment,' said George stiffly.

'Pearls are as good as 3 per cents. We can sell them when I tire of 'em.' She patted his arm, then took her glove off to brush away the mark she had left on his sleeve.

As he walked away, back into the house, he decided that neither the gesture nor the smile that went with it had been at all conciliatory. She treated him, he thought, like a boy. Like a boy who could be cajoled into and out of anything. One day she would find out her mistake. Of course he still desired her, that was one of the troubles; when she permitted him to enter her bed he enjoyed her as he had enjoyed no other woman; it inhibited his freedom of action and criticism during the day.

He thought sometimes about her first marriage. Once in the early days, when she had drunk more than usual, she had told him of the terrible quarrels she had had with Toby Carter. Toby, though a mad huntsman himself, had objected to his wife hunting more than four days a week. So in the end when she had defied him he had had her carried struggling to her bedroom where she was locked in until the hunt was over. Harriet chuckled lazily while she told George of the way she smashed all the glass in her bedroom, tore up the curtains, broke the furniture and in the end broke a panel of her door. Twice she had climbed out of her bedroom window, slid along the roof and climbed down the ivy and so to the stables. Later Toby had had bars put to the windows, but shortly after that, God rest his Catholic soul, and R I P and Ave Maria, etc., etc., he had broken his beastly neck in the field and she had found herself totally free and sole inheritor of a bankrupt estate.

George found it quite difficult to believe that this strong-limbed but lazily dignified creature lying beside him could have been capable of such behaviour when crossed. Only perhaps in the sexual act did he see into the depths of her nature.

Had she learned so much from her first marriage that now she knew just how to turn away a man's wrath and indeed turn it to her own advantage? Or was he so much weaker, or more malleable, or less stupidly obstinate than Sir Toby Carter? The grim thought struck George to ask himself if he had ever crossed her at all? Had she not always had her way? Had he not given in all along the line? Generally it had been a gracious persuasion she had used, if in the exercise of it there was a touch of the arrogance proper to a duke's daughter. Here perhaps lay the crux of the whole thing. Sir Toby, being presumably of noble birth himself, was less in awe of the blood in his wife's veins.

George stiffened his back as he walked. He was perfectly certain that, whatever might have been said or implied today, however firm his reprimand, Harriet would not alter her behaviour or her regime in the very least. She would feed him half-promises and go her own way entirely. That in the end could only lead to trouble. He would have to prepare his ground carefully. If there were to be a real conflict of wills he could not afford to be without ammunition.

IV

A week later, when George was in the counting house in Truro with his Uncle Cary, the chief clerk of the bank, a man called Lander, sent word that he would like to see Sir George when he had a moment, and please might it be private?

George assumed that this meant without the meeting being supervised by the censorious Cary, and so went downstairs into the Bank. Lander, who was forty-five, a man with bad teeth and disagreeable breath but with the quickest eye for figures between Plymouth and Penzance, sweated around his starched collar and said he assumed Sir George well remembered the robbery which had taken place in January of this year, when the Warleggan & Willyams Bank was robbed of several thousand pounds in gold, in securities, in notes –'

'Am I likely to forget it?' said George.

'No, sir. And you will remember, sir, that we published in the newspaper the numbers of various of the notes – those that we knew – so that they would become valueless in the hands of the thieves.'

'Of course,' said George again, testy as always when being told something he already knew.

Lander persevered. 'And you will remember, sir, at your suggestion, five, I think, or six notes, sir, whose numbers we possessed were withheld –'

'Five.'

'Exactly, sir. We actually knew the numbers of these five as well, sir, but you suggested they should not be published in the newspaper along with the others so that the thieves might be encouraged –'

'I recollect all that perfectly, Lander.'

'– Encouraged to spend them and thus might be traced.' Lander paused for breath and sweated a bit more. 'Well, sir, one of those notes came into our possession yesterday.'

George turned the guineas in his fob.

'Did it indeed, by God! You're sure of the number?'

'Certainly, sir.'

'Yes, of course, you would be. How into our possession? Paid into the bank or –'

'Paid into the bank, sir.'

George went to the window, frowned his concentration on the dusty pane.

'Was it noticed early enough? Could you be sure who paid it in?'

'Yes, sir. Greet noticed it because it had been folded smaller than usual at some time and the creases had been marked by damp. That is how he can be sure. I have questioned him repeatedly, sir, to be certain positive he has made no mistake . . .'

George waited. 'Well, then, who paid it in? We must move as soon as possible.'

Lander took out a kerchief to mop his brow and did not know where to look; certainly not at Sir George.

'It was your wife, sir.'

Chapter Thirteen

I

Saturday the ninth of October was dry and bright. The wind had died after several boisterous days and the roads and lanes generally were dry enough to support carriages without the risk of their becoming bogged down. Not that many carriages were expected at Trenwith, the tracks away from the turnpikes being scarcely of a sort to support four wheels at a time. Lord and Lady de Dunstanville might have come in a carriage, but they were in London.

Feverish activity had been going on since the early hours, in which Demelza, Clowance and Isabella-Rose had reluctantly been allowed to take a hand. No matter how one prepares for a party, some preparations have to wait for the day, and then there is never time enough. About noon Demelza and Geoffrey Charles persuaded Amadora up to her bedroom to lie still for an hour, otherwise, they said, she'd be too tired to enjoy it when it really began.

Which was at five. Guests were invited for five and to take tea in either of the drawing rooms while they rested after their ride. The gun room had been reserved for men who wished to change, two sewing rooms on the first floor for ladies; but in the main, the day being so fine, the near-by guests had ridden over in their finery and the more distant ones had already changed at the houses where they were to spend the night.

The great table had been vanquished at last, but as Jeremy had predicted, had proved unremovable from the room, so it stood on its end in a corner propped against the edge of the minstrel gallery. The floor from which it had been uprooted had been hastily filled with sand and cement and new flags laid so that, apart from a difference in colour, one would not have known. A four-piece band played gentle airs from the gallery. The airs would become less gentle after supper when the dancing began.

By the time the sun had set about fifty guests had arrived and a few late comers were trickling in. The great window in the hall, though its multiple panes were all clear glass, reflected and refracted stains of colour from the sky upon people passing to and fro below it. Among the latest to arrive was the party of six from Killewarren: Dr Dwight Enys, Mrs Caroline Enys, the Misses Sophie and Meliora Enys, and Sir George and Lady Harriet Warleggan.

They were welcomed at the door by their host and hostess; it was a peculiar confrontation between the two men; Geoffrey Charles extended his hand with a 'Pray come in Step-father.' They clasped briefly and Geoffrey Charles wondered if it was the first time they had *ever* shaken hands. (Yet once as a very little boy he had adored Uncle George, who always brought him presents.) 'Soldier bright,' said Lady Harriet, and kissed him lightly on the cheek. 'Pray excuse me,' said Geoffrey Charles, smiling, 'I have had no time to renew my uniform.' 'But it is better that way. Amadora!' said Harriet, with another kiss, '*Cómo está usted*?' And they were in.

Caroline at once spotted Ross and Demelza and would have liked to go over, but with George and Harriet in tow and in a somewhat alien environment she felt she could not instantly desert them.

The Popes arrived directly after them, that is to say Mrs Selina Pope, brilliant in black lace, and her two daughters whose mourning clothes had a more normal dampening effect on their looks. With them was Valentine Warleggan, and he had brought Conan Whitworth, who could hardly have been invited by Geoffrey Charles. And making up their party were Augustus Bettesworth and Clemency and Cuby Trevanion.

Spending a night at Nampara – or two if Demelza could persuade them – were the Blameys, Verity and the two Andrews, father and son. Five of the Treneglosses had come from Mingoose House, and all four of the Kellows from Fernmore: Paul, with the darkly saturnine but feminine looks which had enabled him so well to take the part of a clergyman's wife when a certain stage coach was robbed; his fat ineffectual beery father; Mrs Kellow, downtrodden, with eyes that never focused and a not entirely misplaced conviction that death hovered over her family; and her surviving daughter, Daisy, hectically vivacious and hoping still to marry Jeremy, even if only on the rebound. She, like a number of others here tonight, was anxious to see Cuby for the first time.

Cuby Trevanion was in a white Indian muslin frock, high at the throat and tight at the waist and wrists. She seemed in the last year or so to have slimmed off and grown taller, neither of which had had the least ill effect on her looks. And the vivacity that was sometimes lacking was not at all lacking tonight.

In fact Cuby knew herself on trial. She had come to the north coast, against her brother's and her mother's wishes, into the heart of the district and to a house party where too many people were called Poldark or were related to or old friends of the Poldarks; and they were waiting to judge her. She did not know how far her friendship with Jeremy, his courting of her, and her family's refusal of him was generally known; but she suspected it was not a secret. She had therefore put herself out to wear something of style and to be at her most charming. Like her elder brother, she had changed her name from Bettesworth to Trevanion, and was intensely proud of her Trevanion ancestry. Was she really, she asked herself, a scheming woman, selfish, hard and mercenary? Was marrying someone she did not love – or certainly did not care for as she cared for Jeremy – out of a heartfelt sense of pride and obligation and family duty, was that altogether to be condemned and despised? Did not the royal families of Europe follow this precept all their lives, and were they condemned for it? And if she did not belong to a family of dynastic importance whose couplings might mean the difference between war and peace, yet to her and to her mother and perhaps still more to her loving but culpable brother, the Trevanion family and the Trevanion family home were of deep-rooted importance.

So she had come tonight, on the defensive but with a burning pride, determined to look her best and be her best, and make it clear to every Poldark there that the Trevanions had something to be proud about.

The knife that stabbed instantly into Jeremy was that Valentine, by contriving to stay with the Popes, had come as one of Cuby's party. (Not that he needed any contrivance: clearly he did not. Valentine, by mutual agreement, was the destined suitable bridegroom.)

Supper was informal, smaller and more removable tables being laid in the hall; but the large parlour was also utilized, and the winter parlour; so people sat where they chose and ate what they chose. Amadora could scarcely be persuaded to sit down or eat anything, so concerned was she that everyone else was doing so; and Geoffrey Charles hardly left her side, watching that nothing that was said to her, or that she said, was misunderstood. Clowance, who was wearing one of her frocks bought for Bowood, an olive green shot sarsenet fastened with brooches at the shoulders, sat for part of the supper between her cousin, young Andrew Blamey, and the eldest surviving Treneglos boy, Jonathan, who finding himself temporarily not overshadowed by more attractive young men, was making a great fuss of her.

When he could get a word in Andrew said to her: 'It is provoking I shall have to leave soon after midnight, for we sail with the morning tide.'

'Your packet ship?'

'Er – yes. The *Countess of Leicester*. A hundred and ninety tons burthen. Crew of twenty-eight. Five officers. Second officer Andrew Blamey. Outward bound for Lisbon.'

'What time is that – about six?'

'What time is what?' Andrew asked. In spite of his rote-type recitation of details it seemed that he had allowed his attention to wander.

'Full tide, I mean.'

'Oh, full tide's at five. We shall – we shall leave at dawn, which will be about six. I suppose I should count my luck being home for this at all.'

Clowance gazed round her. In three months Trenwith had been transformed from the gaunt empty echoing vault in which she had first met Sir George Warleggan and later had had love trysts with Stephen Carrington, into a warm and happy home. The house, even with a mere two people and three guests and five servants living in it, had already come alive: but tonight, as dusk fell, dozens of candles were lit and glimmered over an animated scene. How good that Geoffrey Charles had come back; and with a pretty foreign wife who reminded Clowance of a hedge rose – you had to get through the prickles to reach the flower. But why did they have to *go* again, putting all this at risk?

'I'm sorry,' she said to Andrew.

'I was only asking you if everything between you and Stephen Carrington was really over.'

'Why, yes.'

Andrew rubbed his sandy sidewhiskers in some hesitation. 'Only I met him again last time I was ashore – at Cardew, you know, the Warleggans' residence.'

'At Cardew?' said Clowance in surprise. 'Stephen there? Are you sure?'

'Oh, yes. Valentine invited him. We all played cards together. I lost too much.' He laughed self-consciously. 'Always losing. Left me a bit embarrassed. I'm heavy in debt now, but a lucky streak'll come along; I know; it always does . . . Stephen lost too. There was eight or nine of us.'

'I didn't realize they were friends,' said Clowance. 'Where did they meet?'

'Don't know. Wasn't it at the races last year? Anyway, I've met him since, two or three times. He's a likeable fellow, Stephen is. What made you claw away to windward of him?'

Clowance wrinkled her brow. 'What?'

'I mean break off the engagement. Twas not to do with me saying I thought I'd seen him in the Ring O' Bells in Plymouth Dock when the matelot got stabbed, was it?'

'Oh, no. Good gracious, no!'

'Because come to think of it, you understand, it is not

uncommon for a man to fight for his freedom – for that is what that man was doing. Maybe he jabbed just too hard with his knife to *gain* his freedom, but when you're in a corner it is hard to judge these things to a nicety. Or maybe the matelot was lightly wounded and then died of something else, and the naval folk of Plymouth issued it out that he had been murdered. I'd not put it past them.'

These had been so much Stephen's arguments that Clowance looked at her cousin in surprise.

Andrew said: 'Resemblances are funny things. I know that day I could easily have been mistaken. And him being your affianced . . . So all I could do was put the helm over and make all sail I could on a different tack. Well, when I saw him at Cardew recently I was more than ever taken by the resemblance . . .'

Katie Carter, who was waiting at their table, took away their plates and edged towards them a large wooden platter containing damson tarts, raspberry puffs, and Black Caps in custard and blancmange.

After she had gone, Andrew took a large bite of his tart and said: 'It was his eyes, you know. Very noticeable colour, his eyes are, such a bright blue with a sort of fleck of tawny in the whites; it is hard to forget.'

'All the same,' said Clowance, surprised at the apprehension stirring within her, 'there's no reason to disbelieve him. You could still easily be mistaken.'

'Well, no, not so, my dear cousin. I have transacted one or two little bits of business with Stephen since we met at Cardew – surprising enough, yes, I have, I have – and to do business with a man you have to have a sense of *trust*. So I tackled him in a roundabout way; and in a roundabout way he answered. No need to ask more. No need to say more. Understanding both sides . . . But I'm glad it was not for that reason that you broke off from him. For it would hardly have been a fair reason, would it. A man has a right to fight for his freedom.'

'Why are you telling me this?'

'I felt I had to. Just to clear up any feeling that I'd done his cause any harm with you that day.'

'No.'

'I'm glad we have come to this understanding, he and I, for tonight I would have been so much surer of my ground.'

'What do you mean?' Jonathan Treneglos was trying to draw her attention but she would not turn her head.

'You remember me saying there was another young man with him when the fighting began. Slim young feller with dark eyes and a sallow complexion?' Andrew Blamey chewed and swallowed and dabbed his mouth with his napkin. 'He's here tonight.'

II

Ross said to Dwight: 'Andrew Blamey senior brought news with him that Wellington has just broken through the extended positions along the Bidassoa and has crossed the river into France.'

They had edged their way together at last, as, similarly, Caroline had found Demelza and was telling her gleefully of a splendid new novel she had just read called *Pride and Prejudice*; the author was anonymous, but such was its comic insight that Caroline was not surprised to discover it had been written 'by a lady'.

'I can understand Geoffrey Charles wanting to be back,' said Dwight. 'But it depends very much what happens at Leipzig, or thereabouts, does it not? Unless Napoleon can be contained or defeated . . .'

'I'd be happier if it were British soldiers he had to fight. All we shall contribute on that front will be the encouragement and the gold.'

'You knew that Detroit had been re-taken by the Americans?'

'No, I did not. I suppose it was inevitable given the weakness of the British forces.'

They sipped wine and looked at their respective wives, who were laughing together with Isabella-Rose who was claiming their attention.

Ross said: 'That offer Buonaparte made to Humphry Davy, to allow him in to France to meet the French scientists. Did it come to nothing?'

'It came to everything. They are leaving Plymouth this week. They are crossing to Morlaix in Brittany in a cartel-ship and taking their own carriage. From Morlaix it will be at least a week before they reach Paris.'

'You thought no more of Davy's invitation that you should go with him?'

'I thought a good deal more of it. But there we are . . . it was simply not practical for me.'

Very soon now the supper would be cleared and it would be time for dancing. The larger parlour would remain with tables and food and wine available for the rest of the night. Ross saw that Jeremy was talking to the Trevanion girl and they were smiling at each other. Valentine had left his party and was making a fuss of Amadora.

'Will anyone go in your place?' Ross asked.

'To France? Yes, Humphry is taking a young man he thinks well of. Faraday is his name,' Dwight said. 'Michael Faraday. I know no more of him than that.'

Jeremy was bringing the girl across. It seemed a maladroit thing to do, but there was no way of stopping him now.

'Father, may I present Miss Cuby Trevanion? My father, Cuby. And Dr Dwight Enys.'

'How d'you do, sir . . . Dr Enys.' She curtsied, they bowed.

She'd certainly got looks, but of an unusual sort. Teeth and eyes brilliant, a candid glance which never wavered for an instant, an elegant manner; elegantly dressed; a lady. Arrogant, scheming, mercenary creature.

'I knew your father,' said Ross, 'and know your elder brother – John I mean – who is not here tonight?'

'No, sir. He is away in Devon.'

'With his horses?'

She flushed. 'Yes, Captain Poldark, I believe so.'

Ross noticed that, as he was speaking to the girl, Clowance got up from the table and walked away. So much for *her* feelings.

Jeremy said: 'It is the first time ever that Miss Trevanion has been on the north coast. I tell her that she must observe the native rituals and dances and then write a paper on them for the Royal Institution.'

'Yes,' said Ross, smiling grimly, 'we are back in the dark ages here.'

'On the contrary, sir,' said Cuby, 'if I may be forgiven for taking a different view, these are the light ages, for I have never been to a more agreeable party. The other Captain Poldark, the younger Captain Poldark, is as charming a gentleman as one could conjure out, and I am much obliged to Jeremy for this invitation.'

So she had plenty to say for herself.

'You have come with your brother and sister, I understand?'

'Yes, sir. Augustus has a post in the Treasury in London, but is at present on leave. Clemency, of course, is my constant companion at Caerhays.'

'Some day you must come and see us,' said Ross. 'We are but four miles up the coast, largely surrounded by mines and the outcrop of mining, but still civilized in our household ways.'

'Thank you, sir. I'm sure I should be honoured.'

Jeremy, who had been listening to the exchange and observing his father's stiff back with apprehension, encouraged the conversation for a few minutes more and then took Cuby's arm.

'Come, you must meet my mother,' he said, and they passed on.

'Does Jeremy have renewed hopes in that direction?' Dwight murmured.

'The last time he spoke on the subject — and he rarely speaks of it — he had no hope at all.'

'An engaging young lady.'

'I question what Demelza will make of her.'

What Demelza made of her was not immediately obvious, for in the noise of general conversation they could not hear what was said; but it seemed to be on an affable plane.

Later, when they had a moment together, Ross said:

'So Jeremy has at last produced The Cause of all the Trouble.'

'Yes, Ross. She has a strong personality, don't you think? Not one who would be told what to do by her brother.'

'No, I think she's just a money-grubbing little she-goat, with no more principles than a high class harlot.'

'Oh, *Ross* . . . I can see how attractive she would be to a young man.'

'Or to an old one, if he had enough money and she set out to please him.'

'You must not be too hard, Ross, simply because she has refused our son.'

'I am not hard for her refusal but for her brazenly stated reason for the refusal – his lack of ten or twenty thousand pounds. I think she cares nothing for Jeremy.'

Demelza sipped her port. It was a specially good port which, Geoffrey Charles told her, had spent fifteen years in wood and which, since he had been able only to obtain two bottles from the steward of the packet ship, he was reserving specially for her.

'I don't think she cares nothing for Jeremy. It is just whether she cares enough.'

'What did you *say* to her?'

'I asked her if she was enjoying her evening among all Jeremy's cousins, and she said she was. Then I admired her frock; then she admired mine. Then she asked to meet Isabella-Rose, and then we all talked about music and songs for several minutes, and then Jeremy bore her away.'

'Does this mean you think the girl is going to change her mind about Jeremy?'

'No-o . . . She has a very strong personality.'

'You said that before.'

'I think she will keep to her decision – to her principles –'

'Principles indeed!'

'Well, whatever you may call them –'

'So all was sweetness and light between you!'

'No, Ross. Far from it indeed in my heart. But if she chooses to marry in the way she says she will . . . She cannot altogether be accountable for Jeremy's passion for her, which amounts sometimes, I believe, to a mania. It is – or could be – a fearful tragedy . . . but unless she has encouraged him wantonly and *then* turned her back . . . I don't believe that to be so, not from what he says. Right at the beginning she tried to warn him.'

Ross took his brandy. 'Well, if it were not for Jeremy's sake I should be pleased not to be having a Trevanion in the family. They're a feckless, overweening lot.' He frowned down at the flag floor. 'Perhaps your kindness to Miss Cuby will help to ease her conscience – always supposing she has one.'

'I did not show any special kindness to her,' said Demelza. 'No special kindness at all. We both understood each other perfectly well.'

III

Soon after the dancing began the staff in the kitchen sat down to their supper. In addition to the five Geoffrey Charles had temporarily engaged, there was Jane Gimlett and Cal Trevail and Ena and Betsy Martin, all from Nampara, there was Music Thomas and Katie Carter and a kitchen maid called Dorothy Ellery, all from Place House, and Wallace Bartle and two girls from Killewarren. Two others, Polly Odgers and Beth Bate, were upstairs, but they would eat later. Jane Gimlett, by consent and by seniority, was in charge.

Music Thomas, though confined to the kitchen and only allowed an occasional peep into the house proper, was in his seventh heaven, being in close contact with Katie, taking dirty plates and glasses from her, fetching bottles up from the cellar for her, accepting a candelabra from her and changing the candles which had guttered in a draught, drawing water from the well, brushing up the mess when Betsy Martin – not he, not he! – had dropped a tray of cream cakes. Katie, being herself clumsy and in haste tonight, had twice nearly had an accident, but twice just saved herself, and she had laughed at the nearness of the escape and her face all night was flushed and animated, and she had spoken to him and smiled at him as if he was her chosen friend.

Ever since the death of Mr Pope they had seen a little more of each other; there is nothing so cementing as a secret shared; and Music had shamelessly made use of his knowledge to stop her in a passage or going by the kitchens to ask her advice on some moral or physical aspect of the secret. Since Music did not have an inventive brain, most of his queries demanded such obvious answers that Katie was irritated by them, but as her job as well as his hung on their silence she could hardly refuse to stop and listen and even answer more politely than she wanted to. It was a kind of blackmail. Aware that he was making himself no more popular with her, he still couldn't resist it. He could see an indefinite future of such encounters, allowing him brief moments of her company which he'd never had before.

But tonight was quite different; in the excitements of the party and the new company they were working with, the usual barriers were down. Katie had confided in him that Wallace Bartle could not carve and on another occasion that all the fine ladies 'in there' were eating just so much as the men.

Now, after the hurry and the labour, came the temporary rest. The big table in the kitchen had been swept clear of the accumulations of the night, and a feast of left-overs was ready for the staff. And beer a-plenty; though Mrs Gimlett was careful to warn them, particularly the men, that their intake should be limited to three mugs each, since the duties of the night were not yet over.

They were all famished and fell upon the food like seagulls; and so for a time they ate in silence, content to reserve their mouths and energies for the more important function. Music had contrived a seat next to Katie, not without difficulty for Cal Trevail also wanted it, not specially to be near Katie but to companion Dorothy Ellery. In the end, after a good deal of shoving and grunting, room was made for them both.

As the mountain of food disappeared, talk broke out again – about Polly Odgers – Mr Valentine's ex-nurse –

coming all the way from St Michael to help tonight – about how Parson Odgers had gone to sleep in the middle of his own sermon on Sunday last – about that dreffulthing that happened to the Poldice bal-maiden last week who went into the stamp-shed and got too near the axle of the stamp, her clothes was caught and she was drawn in and crushed to death – about the old red cow with a wen on the right foreleg missing from Farmer Hancock's just above Pally's Shop: they reckoned she'd fell down a shaft – about picking over the potatoes in the barn and how some had gone poor with rot, gracious knew why.

Katie blew out a breath and leaned back. 'Dear life, I'm full to bust. 'Ope no one in there ask for me yet a-while.' She stretched her hand for the pitcher to refill her beer-mug, but the pitcher was empty.

'There's another on the slab,' said Cal Trevail.

'I'll get'n for ee,' said Music, squeezing to his feet.

'Have a care,' said Jane Gimlett. 'Remember what I warned.'

'I've only 'ad just the one,' said Katie.

'I'll get'n for ee,' said Music, beaming at her.

'Thank ee.'

Music picked up the pitcher, then after a bare hesitation he picked up Katie's mug as well. 'I'll get'n for ee.'

Over on the slate slab was the last pitcher of all. Fingers a-tremble, he poured some out of the pitcher into her mug. Then he fumbled in his pocket. The little earthenware bottle with the worm-eaten cork. He prised at the cork – thing would not come out – they were all talking, noticed nothing so far. Cork popped out and rolled across the slab. He poured the liquid, which was about two wine-glassfuls; it made the beer a bit cloudy. With great ingenuity he found a spoon, stirred; that was better.

He carried the mug back to the table. ''Ere you are, Katie.' He put it down on the table just by her plate.

She smiled contentedly at him.

''Ere what about us folk?' demanded Wallace Bartle. 'Have you got nothing for we?'

''Ere you are, Katie,' Music said, squeezing down into his

seat. It was important where she looked first after she had drunk it.

'Darn 'ee, that's what ye call manners, eh?' said Bartle. 'Wait on yourself, eh?'

''Ere you are, Katie,' said Music, looking as closely into her face as he dared.

'I've said thank ee; what more?'

As a disgruntled Bartle got up, scraping his chair on the stone floor, and walked across for the pitcher, Katie took a long draught of her ale. Music waited expectantly. He would have been baffled if asked to say what he did expect, but the outcome took him entirely by surprise. Her long, pale-skinned face began to redden, it seemed to swell, her eyes started tears, she clutched at her throat, she gave a sort of vomiting cough and sprayed beer all over the table and over Music's face, which had come close to hers.

She was on her feet hawking and spitting. Everyone was up, patting her on the back, pulling the remains of the food away from the wet table, saying, 'There, there, me dear, what's amiss – go the wrong way did it?' 'Vomit in the scullery. Get the pail, Ena,' and 'My dear life and body, poisoned are ee?'

It remained for Cal Trevail to see the thing in its true colours. He gave a screech of laughter and pointed to the beer, which seemed to be frothing over the top, as if it were fermenting.

'Ho, Music, you've done for yerself this time! You was always a one for jokes! My blessed Parliament, that were a tease, that were!'

Music, wiping the beer off his face, strove to protest, but clearly no one believed him. The beer was there as witness. The younger ones were laughing at the joke, which to them was very funny, the older ones were half frowning, chiefly because it should not have been perpetrated in someone else's house. The mouse in the soup, the frog in the pie, the dog-dirt in the pasty: these were routine jokes in a community that liked its humour broad and obvious.

'Katie!' Music said. 'I tell ee as God is my witness –'

He did not get any further. With all the strength that fury

could give to a very strong right arm, Katie slapped his face. It knocked him over, and staggering back he upset a chair and fell to the floor. More laughter.

'Ssh,' said Jane Gimlett disapprovingly. 'Remember where you be! *Quiet*, all of you. How *dare* you, Music! Katie . . .'

But Katie had already disappeared into the scullery to try to make herself sick over again, just in case whatever it was that doltish man had fed her might be poison.

IV

Although the two bottles were very similar, Music would not admit even to himself, in this tragedy for him, that he might have made a mistake. Only three months later, towards Christmas time when Widow Permewan had occasion to use the chilblain cure, did he admit his total fault.

Then it seemed perfectly reasonable to him that two weeks after first using the mixture on her feet, Edie Permewan should at last give way to Art Thomas's blandishments and agree to marry him.

Chapter Fourteen

I

At eleven the dancing stopped and Isabella-Rose sang. They had carried Demelza's old spinet from Nampara, and this they now brought into the room and Mrs Kemp played the accompaniment. It seemed to have no effect upon Isabella-Rose that she was being listened to by a group of grown-up and relatively sophisticated people.

First she sang: *Ripe Sparergrass*. Her voice, so strong in one so young, did not sound quite so harsh or discordant in the bigger room, and the song was like a 'cry of London'; if the voice didn't keep on key it didn't really matter. Demelza remembered that when she herself had first begun to sing she had been off the note. Perhaps it came from her. Ross had sung as a boy, but seldom did now; certainly he didn't wobble like Bella.

There was polite applause at the end. The second song was called *The Frog and the Mouse*, and was one Jeremy had bought. It had strange choruses of mock Latin and bits of old Cornish, making a remarkable jumble of nonsense, which no one supposed Bella would learn in time. But she had.

> 'There was a mouse lived in a mill.
> With a ring-num, bulladimmy, coy-me.
> A merry frog lived in a well
> With a ring-num, bulladimmy, coy-me.
>   Coy-menaro, kilto-caro, coy-menaro,
>   Coy-me, prim-strim, stramadiddle,
>   Larrabong, ring-ting, bulladimmy, coy-me.
> The frog he would a-wooing ride
> To my ring-dom, somminary, ky-me
> And on a snail he got astride.

To my ring-dom, somminary, ky-me.
            Kymenare, gildecare, kymenare, ky-me.
            String-strang, dan-a-dilla, lana-pana,
            Rag-tag, rig-dom, bomminary, ky-me.
When he was on his high-horse set
His boots they shone as bright as jet . . .'

And so it went on for another four verses. The tune, such as it was, showed up the harshness of Bella's voice, but the audience did not seem to notice this. They saw a black-haired, black-eyed little girl, singing vigorously – almost as if she were a man – and giving to the world all the enthusiasm for life and living that she possessed.

Enormous applause.

The plan was that she should sing two songs and then, if really pressed, one – quieter – encore, *Cherry Ripe*. (Bella had badly wanted to sing *The Highwayman* but had been bullied out of it, for it was really a baritone song.) There was no question: an encore was demanded. Everyone called for it. Bella put impatient hands up to her curls. Eyes agleam, she cleared her throat, Mrs Kemp turned over the music, and then a loud, strongly Cornish voice shouted:

'Sing *The Barley Mow*, Bella!'

Isabella-Rose had won much popularity by singing *The Barley Mow* to the farm hands and the miners this last August and September. It was a rousing, catchy song, and no one before in the Nampara area had ever done it as well as she had.

In all the people at Trenwith that night there was no one, except in the kitchen, with so strong a Cornish accent, but Demelza, knowing her son, instantly suspected Jeremy. Whoever it was, he only had to say it three times, which he proceeded to do, and all the guests, knowing the tune and the frolic, began to shout too.

Miss Isabella-Rose Poldark glanced towards where her mother was sitting, then looked at Mrs Kemp, who was so flustered she couldn't offer advice in time. So,

'*The Barley Mow*,' announced Bella.

Mrs Kemp trembled in her case and eventually produced

the music. She whispered with Bella, and Bella adjusted the bow of her frock. Then, with spinet accompaniment, she began to sing, and, at appropriate intervals, the audience sang with her.

'Oh, I will drink out of the nipperkin, boys.'

'*So here's a good health,*' the audience sang, '*to the barley mow.*'

'The nipperkin and the brown bowl,' shouted Bella.

'*So here's a good health,*' came the reply, '*to the barley mow.*'

'Oh, I will drink out of the pint, my boys.'

'*So here's a good health to the barley mow.*'

'The pint, the nipperkin and the brown bowl.'

'*So here's a good health to the barley mow.*'

'Oh, I will drink out of the quart, my boys.'

'*So here's a good health to the barley mow.*'

'The quart, the pint, the nipperkin and the brown bowl.'

'*So here's a good health to the barley mow.*'

The point, as in all these cumulative songs, was that the singer always added something else to the list of the things he intended to drink out of. The responses, though identical each time as to words, varied considerably in tune, and it was about four verses before the audience got the hang of it. Then it went really with a will.

At the fourteenth and last verse Bella sang:

'Oh, I will drink out of the clouds, my boys;'

'*So here's a good health to the barley mow.*'

'The clouds, the ocean, the sea, the river,' sang Bella; 'the well, the tub, the bath, the hogshead, the keg, the gallon, the quart, the pint, the nipperkin *and* the brown bowl.'

'*So here's a good HEALTH to the barley mow!!!*'

There was a tremendous yell of delight when it was over, and people broke the circle to cluster round the little girl to kiss and congratulate her. Oh, dear life, thought Demelza, she'll be *impossible* now! Yet she could not but feel a surge of pleasure at her daughter's success.

George Warleggan had watched this with the observant distaste he had brought to the rest of the evening. He was particularly annoyed the de Dunstanvilles were not here, and it made it worse to see this precocious Poldark child making an exhibition of herself. If the evening anyway was to be intolerable he had at least hoped to take the opportunity of mending a few bridges between himself and Francis Basset, Baron de Dunstanville. After all it was five years since all that banking business; and George felt Francis could hardly blame him for having been drawn in as Sir Christopher Hawkins's second in the duel they had fought. Francis was more than ever the richest and most active man in public affairs in Cornwall, and it served no good purpose not to be on terms with such a personage. But he was not here, so one had to make do with such few other people as were worth speaking to.

He and Harriet were separated, for she had gone to dance. Rather against his wishes she had gone to dance with Dr Enys. Her black hair was down to her shoulders and shone like patent leather in the candlelight. The new pearl earrings with their diamond setting glinted through the heavy strands of her hair.

He had questioned her, of course. Tactfully but thoroughly. It was not her custom, she amiably admitted, to pay money *into* the bank, into the account which as a special favour – she being a married woman – Warleggan & Willyams Bank had opened for her. On the contrary, it was her regular custom to take money *out*. But this time – well, this time the only source of the tainted money, the suspect banknote, seemed to be the Faro table.

Of course any one of the players might have paid it in, and any one of them might have handled the note innocently enough. It could have been through a half-dozen pairs of hands since January. Nevertheless there was always the possibility that it had not, and George had made a list of the people playing at his house on the evening two days before the banknote was identified. There was Anthony Trefusis and Ben Sampson and Stephen Carrington and Andrew Blamey and Percy Hill and George Trevethan and Michael Smith. According to Harriet the chief losers had been Anthony Trefusis and Stephen Carrington and Andrew Blamey, so these were most obviously suspect. George had his sources of information and his creatures who could obtain more. Earlier today, before setting out to this party, he had ordered further inquiries to be made. Was Andrew Blamey in England or at sea when the robbery took place? Where were Carrington and Trefusis? Even if the inquiry promised no definite conclusion, it was worth putting in hand. It was the very first lead they had had in all this time.

Trefusis was a younger brother and a bit of a wastrel — perpetually short of money, quarrelling with his father and elder brother for the lack of it, exactly the sort of young man Valentine seemed to attract. Andrew Blamey was half Poldark, the son of a packet captain and himself in the service. But when ashore he was always drinking and gaming and no doubt companioning Valentine in his pursuit of the light girls of Falmouth and Penryn. Carrington was the unknown quantity, rescued from the sea, someone said; had caught a Poldark and then lost her, always in and out of Cornwall since he first arrived, picking up trade or business here and there, turning a presumably honest penny. But recently buying a French prize in St Ives, according to Valentine. *With whose money?*

In addition to the heavy loss sustained by the banks as a result of the robbery, there had been other irritating after-effects. Harriet's aunt, Miss Darcy, had lost her father's signet ring, and a loving cup that had been in the family for years; they had been in care of the Devon & Cornwall Bank, now partners of Warleggan & Willyams, and were being sent down to Godolphin. Miss Darcy, who did not care for George, appeared to hold him personally responsible that her property had been lost with everything else.

It was clear from the start that the thieves had been gentlemen, or people of at least sufficient education to play the gentleman. Your ordinary highwayman or cut-purse could never put on the airs or the accent of a clergyman or a naval lieutenant. (The woman, they said, had spoken little, so she could have been any doxy they picked up to play the part.) The woman would be impossible to find; but not perhaps the two men. At least there was a lead now, and Stephen Carrington possibly the likeliest suspect.

But George's native caution warned him that, of all the gamblers at his house that night, Carrington was the most likely to have received the note from someone else, being in and out of trade so much, and himself innocent. One must simply pursue the lead for a little while and see what happened.

Something was happening, now the tedious singing was over in the great hall. His enemy and old rival was making a speech. George edged towards the door where he could listen and sneer. It was, Ross said, a few words of hail and farewell. It had been of the extremest pleasure to him – indeed to everyone – to see his cousin return to claim the family home that was his; and the pleasure had been doubled by the presence at his side of a lovely and gracious Spanish wife. In less than three months they had together repaired the ravages of almost ten years' neglect. This was the way Trenwith had been when he, Ross, was a boy; it was the way it had been, he guessed, through several centuries before; it was the way it was going to be, he earnestly trusted, for many years to come. But the war with France still raged, and Geoffrey Charles felt himself obligated to return to his regiment. So two weeks from today they had arranged to take ship for San Sebastian. (There was a groan from the company.) From there young Mrs Poldark would return to her own family, who were themselves shortly returning to Madrid, and her husband would travel to take command of his company of the Light Brigade, the 43rd Monmouthshires. Indeed, Ross said, although his cousin had requested that he should keep the information private, he felt it his duty to inform the company that Geoffrey Charles Poldark had been promoted to the rank of Acting Major, as from the date of his return. (There were cries of congratulations.) So, Ross said, it only remained for him to ask the company to charge their glasses and drink to the love, happiness, safety and eventual return to this old family house of Major and Mrs Geoffrey Charles Poldark.

Everyone drank. 'You're not drinking, sir!' said some strange man, glaring at George. 'Lost my glass,' said George austerely, staring him down. The strange man ducked out of sight and reappeared almost immediately with a glass full, it turned out, of neat brandy and thrust it into George's hand. 'Drink now, sir!'

After everyone had toasted them, Geoffrey Charles took Amadora's hand, she being reluctant to come forward, and said how grateful he was for the welcome, the love and the warmth which had been extended to them both for their all-too-brief stay. He felt, as probably many here tonight felt, that the long war was at last at a turning point, that at last it was nearly won. Having himself been through so many of the difficult times, militarily, most particularly the defeat and death, in impossible circumstances, of Sir John Moore, he was really looking forward to participating in a campaign which, for once, promised victory. (There was a laugh.) But when the final victory was won, he hoped and believed that he and his beloved wife would return to settle down here in their house, as his forbears had done for centuries before him. Not, he added, amid more laughter, that he would be at all unwilling to spend a part of each year in Spain!

The speech ended in a general toast which Geoffrey Charles proposed to his Poldark relatives. Almost before it was drunk he was speaking again, saying that he and Amadora were intending to lead the dancing with a new dance called the waltz. Many here already knew it; those who did not would quickly learn.

As it turned out many did not, but three couples began it, and soon another half dozen tried. Lady Harriet knew it, but unfortunately for her Dwight was called away because someone was ill in the winter parlour. She was about to walk slowly off the floor when Ross Poldark asked her if she would dance.

She was very surprised; and so was he; because it was Demelza's idea. 'Go *on*,' she had whispered. 'I dare you. Quick! Go *on*.'

'Don't be *stupid*!'

'I am not stupid. It is unmannerly to leave her to walk off the floor on her own – I'm a little surprised at Dwight – you must go as a *duty*!'

'Rubbish!'

'It is a time of good will. I dare you. Or perhaps you will *annoy* George! I'm sure *she* won't mind!'

Ross ground his teeth. 'Damn you! If I fall in love with her and leave you it will be your own fault . . .' He strode across the floor.

'Captain Poldark . . . What an honour!' Lady Harriet's eyes were lit with cool amusement.

Ross said: 'Lady Harriet, the honour would be on the other foot, if I knew which foot to put forward.'

'Do you not waltz?'

'Is it very different?'

'Quite different.'

'Then shall we sit out?'

'It's not my way to refuse a gentleman's offer.'

'That I can't for a moment believe, if the gentleman displeased you.'

She gave a low chuckle. 'Then let me explain. It is half way between a formal dance and a country dance. See, the way they go.'

'You do not change partners?'

'You do not change partners. Really, it is rather a lascivious dance. Can you not hear the beat? *terrer-um, terrer-um, terrer-um, tum, tum*. Look, take me round the waist, the way they are doing. See? Hold me closer. Forget the steps if you can listen to me: *terrer-um, terrer-um, terrer-um, tum, tum*. Now start with the right foot: you do not need to make much progress, you may if you want, almost pivot on one spot.'

'If we did that we should be trampled underfoot.'

'Very well, then, just gently, out into the stream.'

They ventured out into the stream.

Clowance, coming up behind Demelza, breathed in her ear: 'Papa dancing with Lady Harriet! There's a topsy-turvy! What *can* have induced him . . .' When her mother did not speak she said: 'Don't tell me *you* induced him!'

'I think in his heart he rather wanted to,' said Demelza, 'otherwise I doubt me that anything I could have said would have persuaded him.'

They watched the dancers for a few moments. 'He's doing real well,' said Demelza. 'Now he'll be able to teach me.'

'*I* could teach you,' said Clowance.

'Well your father was always one for pretty women.'

'Yes, I notice he married one.'

'That was a long time ago.'

'Go on, you started young. And I know you. You'll attract men till you're sixty.'

'Really, Clowance – oh, my dear life, I trust John Treneglos is not coming over! You take him, will you, my dear. Perhaps he is coming for you – I *trust* so – I *pray* so – I'll say I am a small matter tired!'

II

It had been a very unfortunate occurrence in the small winter parlour, to which Dwight Enys had been summoned. A woman had fainted, and she was very slow to come out of her faint. They did the conventional things, patting her hands, burning a feather under her nose, fetching smelling salts, but it took quite a time to bring her round; and when she did come to it was as if her mind was troubled, as if she needed some reassurance that none of the people round her, not even her husband, could give her.

Drake and Morwenna, having been persuaded to stay on week after week, had taken their full share in preparing for the party; they had enjoyed that to the full. But at the party itself they had wanted to take a back place, and only the joint commands of the two young Poldarks had brought them out to share in the evening as guests. Even so during tea and supper they had been inconspicuous, and when the dancing began they took no active part. Drake had never learned, and Morwenna was content to watch. Her own experience of dancing had been confined to a short and unhappy period in her life when George had brought her out and was considering what husband he might find for her most suitable to his own ambitions.

So when Drake went across to help move the spinet after

Isabella-Rose's performance, Morwenna strolled on her own back into the small winter parlour. It was the one room in the house which had really happy associations for her. It was here that she and Drake had met all through the early part of the winter of 1794 – *nineteen* years ago; it hardly seemed possible. She was then only eighteen, Drake the same. They had met here in the presence of the boy Geoffrey Charles, now the owner of this house, and had silently declared their love for each other.

It had always been rather a neglected room, and because of that little in it had been altered, even when George closed the house down and carried the best furniture to Cardew. The heavy blue velvet curtains which pulled together on rusty brass rings; the turkey carpet, part worn through at door and fireplace. And the old spinning wheel. Elizabeth's spinning wheel. Strange that George had left that.

There were only three people in the room when she entered, and presently they moved out to dance. Morwenna went to the fireplace, remembering that in those days there had been miniatures on the mantelshelf of Jonathan and Joan Chynoweth, her aunt and uncle. They at least had gone. She wondered if George had taken them to Cardew or whether they had been pilfered by some straying thief.

It had not *all* been happiness in this room of course; there had been heartgrief too when she had had to break the news to Drake that she was expected to marry the Reverend Osborne Whitworth. Even to think that name in her own mind gave her an unpleasant *frisson*. The thought of him even after all these years still filled her with a sensation of nausea and dread. Whitworth with his arrogance, his booming voice, his conceit, his thick legs and heavy body, the peculiar oppressive driving dominance of his personality, the way in which he used his considerable knowledge of the Bible to quote and reinforce his purposes; and that with never a thought in his head that he might be mis-using it. The small, evil, petty and cruel practices that he associated with sex. His affair with her sister Rowella. The very memory of his great body, great in all ways, his smell – which was not offensive in itself but offensive by association; the stirring of him in the night, the heavy breathing; the lowering eyes when he came to her bed and said, 'First I will say a little prayer' . . . the pain and the dread.

Even at this remove of time she felt breathless, sick at the recollection. She had learned to fight the memory, to turn her back on it in her mind and to face outwards to the present where she was truly loved by a man she truly loved and they had one child of their union, Loveday.

Loveday was here tonight and happily joining in the party. So was Drake, her husband, who through the years by the most endearing patience had conjured her back to normality. So was *she*, until this minute when the happy thoughts connected with this room had somehow turned sour on her, brought to her mind the memories she most feared.

There was a footstep in the room, quite close behind her. It was a heavy footstep and reminiscent nerves lurched at the sound of it. She clutched the mantelpiece and turned.

Facing her was a tall boy, almost a young man. His face was fatter than his body; the short-sighted spectacled button eyes were squeezed between accumulations of fat, the skin pale and pimply. His hair grew very short and tight and fur-brown upon his head. He was dressed in a red silk corduroy coat gilt-buttoned from neck to hem, black silk trousers and patent shoes. He was staring at her intently. He smelled like Osborne Whitworth.

The thick lips parted. The voice came.

'Good evening, Mama.'

Chapter Fifteen

I

When Andrew Blamey left Trenwith at midnight Clowance went with him out to his waiting horse. Music drifted after them, pulsing, beating into the lonely night.

'How long will it take you to reach Falmouth?' she asked.

'Oh . . . four hours, I suppose. Thereabouts. I'll have a beam wind – what there is of it.'

'Take care for footpads.'

Andrew patted the pistol attached to his saddle.

'Let 'em try.'

'How long before you are home again?'

'Not sure – there's all sorts of comings and goings these days.'

'Well, let us know next time you get some leave.'

Andrew hesitated. 'Of course. Yes. Of course. That goes without saying.'

The groom had drifted away.

Andrew patted his horse's nose but made no attempt to mount. 'I hope that – what's her name – Morwenna Carne, your aunt – hope she will be better. Strange to keel over like that.'

'We've put her to bed with a hot drink. She was shivering when she came round. I expect she has been overdoing it. Though Dr Enys seemed to think she'd had a shock. I asked my mother what he meant, but she didn't seem to want to talk about it.'

'Well, I suppose I had better be on my way.'

'Andrew,' Clowance said.

'Yes?'

'I suppose you know now the name of the other young man you saw in Plymouth Dock that night.'

'Here, you mean? Yes. Paul Kellow. I asked. Then I went

to speak to him. Not about *that* of course! That's better forgot.'

'I am so glad you think so.'

'Well, who's to benefit? Not the poor fellow that got the knife in his guts.'

Clowance shivered. 'I hope you'll not mention your suspicion to anyone – ever.'

He said jocularly: 'To think I thought you were coming out of the party to bid me a personal farewell! I had hopes of my pretty cousin!'

'Oh, Andrew . . .'

He kissed her. 'Well, why not. Cousins have become more than cousins ere this. However, I am not too downcast – only curious.'

'Curious?'

'As to which of the two miscreants is the lucky one you are so anxious to protect. If it is not Stephen, perhaps it is Paul! Or do you still have a soft spot for Carrington? I promise not to tell him!'

She shook her head. 'Don't ask me, Andrew. Anyway . . .'

He unhitched the reins from the mounting post. 'You really are my one and only favourite cousin . . . I think I have to tell *you* something. If you will promise first not to repeat a word of it in there – especially not to my father and mother.'

'What?'

'Swear not to tell.'

'Of course I swear not to tell. But what is it?'

He mused, looking over the dark garden with its wide glooming shadows. 'It will all be out in two days, so . . . But it could be inconvenient to say the least if it were out in less . . . Why do I tell you this now, Clowance? Only because I am a little bit in love with you. Put it down to the wine! *In vino veritas*! . . . Cousin, I am not returning to my ship at dawn tomorrow.'

She stared at him, thinking him drunker than she had supposed.

'The second officer of the *Countess of Leicester* is about to fail to turn up! She will sail without him. Captain West will be in a passion. I know I should have let 'em know, but had I done so it would have been made public too soon, and then the bailiffs would have been around!'

'Andrew, what are you trying to tell me?'

'Remember your promise!'

'Yes, yes, I remember my promise, but what is happening? I am totally mystified! And quite appalled!'

'Well, no doubt it *is* all very sad for a young man making a steady and sober career in the Packet Service. But, Cousin, this young man has never quite been sober or steady enough. So he has run himself into debt. Very considerable debt, this time. Only my profession and my guaranteed income from it saves me from immediate distraint. But I have promised my debtors more, when I return in two weeks' time, than I can possibly give 'em. So I estimate that I shall lose my position before the end of October in any case and no doubt cool my heels for a while in prison!'

'But Andrew –'

'So I have decided to embark on an adventure which may, while being a trifle more hazardous, yet bring me in far more money than the Packet Service . . .' He touched her on the shoulder. 'Do not suppose that I am unaware of the distress this will give my parents. Do not suppose that, before this, I have not accepted my father's help in bailing myself out of financial scrapes. But one cannot go on doing that indefinitely. I have writ them a letter which I will leave in their house for their return. If it does not excuse all, I trust it will explain all. When I come back . . .'

'But where are you *going*?'

'Didn't I say? Perhaps I had better not say! It is barely a week since I saw Stephen Carrington in Falmouth. We conversed a while in The Royal Standard, and I told him of my plight. He told me then of his plans to sail with two vessels to Genoa loaded with barrels of pilchards, and he offered me command of his new vessel which was launched at Looe only last week. There's no money in it save subsistence, until we *make* money; but then there's a likelihood of a high profit. She's in Penryn at the moment, my ship; Stephen brought her round. I'm sailing on the morning tide to pick up my cargo in Mevagissey – then we're off and shall sail more or less together; Stephen rendezvousing with me in the Scillies; he's coming from St Ives, you see. We shall not be back before March, but then, if all has gone well . . .'

'Andrew, have you not thought about your whole career in the Packet Service? Like your father, you could have –'

'Thought of it often, sweet Cousin. Though I may seem to you a bit of a scatterbrain, this has not been done easy-like.'

'Oh, Andrew, I *wish* that you were not doing this! If you –'

'Perhaps I should not have told you. It is not a nice secret to ask you to keep for forty-eight hours, but now it is on your conscience as well as mine.' He put his face close to hers again. 'Time only will say whether I'm as stupid as you think. But many young men sow their wild oats. It is no use getting to thirty and wishing you had enjoyed yourself while you were young. I – have enjoyed myself. I drink too much and wench too much and gamble too much. So my father gets ever more angry and my mother ever more anxious; and maybe a clean break like this will be for the best and may even help to let some of the fever from my blood. Stephen is a great character, even if once in a while he does thrust in the knife too deep . . .' He kissed her again. 'You know you really are very, very pretty.'

'Andrew, I will keep my promise but . . .'

He mounted his horse, and the animal adjusting to his weight, took a few steps away.

'Will you write?' she said. '*Try* to if you can. You know we shall all be – waiting to hear.'

'If I can,' he said. 'We're hoping not to put into port more than we can help betwixt St Mary's and Genoa . . . I'll do my best. By the way – d'you know what my new vessel has been called? I give you two guesses.'

'Of course not. I've no idea.'

'Stephen has called her the *Lady Clowance*.'

Andrew took off his hat, dug his heels into the horse and they went clattering off down the drive.

II

Looking back, Jeremy could not quite decide at what moment the evening began to go downhill.

At first, having got over the initial unpleasant surprise of discovering that Valentine had somehow become one of the Trevanion party, he had been delighted with everything about Cuby: her looks, her elegant pride, her attitude towards him, the ease and grace with which she came forward to meet his father and mother. Cuby had joined in the fun with him, had danced with him, had even agreed to essay the waltz with him, which was a delicious experience. In all their intermittent, restricted associations stretching now for two and a half years, it was a pitiable commentary that except for the short meeting at the races a year ago he had never held her so close as this before. Now while they danced he just breathed in the joy of it all, her lips, her smile, her body close to his, the feel of her hair brushing his face, the scented violet gloves, the bare rounded forearms, the curve of her cheek, the long dark eyelashes, her smile, her lips.

Another pleasure of the moment was that Valentine was dancing with Mrs Pope and, inevitably for a womanizer like him, was making a great fuss of her. It was at least a couple of dances after this that Valentine, with a for him singularly purposeful approach, claimed Cuby, and thereafter monopolized her. The fact that it looked a little as if he had received such instructions from his father in no way sugared the pill. That was what was expected of him – of them both. Again this could be no impediment for Valentine: he adored all pretty women and it could be no hardship at all to admire and lust after Cuby tonight. What turned the evening sour was that Cuby for her part behaved with just the same sparkle and animation and zest towards Valentine as she had towards Jeremy.

Jeremy in turn paired himself with Mrs Selina Pope.

It was a country dance, and there were other pretty girls on the floor, including Daisy Kellow, whose bright looks had slightly faded this year, as if she saw her chances of marrying Jeremy receding. Also Davida Treneglos, John and Ruth's second daughter, the one after the problem child Agneta; she had suddenly blossomed with auburn hair and a peach skin which so seldom went with that colouring. And there was his sister Clowance, blonde and lovely: not for him of course but representing all the other girls in the world he might find and court and learn to love. And little minx Bella dancing with the best. And tall handsome Caroline Enys and his own delightful mother. And all – all of them were as nothing because one girl would not have him.

He watched Cuby and Valentine move off together towards the larger parlour; no doubt to drink canary and to laugh and joke between themselves, partners, not just for now but for life. This was what was ordained. This was what had been financially and legally arranged between Sir George Warleggan and Major John Trevanion. It was sealed. It was settled.

He excused himself and strode out into the garden, his mood being not improved by discovering Horrie Treneglos cuddling Letitia Pope, and another couple in the garden he could not recognize. So he saw nothing of the brush between Valentine and Geoffrey Charles.

Only a half-dozen people noticed the extra tightness of Geoffrey Charles's face as, at the end of a dance, he requested a word with Valentine in private.

They met in the parlour where Morwenna had met her son.

There had been a little incident earlier in the evening when Amadora, being greeted by Valentine for the first time, had been offended and frightened by his amorous familiarity. To tell the truth Amadora, born into a family of Spanish hidalgos and raised in a convent, had found English society and Cornish society clumsy and unpolished and brusque. They were noisy, overt, a trifle discourteous by the standards she had been brought up to know. But such was her admiration for the English in other ways, and such was her love for Geoffrey Charles, that these little buffetings were taken in her stride. When you went into another country you did not expect it to be exactly like your own. She looked on it as a challenge.

But when a young man came suddenly upon you, terribly good looking but in a narrow, long nosed, bent sort of way, and kissed you at once on the lips, not quite content that your lips should remain closed, and stroked your elbow and arm and put a hand familiarly on your knee and said that he was your one and only brother-in-law, and they must get to know each other instantly and intimately, and looked as if he meant it, Amadora took affront. It was really more shock and indignation than fright, she explained to Geoffrey Charles afterwards; she was not one to be easily intimidated; but in the momentary shock she had passed on the message to her husband that she did not approve of this step-brother of his.

So that had not endeared Geoffrey Charles to Valentine at the beginning of the event.

But the later thing . . .

'Yes?' said Valentine lazily when they got in the room and found it empty. He had drunk more than most, but it scarcely showed. 'What can I do for you, brother?'

'What in Hell,' said Geoffrey Charles, 'do you mean by bringing that God damned boy here?'

'What?' Valentine dabbed the end of his nose with a lace handkerchief. 'What boy? Oh, you mean Conan Whitworth. Did it matter? He asked to come. Is he offensive to you?'

'Of *course* he's offensive! Didn't you know his mother was to be here? Didn't you appreciate the shock it would be to her!'

''Fraid I didn't. Should I have? Sons and mothers are not usually so antipathetic to each other.'

'For God's sake you could have written and asked me! Jeremy had the manners to do that when he wanted to invite someone I did not know!'

'Oh, Cuby and the Trevanions!' Valentine beamed. 'That was a truly excellent idea, wasn't it.'

'To hell with that! I want to know why you brought that boy here!'

Valentine's smile was wearing thin, but he did not relinquish it.

'My dear step-brother, I have told you. He wanted to come. I brought him. Why should I not? I was a babe in arms almost when his father was killed and his mother married again. You were but a lad yourself. How am I to know all the ins and outs of the affairs of your tedious friends?'

Geoffrey Charles's anger was blunted on the realization that probably Valentine spoke the partial truth. But the anger did not go away.

He said: 'I suppose you have always felt you owned this house!'

'Not at all, brother. Merely a residual interest, as it were. Do you wish to make an issue of it?'

'Only to the extent of ensuring you do not become over-familiar in the uses to which you put your relationship.'

Valentine's temper was rising, but he was the junior by ten years and authority was not on his side.

He said: 'Are the royal toes sore with being trodden on? You have only to say.'

'I've said all I have to say.' It was impossible to bring up Amadora's name without making her seem over-careful of her dignity.

'Then may I rejoin the ladies? Or do you wish me to leave?'

'Do whichever you damned please,' said Geoffrey Charles, turning away. 'Leave by all means if you have neither the wit nor the manners to offer an apology.'

'Apology?' said a voice from the door. 'Between brothers?' It was, of all people, Sir George, his voice even colder than usual. Although his black silk suit had been cut by the best tailor in London it sat uneasily on him; his sturdy bull-necked body would not adapt to its elegance. 'I came to tell you, Valentine, that we shall be leaving shortly . . . Is your wife not here, Geoffrey Charles?'

'No, she's upstairs,' said Geoffrey Charles woodenly. Amadora was with Morwenna.

'An apology?' said Valentine. His confidence had come

back with another person in the room, and he resented his brief loss of it. 'Between brothers? Between half-brothers anyway. Will a half apology do?'

'Make it what you will,' said Geoffrey Charles. 'So long as you understand what I have said.'

'And what has he said?' asked George.

No one spoke. George walked across the room, eyeing it, for he had not been in here before tonight.

He said: 'This spinning wheel belonged to your mother. Perhaps if you don't treasure it you could give it to Valentine.'

'I do treasure it,' said Geoffrey Charles.

'It is in very poor condition. It needs attention.'

'It has been neglected for a great number of years – like the rest of the house.'

'Just so. The Harry brothers were never very satisfactory.'

'I have discharged them.'

George raised his eyebrows and put his fingers on the spinning wheel, as if sampling it for dust.

'And what has Valentine said?'

'What?'

'What has Valentine said that you expect him to understand?'

'Oh, a mere trifle,' volunteered Valentine. 'That I must mind my Ps and Qs while in this house and take care whom I invite to it without the permission of the owner.'

'I do not think you need to put yourself in such a situation again,' said George. 'You will have your own inheritance soon enough.'

'I wish him good fortune with it!' said Geoffrey Charles.

'What do you know about it?' George snarled.

'*Nothing*. Should I? I have been away far too long to have any idea what damned plans you have in mind! So long as they do not involve me, I don't care.'

'I can promise they do not involve you in any way. You are at full liberty to spend your wife's money restoring this place to its former glory – such as it ever was.'

It seemed that even George had been drinking more than his norm.

'I won't detain you,' said Geoffrey Charles, 'a moment longer than you wish to stay.'

'Come, Valentine.' George turned back towards the door as Amadora came in followed by Ross.

'Oh,' said Amadora. 'Geoffrey, I shall be just here to tell you that Morwenna is gone to sleep . . .'

She paused and looked from one to the other.

'Ah, Ross,' said George.

'Ah, George,' said Ross. It was the encounter neither of them had been seeking.

Geoffrey Charles said: 'Is Drake with her still?'

'Yes. I think it shall have been some shock she has received.'

'That's what it was.'

George said to Ross: 'I have been observing the repairs that have been wrought in this house. It must have cost Geoffrey Charles a pretty penny. Or I suppose I should say *Mrs* Geoffrey Charles.'

'Oh, a great deal of it has been done cheaply,' Ross said. 'There has been tremendous good will in the villages.'

George sneered. 'No doubt.'

'And relief.'

'Relief?'

Ross said: 'That the house is to come alive again in the way most proper and suitable to it.'

George said: 'Are you suggesting that my occupancy of the house was *im*-proper?'

'Most people think so.'

George breathed down his nose. 'It is a Poldark house, I know. And that makes it sacrosanct. At least I did not commit the vandalism of having the great table torn up to accommodate a mere dance.'

'It will go back unchanged,' snapped Geoffrey Charles. 'Have no fear.'

'Oh, I have no fear, for the property is out of my hands. It is no longer my concern.'

'Was it ever?' asked Ross.

'That's as maybe. I will leave you to your parochial triumphs. Come, Valentine.'

In the last few minutes Valentine had discovered two glasses half full of claret left by someone on the bookshelf and had finished them off.

'Tell me, father,' he said, 'there was this great fight you once had with Cousin Ross, and you threw him out of the window. Was it in this room?'

There was a gaping silence. Geoffrey Charles broke it by saying:

'Get out, you stupid fool! Go home!'

'He's but a little drunk,' said Ross. And then to Valentine: 'No, it was not. In here we should have had no room to fight, should we, George?'

Geoffrey Charles said incredulously to Ross: 'And Sir George threw you out? I don't believe that!'

Valentine dabbed at a spot of wine on his lace cuff. 'Oh, but it was told me often when I was a little boy. The servants all talked. Polly Odgers used to tell me of it when I was recovering from the rickets. It used to make me laugh. I used to wonder how it came about that my father should ever have been able to throw Uncle Ross through the window!'

'As I remember it,' said Ross, 'three servants threw me out.'

There was a gust of half controlled laughter.

'And I remember,' said George suddenly, contemptuously, 'the cause of the quarrel. Perhaps you have forgotten, Uncle Ross. You were at that time in the process of defrauding your nephew, Geoffrey Charles, of a substantial share in your successful mine by having persuaded his mother to sell the shares to you at a knock-down price. Do *you* remember that?'

Ross tried to think of his age and the age of the man opposite him.

He said: 'I remember the ridiculous story you told. Perhaps the woman you'd then just married began to realize her mistake when she heard all the fabrications that you invented.'

'Don't ever speak her name in my presence!' said George.

'Why, does it upset you?'

'It upsets me to think that you ever touched her!'

The little parlour was suddenly full of terrible portents and terrible memories, portents and memories which concerned very gravely the interests of the two young men – particularly of Valentine. 'Touched', the word that George had accidentally used, could mean anything to them. This was a moment nearer to a clash between George and Ross – on the most important subject to them both – than there had been for many years – perhaps ever been. Another step, and there could be no withdrawing. Cheerfully they would have killed each other.

Ross said: 'In fact, I threw a servant through the window first. It made an unattractive mess of wood and glass on the lawn. When I followed I was quite cut about the hands. However . . .' He broke off, conscious that only he could defuse the situation. 'However, *Mrs* Geoffrey Charles, may I assure you that it will never happen in your presence, and only old men could boast of what they did then. Sir George is about to leave. And Valentine, having no other glasses to drain in this room, will no doubt accompany his father. It has been an enchanting evening, Amadora, and you have graced it as perhaps no Englishwoman could have done. We're all grateful to you for coming here and bringing Geoffrey Charles back.'

'You have already said this once in your tiresome speech,' observed George, still playing with fire.

'Yes,' said Ross. 'Good things are always worth repeating. Evil things should be strangled at birth.'

'Or live on the other side of the county, eh?' said Valentine. 'Amadora, delicious one, allow me a good-night kiss, and then I shall not darken your door for many a long day.'

Amadora glanced swiftly at Geoffrey Charles but his face was without expression. She allowed herself to receive a considerable hug and a lingering kiss from Valentine, and when they had separated she tried not to put a handkerchief to her lips.

'And a half kiss for a half-brother,' said Valentine, blowing one. 'Is there more wine outside?'

'You have had enough,' snapped George.

'Yes, Father. But the difficulty is my party may not be leaving yet, so all these adieus may be premature. You know how I hate to be without a glass in my hand.'

The relative smallness of the room had made the tension greater; no one could get far enough away except by leaving; and for a few more seconds not a person stirred. Far more than enough had been said for a challenge to be issued by either of the older men, for one to call the other out; and neither in the presence of the younger generation would have felt able to refuse. And the danger was still present. Only one more wrong word needed to be said.

Acutely aware of this, Geoffrey Charles made a great effort to swallow his own annoyance.

'We have all become over-serious, talking of old times that were best forgot . . .'

Again there was silence.

Geoffrey Charles went on: 'At least there are *many* things which may pleasantly be remembered about this evening, and when I am back on the Pyrenees, those are what I shall think of.'

Valentine, who had provoked everything, said: 'Avoid the Frenchie bullets, brother. Amadora is too pretty to become a widow. For my part . . .' He did not finish.

Geoffrey Charles gave a cynical smile, which was not really a relenting of his former expression.

'I'm sure you have better things to do.'

'Of course,' said Sir George, brusquely turning away. 'He has better things to do.'

III

Ross and Demelza rode home about an hour later following the shadowy figures of Andrew and Verity Blamey who were a hundred yards ahead, and followed by Isabella-Rose in the charge of Mrs Kemp.

'Why were you so long?' Ross asked. 'I was waiting around . . .'

'I went up to see Morwenna.'

'Oh, I didn't know.'

'I thought she was sleeping and began to steal out, but she called me back. I said sorry, sorry, but she said she *wanted* company – at least company who understood.'

'I think Geoffrey Charles was nearly ready to kill his half-brother.'

'It was a *wicked* mistake the boy ever came. I haven't seen him before. He *is* like Ossie. There's no resemblance to his mother in him at all!'

'How did Morwenna seem?'

'She badly wanted to talk.'

'About what? Tonight?'

'About everything. It seems Geoffrey Charles has offered them – invited them to come back to Trenwith permanently, to look after it while he is abroad – making Drake into his factor, as he had always wanted to when he was a boy. She said they were both very tempted – not because they are not happy in Looe but because she very much likes Amadora and because it would re-cement the old friendship between the two men. But this, I think, this meeting . . .'

Ross said: 'Well, the boy exists. If he continues to live with his grandmother near Mevagissey he will be nearer her there than if she were living here.'

'I suppose. But somehow his connection with the Warleggans and the Poldarks makes him more likely to turn up, like an evil goblin, at Trenwith than he would at Looe.'

They rode on for a while.

Ross said: 'All this prancing around. I shall be as lame as Jago's donkey tomorrow.'

'Could she dance?'

'Who?'

'Lady Harriet, of course.'

'You might better ask could *I* dance, with my lame ankle and my ignorance of modern steps!'

'The waltz,' said Demelza, 'is one of those dances where it is hard to be good if your partner is bad, and vice versa. So I presume you dropped into it nicely.'

'Why did you not dance with John Treneglos? I saw him ask you.'

'I would better prefer to take the floor with a performing bear. Later I stood up with Paul Kellow.'

'So I noticed. So did *John*!'

'What did she talk about?'

'Lady Harriet?'

'Yes, yes, yes, yes.'

'We had very little to say to each other, I assure you, being, as we both were, preoccupied with not stumbling over each other's feet. She congratulated me on Isabella-Rose's singing.'

'Serious?'

'She appeared to be serious. I said I could not stand it, it was like a corn-crake, but she said that was rude and unsympathetic.'

'So it is!'

'How can you equate singing with shouting? Though I have to confess it seemed to please . . . You must not let her get too big for her boots while I am away.'

'Lady Harriet?' said Demelza.

'Well, her too if you like. You certainly seemed to find something in common when I brought her over.'

'Horses mainly,' said Demelza.

'Horses?'

'Well, that fable there is about me knowing all about 'em.'

'You know more than most.'

'She asked me about *our* stables, as if we had anything to compare to theirs! They are just having their stables whitewashed and I told her not to use white but pale green which was better for the horses' eyes. Tis only common sense and a few simple remedies I know —'

'Could you make a friend of her?'

'D'you mean if she was not married to George? I don't know. She's too high bred for me. You can see how she can be such a friend of Caroline's.'

'But you're a friend of Caroline's.'

'*Yes*, of course. But Caroline's hardness is only a shell.'

'Perhaps Harriet's is.'

'Are you tempted to tap and find out?'

'No, thank you, my love. I have enough at issue with George. We nearly came to blows again tonight.'

Demelza stared at Ross in the dark to see if he was serious. 'Don't tell me *that*! I thought it had all passed off beautifully, except for that terrible boy upsetting Morwenna.'

'That started it.' Ross went on to explain what had happened. By now they were passing through Grambler village, which was as dark as death. The sweet westerly air was contaminated by a whiff from an open cess-pit.

'My dear,' said Demelza, 'George is such a . . . I don't know if evil is too bad a word. Perhaps it is. *Nasty* man. Yet he can marry someone like Elizabeth who, if I can forget what she meant to you, was a *good* person. And now he marries again – a – a woman of character and – and looks. But George himself . . . And you. It is *fatal*, fatal ever for you two to meet! When you are both in your chairs at Bath being wheeled to the Pump Room your nurses will have to receive instructions to keep you well apart, otherwise gracious knows what the consequences will be!'

Ross said: 'Valentine *created* the situation, seemed as if he were delighting in it, egging us on. He has a sense of ill-considered mischief. I wonder if he brought Conan Whitworth deliberately.'

'Oh, would he *know*? Surely it was ignorance.'

'I trust so. But it has left a bad feeling between the brothers . . .'

'Valentine and Geoffrey Charles?'

'Yes.'

'Half-brothers.'

'No matter. It is an ill thing when two young men show such antagonism. A small breach like this can so easily widen, become a permanent ugly rift, a danger for them both . . .'

Demelza pulled her cloak more tightly around her; after the heat of Trenwith the night air was chill.

'Jeremy was not involved in this?'

'No, I did not see him until a few minutes before I left. He had been out.'

'With Cuby?'

'No, when I saw him he was escorting Mrs Pope.'

'Something more went wrong for him tonight, I b'lieve. Although he brought Cuby across I do not think the evening turned well for him.'

'What makes you say that?'

'Just noticing things.'

They could see the unsymmetrical spire of Sawle Church against the cloudy sky. A dog was howling. It was a forlorn, lost sound.

'You had quite a conversation with Mrs Pope after supper,' she said. 'Was she telling you her plans?'

'No, asking my advice. It does not seem that she will be leaving.'

It was better to have the churchyard behind. Whether one believed in ghosts or not, after dark there was a kind of spiritual miasma about the place more dangerous, Demelza felt, than the organic smells they had just passed through.

Ross said: 'She asked me about mineral rights.'

'Why that?'

'When Pope bought the place Unwin Trevaunance retained the mineral rights. It's a course which often leads to litigation. But you remember only a couple of years ago Chenhalls, from Bodmin, with Trevaunance's cooperation, had already proposed a new mining operation only a hundred yards from Mr Pope's front door. It coincided with Mr Pope's illness, and there were some who thought that worry or annoyance were partly the cause of his indisposition.'

'I remember you talking about it. But didn't . . .?'

'Yes, it came to nothing. The price of copper fell and Chenhalls lost his enthusiasm. Unwin Trevaunance told me he had thought of continuing on his own but he didn't want to put out that much money and it was, as he remarked, "such a pesky, uncomfortable way from London."'

Now there were pleasanter smells, scents of the countryside and the sea: stubble and turned earth, a wisp of wood smoke from a dying fire, cows munching in a neighbouring field. Demelza kicked with her heel at Hollyhock who seemed to be falling asleep as she walked.

'Well?'

'Selina Pope says she has been advised by her lawyer to make an offer to Unwin Trevaunance for the mineral rights – so that, as she says, she will never again suffer the inconvenience of men trespassing on her land and proposing the opening of exploratory diggings within sight of her front door.'

'And what was your advice?'

'If she has money to spare, I believe it's worth doing. She asked me what she should offer, and I told her what I thought, and she said it was not far from the offer she had been advised to make.'

Demelza said thoughtfully: 'I hope Clowance will come safely home.'

'Why should she not? Jeremy said he would bring her.'

She turned and looked behind her. 'Bella is *still* talking to Mrs Kemp.' And then: 'I hope Henry hasn't wakened.'

'The more chickens one has, the more one has to cluck over.'

'And the more pleasures; the more fully one lives. I shall need them all when you are gone.'

'You will have one worry the less.'

'I trust you to be safe in London. So long as you are faithful to your promise not to accept some mission overseas again.'

'This war is nearing its end. I do not see how it can long continue. When it does end I have made arrangements with Dwight that we should all go to Paris together to celebrate.'

Demelza said: 'I think I should like that.'

IV

Captain Andrew Blamey said: 'I am glad Andrew got away in good time. And he seemed more modest in his drinking tonight.'

Verity checked her horse to keep on a level with her husband. 'I thought he was a little – strange.'

'In what way?'

'Perhaps I should say strained.'

'D'you think it is debt again?'

'Well, he has been home little enough this leave, so I have hardly had a chance of getting him to talk. But, as you know, there have been collectors about.'

'I detest the fellows!' snapped Andrew Blamey. 'It shocks and affronts me that they should be seen hanging around my house!'

'I think he feels that.'

'Then why the devil does he get into their hands? Twice I have paid his debts, so that he can start clean again. Straight away he plunges into more!'

'His pay is not very high, my dear. He has all a sailor's temptations.'

'I managed on it – and married on it.' Blamey stopped. 'Though God knows no one could have made a more sorry mess of things than I did! Yet it is because of that . . .'

'I know, my dear.'

'It is because of that that I am so anxious he shall not become a drunkard and a rake. At least I was not a rake, though God forbid that I take any credit for that either! My drinking was my damnation.'

'Well, you came out of it, came through it. For the last twenty-three or four years I do not believe you have been suffering damnation –'

'No, thanks to you –'

'Ah, no. Before ever you met me you had changed. I know, I know: it needed a tragedy to change you. But you did change. Why should not Andrew; and without the necessity of any tragedy at all? He's still so young. You forget he is so young. Give him a little time yet. Have a little patience.'

Captain Blamey sighed. 'Oh, I know. You always tell me this. And I always forget . . . At least let us chalk up tonight that he did not get drunk and that he left promptly.'

'I was pleased,' Verity said. 'He kissed me with so much more warmth when he left me tonight. It was like old times.'

Chapter Sixteen

A week later another trio were on their way home.

The Carnes lived just in West Looe, in a small corner cottage on the cobbled and mired lane that ran down towards the fifteen arch bridge of stone and creaking timber that spanned the river. It was a long bridge – six bow-shot lengths, even it had, once been estimated by William of Worcester – and narrow – less than seven feet wide in places, and it carried the considerable traffic between the two small towns. Someone had once called East and West Looe the Scylla and Charybdis of Cornwall, though what particular rival dangers they represented was not quite clear, for once a vessel was within the arm of the river it was fairly safe from storm. It was also well protected from seaward attack by eleven guns mounted on a platform in East Looe guarding the entrance to the river.

The little cavalcade bringing the Carnes home had not talked much on the long trek from Trenwith. They had picnicked under a hedge sheltered from the strong wind, but rain was threatening and there were only a few hours of daylight left, so they had eaten their pasties quickly and resumed the journey with the minimum of delay.

Dusk was not far away as they reached their home. Drake led the mare and the ponies round to the stable at the rear, and Morwenna and Loveday went in. When Drake came back Morwenna was on her knees lighting the fire.

'Leave me do that.'

'No, I think I can coax it better than you.'

'Where is Loveday?'

'I have sent her to Ada Greet's for some fresh milk.'

Drake lifted his pack onto the table. 'I reckon they've give us enough food to last a week. Really, they'd no need.'

'Geoffrey Charles is very generous. So is Amadora, but on a different level.'

'How do you mean?'

'Well, I think she's afraid to seem to patronize us. She herself would be too proud to accept gifts in kind from anyone. But it never occurs to Geoffrey Charles: he just piles everything upon us.'

'He's a rare good man. Tis a pity he feels he have to go back to fight.'

Morwenna picked up the tongs and began to feed the infant fire with small pieces of coal. Her glasses had slipped down her nose and she moved to push them up, but then looked at her dirty fingers and hesitated. He did it for her. She smiled.

'Still cosseting me, Drake?'

'Just a little now an' then, m' dear.'

'Just a little always,' she said, 'ever since we were married.'

'You needed it.'

'Yes. Yes, I suppose I did.'

He began to unpack the bag and put the items of food on the table. Then he went into the back yard and drew some water from the pump, emptied it into the big kettle which was suspended over the fire and adjusted the ratchet so that the bottom of the kettle should be near the flames.

Morwenna got up, her hair falling across her face, but was able to push it back herself with her forearm. He had made a movement but she smiled and said: 'No, I can do it myself. I think it is time I did more for myself.'

'That's a rare old nonsense,' he said. 'You've always done much for yourself. And for me. And for Loveday.'

She said: 'I have worked, have I not? I have been a good wife? I've worked like any other woman, stitching and scrubbing and cooking and sewing. I've made you happy, Drake?'

He stared at her, startled. 'Happy? Of *course*. I've been – all these years – can ye suppose I've not been happy – and would have been with the half of what you've given me? I'd have been content even with only the half that you promised me when we was wed! But it hasn't been that way, as you well d'know. There's been so much love . . .'

She blinked as if trying to come out of a reverie. 'So much love. Yes. So much love.'

The house was very dusty, a cobweb on the window.

Drake picked up a cloth and rubbed the cobweb away. 'Are you hungry?'

'No. But I expect you are.'

'Not yet. I reckon you must be tired after such a long ride, so why don't you go up to bed and I'll bring you a cup of tea when the kettle boils?'

'There you are,' she said, 'cosseting.'

'Do it matter? Tis good for you, and I enjoy it.'

She turned over one or two of the items of food, and then carried the butter and the cheese and the cream into the larder. When she came back she said:

'It's good to be home.'

'Yes. You must feel that.'

'Don't you?'

'Yes, no measure! But *you*, I mean, after – after what happened at Trenwith.'

'Oh, yes. Oh, yes . . . Drake, the clock needs winding.'

'I'll do it in a moment.' He put his arm round her shoulders. She leaned her face against his.

'I know what's keeping Loveday,' she said. 'Sarah Greet will be home from school and will have persuaded her in to exchange all the gossip. We shall get our milk sometime!'

'Well, the kettle will take a while yet.'

'Drake,' she said, 'I'm sorry.'

'Sorry? What for?'

'For everything that has happened – between ourselves and those at Trenwith.'

'M'dear, it is all nothing so long as you are not left too unhappy by it. After what happened there with that boy.'

She shivered. '*I* am not unhappy – now. But I feel you would have preferred to make your life there with Geoffrey Charles. Would you not?'

'I dunno.'

'I could see the accord – the deep affection between you; it has hardly changed from those days when he was a small boy and I his governess. Now he is married and coming home to live as soon as the war is over. It was — is — the realization of a dream. You are part of that dream and it will not be quite complete without you.'

'Well,' said Drake, with a sigh. 'There may be a morsel of truth in what you d'say; and I'm sad for that. But you are the only one that matters — to me, I mean. We live where you want to live and that's an end on it. If you are happy I am happy, and if not, neither am I. Looe is my home now just so much as tis yours. And Geoffrey Charles fully understands that.'

'He does now, yes; but I still have a guilty conscience.'

He kissed her. 'Stuff and nonsense. The kettle is singing. It look to me I shall have to go get the milk myself.'

Morwenna put a restraining hand on his arm. 'Drake, all these years you have looked after me as if I were an invalid, as if I were the victim of some terrible accident —'

'So you were.'

'Well, but only in a way. I am not halt, I am not blind, I am not *really* an invalid, as you know! I am strong and have worked hard, as I have just said —'

'Of course you have worked hard —'

'Tried to be a good wife and a good mother.'

'And been both in a wonderful way.'

'But meeting Conan — my other child — like that, and seeing him so like Ossie, was like having all the injuries done again. Like having delicate bones re-broken —'

'It was a bitter thing to happen!'

'But these last few days — *since* then — I have been asking myself if it was not a sort of favour.'

'Favour, by the Lord! Favour!'

'Sort of. Because really, all these years, Ossie has been a nightmare, something I have run away from. Often *really* a nightmare, something I've wakened up from in terrible distress —'

'I know, m'dear.'

'— thinking he was there beside me, feeling his terrible presence, breathing, grunting, pawing. Oh, the relief to wake, to discover it was not so!'

'Why recollect it all?'

'And not only in the night. There have been days when – when everything was physically repugnant to me, when merely contact with another human being has seemed intolerable, because *his* flesh was there, in the contact, turning the good into the bad, the clean into the vile . . .'

'Yes, I truly understand.'

'This awful encounter with Conan brought it all up again, as freshly cut as a new piece of meat, the blood oozing . . .'

'Morwenna –'

'But since it happened, since it has happened I have tried to – to face up to it as I have never tried before. I have kept saying to myself, Ossie is dead, Ossie is dead, Ossie is dead. Over and over and over – Ossie has been dead for *fourteen* years. He *cannot* hurt me. He just cannot. Nor can his son hurt me. This is a challenge to my *mind*. I can only hurt myself!'

'Yes, I suppose. But –'

'It is to my mind that the injury has been done. Isn't it? So in meeting Conan and in *fainting* and in the first horrors of coming round, and in all that followed I am really only hurting myself. Am I not? But if I hurt myself in this way I also hurt you and Loveday. Therefore, is my love for you and her stronger or weaker than this thing, this fear in my mind? If it is weaker then I am a weakling indeed. If it is stronger then I must not allow such a thing to happen ever again. I must not close my mind to memory, for that way it builds up and becomes unmanageable –'

'Do not agitate yourself, m'love –'

'I am *not* agitating myself!' said Morwenna, tears streaming down her cheeks. 'I am trying to learn to be *strong*. It is time, for God's sake, that I was strong! If I meet Conan again – for that cannot be unlikely wherever we live – I shall hold tight to your hand and stare him out. And whether you are there, actually there, or not, I shall be holding tight to your hand. And after he has gone I shall go into a corner and be sick at having seen his face again. But I shall not *hide* from it! I shall not hide from him – or allow him to do us hurt – any more!'

She was gripping his hand so hard that her nails were digging into his skin.

'There, there, my dear,' he said quietly. 'I see just what you d'mean.'

'Do you, Drake? I wonder. But does it matter, only so long as I keep to my resolve? I think, I hope, I *believe* I can keep to my resolve.'

He held her for a while, neither of them speaking. A thin worm of steam began to come from the spout of the kettle. Her harsh grip relaxed, became no more than warm and confiding.

Presently in the distance they heard a whistle. It was Loveday with the milk.

Morwenna sighed and said: 'It is not polite for a young lady to whistle. I think we shall have to mention it to her, Drake.'

'She's happy,' said Drake. 'Does anything else matter?'

Morwenna took off her glasses and hastily wiped her eyes dry. Then she put some spoonfuls of tea into the pot.

Chapter Seventeen

I

Letter from Jeremy Poldark to Dr Goldsworthy Gurney, dated 18 October, 1813.

Dear Gurney,

I am writing to tell you that I have decided not to proceed with our collaboration on the steam road carriage – at least not for the present. Let me say right away that this is not for any personal reason which involves you. I have not taken this decision because of any feeling that we could not work together, fund the building of the machine together and launch it together. On the contrary.

Unhappily, for reasons that I prefer not to explain, my life in Cornwall is no longer acceptable to me. I must explain I have been struggling with this situation for much more than a year – so it all existed long before we met – and your interest helped to revive a prepossession with steam that I had almost abandoned. But the prepossession, I have now come to realize, is not quite enough to drive out this other prepossession, and for the time being I have to go away.

So – do not laugh! – I am joining the Army. With my cousin's, Major Geoffrey Charles Poldark's, somewhat reluctant cooperation, I have been to Plymouth and obtained for myself a commission in the 52nd Oxfordshires; and I leave to join them next week.

It will be a new experience, at least, and I trust I shall feel less squeamish about killing a Frenchie than I generally do about a mouse!

In the meantime, of course, please make all use you care to of any of the sketches and plans I left with you. There are a few more I still have at home if you should need them. What remains of my machine at Hayle is also yours for experimentation, if you choose to use it.

As I said to you when last we met, I am not convinced by your arguments that a machine needs struts or legs to propel it first into motion; and I urge you to consider further the problems of adhesion before you launch upon the construction of the vehicle. I know some modern scientific opinion is on your side; but if a machine may start on rails without extra propulsion I *cannot* believe it may not be persuaded to start on the much more uneven surface of a road. I would rather consider the use of grit or gravel which could be contained in canisters and shed in front of the driving wheels when the occasion needed.

This is the last letter you will be receiving from me for some time, but if you wish to answer it, or in due course have new information to impart, pray direct your letter to me at Nampara, and my parents will see it is forwarded on.

I trust that, contrary to your fears, Dr Avery will come well and thus leave you more time to devote to your many stimulating experiments.
Ever yours most sincerely,
Jeremy Poldark.

II

The night before he left he walked up to a Wheal Leisure. By a wry coincidence there had been trouble with the engine last week. For eighteen months since the engine began to run it had been almost trouble-free – a testimony to Jeremy's design and Harvey & Co.'s manufacture. They had occasionally stopped it for ten minutes to make some adjustment or minor repair – ten minutes being about the maximum a good engine would stand without the necessity of blowing afresh – but most of the ordinary maintenance could be done while the pump was in motion. However, last week the other Curnow, Dan, had come to the house and reported that he was not happy with the engine: the stroke, he thought, was erratic, the vacuum not good, everything was a bit sluggish. Jeremy had gone with him, found Peter Curnow there too, and Ben Carter.

They waited for him, though he was by years the youngest – not because he was the boss's son, which would have counted for little – but because he was the expert; he had designed the engine; it was his creation, his baby. He went round, peering here and there, listening, up and down the stairs, probing, questing, shutting off this valve and that, half stopping the stroke and then allowing it to go through. After half an hour he said he thought there was a leak in the condenser; the engine was not making a proper vacuum; hot water was escaping in such a way as to suggest the eduction pipe; his guess was a fault in the actual air pump.

The Curnows nodded wisely as if they had been sure of this all along, but Ben groaned. It meant shutting down the engine, possibly for as long as a week, and at a wet time of year; the lowest levels would have to be evacuated.

The separate condenser – long ago invented and patented by Watt – was in a pit in the basement of the engine house, a masonry pit full to the brim with cold water, the condenser itself being inside the pit and containing a certain amount of water which originally had been hot steam and which condensed as it came into the cylinder and so created a vacuum.

Once the engine was stopped, the first task was to pump the water out of the masonry pit with a hand pump. The pit itself was about six feet deep by eight broad, and had bracing bars across it to support and keep rigid the condenser cistern; so even when this was empty the examination of the cistern was neither easy nor comfortable, especially as it had to be done in the almost total darkness of a cold, dripping cellar. Jeremy was lowered in first, with a miner's candle in his hat and two lanterns to help.

He was down an hour, Ben with him part of the time. Then he came up for hot tea and Dan Curnow went down. About midday, on his second turn, Jeremy found what he was looking for. The air pump was made of cast iron and there had been a small flaw in the casting. At the time, this had been filled up with scale and so had been undetectable; but over the months the scale had been dissolved by the action of impurities in the outside water – which was water brought up from the mine and not the purer rain or stream water used directly for the engine. As a result the original hair-line crack had reappeared, and at one end of it a pin-prick of a hole through which the water had been seeping in. So the engine had been sucking up a mixture of air and water instead of air only.

They had cleaned and dried off the part, filled the crack and the hole with iron cement, tested it, and the engine had been restarted only two days after it was brought to a stop.

Of course the Curnows would probably have come to the same conclusion in the end, and made the same discovery and the same repair. It simply was that Jeremy with his intimate knowledge of the construction of the engine had been that much quicker off the mark. With him gone, timely repairs would be a little less frequent; a serious breakdown, if it was a complex one as well, would require another expert to be called in.

The same with Wheal Grace – so long as it continued to run. Nampara was to lose its chief engineer.

'When d'you leave?' Ben asked.

'First light.'

'For Plymouth?'

'No, Falmouth – to Chatham.'

'D'you expect to sail overseas soon, then?'

'I don't know. I'm told there's a contingent leaving for Holland sometime this month to bring the regiment up to strength.'

'Holland, eh? Been fighting there, have they?'

'So it seems. But I don't know much except the name of the commanding officer and the depot I'm to report to in Chatham.'

'So you'll not be going to Spain like your cousin.'

'Not at present, it seems.'

Ben glanced at his friend. 'Got all your uniform, have you?'

'Not yet. My father has given me his sword, which has saved something; but a spy glass and compass have cost me £55! The uniform and bedding and other equipment I shall get at Chatham. Also a horse. I would have taken Colley – but the cost and risk of transportation is too great.'

'A horse in a foot regiment, like?'

'It is usual for an officer, if he can afford it . . . You know Geoffrey Charles is to be a major?'

'Yes. I heard tell.'

'Well, his new rank has enabled him to give me the recommendation I needed to get a commission. That at least cost me nothing, so long as I did not mind which regiment I was appointed to. I said I did not, rather expecting every recruit would go to Spain . . . In fact it is a good regiment, one of the Light Division. I think my cousin had some hand in the choice, though he would admit nothing.'

They had climbed to the third floor of the engine house and out on to the bob plat.

Jeremy said: 'Even though I have spent nothing for my commission it is no inexpensive thing to be an officer. I am told that even after the initial costs I shall need about £100 a year above my pay to make ends meet.'

'What pay do you get?'

'Five shillings and threepence a day, which after deductions will come down to about 4/-.'

'What, 28/- a week as a lieutenant?'

'As an ensign.'

'You'd be better off at home, Jeremy. Looking after this mine engine like you did last week.'

'It is not for the money I'm going, Ben – nor yet for the glory.'

They stared out over the beach which had meant so much to them both. It was an errantly windy day. Black clumsy clouds were driving up from the north-west, imposing themselves upon a sky of an unusual shamrock green. The surf reared itself and tumbled in disarray as the gusts caught it, throwing up sharp spirals of spume like the blowing of sperm whales.

Jeremy said: 'I wish I were more like my father.'

'What way?'

'Well . . . for one obvious thing at the moment. My father is a natural soldier and a brave man.'

'We-ll. I don't know as I'd say he ever became a soldier from the real wish to be.'

'Then should I say he appears to take to it far more than I do. He seems not to have any conscious, physical fear – I mean for himself, such as I do.'

'Well, I don't know 'bout that neither.'

Jeremy pushed the hair out of his eyes. 'To tell the truth, dear Ben, I'm a rank coward. I am sickened at the sight of pain being inflicted and I am more than a small matter concerned at the thought of pain being inflicted on me. I like to tend an animal when it is ill, but if it is finally decided that the animal will not recover, someone else has to put it out of its misery. Bella is made of far sterner stuff than I am; she can superintend the slaughter of mice; I absent myself quickly. Could there ever be a more unsuitable man to lead other men into battle?'

Ben leaned back against a sudden gust of wind that threatened to push him over the edge of the unrailed platform.

'You say harder things 'bout yourself than is the honest truth. But – well . . .'

'No one made me go, eh? Quite true. So why should I come dwaling to you at this late stage? Perhaps because these thoughts of mine are best hid from my own family, and yet I still have the wish to express them! However, that is now done . . . Let us go down into the warmth of the house. It grows cold here.'

Ben said: 'Your father's in London. Your cousin is on his way back to Spain. Nampara will lack a man.'

'True enough.'

'Even Trenwith is bereft. That Trewinnard boy, he's a nice 'nough kind of man but he's got no strength, no . . . authority.'

There was a long silence.

Ben said: 'Wonder what Miss Clowance will do if that

man come round again, that Stephen Carrington. I hear tell he's somewhere about again.'

'He's at sea, and likely to remain so for some months. But I don't think you need worry about one thing, Ben. He could never prevail upon Clowance to do anything by force. He's not as bad as that. And if he tried to be as bad as that, can you imagine Clowance being – forced to do anything she was not willing to do?'

Ben smiled uneasily. He acknowledged – or was prepared to acknowledge – Clowance's physical strength. It was her *mental* strength, her *moral* strength against the seductive persuasions of that carnal, cunning man that he had reason to doubt. A fine thing Ross Poldark and his son would have done if one came back from his parliament and the other from the wars to find that their daughter and sister had fallen again under the wiles of Stephen Carrington and had married him. Ben knew he had little or no hopes for himself. But he could have accepted that Lord Something, who had been interested, and whom, it was said, she had refused. He could have accepted the Guildford fellow – who had been conspicuous by his absence since January. All he could not tolerate, could not live with, was the thought of Stephen Carrington still succeeding in carrying her off.

Jeremy said: 'I know you don't like or trust Stephen, Ben – my *own* feelings are mixed about him. But you have to admit he has initiative. He has got these two vessels, both fast fishing vessels, one built in our yard in Looe, the other a French prize brought in at St Ives. He bought it at auction there and has been refitting it to suit his purposes. He's persuaded my cousin, Andrew Blamey, to join him; did you know that?'

'No . . . Is that the young officer in the Packet Service?'

'Yes.'

'I seen him once. Ginger haired almost, wi' big side chucks . . . Do it please your family, him going off wi' Carrington?'

'Of course not. Particularly his mother and father. They naturally think he has thrown away a secure position in a respected government service for this wild venture. They're right. Any number of things may go wrong with Stephen's plans. But according to Clowance, to whom Andrew spoke just before he left, Andrew had got into some difficulty with his debts, and it was only because he told Stephen of these that Stephen offered him the chance of sharing in his adventure. There seems to be no question of Stephen having lured him away.'

'What are they about?'

'Stephen has crammed both his vessels full to the gunnels of pilchards, salted in their barrels – all of which he has bought cheap in Cornwall – and is going to run the French blockade and take them to Genoa. If all goes well you can see what he might gain. At any rate, as I have told you – even if he catches the Portuguese trades as he hopes on the way south, he will certainly not be back in England until March at the earliest. Clowance will be safe till then.'

Ben grunted. 'He have made some money from what he put into this mine, but not near enough for what he must 've laid out. Where's he gotten the rest of the money?'

There was a silence. Jeremy said: 'He may have borrowed some of it. Also he tells people he has inherited from an uncle.'

'A likely story.'

'I am only telling you that he has gone away for some months, so you do not need to worry on that score.'

They went down to the second floor. Here for a few minutes they watched in silence while the sword-coloured piston rod slid up and down, steam rising round it as it moved. *Grunt, pause, breath*; *grunt, pause, breath*; so for eighteen months it had been working, working all the time except for the occasional regular halts, and except for the stoppage last week. It had been well designed, and he had designed it, with some outside advice. This at least was something to be proud of. Thirty tons of rods to lift; then down, down, pushing the water so that it was forced up to the tanks to gush away down the surface adit. There were beads of sweat on the piston, like those on the brow of a working man.

He, Jeremy, had made this. He and the engineers and

craftsmen working under him. He still felt as if he had created something *alive*, out of iron and brick and water and fire. Something of great power, of sentience, of mood and temperament, of *character*. He was leaving this behind.

He said: 'I expect the war to be over within the year. Napoleon is tottering. Once he has gone I don't believe the Americans will be unwilling to make peace. I should be back within two years – perhaps less than that. When I do come back, there are all sorts of improvements I would like to try. There is a roll-crusher I have seen written of. And there is a mechanical buddle for processing slimes. These and other things. And I'd like to make some experiments into why iron castings containing gunmetal inserts sometimes collapse. Is it because they have been in contact with impure water? There is much to do here . . . But, I suppose, for the moment there is much to do elsewhere. Peace of mind. Is that what I seek? Peace of mind? In war? It is an odd question.'

They went down to the ground floor where the grey-haired, balding Peter Curnow had the fire door open and was shovelling in coal. They watched in silence, as the ashes fell glowing and the new coal sent clouds of grey smoke up the chimney. Presently the door clanged shut and Peter picked up his oil can and began to drip oil on the levers which automatically opened and shut the valves. He grinned as he went up the stairs.

'Just going put a drop on the gudgeon pins. You don't want me, do ee?'

'No, Peter. Thank you.'

A great grey striped cat raised his head and looked at them from his chair, eyes narrowing to slits as if the light had become suddenly brighter; then turned luxuriously and tucked his head under his paws. Vlow, as he was called after an extinct mine further along the beach. Cats always appeared out of nowhere to adopt or be adopted by a working mine. They knew a warm place.

'It's passing odd,' said Jeremy, 'that when you and I first prospected this old mine and I persuaded my father and Mr Treneglos to put up the money, though we all knew about Trevorgie and the possibility of linking up with her, I never *really* believed we should – or if we did that the old ground would be much worth the working. But it's Trevorgie now that is keeping us going and showing a profit. If you had not made that discovery that day the whole mine would have been shut down six months ago.'

'I suppose. Though we might've gone deeper and found something. The beauty o' the Trevorgie workings is that they're more or less shallow and don't impose extra strain on your engine.'

'The beauty also of going into old tin workings and finding copper. D'you still get complaints?'

'What about?'

'It being haunted.'

'Yes. A dozen or more 've given up their better pitches and gone into the newer work. But there's enough'll brave the knockers for the sake of profit.'

'What do they complain of – Roman soldiers?'

'Just noises. Tis a superstition. Knockers are supposed to be three feet tall with legs like sticks and big ugly heads and hook noses; but no one never sees 'em. They just 'ear 'em on the other side of the wall.'

Jeremy put a finger under Vlow's chin and tickled him. The cat grunted and buried his chin deeper.

'What do they fear – is it supposed to predict a fall of rock?'

'Gracious knows. Bad luck, I reckon.'

'What's our profit likely to be next quarter?'

'Zacky'll know for sure, but eight or nine hundred, maybe. You know that black tin we sold from the east workings of the 40 fathom level? When twas put into the burning house a great part of what was thought to be tin turned out to be iron. So twas only half a ton 'stead of a ton.'

'Well . . . not riches yet, but a fair return on capital.'

'Your share'll pay for your uniform no doubt,' said Ben with a hint of bitterness.

'Ben . . .'

'Yes?'

'You cannot suppose I leave you with a light heart. It has been – a hard decision for me to come by. For more than a year now . . . Oh, except for my cowardice I would have been away at the beginning of this year instead of the end of it. It leaves us, as you say, thin on the ground for men . . .'

'Men who take responsibility,' said Ben. 'Men who make decisions. There's plenty of others around.'

'My father expects to be back from Westminster in a few weeks. Because of my not being here he will be home well before Christmas.'

'Does he *like* you going?'

'Like? That is not the word. At least he has not stood in the way. We had a family council – with Geoffrey Charles before he left. It was not an easy meeting, but in the end we all agreed.'

Ben stirred the coal dust with his foot. 'Have you seen Zacky yet?'

'No, I shall call in there now. Good that he's better.'

'Yes . . . he's better. But he's *old*, Jeremy. My grandfather, ye know.'

Peter Curnow trotted down again, can in hand, put it on the shelf, rubbed his hands on a rag. 'She's going proper now, Mr Jeremy.'

They talked mining for a while. All these good-byes, Jeremy thought; it would be better when they were over and he was at last away. Last night he had seen Paul Kellow . . .

Paul had said: 'How much have you taken?'

'Four hundred. That's for my uniform etc.'

'Stephen's had all of his.'

'And you?'

'Some left. But I've had most of it from the cave.'

'Why?'

'It feels safer. Why don't you take more?'

'Some day. When next I'm back.'

Paul sipped his beer.

'What I have will about see us through next year. That's if I can continue to deceive my father as to how it is come by.'

Jeremy did not suppose Mr Kellow would bother to enquire too closely so long as the supply did not dry up. But he did not say so. Paul, apart from buying a few extravagant items of clothing, had behaved far the best of any of them by putting most of his ill-gotten gains towards the preservation of his family. Being the sort of young man he was, fond of display, it must have needed considerable restraint not to break out in some more obvious manner himself. Or fear . . .

Paul said: 'And it *was* hard come-by, by God! All the time in that coach I felt as if the rope was tightening around my neck. I dream still at night sometimes of the back of the coach broken open and the two strong boxes on the seats for any to see if the coach stopped, and none of us able to break into the cursed things! I wake up in a fever, sweat pouring off me as if I were taken with the ague! Then I am afraid to fall asleep again lest the nightmare shall re-start.'

'No doubt,' said Jeremy.

'I asked Stephen once if thoughts of it ever disturbed his sleep. He said, no, and he never dreamed, he said. Yet at the time I'll swear he was just as worked upon, as anxious, yes, and as scared as we were! I recall him cursing and swearing with that crowbar, and his face all running with sweat.'

'I recall it all,' said Jeremy.

They finished their beer.

Paul said: 'The success of the coaching business depends on the ending of the war. With luck we can survive another year. Then we are expecting an expansion of travel. Sooner or later it is bound to come. People scarcely stir in Cornwall from one place to the next unless driven by some dire necessity . . . Are you going to say good-bye to Daisy?'

'I think so. Later tomorrow.' Which was now today . . .

(Early this morning, just before daybreak he had been out to Kellow's Ladder and had taken the money he needed. It was all in his purse now, some of it paper, some of it clinking; in a purse about his waist where it must never leave him . . .)

After parting from Ben Carter, Jeremy went to take leave of Zacky Martin, who was the official purser to both mines but who now was mainly confined to his chair; and there were few easeful breaths he took in a day; then on to a few of his many other friends in and around Mellin and Grambler.

These preparations to go did not so much matter; it was leaving early tomorrow morning that was going to be emotionally charged. His mother, he knew, would be full up, but was unlikely to give way. Isabella-Rose, of course, looked on it all as a prime lark, only envious that she could not go with him, comically bitter that she could never be a soldier. Clowance he was not so sure of. She might unexpectedly burst into tears, and the awful, humiliating thing was that when they had been children he had never been able to keep his eyes dry if she once started crying. It had happened once when he was eighteen and she fifteen. It had been humiliating enough then. Tomorrow morning if it happened it would be quite *intolerable*. A soldier going to the wars in *tears*. Somehow he must get at Clowance tonight to warn her, even threaten her, that *nothing* must be emotional in the morning.

He had not written to Cuby since the party. There was no point. Let her find out in whatever way she would. At least he hoped to be far away at the time of her wedding. There was no risk of his being able to accept an invitation to attend.

Now that the time had come for him to leave, he welcomed it. Or a part of his complex nature welcomed it. All his life, he told himself, he had had it soft. All his life, except for the self-imposed dangers of the coach robbery, he had been cosseted and protected, a privileged member of the Poldark clan, of a Cornish county family, his only revolt against parental discipline being a daring decision to learn the principles of high pressure steam without their knowledge or consent. If he had slept rough or lived rough or gone hungry it had been with the sure knowledge of the open door of comfort awaiting his return. Well, now he was going out into the real world of hardship, privation and adventure. There were to be no easy escapes any more. Life – real life – was on his doorstep. So was death. His childhood and his youth were over. Now he was to come of age.

III

In the week that Jeremy left Sir George Warleggan sent his lawyer, Hector Trembath, to call on another lawyer, Mr Arthur Williams Rose, who lived and practised in Liskeard. Always a man to proceed with circumspection – and careful never to allow any one of his employees to see the whole of his mind – George had engaged two of his other clerkly servants to make the preliminary inquiries on another front. These had been slow in coming in. Now they were complete. Of the seven young men playing Faro with Harriet on the significant date, two had satisfactory alibis for Monday the 25th January. Of the remaining five, it seemed improbable that Andrew Blamey should have been involved. His packet ship was indeed in Falmouth on the 25th but had left on the dawn tide of Tuesday. This made his physical presence possible on the coach, but the *Countess of Leicester* had only arrived on the Saturday afternoon, and it seemed unlikely that young Blamey could ever have got to Plymouth and played his part as Lieutenant Morgan Lean in an enterprise that must have needed careful planning in advance of the robbery. Still, George was reluctant to strike him off altogether, for it would be so gratifying to accuse a Poldark.

In January Stephen Carrington had been in employment as an assistant to Wilf Jonas, the miller, of Bargus Cross-lanes, not very far from Nampara, and had still been more or less officially living at an old Tudor cottage called the Gatehouse on the edge of Poldark land. But inquiries showed that Carrington had taken a day off from the mill whenever he fancied. Jonas, even when offered money for the information, had said gruffly he had no idea and no record of Carrington's attendances in January. All that was known was that three weeks afterwards Carrington had left for his home town, Bristol, and had not returned until July, when he had spoken of an inheritance and spent money freely.

Anthony Trefusis had been living at home at Trefusis with his parents and elder brother at the time, but his appearances and his departures were always so erratic that he could well have absented himself for a couple of days and scarcely any remark made on it. Nothing could be obtained from the servants. But the week following he had been to the races at Newton Abbot, and apparently had been lucky. Although not paying all his debts, he had seemed more flush than usual.

George Trevethan, whose father ran a gunpowder mill in Penryn, was seldom short of money, and therefore not a likely suspect. But he had been away visiting friends in Exeter in late January, so he could not be altogether excluded. The remaining suspect was Michael Smith who came of a wealthy but drunken family near Kea. A witty young man, with a fine voice when sober, he readily volunteered, when asked, that he had been indoors for the last two weeks in January with a severe attack of influenza. Too readily volunteered? But there seemed no later special access of affluence to make him a prime suspect.

George, of course, never lost sight of the fact that this at present was *all* supposition, that the note might have passed through half a dozen hands before coming to light in Harriet's winnings. That was why he sent Mr Trembath to see Mr Rose.

He had been, Mr Trembath reported in his effeminate, high-pitched voice, to call on Mr Rose at his office in Liskeard, but Mr Rose was confined to his room with an attack of gout, and only consented to see him after some insistence and after mentioning his client's name.

Mr Rose, Mr Trembath explained, was a very stout elderly man who distinctly reminded him of drawings he had seen of Dr Samuel Johnson; with a high colour and thick white hair, all his own –

'Yes, yes,' said George testily. 'What was the outcome?' Hector Trembath, although a good and serviceable friend in law, was not George's ideal of a grave and laconic solicitor. He always wished to embroider his conversation with inessentials.

'The outcome, Sir George? Why, very different from when we put the questions to the coachmen, Marshall and

Stevens. Mr Rose says he remembers his fellow passengers perfectly. He says that the lady wore a veil the whole time and he would be in some difficulty in recognizing her instantly again. He says he did notice that she had a small mole on her chin and that she was left handed; but little more. However, as to the clergyman and the naval lieutenant, he declares he would know them anywhere.'

'Ah,' said George, turning the money in his fob. 'So?'

'At first he seemed to have the wrong impression, that some suspects had been arrested and needed identifying. I explained that such was not the case. But I did put to him the fact, *significantly*, if I may say so, that you would like him to visit you at Cardew in the not too distant future, and to spend a few days there as your guest. He pulled a face at the thought of travelling so far in the bad weather; but when I explained it would likely not be until the early spring he brightened up. I also said you would like him to do some business for you.'

'Did you mention that the reward of £400 would be paid instantly for the identification of one or more of the criminals?'

'I did, sir. I fancy I left him in a much more cheerful mood than when I called.'

Book Two

Chapter One

I

In November Wellington again defeated Soult and began to invest Bayonne. On 11 November, Dresden fell, on 21 November, Stettin, on 5 December, Lübeck. The Allied Sovereigns entered Frankfurt. Everywhere Napoleon was reeling, but defeat, submission, were not words in his vocabulary as applied to himself. The Allies offered him peace, with France uninvaded and allowed to keep her natural frontiers – even to the Rhine – and with almost all British conquests overseas returned to the French. Buonaparte returned evasive answers, proclaiming publicly his utter commitment to peace while threatening in private that if he lost his throne he would bury the world in its ruins.

In late December Aunt Edie Permewan was finally edged into church and became Mrs Art Thomas. She gave her age as 41, which was a lie by more than ten years. Art told the truth; he was 23. He didn't mind the sniggers, the digs in the ribs, the bawdy jokes. By the marriage he entered into his promised land, a languishing tannery business. Music did not like to claim his share in the successful wooing. After all, his mistake had cost him dear: the friendship of the girl he cared for more than all the world. Despite his stuttering efforts to explain, Katie still refused to speak to him.

In November Geoffrey Charles wrote a brief note saying Amadora was now safely back with her parents in Madrid, and that he was on the way to rejoin his regiment *in France*. He thanked all his cousins for their warmth and kindness, especially to a little Spanish girl who had come as a stranger among them and become so quickly their friend.

Jeremy eventually wrote his first letter home.

My dear family,

Here I am at Willemstad, billeted on a farmer and his wife just on the outskirts of the town. The long story is that we landed at Chatham on the afternoon of the 9th December and I proceeded at once to report to my depot and then to provide myself with a uniform and a greatcoat and all the other paraphernalia and utensils of an officer of the British Army. This took me several days and a visit to Rochester, but in the end I was equipped and spent two more days idly observing the scene – among it a ship being loaded with cannon balls, the sailors and the dock workers *throwing* the balls from one pair of hands to another as if they were building bricks, which when I lifted one, they certainly are not! – before I was called again and reported to a Captain John Sheddon, who was to be in charge of us. It seems that I have been unfortunate in that *all the rest* of the 52nd are in France under Wellington, but the 2nd battalion has been detached for service in Holland, and we – those who sailed in the *Mary Morris* – were a small reinforcement. Apart from Captain Sheddon and myself – captain and ensign – there were four sergeants, one bugler, and 69 rank and file.

I did not buy a horse, for I was told it was easier to get one in Holland – which has hardly proved to be the case; although I now possess one, I am not sure if I did not pay far too much for so indifferent a mount.

We marched to Ramsgate, and embarked on the 16th, arriving at Stevense, on the Dutch coast, on the 23rd. I thought, this is the strangest Christmas! Our instructions have been to join the rest of the 52nd, which arrived from Dover three weeks ago, and to form part of the army of Holland under General Sir

Thomas Graham – a man with a great reputation from the Peninsula. More particularly we are part of the light brigade commanded by Major General Kenneth Mackenzie, and with us now, though not exactly near enough to be on terms of *fraternization*, is part of a Prussian corps under Prince Berkendorff and a German army under General von Bülow.

So far we have seen little to disturb or affright, but I am told we are probably going to invest Antwerp before long.

It is bitter cold here, and all the lakes and canals are frozen. Many of the inhabitants use the canals to skate from one village to another, and some of the English soldiers do the same. Coming from a county where the frost is seldom hard enough, I don't remember ever having a skate on in my life! I have tried a couple of times and it is deuced difficult, I assure you. But I shall persist!

The windmills here are *huge*. They say that sometimes a single sail in one arm stretches to 120 feet. A friend I have made called Lieutenant Barton, who comes from Devonshire, tells me the name Holland is a corruption of Hollowland – and I can well believe it, for everywhere the sea seems to be prevented from bursting in on us only by dykes and embankments. There are marvellous sea birds, some of kinds I have never seen before, and in great quantity. In this harsh weather many are in distress, and I began to feed them, only to be called in to see Captain Sheddon and ordered to desist – otherwise, he said, the camp would be covered in guano!

In addition to Frederick Barton, I have made particular friends with two other ensigns, both men of about my age: John Peters, who is a farmer's son, and David Lake, who went to Eton and knows Valentine.

Well, that is all there is to tell, I rather think. In addition to the wish that I could skate is the regret that I learned no modern language at school. No one expects you to speak Dutch, but a little French can be a great help, since France has run this country for twelve years.

A happy New Year and love to you all.
Jeremy.

In early January Tom Guildford, on a short visit to Cornwall, came to see Clowance and asked her to be his wife. She refused, but in thoughtful, hesitant terms that encouraged him to suggest that they might continue to see each other.

'Of course,' she said. 'I'd like that, Tom, please.'

He looked at her with grave dark eyes. 'We enjoy each other's company, do we not.'

'Very much.'

'Then do you not suppose that this is the basis on which a warmer affection could be built?'

'Oh, affection,' she said. 'That I already have for you in some measure. You are so . . .' She hesitated to find the word.

'You have a sisterly affection for me, eh?'

'No . . .' She laughed in embarrassment. 'It is not quite that.'

'More – or less?'

'Different.'

'In that case I shall take heart and invite myself to call upon you again tomorrow.'

'Pray do. I should like that. Come to dinner. I know my father and mother would be pleased.'

They were alone in the library, where they were a little removed from the rest of the house and from risk of interruption. Tom was in a mole-coloured velvet jacket, with wide lapels, a darker waistcoat with pearl buttons, yellow cord breeches, highly polished shoes. The light fell across his dark hair which he wore long and tied at the back. He had poor skin, white, uneven teeth; there was something very solid and reliable about him.

He said: 'Now that my mother is past my aid or the need of my company, I can make this journey more often.'

'Tom, believe me, I am so very sorry. And believe me also

that I could almost love you for preferring her to me last summer.'

'We make a little progress, then. What I was about to say was that, excepting my studies for the law, I now no longer have any ties in London. My father is one who will survive everything because his personal self-esteem is great enough to rise above the inconveniences of bereavement. I shall be happy to come to Cornwall whenever I can, not merely to escape from a home which is no longer desirable to me but in the hope that what *is* desirable to me in Cornwall is at least within my sights. Now wait, my dear, before you protest, for I know you have said no, to me, and I fully understand you are not a girl who would trifle easily with a man's affections. In other words, no, means no. But there are degrees of *no*, if I may venture to say so. The first degree of *no*, means that you cannot bear my company, that your flesh crawls at the sight of me, that, if my hide is not too thick to take the hint, I should leave this room and this house, never to return. The second degree of *no*, means that you acknowledge me as a human being, as a man, as a person of about your own age, who can be useful to pass the time with, who has the merit of a certain breeding and address, who is acceptable as a companion, and, within reason, as a friend; but whose personality means nothing to you at all. The third degree of *no*, means that you find me of reasonable interest, of reasonable attraction, that you enjoy the thought of my company, that life is the better for my being around; but that the vital spark, the vital charge of electricity and energy which transforms liking to love, is at present missing ... How would you assess your feelings?'

Clowance said: 'I believe you will become a very clever lawyer, Tom.'

'Thank you. So I intend to be. But would you, as the honest girl you are, tell me in which category you rate me in the three I have suggested?'

Clowance was silent.

He said: 'Can it be the third?'

'Of course it is the third, Tom!'

'Then I feel my future journeys will be worth while.'

'Perhaps you will meet someone in London soon.'

'Perhaps I shall. I do not intend to be an anchorite on your account; but it will be very difficult to find someone else who will bear any comparison with you.'

'Do you not think it time we changed the subject?'

'Not at all; it is a very pleasant subject, even though its main purpose is blighted.'

'What time will you be here tomorrow?'

'When you say.'

'Would eleven be too early? Then I will wait to canter across the beach until you come.'

'That will be very pleasant.'

'This frosty weather is likely to last. I'll have a fresh horse for you. The tide is right and we can reach the end and be back for dinner.'

'Clowance.'

'Yes?'

'You know I love you.'

'So you have just said.'

'But I do not intend to join the army on account of frustration, as Jeremy has, it seems.'

'Who told you that?'

'Valentine.'

'It's very strange . . .'

'What is?'

'No matter.'

'Given the encouragement,' said Tom, 'of being in the third degree of *no*, I intend to pursue my suit. I would warn you that I am a very persistent person. I almost drove my Nanny mad.'

'You wouldn't take no for an answer?'

'That is correct.'

Clowance bent to put coal on the fire, but he was too quick and did it for her.

'Oh, Tom,' she said.

'Good, good, that is a nice voice.'

'I almost wish it were *not* no. Life would be so much easier for me, less fretful, less hateful.'

'Does it have to be hateful?'

'A little. Just at present. Perhaps in a little time . . .'

Tom said: 'I'll give you time.'

II

In the late January the Thames froze; it was the hardest winter for many years. The Allies were over-running France, and it seemed there was little to stop them from entering Paris. At La Rothière on the first of February the Germans under Blücher, and aided later by the Russians, gained a decisive victory over the French. Wellington, however, when he learned of the disposition of the allied troops, did not approve at all: they were too strung out. And so it proved. With his old genius Napoleon gathered his troops, many of them young and raw, and struck first at the Germans under Blücher, defeating him and his commanders four times, and annihilating a Russian division by the way. Then while they reeled back he flung his exhausted troops against two other German and Russian armies, swept them from his path and confronted the Austrians under Prince Schwarzenberg who were advancing with dignified caution on Paris. The Austrians lost their dignity and beat a hasty retreat, and by the end of the month were in the foothills of the Vosges once again considering a separate peace.

In Holland Jeremy, unaware of the noble part being played by the 1st Battalion of the 52nd beyond the River Adour in France, was with the 2nd Battalion undergoing his baptism of fire. They had driven the French out of Merxen, without loss to themselves, and then after staying there a few days had advanced into the suburbs of Antwerp. From the position they now reached the British were able to survey the French fleet frozen into the basin of the city, and it seemed a profitable idea to bombard them from this vantage point.

One day they were surprised by the arrival of William, Duke of Clarence, the Prince Regent's brother, come to observe the scene, but unfortunately it coincided with a French retaliatory bombardment. The Duke showed no signs of fear and continued to watch from his horse until a bullet pierced the skirt of his greatcoat and Captain Love, the commander in the field, was blown from his horse, without serious injury to himself, and the sentry beside him was killed and three others seriously wounded.

In spite of the little scuffles near Merxen, this was the first time Jeremy had seen the shambles of a direct hit by cannon. Blood and bones spurted, a man held his hand to a shoulder that lacked an arm, another writhed on the ground breathing blood and vomit on the grass. But it was Love's horse that finished Jeremy. He moved a few feet away and was sick into the bushes.

'Feeling a trifle off-colour, Poldark?' Lieutenant Barton asked with a grin.

'No, no,' said Jeremy straightening up and wiping his mouth. 'I do this for pleasure.'

The bombardment having stopped on both sides, as if by mutual agreement, there followed a period of consolidation while breastworks were built and batteries were brought forward. The bombardment of the ships had been considered a failure, because the ships were relatively small and there was so much ice on which the cannon balls could bounce harmlessly away. Antwerp should now be bombarded instead, to soften it up before the troops moved in to take it.

This cannonade went on for four days, but the enemy return fire, after that one spectacular hit, was sporadic and usually harmless. The army waited for an order to advance which never came. Instead they were ordered to retreat – to Odenbach, where they had been for a few days on the advance. Captain Love explained that the Germans under von Bülow had received orders to move south and to pass by Antwerp; it was part of a grand design, though whose design no one knew. Some Russian troops, some Cossacks, remained behind. A menacing lot of men, with their shaggy ponies, their sheepskin cloaks, their long lances and straggling beards. On the whole they maintained a sort of discipline, but one could imagine how quickly it would slip away in a war of conquest and pillage.

Jeremy mentioned little of all this in his second letter to his family, being full of amusing anecdotes about his fellow officers, of which there were plenty. He was interested in the way the Dutch kept pigs, what fine cattle they bred, the oddity of the Dutch cheeses ('why do they not thread a wick in them and use them for candles?'), the lovely dyed silks and silk-stuffs they made. In the meantime what was this exciting news about two new finds of copper at Wheal Leisure? Extraordinary those old Trevorgie levels, which had been mined so extensively for tin . . .

In early January the *Chasse Marée* and the *Lady Clowance*, one only a day behind the other, arrived at Livorno and unloaded and sold their hogsheads of pilchards at 182/6 a hogshead. After a week ashore they reloaded with Italian white wine, tubs of liqueurs from the monasteries, silks, laces and velvets; but when about to leave they were embayed for two weeks by a vicious winter storm that sank six vessels in the port and did some damage to the *Chasse Marée*, so it was near the end of the month before the brooding mountainous landscape of Italy was out of sight.

It had been an eventless trip out, except for a few tense hours weathering Gibraltar, and except for the fact that two members of the seven crew of the *Chasse Marée* had been struck with a mysterious illness from which they had nearly died. Andrew Blamey thought sometimes that they had come through so far as much by good luck as by good management; Stephen's knowledge of navigation was cursory to say the least; even he, who had been skipping his exams lately, knew far more. One of the fishermen crew, Bert Blount, who came from St Erth, knew more than either of them.

Ross had been at Westminster almost three weeks before he saw Canning, who had been at Hinckley with his ailing son. Canning was again in a mood of despondency – not because of the state of the war but because of the state of his personal affairs.

'Naturally,' he said, 'I'm delighted that things are moving

so well for us at present. All the same, I would have dearly wished to play some part in these ultimate stages, some part other than that of an uninformed back bencher, listening with anxious ears for the drops of information leaked out by the relevant ministers. Especially from Castlereagh.'

Castlereagh was the man with whom Canning had fought a duel five years ago. Reconciliations had taken place between them since then, yet their inability to work together had as much as anything contributed to Canning being left out in the cold.

'If Castlereagh plays his cards right – or perhaps I should say uses our gold right . . . But I know it still all trembles in the balance. Napoleon's latest successes make one fear Marengo all over. He is trying to divide us once again.'

'Austria surely cannot make a separate peace this time,' Ross said.

'Well, one still has to consider that our allies are really only allied in their opposition to Napoleon. The Austrians have far more in common with the French than with the Russians or the Prussians, whom they consider the ultimate barbarians – and one has to admit they are not so far wrong. The Empress of France is the daughter of the Emperor of Austria. *Her* son is Napoleon's heir. If Napoleon has the good sense to accept his defeat so far as it now goes, agree to the old frontiers and begin to act like a reasonable man, the Austrians would far rather he retain his throne than that he should lose it and have Europe living under a Russian-Prussian hegemony.'

'But France will continue to exist. We have no intention of destroying it – only Napoleon.'

Canning made a sudden impatient movement. You could see he wanted the dispatch boxes of office under his hands. 'That is Castlereagh's task – to make that clear. He must use all the influence we have, especially our money, to prevent the Austrians weakening. *And* the Russians: I'm told Tsar Alexander is very depressed by the latest reverses. What we really need – what we must have – is a formal treaty between all the Allies, guaranteeing that none shall make peace without the others!'

It occurred to Ross that Canning did not appear to be badly informed about the diplomatic and military situations as they stood at that time. It was said by his enemies that he behaved as if he ran a little government of his own.

'You have heard of Sir Humphry Davy's adventures in France?' Ross asked.

'In France? No.'

Ross explained. 'They are well, it seems, and in Paris, staying in a hotel, having been twice arrested on suspicion, and having had great difficulty in obtaining passports. Nevertheless he has met Ampère, Gay-Lussac, Humboldt, Laplace. And they are permitted now to roam abroad at will. They have been to the theatre, have met the Empress Josephine. The few Americans living in Paris are astonished. I wonder if a revolutionary French scientist would be given so much freedom in London.'

'I think we should not be unmatched in such civilities.'

'But should we *invite* him?'

'Ah, it is one of Napoleon's virtues and advantages not merely to be able to do a good if eccentric thing, but as an absolute monarch to have to answer to nobody for his actions. Just supposing Lord Liverpool were to invite some eminent French scientist to pay us a courtesy call, imagine the questions in the House!'

Ross said: 'There may well be rioting in Paris and civil war if the Emperor falls.'

'As he must within a month or so,' said Canning. 'Granting only that we stay together.'

Chapter Two

I

In early March Wellington's army including the 43rd Monmouthshires penetrated further into Aquitaine. Word had
gone ahead of them that the men did not rape and pillage
but behaved under a strict if brutally imposed discipline. It
was told that Wellington even invited the mayors of the
towns and villages through which he passed to dine at his
table, something a French general, for all his ideas of
equality, would never have done. What was more the British
paid for what they took. By the time they entered St Sever,
and Brinquet, they were greeted almost as a relieving army.
Bunting was hung from windows, and here and there a
Union Jack. The Army basked in its popularity and brief rest.

Luckier than his cousin, who was to be in the forefront of
the last bloody battle for Toulouse, Jeremy's battalion was
not involved in the attack on Antwerp and Bergen-op-
Zoom, which was a disastrous and costly failure. The 52nd
were kept in reserve all through the 8th March and on the
9th they were deployed to cover the retreating troops when
the attack was abandoned. Jeremy was sickened by the
procession of wounded soldiers, groaning in carts, limping
along the frozen tracks, leaving stains of blood behind like
little signatures in the snow.

So April dawned, and in Cornwall the daffodils, the
primroses, the snowdrops flowered, all late because of the
bitter winter. The sun seemed like a stranger, and for a
whole week persisted before its warmth could be felt
through the cold grip of the dying frosts. In very bad winters
such as this Demelza felt a little anxious lest – who knew? –
the miracle of spring wouldn't happen. It seemed to her that
whoever controlled the weather was absent-minded, busy
perhaps with some other world; he turned his back and

forgot about it; then, at the last moment he remembered and turned round and pulled a lever like those which started the engine of a mine, and behold there was a gentler beginning to the next day, and a bird sang, and softer rain fell, and the daffodils lifted their wrapped heads looking for the warmth from the sun, and it was going to be spring after all. Henry now was sixteen months old and most like Clowance of all her children, except that his was a darkness which was likely to last: *she* had begun with some dark redness in her hair which had soon changed to blonde.

And Isabella-Rose was just twelve and becoming a handful in a way none of the other children quite had been. She was cheerfully disobedient and took any mild punishment meted out in such a vociferous but good tempered way that one did not know quite what to do about her.

And Clowance was not yet twenty: still so young for all the marriage proposals she had already received. And Jeremy – the only one of her children who had been delicate as a child – was nearly twenty-three and enduring, she was certain, agonies of discomfort in the intense cold of Holland, if not every moment of the day in danger of his life.

And this month, in spite of the absence of its proprietor for part of the time, Wheal Leisure showed a startling increase in profits. The quantity of good ore raised had doubled and with it the money available for distribution. When he came home Ross gave a dinner for the shareholders, at which were the two Tregloses, father and son, who were keenly delighted at the turn of events, and six of the smaller shareholders who held between them twelve of the outside shares. Notably missing was Stephen Carrington, who stood now to benefit materially – by in fact two-fifths of the amount that Jeremy did.

On the same day in the evening Jeremy was in Mechelen, on the road to Brussels, eating broiled kidneys in a farmhouse with four other officers and speculating on the wild rumours that were flying about, that Napoleon was defeated, that he was dead, that he was on his way with a new army to attack Wellington on his flank, that the Russians were on the outskirts of Paris.

The young men drank noisily to the end of the war. Contrary to what Demelza pictured, it was a jolly, comfortable supper, during which they toasted the end of the war so often that only two out of the four remained upright, and all of them had to be helped waveringly to bed.

That night at Gunwalloe the *Lady Clowance* and the *Chasse Marée* discharged their cargoes of contraband, having hovered out of sight of land for a day while two men they had put ashore the previous night made contact with the people Stephen had arranged to meet there. In the weeks before sailing he had done some speculative travelling along the south coast, and at Gunwalloe he had come across a man called Nancarrow who owned a brickyard and had possibly the best distributive centre for contraband goods in West Cornwall.

It had not been a good trip home. Although they had been doing their best to close their eyes to the fact, the two men who had been so ill on the outward journey were suffering from typhus fever, and on the return journey four others had developed it and one had died.

Among the four was Stephen himself. For thirteen days he lay in his berth with terrible pains in his head and limbs and back, and skin so sensitive that he could not bear to have it touched, then becoming delirious with a fit of shivering, and a mulberry coloured rash grew round his mouth and spread across his face and chest.

All the illness was on the *Chasse Marée*; and when it looked as if Stephen might follow the man who had just died, Andrew transferred from the *Lady Clowance* to take charge, leaving Blount in command of the *Lady Clowance*.

The weather turned bad in the Atlantic and they became separated. Only by the sheerest luck were they able to keep to their original plan and rendezvous in the Scillies. With three men sick at one time the *Chasse Marée* was badly undermanned and could have foundered.

By the time they reached St Mary's Stephen was past the crisis. He was like a ghost and could hardly walk, but his appetite, which had not existed for two weeks, was ravenous. They would have stayed there longer, for everyone, particularly in the French ship, was exhausted; but they were afraid of being boarded by the excise men. One official vessel approached them as soon as it was light, but the word typhus was enough to scare it off for the time being. By the following morning they were gone.

So the landing at Gunwalloe. A gusty night but no sea. No moon either. (Stephen had planned to be back a month earlier during the previous lack of moon.) A few remote stars hiding themselves behind racks of cloud scarcely disturbed the shadows. The unloading went without a hitch. Although still very weak, Stephen insisted on superintending it all and in going ashore to see Nancarrow and to arrange the settlement.

He was back just before daylight, when Andrew was anxiously waiting to put out to a safe distance. The *Lady Clowance* had already gone. Stephen grinned, his teeth looking ghastly in his drawn, bearded face.

'All is well. Weigh anchor. If this breeze holds we shall be in Falmouth today.'

II

One of the lieutenants under Major Geoffrey Charles Poldark was a young man called Christopher Havergal, who had a reputation for wildness and eccentricity – a reputation which took some earning in an army where singularities ran high. He had only recently been transferred into the 43rd, and he arrived on a black charger, in a blue frock coat and green silk waistcoat, with two servants, a Portuguese mistress on a donkey and his own silver eating utensils. He was just 21, rich and related to titles, though none was his, nor, he said, ever likely to become his.

Newly in command of a company, Geoffrey Charles's first instinct was to distrust him. He wanted officers who lived happily and high-spiritedly together but he did not want insubordination or stupid pranks. However, he perceived that under his somewhat pretentious mannerisms Havergal had a cool and astute brain and was not afraid to use it. Indeed he was not afraid of anything, either bullets or reprimands. And it seemed as if, working in the back of his mind, was an awareness that the war would soon be over and that he wished to savour every moment of danger while it lasted. If in the process he could in some way distinguish himself, so much the better.

The battle for Toulouse was undertaken by Wellington after the rest of the war had ended. He knew that Paris had surrendered, but not what had happened to the Emperor, and he feared that if he left Soult in possession of Toulouse Napoleon might join him there and, together with Suchet, form a large enough army to counter-attack and perhaps regain his capital. So while the news was spreading throughout England that Napoleon had at last been forced to abdicate and that the Senate had decreed his deposition and the return of the Bourbon king, the Peninsular Army set about one of its most daunting tasks. Protected on three sides by flood water and dominated by a ridge to the east from which Soult outgunned the British by two to one, Toulouse and its defences withstood and repelled three fierce attacks. In the second of these the Monmouthshires were deeply involved, for the two Spanish divisions, having proudly demanded that they should be given a share in the glory of the occasion, as proudly disobeyed orders and attacked too soon, whereupon they suffered a devastating repulse and the British light division was thrown into the battle to plug the gaping hole their retreat left. Geoffrey Charles had his horse killed under him and two bullet scratches that he did not notice until afterwards. Six of his company were killed and sixteen wounded.

It was after the cannonade had finished and while they were re-grouping and awaiting fresh orders that a horseman was seen galloping wildly across the flank of the hill immediately under the enemy guns. It did not take exceptional eyesight to see that he was wearing the uniform of an officer of the 43rd, nor more than a moment or two longer to recognize the long blond hair of Lieutenant Havergal. He was riding at full speed, but twisting and turning and bending in his saddle as if unable to control his movements.

'Poor devil's half mad wi' pain!' a man grunted near Geoffrey Charles.

This wild riding went on for a full two minutes. The French did not fire, assuming him to be in his death throes. And so indeed it seemed; for at last the black horse came to a sudden stop, so sharply that the rider was flung out of the saddle and on to the ground, where he twitched once or twice and then lay still.

Too many had been killed for this to be an exceptional event, and eyes were straying off towards the horse and wondering if he could be safely caught and brought in; when the figure on the ground came sharply to its feet and leapt into the saddle again. Then with his back to the enemy and paying no regard for them at all, he trotted amiably back to his own lines. As he came nearer they saw he was holding a dead hare by its long ears.

'Caught him, by God,' he said as he came up. 'I thought he was going to get away.'

Nothing could be said then, because an order for a resumed barrage and slow advance came through, to coincide with and cover Cole's 4th Division on their left; but in the evening when, after a series of bloody battles the British captured the whole ridge and had Toulouse at their mercy and were settling down to tend their wounded and bury their dead, a message came through from the Commander-in-Chief.

'Major Poldark. You led your men well, but in the middle of a battle it is the French who are our prey. Your officers should not chase the wrong hare.'

As usual, nothing had escaped his eye. Geoffrey Charles sent for Lieutenant Havergal.

'Sir?' He came in casually, with an affected stroll, but straightened up well enough to salute.

'Havergal, your behaviour this afternoon did not please me, nor my superior officers who witnessed it.'

'Have they said so, sir?'

'Yes, they have. *He* has.'

'Oh . . .' He was a grey-eyed, good looking blond young man with something of the narrowness of countenance of

Valentine. In age it might become vulpine, but at present it was in the full glow of youth.

'Sir?'

'Yes?'

'Might I make a suggestion?'

'What is it?'

'With respect, sir.'

'Well, go on.'

'That we send him over some of the soup?'

Geoffrey Charles did not allow any alteration of his own expression. 'On practical grounds I would discourage the idea. The soup would get cold.'

Lieutenant Havergal stifled a little smile.

'Might *I* make a suggestion?' Geoffrey Charles said.

'Sir? But of course.'

'I believe our casualties are about six hundred dead today. And about three thousand wounded. The war is *almost* over. Perhaps this battle need never have been fought. If tomorrow there is more fighting let your heroics be on behalf of some better cause.'

Havergal flushed. 'Sir.'

'Courage, Havergal, comes in a variety of forms, but should not be confused with bravado.'

'No, sir.'

'You understand?'

'Yes, sir.'

'Very well, then.'

As he was turning to leave Geoffrey Charles said: 'Oh, and Lieutenant Havergal.'

'Yes, sir?'

'*I* will have some of the soup.'

III

England was *en fête*. The 'dreadful scourge' of Napoleon 'was at last removed'. No more war – except some trouble 3,000 miles away which did not really count. Church bells rang. Bonfires blazed. Crowds danced in the streets. Twenty years of menace had finally gone. Peace would soon be formally signed. Louis XVIII restored to his Throne, the Prince of Orange, after nearly two generations in exile, established in his new capital of Brussels, the conquering forces of Russia, Prussia and the rest concerned only with the end of all hostilities. Brotherhood would reign.

Cornwall rejoiced with the rest. Truro, Falmouth, St Austell, Penzance, each vied with the other in their jubilations. The weather just after Easter had finally relented, and spring came with a sudden rush, more like some subtropical country than the graduations of England.

Ross gave a celebration dinner out of doors, on the wasteland on which the attle from Wheal Grace had encroached; just above Demelza's garden. The 2 p.m.–10 p.m. and the 10 p.m.–6 a.m. cores were excused attendance at the two mines. Flushed with the success of Wheal Leisure, he ordered no expense to be spared, at least so far as food was concerned. (Nothing stronger than ale lest the party ran into trouble.)

The afternoon was fine with nothing worse than a stiff south-easterly breeze, from which this land was partly sheltered by the rising ground beyond Mellin, and the party – over a hundred and twenty people turned up – was at its height when a young man rode down the valley. He was in semi-naval uniform which had obviously had much hard wear, his hair was bushy under his flat peaked cap and of a reddish tinge. Mostly screened by the hawthorn and the nut trees, which were only just showing traces of green, he had almost reached Nampara, before Ena Daniel on her way back to the feast with jugs in hand, smiled and bobbed at him; and when she had reached the feast told her mistress.

By the time Demelza arrived at the house he had dismounted.

'Andrew!' she said, smiling her pleasure and being kissed on the cheek. 'But that's some lovely! I didn't know you were *home*! Look, we are giving a feast to celebrate the end of the war; why do you not join us? Everyone is here! Everyone, that is, except Jeremy, whom I heard from yesterday and is safe and well, thank God. When did you return?'

'Last Wednesday,' said Andrew. There was an awkwardness in his manner, which Demelza took to be uncertainty on his part as to the reception he would receive, having upset his father and mother so much in October.

'Are you well? You look well. *Thinner*, but some brown!'

'Yes, thank you, aunt, *I* am. I came just to see you and . . .' He trailed off, gazing at the crowd on the common.

'Are you at Flushing? . . . I mean, are you staying with your father and mother?'

'Yes . . .'

'I hope all is well between you again.'

Andrew half smiled. 'My father has not spoken to me yet, but my mother has welcomed me in her usual warm, loving way. I am living at home at the moment, for – a particular reason.'

Demelza glanced at his clothes. 'And – has it been a success, what you went out to do?'

'The shipments of pilchards? Oh, yes. I have made far more money, we have all made money. So far as money is concerned . . .'

He still seemed ill at ease, fumbled a finger round his neckband.

'Then do come and join us. Everyone will be so delighted to see you. Oh, here is –'

Clowance came running across the lawn, sleeves rolled up, hat clinging to the back of her neck by a ribbon.

'Andrew!'

There were the usual kisses and exchange of greetings. Clowance's questions ran on identical lines with those of her mother's, and they half led him across the lawn towards the feast. But then he stopped.

Red-faced he said: 'I have to tell you about Stephen.'

There was a brief silence. 'What is it?' said Clowance.

'Make no mistake,' Andrew said, 'the venture has been a grand success. I can hardly believe it could have been so profitable. But on the way out two of the crew of the *Chasse Marée* were sick with spotted typhus. On the return four others took it. One of them was Stephen. One of them, Cyrus Pagen, died. The others recovered. But soon after we berthed in Penryn Stephen was taken poorly again. I believe he caught a chill being up all night the day before we dropped anchor. He is ill in Penryn now. The apothecary says it is the putrid peripneumonia. I felt I had to tell you.'

Why, said Demelza in her heart, but did not speak.

'*How* ill?' asked Clowance.

'The apothecary does not think he will live. Both lungs are choked, he says. It is a matter of a day or so.'

In the field they were laughing at something. The women were laughing, coarse, hearty, likeable shrieks.

Andrew said: 'Believe me, I didn't know what to do. He keeps asking for Clowance. I was — pulled both ways. I know well enough that you have broken up. It is none of my business to ask why. It is none of my business to try to bring you together again. But when a shipmate of yours, who you've been on terms with for all of five months, seems about to *die* and says all the time, *Clowance, where is Clowance? I want to see her before it is too late . . .* what do you say, what do you do? If I have done wrong, forgive me — both of you . . .'

After a long pause Demelza said: 'Pray come indoors, Andrew. Probably this is not an occasion just at once to — to join our party.'

They went in. In the parlour Demelza poured Verity's son a glass of port. Andrew swore he was not hungry, but when some cake was brought he ate three pieces of it. Clowance had been helping him, but suddenly she disappeared.

Demelza and Andrew talked. Stephen, it seemed, had taken a room in Penryn. In the first few days ashore he had been busy with his two vessels, arranging for their anchorage, for tackle and trim to be made good, for future contracts to be considered, for paying off the crew and giving them their agreed share of the profit. Andrew had gone home, had received the sort of welcome he anticipated but had decided to stick it out for his mother's sake and because, when he let it be known he would be able to pay off all his debts, he believed his father would come round. He had called to see Stephen — what was today? Wednesday — he had called to see Stephen on Sunday evening and found him lying in his bed with what he called a feverish chill. But it was clearly more than that. On the Monday, when Andrew insisted on calling the local apothecary, the man had said that both lungs were inflamed and that it would be touch and go whether Stephen pulled through. Since then he had been losing ground all the time. This morning . . .

After a couple more minutes Demelza excused herself and went upstairs, found Clowance in her room, sitting on the bed, a valise, half full at her feet. She looked at her mother with full eyes, then blinked out at the bright day.

Demelza said: 'Can I help you pack?'

Clowance choked. 'Oh, Mama, you are so *kind*! I thought you might . . . What else can I *do*?'

'What else can you do?' said Demelza with a degree of bitterness in her heart but none in her voice.

'You see . . . I still care something for him.'

'I know.'

'But even if I did not . . . If he is dying . . .'

'Andrew will go back with you. He must, of course. Shall I get someone to saddle Nero?'

'Thank you, Mama.' As she reached the door. 'Please, don't go for a moment.'

Demelza waited.

'I shall not come back tonight. Or perhaps tomorrow unless he – unless he . . . I shall stay with Aunt Verity.'

'Of course.'

'Will you tell Papa, please? *Explain*. Tell him how it is. And tell him I couldn't *bear* to come out among all those people and try to explain to him! I wouldn't want him to feel I had gone without his permission.'

'Yes, I'll tell him.'

'Do you think he will mind?'

'I think we both mind.'

'But if Stephen is so ill . . . if he is dying . . . perhaps I shall not get there in time . . .'

'We can only hope . . .'

'And Mama.'

'Yes?'

'Do you think there would be any way – any way at all –

of Uncle Dwight travelling as far as Penryn? I know it is a lot to ask . . .'

'I will go and see him myself this evening.'

Tears were now streaming down Clowance's face. She wiped them away impatiently.

'I am such a *fool*. But this has come so sudden. Like a stab in the back. *Thank* you. Thank you again for being so good about it . . . I wish I were as strong as you.'

'I'm older,' said Demelza. 'But as for being stronger . . . I'm not so sure.'

IV

'So you let her go,' said Ross. 'Without telling me.'

'She asked me not to. She was afraid of what you'd say.'

'No wonder.'

'And do you think if I had refused her permission to go she would have heeded me?'

'Yes!'

'And if he dies tomorrow?'

They were standing in the dark amid the ruins of the feast while their servants and willing helpers from the villages were clearing up by the light of storm lanterns and a quarter moon striped with cloud.

Though neither of them had mentioned it and under no circumstances would ever have considered mentioning it, their thoughts had individually slid away to an occasion when a young naval lieutenant had lain dying of some brain fever at Tregothnan eighteen odd years ago. His passion for Demelza had kindled some corresponding spark of sympathy and love in her which briefly she had been unable to withstand. She had not been at his side when he died; Ross wondered, had her sympathy for Clowance been the greater for her own memory of that time?

At least the two young men could hardly have been more different, and most of the advantages of comparison lay on Hugh Armitage's side; Ross had to admit this – and could admit it to himself more freely now with the passage of the years. In fact he would much have preferred the competition of someone like Carrington – in the very unlikely event of Demelza's ever falling in love with anyone so bold and obvious as Stephen. Armitage had been artistic, well-educated, intellectual, thoughtful, sensitive; infinitely difficult qualities to compete with. And he had died before there was any resolution of the test.

Ross's hand on his wife's shoulder was heavier than usual, and she glanced up at him quietly, trying to see his expression.

'What would you have done?'

Ross sighed. 'Damned Andrew.'

'For coming to tell us?'

'Yes, if viewed in a cold-blooded fashion. If Stephen dies tomorrow Clowance would have known nothing about it till too late. If he recovers, she is thrown into his lap again.'

'She has never been free of him,' Demelza said. 'Especially these last few months. Since she refused Tom. I believe Tom forced her to face up to something she hadn't faced before.'

There was an uneasy pause. As if their minds worked in accord, each was now thinking of another occasion still further back, when Francis Poldark and Geoffrey Charles had lain dangerously ill of the morbid sore throat, and Demelza had gone over to help Elizabeth and had caught the infection herself.

Eventually Ross said: 'Do you think Dwight will go to Penryn?'

'I said I would see Dwight and ask him myself; but it was impossible with Henry so teasy. I wrote him a long letter – long for me! – telling him all about it; sent it with Music Thomas who said he would take it on his way home.'

Ross put his arm round Demelza. 'Life is like a gaming table, isn't it. One has so many pieces on the board. With them one gains a little, loses a little.'

'We are still gaining,' said Demelza. 'With peace Jeremy is safe – or as safe as is reasonable. With Wheal Leisure we are almost rich again. But I'm sorry, sorry, sorry for Clowance. My heart aches for her. And because of her. And I am anxious . . .'

Chapter Three

I

Dwight found the cottage at the third attempt. Like its
upstart relative Falmouth, Penryn climbed the hill beside its
river, steps and cottages reproducing themselves up and
down steep slopes, with narrow lanes and passages bisect-
ing the slopes laterally to allow of the carriage of produce
and to make room for short lines of washing between the
first and second floors.

Stephen had found a landlady at the end of a row. It was a
not unpleasant room except that the roof enabled one to
stand upright only in the centre space. Low windows, hung
with threadbare curtains of faded pink cotton, and longer
laterally than they were high, looked out both ways, down
towards the tidal river and up towards the rampant woods
that surrounded the turn-pike road to Truro. The entrance
to the house was dingy, with an open drain trickling over
cobbles towards a ditch, and tattered, half-naked children
with scabrous lips and running nasal mucus playing on the
door step. Upstairs was moderately clean, if the air could
and should have been fresher.

Stephen was lying on a sort of truckle-bed – except that
the castors had long since broken off. He was conscious,
very flushed, breathing fast. Clowance was on a low chair
beside him, still in the frock she had been wearing at the
celebration, her blonde hair caught in a trim blue ribbon.
She looked very pale, and suddenly much older.

'Oh, Uncle Dwight, how good of you to come!' She got
up, kissed him on the cheek.

'Good day to you, Stephen,' Dwight said, having
squeezed Clowance's hand.

'Good – ur . . .' His voice was choked by a cough, and a
grimace of pain narrowed his eyebrows.

They exchanged glances over him. Clowance said: 'Mr Wheeling was here this morning. He says there is no change and nothing more he can do.'

Dwight took his time examining the sick man. Then he went through the remedies Mr Wheeling had left, raising his eyebrows at one or two of them.

'Who is looking after him?'

'I am,' said Clowance.

'But before you came?'

'Andrew did his best. And Mrs Nye, the landlady, came up when she could.'

'You cannot do it all yourself. Did you have any sleep last night?'

'Andrew is coming in tonight. And Aunt Verity will take a turn when she can.'

'How often is he bled?'

'Every time Mr Wheeling calls. Which is three times a day.'

'Well, that must only be once a day – if you accept my decision on these matters.'

'Of course.'

'It is difficult for me to come and issue these commands and then go away again. But clearly I cannot stay for long, with my own patients to see to . . .' Dwight picked up another bottle and stared at it. 'Tincture of mercury . . . Yes, well. Where does Mr Wheeling live? Perhaps I could see him . . .'

'Tell me what to do,' said Clowance, 'and I'll tell him.'

Dwight smiled at her. 'I believe you will . . . But, my dear, please don't think I have any miracle I can perform . . . How often does he expectorate?'

'Scarcely at all.'

The smile faded. 'But when he coughs?'

'No. Nothing comes up.'

'And what did Mr Wheeling leave him for that?'

'I have to give him this twice a day.'

Dwight took the bottle. 'I think I can improve on that. Clowance, it is vital he shall spit freely, otherwise the congestion will not clear away. It is of the essence of the disease . . . Stephen . . .'

'Yes?'

'When you cough, why do you not spit?'

He lay there as if he had been running a race. 'Don't know. Nothing comes.'

Dwight rubbed his chin. 'Can you try. Now.'

Stephen tried. After a bout of horrible coughing his head went back on the pillow. Clowance dabbed gently at his face and forehead with a cloth.

Dwight sat on the bed. 'Can you hear me, Stephen?'

'Yes.'

'I am going to change some of your medicines. Little bleeding. But something to agitate the cough. And a tea-spoonful of brandy every four hours.'

A tired grin came to his face. 'Like that.'

'But no more. Only that much. Stephen, I expect you know that we doctors can only lend a little outside aid. *You* are the one who is attacked. *You* must fight. D'you understand that?'

'Yes.'

'And *spit*. Force yourself if you possibly can – even if it hurts – however much it hurts – spit out the sputum. For that is the disease you are spitting away from yourself. No help I can give, no help Clowance can give, is half as important as that. D'you understand?'

'Yes. And thank ee.'

In the claustrophobic passage outside, where even Clowance had to bend her head, Dwight said:

'I won't pretend to you that it is a good prognosis. Both lungs are affected, the right more than the left, and the lower part in each case more than the upper. There is scarcely any air getting into the affected lung tissue. I suspect that a certain amount of red hepatization has already taken place. But he is essentially a very strong man. Not that I . . .' He stopped. He had been going to say that a peculiarity of pneumonia was that it often killed the strong and spared the weak. 'Every day that passes is a day in his favour. If he can reach the crisis he may yet pull through. It is perfectly true what I told him in there: *he* is fighting this disease. We are the spectators. One other thing.'

'Yes.'

'Get one of the windows to open if you can. Not to let the air fall directly on him but to keep it stirred in the room. Let's see, you have a fireplace; a small coal fire will help to clean the air, though do not get the room too warm. Keep a kettle boiling. And change that poultice on his chest. It smells as if Wheeling has used tincture of cantharides last time; but I think enough is enough. Anyway the value of blistering is doubtful. Something to soothe now. Goose grease on brown paper, with the singlet over to keep in the warmth.'

'I am so grateful that you came.'

'I will come tomorrow evening if . . .' Again he stopped what he was going to say. '. . . if I can. How long did Andrew say he had been ill?'

'Like this? About four days.'

'Yes, well, the disease should be nearing the crisis. How long is it since he had typhus?'

'Andrew said he had been better a week before this came on.'

'Well . . . avoid his breath. Try to keep the sputum, if it comes, out of contact with other things, and have it emptied quickly away. Our knowledge of these fevers is rudimentary even today, but these are elementary precautions. When is Andrew coming to relieve you?'

'About two he said.'

'And how far is your aunt's house from here?'

'Oh . . . three and a half, four miles.'

'You must get food and sleep, you know.'

She smiled. 'I dozed off last night in the chair. I think he wants me near him.'

II

Most of the second night she was there he was light-headed, rambling. The guttering candle threw monstrous shadows of his head against the unrendered bricks of the bedroom wall, as if the ugly silhouettes as he tossed and turned were reflections of the nightmares going on in his mind. In the end Clowance moved the candle to kill the images and then, having given him his sip of brandy, fell into a doze herself.

When she woke he was struggling to get out of bed. She put her arm about his shoulders to restrain him. He didn't know her and began to talk about some box he wanted to open, for which he had no key. He was using a lever and attempting to force the lock of the box, but the lever kept slipping in his hands. She tried again to wake him and he half woke, stared at her with glazed eyes and called her Jeremy. 'It's no good, Jeremy,' he kept saying. 'Got to leave it, get away, else they'll catch us. Red-handed, eh? Holy Mary, let me try again! Jeremy, let me try again!'

It was as much as she could do to stop him rolling out of the bed, for he was a heavy man, and his shirt and arms were slippery with sweat. Then he began to gasp, taking in each breath as if it were his last, drawn up like deep water from some drying well. She took a damp sponge and wiped his face and forehead with it, but this gave him no ease. Though only two hours had passed since the last dose she poured out another spoonful of brandy and tried to get him to swallow it, but what with her trembling hands and his wavering head most of it ran down his chin.

It was the darkest part of the night, when there seemed no end to her striving and no end to his distress except death. She poked at the sulky fire but it seemed as lifeless as her thoughts and hopes.

He was rambling on again now. Once he brought up Violet's name; twice he mentioned Lottie – presumably Lottie Kempthorne; then he began to talk to Clowance, though as if she were not there, his blue eyes bloodshot and glazed. He told her he had to confess, he had never been a privateer. He began to persuade her to go away with him on some sort of a stage coach which was – to his horror – already approaching Liskeard. She held him down as he again tried to climb out of bed.

Then, whereas before he had been as hot as fire, he began

to shiver, so that she had to keep the blanket close up to his chin. Again and again she wiped his face, until the towel she was now using was wet through. In and out went the lungs, like a mining engine fighting against loss of fuel. The hands grasped at the air, found hers, but as soon as they had found them released them, groping for something more. Groping in fact, she thought, for life; and that was escaping him.

For another hour this went on, and she scarcely had time to light one candle from the guttering end of another to keep away the dreadful and intolerable blackness that would follow. Then he was sick, a sort of black vomit emerging from a corner of his mouth, which she tried to wipe away as it came.

Thereafter the breathing was a little easier and he seemed to have reached the limits of exhaustion, which led either to sleep or to coma. Exhausted herself, she released her hold of him and lay back in her chair, slowly dozing off to sleep . . .

She woke with a start to see a faint smear of light showing through the splits in the stirring curtains. She stared at him anxiously. Either his breathing was quieter or it was not there at all. She jumped up and pulled aside the curtains, glimpsed the creeping greys of dawn, turned back into the tallow yellows of the sick and heavy room.

He was *watching* her.

'Clowance . . .' He tried to moisten his lips.

She came to the bedside, trembling, questioning, staring for signs of good or ill.

'You've . . . been here all night?' he whispered.

'Of course.'

'Dreams . . . nightmares . . .'

'Yes.'

'I dreamt . . . Holy Mary . . . dreams.'

'Do you feel – how do you feel?'

'I've – I don't know.'

She wiped his forehead for the fiftieth time; it was wetter than ever, his mane of tawny hair was as lifeless and bedraggled as if it had been out in a storm. But wasn't the sweat cooler?

He said: 'You stayed. This . . . the second night you stayed.'

'Don't talk now.'

She tried to make the greasy poultice easier on his chest; and then they were quiet together. As the dark room lightened with the reluctant day he stirred again.

'You came – to look after me.'

'Rest now.'

'Want to talk – a little. Sit here.'

She sat on the chair. His hand came wandering out and she took it.

'Clowance. Don't know how this will end.' He made an effort. 'Still can't spit, ye see.'

'Never mind.'

'Can't say all I want to say yet – mebbe never. But – I love you. Ye know that, don't you.'

'Yes.'

'You coming like this – does it mean you care a little?'

'I care a little.'

His hand tightened on hers. 'You don't know how much that means . . .' The hand was definitely cooler.

'Can you sleep again now?'

'Eighteen months I been – like a man bereft. Didn't know – couldn't believe that you . . .'

'Don't go into it now.'

He was still just as much out of breath. 'That sort of thing. Losing you like that. It makes a man humble.'

'Don't say that. That was not what I wanted.'

'I know. I know. But it does . . . Makes ye do strange things . . . Did Andrew go for you?'

'He came over and told me. Otherwise I should not have known.'

'God bless him. And you for coming.'

The daylight crept in like a thief, picking out the other chair, the home-made wardrobe, the tumbled bed, the soiled linen, the foul bucket and the pitcher and the bottles of medicine, last almost it seemed the colours of her face and hair. Pink was in the sky now, staining the hillside above the trees.

He said: 'If I die . . . if I live . . . I'll be happier either way knowing that you care a little.'

He fell into a deep sleep that Clowance was afraid was too much like unconsciousness.

At eight Andrew came and wanted her to leave but she would not. She dozed uncomfortably in the other chair while he brought fresh coal and re-lit the fire, carried out the bucket and the other soiled stuff, made her a cup of tea. She sipped it and they stared together at the man on the bed.

'It is time for his brandy,' said Andrew.

'Let him sleep. I – I think he is sleeping.'

Dwight Enys turned up at eleven, in spite of his having said he would not be able to come until the evening. By then Stephen was just stirring again and beginning to cough.

Dwight felt his pulse, his forehead, looking at his tongue, not very much more.

'This crisis is past,' he said. 'The fever has gone. Now it remains to be seen . . . But with reasonable care. Care such as he has had these last two days . . .' He smiled at Clowance. 'With reasonable care he should recover.'

III

Clowance stayed nearly two weeks, having sent Andrew with a long letter to her parents on the third day, and thereafter writing them regularly by the common post.

After the intense fever Stephen was still a very sick man, still plagued with a racking cough and pains in both lungs. Andrew took the third night, and Stephen would not allow Clowance to return on the fourth. Thereafter she spent each day with him, sleeping at Verity's, and as he recovered taking a little more time off to buy delicacies for him to eat and books and magazines for him to read.

It was a fine month, and the retarded spring was all the more lush for having been kept waiting. There came a day when, walking with a stick, and gingerly like an old man, Stephen took a turn about the town. That really marked the end of his invalidism, though it was four days after that before he risked himself on a horse. It was, he explained apologetically to Clowance, the two fevers, one atop the other, that had brought him so low. Clowance needed no apology; she was only happy to see the life returning to his step.

By the time it came time for her to leave, much had been said between them, much explained. Yet much remained to be said. In all their conversation they had never really got round to the subject of their final quarrel, the cause of their parting. For himself he could still scarcely understand it, for her part she could scarcely explain it. By a common instinct to preserve their new-found accord they sheered away from the danger spot, content that at least for the moment it could be ignored.

A little late in being aware of the proprieties, she now tried each day to leave his lodgings before dark.

He said: 'M' love, I'm not much of a fatalist. I believe on the whole a man makes his own fate, don't wait for it to come to him. But I've had three great strokes of fortune in me life so far, and they were all nothing to do with me as an active party. First was when I was a starving urchin run-away of eight and I happened upon the Elwyn's farm, who were a childless couple and Mrs Elwyn just needing me in place of a son. Second was when I was drifting with a dead man on that raft and Jeremy picked me up. Third was when I was near dead with the peripneumonia and you heard and rode over and spent two nights and three days without break nursing me through it. For I should *never* have recovered wi'out your nursing, you can be sure of that!'

'Oh, I don't know –'

'Oh, I *do* know. So three times my life has been preserved and two out of the three times it has been a Poldark that has done it. D'you not think there is some fate in that?'

'Perhaps.'

He was sitting down so she kissed his forehead, now healthily dry with the hair upgrowing again. He quickly put his arms around her knees, half pinioning her.

He said: 'What will they say when you tell them?'

'I've no idea.'

'Do you care?'

'Very much.'

'Yes.' He sighed. 'That's what I have to get used to.'

'What?'

'That you owe them a love and affection that don't belong to me, that I'm no part of. I think that's mebbe what I *shall* get used to now.'

'I hope so.'

'D'ye know,' he said. 'To tell the sober honest truth, I'm a bit of an egotist. Except for those two times being rescued before this, I've always relied on meself and, most times, not been disappointed. So it's led to me being reliant on meself and confident of what I am and what I think and what I stand for. You've taught me a lesson in that.'

'Believe me, Stephen, that wasn't what I wanted or intended —'

'Well, that's what you got. And if I'm self-sure about anything now, it is that I can learn from experience. Experience has taught me never to take anything about *you* for granted, f' instance. And I promise you I never shall.'

'Not even my legs?' she said.

He released her instantly, and gave a little gurgle of laughter, which ended in a cough. 'Oh, Clowance, we'll make a good pair, I swear it! Promise you will always be like this — loving, *warm*; but always, always one on your own, *quick* as me or quicker, and ready to hit back if I take liberties!'

'I'll do my best.'

'I'm sure you will. My dear . . .' He cleared his throat and waited for his breath. 'Don't come back again. Send me a letter — quite short — just saying what they say and telling me when I can come to Nampara — or *if* I can come. Take a week. There's no hurry now. I've business to do with my two vessels — d'ye realize I'm a ship-owner!'

'You've said so before.'

'This week I shall take it easy — just going down for a few hours a day — and eating . . . and, when I can, sitting in the sun. Andrew's been a real help to me, on this voyage and while I been ill. I hope he'll stay along with me as me second-in-command. Then by the time your summons comes I'll be total fit and well again and ready to ride over and face the music.'

'It's I who will have to face the music first.'

'I know. But surely by now they will have guessed.'

'I think Mama did before I left. It is my father I am in doubt of.' She tied a scarf about her head. 'But not so *much* in doubt of. All his life he has been far too indulgent to me.'

'I don't blame him. What time will you leave in the morning?'

'About eight.'

He took her hand. 'There are some things I reckon I still ought to say to you, me darling. But twill not be easy.'

'Then don't try. If we quarrelled –'

'No, tis not altogether that. There's things still not quite straight between us, you and me. If I'm to marry you, as I hope and pray, I'd wish you to come to me knowing all me faults, all the things I've done in life that don't lie altogether easy on the conscience.'

'While you were delirious you were anxious to tell me that you had never been a privateer.'

He sighed. 'Quite true. I never have. Else I should not 've been so scared of the press-gang when I was at sea, as I once told you. Crews of privateers don't often get pressed – should not at all! I went – adventuring with Captain Fraser, Budi Halim, Stevenson, and one other, Hawker, but we did not have letters of marque. Twas a sordid expedition, I can tell you, to seize what we could find; but all the rest was true – we were cornered by a French sloop, shipwrecked, sunk. From there on, until Jeremy and the others picked me up, twas all true . . .'

'And should I be shocked by that?'

'Nay, there are worse things about me, Clowance, as you may guess. God knows whether I shall gather the courage to tell you it all before we marry. I *should*. But I couldn't bear to lose you again.'

'You're not married to someone else, are you?'

'Holy Mary, *no*! What made you say that?'

'That's the only reason I can think of why I shouldn't marry you.'

He kissed her hand.

'Ride safe and ride careful. I'll come for you soon.'

IV

Clowance said: 'You must think me an impossible daughter.'

'Not impossible,' said Ross; 'people have been known to change their minds. But I am concerned to learn the reasons.'

It had been a frustrating day. She had got home about twelve to find her father gone to Truro for a bank meeting and not expected back till dark. Instead of being able to explain to them both together, so that both had the same information at the same time – and she was not appearing to persuade one in the other's absence – she had sat down to a noisy dinner at which Isabella-Rose was particularly exasperating by wanting to know all about Clowance's two weeks away, being relentless in her questions and refusing even to accept her mother's veto on the subject; while young Henry, newly promoted to a baby chair at the table, syncopated the meal by beating on his table top with a spoon. Eventually about four Clowance had disentangled her mother from the claims of the household and had walked her on the beach for an hour, pouring out her heart.

Now, belatedly, she had to do the same all over again while her father ate his supper. (She had said she would prefer to wait until he finished but he said, no, he'd like to hear at once.) And speaking to her father with her mother listening was, she found, quite different, in spite of all her effort not to let it be so. It seemed to centre on the practical rather than the emotional, even though the latter at the final resort must be the one that counted most.

'Stephen now owns these two boats and has made money out of the one voyage to Italy and back. He says that, though the outward trip was perfectly legal, he took a deliberate risk bringing home wine and silks. These have all been safely landed – were landed before he was taken ill a second time – and he has been paid for most of them. He says that now the war is over he knows he can never make this sort of money again, so he intends to use the vessels for coastal trading and at pilchard time to take the fish wherever they are most wanted; it might be Italy again; but if so he will probably not go himself. He says that with the end of the war there must be an enormous expansion of trade with Europe, and he is hoping to buy a third vessel to take advantage of this situation.'

Ross thought: these are his words; I can hear him saying them.

'And the smuggling?'

'He wants to avoid it if he can. He says that with the end of the war – except the war in America – there will be many more resources available in England to put smuggling down. He believes there is plenty of money to be made out of legitimate trade.'

Ross waved Demelza to stay where she was and took another piece of pigeon pie.

'And where does he intend to operate this business?'

'Penryn. It has good facilities for small trading vessels. He also thinks we should live in Penryn, where he can be near all the furnishings of his trade. The Gatehouse . . . would be too far away.'

Ross nodded and ate quietly, reflectively.

'I should be near Aunt Verity,' Clowance said quickly.

'Yes . . . yes. Bear with me if I go back a little, Clowance. Perhaps you have already explained it to your mother . . . But you parted from Stephen eighteen months ago after a – a quarrel, a difference between you that seemed to be final. Do you suppose it is likely to occur again? – for once you are married it is much harder to separate, indeed you are bound irrevocably together. You may separate physically but neither of you may marry anyone else.'

Clowance glanced from one parent to the other. 'I think we have both learned from that. What I have learned is that there is nobody who can take his place.'

'And what has *he* learned?'

She hesitated. 'I think a good deal. So he says. And he has spoken in a way that has made me entirely believe him. I think . . .'

'Yes?'

'I think, whatever else, that he loves me. He's not a saint. He has never pretended to be. We quarrelled and separated, and I thought I was right. Now I know I was wrong.'

'You mean you were *in* the wrong?'

'No, no, no. We have not – to be truthful we've not gone back over it word for word; but I think he believes *he* was in the wrong. Where *I* was wrong was in supposing that such a quarrel was a sufficient reason for parting. If you – love someone – it doesn't happen – that way.'

'And you are sure you love him that way now?'

'Yes, Papa. Quite sure.'

'Then there is nothing more to be said.'

Silence fell again. Demelza rose and poured out some wine for him, a glass of port for herself. Clowance had already shaken her head.

'And what part has Andrew played in all this?' Ross asked.

'He and Stephen have grown to a firm friendship. He has done well out of the voyage and is now Stephen's junior partner. He came to tell me about Stephen, as you know. He had been nursing Stephen himself . . . He is living at home, is reconciled with Aunt Verity . . . He has exchanged a few words with his father, but Uncle Andrew finds it hard to forgive him for abandoning his position in the Packet Service.'

'Well, it's understandable,' Ross said. 'Andrew Blamey made his life in the Packet Service, and he expected his son to do the same. I hope this new venture works.'

'So do I,' said Clowance. 'Oh, one thing I should say. Stephen is trying to persuade Andrew to drink less. He says he is no use to him unless he can hold his drink. That at least should please Uncle Andrew.'

Ross glanced at his wife. 'And does Stephen believe he can support you?'

'Oh, yes. This last week, when he was feeling so much better, we looked at one or two places in Penryn. There is a half house to let just outside the town; quite small and it looks towards the river. The rent is not high. We should have to furnish it, of course. But apart from the capital Stephen now has – and a good chance of a reasonable income from his trading vessels – there are his shares in Wheal Leisure, which at present are bringing in an extra income.'

'And have you talked it over with him or with your mother, when you think of getting married?'

'We thought the middle of next month, Papa. But that would depend entirely on your approval.'

'Entirely?' Ross said with a little smile.

'Well . . . yes. Or almost entirely. I desperately want – we both want – your approval. And we couldn't marry if you were in Westminster.'

'I doubt if you will encounter any obstacle in the latter,' said Ross. 'Europe is going mad with joy, and so is London, and I better prefer to sit at home and read about it in comfort.'

'And the former?'

He looked at her for a long moment. 'You tell us you're sure. You told us that two years ago. Do you remember?'

She flushed. 'Yes, I remember.'

'But you're more sure now?'

'I'm more sure now. I have learned a lot about myself since then.'

'And about him?'

'No. Not much more about him. But I have learned to *accept* him, the way he is, not the way I presumed he ought to be. Whether I shall be happy all the time I am married I don't know. But I know I don't want to face my life unmarried to him.' She got up and put her hand on her father's arm. 'I am sorry to give you so much worry, Papa. I am indeed sorry if I disappoint you. But please will you give us your approval?'

He put his hand over hers. 'Have we ever denied you anything that you set your heart on?'

V

On the beach Clowance had said: 'There is all the difference, isn't there, between friendship and love. I am sure you must know far more about all this than I do, Mama . . . But – but friendship is almost a matter of choice, isn't it. The other person is nice to you and you like him and you find you have the same tastes in common and you welcome his companionship and you become attached. It is half in the mind – perhaps more than half. It is *reasonable*, always subject to reason. Almost everything about a friendship you can explain . . . That I can find with Tom Guildford. Perhaps even could have with Lord Edward Fitzmaurice . . .' She stopped and pushed back her hair. 'Love is different. *Is* it not? Love is something that grows in your heart and in your stomach – and lower down – and it is lucky if you find you even have *tastes* in common with the person, for it makes no manner of difference. If you love, then you're in deep water, struggling. Perhaps you don't even struggle – you just go under, *drown*. You and Papa were wise in insisting that we should wait till the October to marry, for that gave me time to see things in Stephen I didn't like; and in the end I came to the surface and drew back from where I was going. My mind, my loyalties, my judgements, all told me to draw back and I obeyed them.' She paused for a long time. 'And then,' she added in a small voice, 'I found it was no good.'

'I see,' said Demelza.

'I believe you have had one or two bitter quarrels with Papa in your earlier life. Did they stop you loving him?'

'No,' said Demelza, then corrected herself. 'Once or twice, yes. For a while. Once at least I hated him.'

'That's easier, isn't it. Love and hate – they aren't that far apart. I don't know if I ever hated Stephen, or even thought I did. It was more a terrible indignation! But *nothing*'s any good, is it, to break the – the tie.'

'Sometimes it happens,' said Demelza. 'It depends.'

'I don't think I shall ever be as much in harmony with Stephen as you are with Papa. There will be more quarrels;

but the fact that we have already had one – and a bitter one at that – shows that they don't alter the inner feeling. We've both learned from it. I sincerely believe that.'

They walked on a way in silence. Then Clowance said:

'It *is* a terrible thing, isn't it.'

'What? Love?'

'Of this sort, yes. Other loves, other loyalties don't count . . . I'm sorry, I didn't mean that. You know what I mean.'

'I believe so. Yes, for sure.'

'One man's voice . . . one man's eyes . . . one man's lips . . . why are they like electric charges when you hear them, see them, feel them? And another man, perhaps just as good looking, perhaps far more worthy . . . his don't connect, cause any current at all! Is there only one such person born into the world to satisfy and electrify one other person? Or are there a number such, floating about like particles of dust in the sunshine and it is all a matter of luck – good or ill – which you meet?'

'That's nearer the truth, I suspect,' said Demelza. 'Yet if you believe the Bible, no one man – or woman – is just like another. Each one of us is unique. So one grain of dust is not just like another. There may be five – or fifty – which will create the spark in you – the electric spark – but twould not be quite the same spark in each case, never altogether the same. Yet . . .'

'Yet?'

'You may go through life only seeing and feeling that electric charge in one man. Or at the most two.'

'Have you felt it in two?'

'I have felt it in two.'

Clowance took her mother's arm companionably. She knew better than to ask more.

'Well, it *is* a terrible thing,' she said again, as if by repeating it she took some of the wildness of it away, domesticated it. 'That women – and men – should be so helpless to guide their own fate! A chance meeting, and that is it! I feel so sorry for Jeremy and Cuby Trevanion. I do not believe her to be the sweetest of young women. But with him it has happened too . . . Perhaps he will find one of his other – his other sparks of electricity in Holland or in France! Like Geoffrey Charles and his little prickly rose.'

'I am so *relieved* the war is over – the main war, I mean.'

'Yes . . . yes. I would dearly love for Jeremy to be here for my wedding. I'll write him as soon as Papa has given his consent to the date. Surely in time of peace there is not much for young officers to do! I shall ask him to apply for leave.'

Chapter Four

I

On the first of April the Allies entered Paris, led by the Tsar, the King of Prussia, and Prince Schwarzenberg of Austria representing his Emperor. Paris, preferring not to suffer like Moscow, had put up a frail resistance. On the eleventh Napoleon abdicated. On the thirteenth he took poison, which did not work. On the fifth of May he entered into possession of his new estate as Emperor and Sovereign of the Isle of Elba, with an annual allowance of a million francs. On his voyage out he designed a new flag for himself and his new possession. He told the sorrowing French that he would return next spring when the violets were in bloom. Lord Byron wrote a poem of grief that the great man had fallen.

At the end of April Viscount Wellington, imminently to become a Duke, but dressed in a plain blue frock coat, white neck-cloth and black top hat, flanked by General Stewart and Lord Castlereagh, made his own triumphant entry into Paris riding a white charger and watched with intense curiosity by the great crowds that lined the route. He had just been offered and had accepted the post of Ambassador to France.

On the 5th May Louis XVIII, swollen with gout and self indulgence, peaceful minded, polite and pathetic, followed, to take his seat on a throne which must have still felt warm from the boiling vitality of his predecessor.

Plans were well ahead for the ruling sovereigns of the alliance to visit England, that country which, through all the bitter disappointments and defeats of two generations, had alone maintained its independence and its resolution. There were to be the greatest of festivities in London and throughout the land. In the meantime Major Geoffrey Charles

Poldark remained at Montech, north of Toulouse, living in abundance and being treated by the French with gay hospitality. Ensign Jeremy Poldark on the 9th May moved with his company into quarters in Brussels, away at last from the bitter frosts of the winter and welcomed by food and wine and girls. It was the biggest city he had ever lived in. But the poverty in parts was ghastly and the army discipline sickened him. He heard with fascination that the London *Times* was shortly to be printed by steam power, and that a north country man called Stephenson was putting Trevithick's designs into practice and had introduced a colliery railway at Darlington whose steam engine pulled coal wagons as far as Stockton and back. There was also an exciting new engine at Wheal Abraham in Cornwall that he wanted to hear about. Jeremy had written twice to Goldsworthy Gurney, but so far had received no reply.

On the 15th May Major Geoffrey Charles Poldark received a letter from his wife telling him she was happy to say she was with child and that she expected their baby to be born in early or mid December. By the same post he heard from Clowance that she was to marry Stephen Carrington at St Sawle Church, Sawle-with-Grambler, on the last Saturday in May at noon.

All May was a beautiful month. There was a chill in the air if you stood about long in the shade; but the sun rose a little earlier each day to warm the winds and bring out the flowers. The gorse was aflame and almost hurt the eye. Wildflowers in the hedges seemed to bloom as never before. Everything appeared to be contributing to a mood of general rejoicing.

At first Clowance had said she could not wear the same wedding dress; it would be bad luck; but Stephen said he wanted it. There must be nothing different about the wedding, nothing different at all; the last eighteen months had just been a terrible mistake, a black chasm in the thoughts which should henceforward be ignored. It was all beginning again, just as it ought to have happened in October 1812. He said to Demelza: 'Arrange it as you please, Mrs Poldark. Lots of guests if Clowance wants 'em – or none at all if she don't. There be only one important thing to me – as there should have been before – so do whatever she wishes.'

An awkward meeting, Stephen's first visit to Nampara since his quarrel. In fact there had never been any quarrel or even hard words between Stephen and Ross or Stephen and Demelza; so there was nothing to forget, nothing to overlook, nothing to ignore. What stood between them was the knowledge that they wished she had made a better match – or at least a securer one. He fell short of their hopes for their future son-in-law by being vaguely unreliable, rash in his decisions, unpredictable, with an exaggerated masculinity, a too easy way of talking. And the gap of eighteen months, because of the way it had happened and what had happened in it, had hardened that feeling instead of alleviating it.

Demelza thought he looked a lot older, but this might have been the effects of his illnesses. Some of the arrogance had gone out of him – temporarily or permanently one did not know. He looked more responsible. He told Ross of his plans to develop the coastal trade, to buy or have built another – a third – vessel. (It was a good mark, Ross thought, that he did not mention having one of them built in their yard in Looe: he sought to make a good impression, not to curry favour.) He was frank about the profit he had made and aware that he was unlikely to repeat it. Nevertheless he had now made a beginning, a firmly based beginning which if followed up intelligently would soon make him a ship owner of some consequence. He thought eventually to offer Andrew Blamey a share of the business. (Always provided he could learn to hold his drink.) Although, he said, he would regret the quarrel with Clowance to his dying day, he did feel that he was now in a much better position financially to marry her. He could offer her a home, small but good enough for a beginning; he would himself limit his trips at sea so that she should not be too much on her own. In any case they were near the Blameys, and after all only about four hours from Nampara. He very much hoped that, even though he might not be a perfect match for Clowance in their eyes, that they would give him a full and fair chance to prove himself and not hold back during these weeks and so diminish Clowance's happiness. He knew now how much she wanted them to be wholehearted in their love and good wishes at the wedding, something he had not understood before. He really understood it now. Could he rely on them?

It was hard to seem grudging after that.

The wedding day was one of the finest of the month, though by a change to a warmer breeze it presaged a change in the weather. They had invited the three Blameys, four Enyses, six Trenegloses, four Kellows, Mrs Selina Pope and her two step-daughters, three Bodrugans, three Teagues, and a round dozen others. Filling the church were the Martins (Zacky looking much better), the Daniels, the Nanfans, the Carters (needless to say, not Ben), Prudie Paynter (but not Jud, who said he was some slight, and who was to deny him the privilege of being ill at his age?), the Scobles, the Curnows, and many others, so that the congregation overflowed into the churchyard and out to the gates beyond.

Demelza had asked Clowance about invitations to such people as the Falmouths and the de Dunstanvilles and the Devorans, but she had said no. Mainly they were Papa's friends and it was not necessary to invite them to a quiet family wedding.

The wedding procession assembled to leave Nampara. Ross had often thought the rough road down the valley to the house ought to be levelled to permit a carriage to come at least as far as the bridge crossing the stream. The best they had managed so far was the occasional bullock cart, but that did not seem quite suitable to convey a bride to church. Clowance pooh-poohed the whole idea. She could well sit a horse in her bridal dress; who cared about some strains on the stitchings of her fine blue satin? And she was certainly not going to jog to church in some pony cart which would be sure to upset before it even got out of the valley. All she agreed was that she should not ride Nero, who would immediately break into a gallop and have her at the church before the others were mounted. She accepted Ladybird, an elderly mare who could be relied on to follow where she was led. The bridesmaids were Isabella-Rose and Sophie Enys, also both in blue satin, with yellow hats trimmed with trailing blue ribbons. Bella had been dancing about on her toes for twenty minutes before anyone else was ready and earning the reproofs of Mrs Kemp for getting her shoes soiled in the long grass by the library wall, when suddenly she uttered a long piercing scream which was discordant even by her standards.

When all other noise in the neighbourhood had necessarily ceased she stood on tip toe and pointed up the valley and said one wailing word:

'Jeremy!'

Then she was gone, frock fluttering, hat flying, across the bridge and up the valley. There was a short pause before several of the others made a move to follow. Through the nut trees and the hawthorns, which were still only in their infant green, a tall thin man in a red jacket and a shiny black hat could be seen riding down the lane.

'I *knew* he'd come!' whispered Clowance. 'I *knew* he'd come!'

The soldier emerged finally into full view at the bridge, with Bella riding in front of him. He vaulted off his horse, letting his younger sister slide down after him, embraced Demelza, then Clowance, then grasped his father about the shoulders.

'Is it over? Am I too late?'

'No, no, no, we are just setting out! Oh, Jeremy –'

'By God, I thought I should never arrive in time. By God, I had given myself two days' leeway but, as you see, it was scarce enough! It would have been a damned long way to travel to arrive after the ceremony was over! . . . And where is Stephen, has he run off at the last minute? No, I see, of course, of course. Mama, you look beautiful: it takes absence to appreciate these things. And as for my sister! . . . Well, now?'

'Which one?' said Bella.

'Both, of course. But more particularly today the one who is shortly to be wed –'

'I shall be wed soon,' said Bella. 'That is if anyone will have me!'

'*I'll* have you!' said Jeremy. 'Any day. You would be just my sort of wife . . . You are well, all of you? It is a *perfect* day. But what a journey! If I am to make my career in the army you must all move to Dover!'

So they chattered like a bunch of starlings, each getting a word in but cut short by another. After ten minutes, when Jeremy was consuming some biscuits and a glass of wine, Mrs Kemp said to Demelza:

'If you please, ma'am. We shall be late.'

'It doesn't matter –'

'Very good,' said Jeremy, overhearing and swallowing a last biscuit, 'this marriage has been delayed before. I shall not be responsible. Mama, I trust you will allow me to partner you into church –'

'What about *me*?' said Bella. 'I saw him first!'

'You're a bridesmaid, my lover,' Demelza said gently. 'As you know very well, you will partner Sophie, and follow behind the bride.'

'Oh, *Sophie*,' said Bella. 'She's not a *man*!'

In the laughter that followed Jeremy took his mother's hand and squeezed it. She was too full to speak, and he knew it. Ross who in his quiet way grieved more about Clowance's marriage than Demelza, thought, well, *he* is home. If you have four children it spreads the pleasure and the anxiety but seems to diminish neither. Hostages to fortune, as someone was saying. But *Demelza* is happy now. It has changed her day. He is home.

II

It was very difficult these days being married by the Rev. Clarence Odgers; his wife as usual had to stand beside him to make sure he remembered the Christian names correctly and did not wander off into the Burial service by mistake. But eventually it was done. Stephen, broad-shouldered but still gaunt, his hair trimmed shorter than usual and smoothed back, in a semi-naval suit that reminded Jeremy uncomfortably of Lieutenant Morgan Lean, RN, passenger on the Elegant Light Post Coach, *Self-Defence* on Monday 25th January 1813, stood by his blue silk-clad bride, who was at least two shades blonder than he, and swore to love, honour and cherish her in sickness and in health – as she had very recently done to him – and so in a comparatively short time they were married till death them did part, in a bond that no man should put asunder. And they emerged into the sunshine and the rice and the smiling faces of all Clowance's friends.

A small dinner for all the invited guests in the library; it lasted till four, but the days were stretching ever longer and the ride home would still be all daylight. Clowance went upstairs and changed into a new plum-purple riding habit, a cockade hat with ribbons, and a plum-purple cloak and fine leather gloves.

All Stephen had had time to say to Jeremy so far was, '*Glad* you're back, boy,' but now it was time to leave.

'How long are ye home?'

'A week. Perhaps a little more. So much of my leave will be taken up with travelling.'

'D'you have to go back?'

'Oh, yes!'

'Maybe next week sometime? Come over. Ye know how your sister has such regard for you.'

'She has not always said so!'

There was a laugh.

'Well, tis true, as you very well know. Isn't it, me love?'

'Oh, I can suffer him,' said Clowance.

'I'll come,' said Jeremy, smiling. 'So long as I am not disturbing the honeymoon.'

'She will be a-tired of me by then. Come Tuesday or Wednesday. One of my vessels will be in, the *Lady Clowance*, built in your own shipyard at Looe. I'd like to show you over her.'

'Then I'll gladly come.'

Stephen moved on. 'Captain Poldark.'

'Well, Stephen.' Their hands clasped, but it meant nothing.

'If I ever give your daughter cause for complaint, I hope she'll send for you.'

Ross smiled. 'I hope she will.'

'With a gun,' said Stephen.

'Unloaded,' said Ross. 'I seldom shoot my relatives.'

'Nevertheless,' said Stephen, 'the sentiment is sincerely meant.'

'I'm glad.'

And so to Demelza.

'Ma'am,' he said. 'I'll take care of your daughter. I promise. God's honour. I'll do me best.'

'I hope you will, Stephen. She will not be a meek wife.'

'Meek compared to Isabella-Rose,' said Stephen.

There was a general laugh.

'Hey, hey!' said Bella. 'What is this you're saying 'bout me?'

'Nothing, old dear . . .' Stephen kissed Demelza. 'Ma'am, I cannot regard you as my mother-in-law. You're too pretty. Yet I have to, I s'pose.'

'I s'pose yes,' said Demelza. 'It is a hazard you must face.'

'Gladly, m'dear.' He paused. 'And seriously . . .'

'Yes.'

'Seriously.' He kissed her again.

So very soon they were ready for off, Clowance this time on Nero, who was already snorting and showing the whites of his eyes, ready for a wild gallop. Stephen's horse was the best he could hire for the day, but it was not of the same quality. Then a clucking to the horses and they clattered across the bridge, waved and began the uneven trek up the lane to the top of the hill. Bal-girls and surface workers at Wheal Grace stood and waved and watched them go.

Clowance carried only a light bag. Those belongings she had wished to take with her had been conveyed over to Penryn yesterday by Matthew Mark Martin.

Clowance restrained Nero as best she could, and they kept pace with each other until they were well past Killewarren. Thereafter, even Nero being temporarily blown, they slowed to a walk at which they could converse. Stephen was himself out of breath, a sign that he was still not fit.

He said: 'Well – it has happened – m'dear.'

'Yes . . . it has.'

'I can still scarce believe it. I've thought on ye so often . . . but these last months I've been in a turmoil. Me being ill – it has been a blessing in disguise. If I had not been – if we had not met this way – would you have married that Tom Guildford?'

'I don't think so.'

'We were meant for each other, ever since those meetings in old empty Trenwith . . . well I *surely* thought so, for I could never get you out of my head. When we were engaged before, I was always counting me luck. Then it suddenly slipped away . . .'

'Don't talk of it.'

'But now, Holy Mary, it has slipped back. But I must not talk of it – ye're right. We are starting afresh – all over again.' They walked a way in silence. The only sound was the comfortable creak of saddle and stirrup, the clopping of the hooves. 'I thought Prudie Paynter was a sight, standing there wi' hair like a donkey's tail and that great straw hat with holes in it. Twas outrageous the way she hugged and kissed you!'

Clowance laughed. 'You should see Jud – but of course you've seen him.'

'What is she to you – taking such liberties?'

'She and Jud were servants to my parents, though that was before I was born. I thought you knew it.'

'Jeremy looks brave in his uniform . . . Sooner he's out of it, the better now. He should attend to his mine, which is bringing in such a steady profit. Glory be! Many's the time I regretted having sunk so much in a hole in the ground, but I shall get the capital back *this* year! Had we known . . .'

After waiting Clowance said: 'What were you going to say?'

'Nothing. No matter. It was just a thought . . . Clowance . . .'

'Yes?'

'When I was lying ill there, watching you move about the room, you tending on me this way and that – like an angel, patient, gentle, kind – did I rave much?'

'A great deal.'

'What did I say?'

'All sorts of things.'

'Did it make sense?'

'Not much.'

'What *did* I say?'

'Oh . . . you were trying to open something, could not get it open. Then you mentioned three girls, three girls whose names I knew. One of them was mine.'

'So it should have been!'

'You seemed to want to escape with me on a coach to Liskeard . . . Then you were bargaining about a lifeboat . . . Then you were on that raft in the sea, floating . . .'

'But little of it made real sense?'

'Little indeed.'

He sighed. 'When I came round, saw you there, *really* saw you, knew – or hoped I knew – why you had come . . . I swore that if we should ever marry I would not come to you unshriven.'

'I don't know quite what you mean.'

'Well . . . you think you know me. You already do better than anyone else in the world. But you don't know all me past. I have told you some of it – picking and choosing a little too much, I suspect. There are still dark corners.'

'Are they dark corners which will affect the future?'

'I should pray not so. But you are so honest, so straight in everything you do –'

'Ho-ho! Don't be too sure!'

'Well compared to me. Compared to the most folk. Lying there watching you, I thought, I cannot ask this girl to marry me unless she knows the worst of me. I *cannot*. And then, when it came to the point, I was that afraid, that much the coward; I thought, first just get her consent. And then, when she had consented I was so full of the pleasure of it all that I could not bear to tarnish it!'

Clowance brushed away a spider which had swung down from the overhanging trees.

'Well, Stephen,' she said, 'if you have left it so long, if you have been unable to bear the thought of telling me before this, if you have wed me under false pretences, then perhaps it is already too late to make amends, to repair the damage, to set it all to rights. You have already committed the unforgivable sin of marrying me – unshriven, as you call it. What good will it do to confess to me now?'

He coughed with laughter. 'When I go to Heaven, if so be as I ever get there, I shall want you beside of me at the gate to put my case so well! Serious, though . . .'

'Is this not all serious?'

'All except the Heavenly gates . . . though I now be married to you I've not yet – possessed you. That is what marriage means to me – possession. So, in a sort of way, the urge is still there, telling me there's still time. I feel that I have not been honest enough with you – showing you the faulty person I really am. Maybe tis all a matter of wanting to be honest with meself, see.'

They rode on. Clowance said: 'And do you suppose these confessions will make *me* happier?'

'That I don't know. I doubt it. But there will be nothing then betwixt us but perfect honesty, like.'

'And if you tell me and I am deeply offended, do you suggest I should turn around and gallop back to Nampara?'

'No, no, no . . . I do not believe me errors are so dreadful that you'd do that! I hope you'd listen with sympathy and understanding like the way you have done to so much in the past.'

'Then do not speak them,' said Clowance with decision. 'Leave my sympathy and understanding until another time, Stephen. If I want to know – when I want to know – then I will ask you. To tell me now would be – would be throwing splashes on a clear screen – and to no purpose.'

The light cool wind was following them at about the pace they made, so it was imperceptible, and the sun beat down. Stephen took out a handkerchief and mopped his face.

'Then there will be no splashes, dear heart. Nor shall I

mention it again. Whatever flaws there may be in me, there's no flaws to what I feel for you, nor ever has been since the day I first set eyes on ye.'

They stopped and took a breather just before joining the turnpike road from Truro. The sun was slanting by now, and presently they could see the glimmer of Penryn Creek winding silver-grey among the trees. The dark woods around were as if stained with a maiden-green dust, which was not yet more than surface deep.

Stephen said: 'Bother, I asked Jeremy for Tuesday next or Wednesday. I had forgot: we have an invitation for Tuesday. The letter came yester morning from Sir George and Lady Warleggan. They send their congratulations on our marriage!'

'Gracious alive!'

'Well, I have been to their house once or twice, you know, last autumn, with Valentine. And you went to that party, you told me, after we had broken up. I suppose Sir George's quarrel is only with your father.'

'What do they invite us to?'

'An evening party. Supper and cards.'

'Oh . . . I have never gambled properly. Are the stakes high?'

'I don't think twill matter whether we play or no. It seems to me it would be proper to accept, us now living in this area and me in business here.'

'Yes. Yes, I suppose so.'

'Maybe there will be dancing too.'

They were proceeding so slowly that Nero was showing a tendency to investigate the hedges that he passed. Clowance checked him.

'But Stephen, it is still May!'

'Yes?'

'Surely Valentine will not be there! His term at Cambridge cannot end until sometime in June. What a strange thing!'

'Maybe he's come back early for some reason. The invitation did not mention him, but . . . Well, I shall surely consider it even a greater compliment if he's not there, for it means we have been invited by Sir George and Lady Harriet for our own sakes!'

'And what shall you do about Jeremy?'

'Oh, send a note – there's just time – asking him to come Wednesday for certain.'

'Perhaps he would like to come to the party too,' suggested Clowance.

Chapter Five

I

George's arrangements were coming along nicely. Mr
Trembath had again been to see Mr Arthur Williams Rose
of Liskeard, who had said he was by no means well but
professed himself honoured at the invitation of so notable a
gentleman as Sir George to spend a few days with him
discussing legal matters – though, being as smart as the
next, he had no doubt at all as to what his real function was
likely to be. Just to make sure of him, Mr Trembath was to
go to Liskeard again and act as Mr Rose's escort, bringing
him to Cardew on the Monday evening so that he would be
here in ample time for Tuesday's party.

George had been lucky in his choice of dates: Anthony
Trefusis was at home and, as always when it was gaming at
cards, immediately accepted. Stephen Carrington, just married to the Poldark girl, was sure to be home and certain to
come. Andrew Blamey was at sea in one of Carrington's
trumpery vessels, but if winds were favourable he was due
back early Tuesday. Michael Smith had already accepted.
The only one likely to be missing was George Trevethan,
who, his father said, was in Exeter; but as a young man
scarcely ever short of money, he was the least likely suspect.

To hide the real purpose of this party even from Harriet,
he had invited a round dozen other people which, with
family, would raise the numbers to about twenty. Valentine
could not be here, but he had invited Cuby Trevanion and
her brother and sister just the same.

Although everything had been virtually settled between
himself and J. T. B. Trevanion eighteen months ago,
the dashing major had never been as good as his word. The
joke about the name Bettesworth, which he had changed to
Trevanion when he was twenty-one, still persisted. He 'bet his

276

worth'. And not even the prospect of lifting the load of debt once and for all from round his neck by marrying his younger sister to the son of a rich merchant and banker had been strong enough to keep him away from his horses. Three times George had discovered him in the process of compounding his debts (in the hope, of course, of discharging them) and three times George had found it necessary to inform him that unless this behaviour ceased, their arrangement for the marriage, the whole complicated legal structure they had built up around deeds of gift, trusts, and inheritances of land, would be pulled down and cease to preserve him, merely by the promise of its existence, from the debtor's prison.

Indeed, had George not himself so set his heart on seeing Valentine master of the splendid Caerhays Castle, he would by now have cast Trevanion off altogether. George had a low tolerance of foolish behaviour, and when that foolish behaviour involved money he was hard put to it to hide his contempt. However, now at last, after more hard bargaining between the sets of lawyers, the matter seemed to be finally, finally settled. Instead of receiving any further interim loans, which he could plunder as he thought fit, John Trevanion had accepted the condition of receiving a monthly payment from George until the wedding took place, whereupon he received a further and final sum of £18,000 and bound himself to vacate the castle within twelve months of the marriage. The castle and its demesnes should pass to his younger sister unencumbered of debt, and no more than personal belongings to the value of £500 should be removed by him when he left.

These were humiliating conditions for a man of ancient lineage who had been Sheriff of Cornwall when he was twenty-five, a member of parliament at twenty-seven and a prominent Whig and a leading figure in the county ever since; but there was no escape, even if he should wish it. He waited on George's nod. And George had made up his mind that the engagement should be made public at another party as soon as Valentine came home; the wedding could follow in September. There was no further need to wait. Valentine would be twenty-one next February, and would continue his studies for one more year. He could take up his permanent residence in the castle in about September 1815, by which time Major Trevanion would be moving out.

George had spent some time considering his position if Mr Rose, as seemed likely, *should* recognize one of the card players as one of the robbers of the coach. He had thought of asking a couple of constables from Truro to be present, but they were such rough, uneducated men; they could never understand the situation in time, and their use would hardly be greater than two of his own servants if it actually came to physical force. He was himself a magistrate, and Lord Devoran, who had been invited without his daughter, another. Between them they could surely deal with any situation which arose. Anyway, identification was all. Summary arrest could follow.

Several of his more trustworthy servants must be alerted beforehand; for if the one arrested were kept in close confinement and constantly questioned he might well give away the identity of his companions in crime. It was important that they should not be allowed to bluster their way out of the house. Young Trefusis, if it were he, would certainly try to fly the country – as probably would young Carrington, disturbed in his honeymoon with the Poldark girl – and the Blamey fellow. Michael Smith, so far as he knew, had no connections with the sea, but, obviously, whoever it was would do his utmost to save his neck. A great deal, it seemed to George, depended on the outcome of the night.

He had also steeled himself to complete disappointment, if Mr Rose should recognize no one.

Harriet, was cynically intrigued by the party; but knowing nothing about the visiting lawyer she could not draw any conclusions from his impending visit. Anyway, lawyers of one sort or another, and their creatures, were always in and out of the house; far too often for her to draw any inferences from their comings and goings. She was intrigued by the party because it was unheard of for George to organize such a thing on his own initiative, without even Valentine to prod him.

'But you know, my pet,' she said, 'cards are not in your line at *all*. You never really understand the theory, and you hate hazarding money on anything except a near certainty. Besides, is it not unwise to invite John Trevanion on such a night, knowing his weaknesses?'

'Trevanion is coming simply so that we may agree for a day for the announcement of the engagement and for a day for the wedding.'

'You mean you will tell him what is most convenient to us, eh? And what day *is* going to be convenient to us, may I ask? Have *you* decided?'

'Valentine will be back in two weeks. I thought Midsummer Day, the 24th of June would be suitable.'

'But how romantic of you! And the wedding?'

'The first of September. That will give them – I mean Valentine and Cuby – a time together before he returns to Cambridge. That is, my dear,' said George, turning the tables with a little of his own irony, 'unless you wish it otherwise.'

Harriet yawned. 'Why should I? He's your son. A lively fellow for all that. I should not be astonished if he leads Miss Cuby a dance. Though, from what little I have seen of her, I should not suppose her easily put on. I admire her for what she's doing.'

'What?' said George. 'What is she doing?'

'Marrying money, of course.'

'Valentine is as personable as she!' said George shortly.

'Of course he is. I find him very personable. Possibly she does too. But you cannot pretend other than that this is an arranged marriage. As I say, I admire her for her clear-sightedness in entering into it. A marriage that is based on money is at least based on something stable.'

George got up, went to the window, looked out on his deer. He did not care for venison and therefore regarded them as useless creatures; but to keep them was expected of him, and it gave him pleasure to know that he had more than either the Falmouths or the Dunstanvilles.

He said: 'The second anniversary of our marriage is scarcely past. On it, as you know, I gave you a new carriage.'

'Indeed. And I thanked you for it – in the only possible way that a wife can thank a husband.'

'Yes, you did.' George passed a finger round his neck-cloth, overwarm at the thought. 'Yet now you speak of marriage in such derogatory terms it might be some disreputable art you are describing. If there ever *is* a good motive for marriage, you say . . .'

'Well, at my time of life,' said Harriet, 'thirty-three, that is – which I regard as the extreme old age of youth – you cannot, I trust, expect me to hold to notions of love and romance. I was stupid enough to marry Toby Carter for love. Hot-blooded, we were; by God, we were hot-blooded! Nothing would stop me, not even his reputation. Nor that he was a Catholic. Nor that he had lost two wives already. Nor that at forty he had already run through one fortune and was in process of dissipating another. Nor did *he* consider that I had only a small personal fortune and precious little hope of inheriting any more, and that I had no intention whatsoever of being the sort of wife he wanted! I swear to you we were in *love*, dear George, but within three months we were fighting like cats. *Physically*, often enough. The scars I have on my thighs are not hunting scars; did I tell you? So you see how I regard marriages for *love*.'

As was often the case, George disliked the tone in which Harriet spoke to him, but did not know what to do about it.

Eventually he said stiffly: 'You cannot generalize from one person's experience. Nor do I think our marriage need be stigmatized as –'

'Oh, our marriage was a convenience, was it not. I was hard drove for money, and very very tired of being so hard drove. You fancied marrying into the Osborne family, and thought I was personable enough to sit at your dinner table . . .' As he was about to speak she added: 'Oh, I think you rather fancied me – as a man does a woman. And I was not – not totally indifferent to you. Those were useful ingredients of the marriage brew – a little of the pepper and the mustard, say. They have remained ingredients, as you well know. But let us not talk about *love*. Fortunately we were both too calculating for that.'

'Calculating?'

'Level-headed, then.' She gave her low chuckle. 'But I conceit that it is not working too ill. You are even becoming accustomed to Castor and Pollux!'

Something had startled the deer; or they were off on some sudden impulse of their own, bounding away over the brow of the hill.

Harriet said: 'If you are making this largely a young people's party, why do you not invite Jeremy Poldark? He is back from his soldiering; that is if he ever did any.'

'I don't care for the fellow,' said George. 'A gangling youth. Doesn't even have the looks of his father . . . How do you know he is home?'

'My God, do not be so suspicious! I met him in Truro last week. He was hiring a horse, and in great haste to be home for his sister's wedding. But very handsome, if I may say so, in his regimentals. What a uniform will do for a man!'

'We have Clowance Carrington coming – that's one Poldark,' George said testily. 'And Andrew Blamey, that's another –'

'Both invited by you!'

'Yes, I know!' Memory of his last clash with Ross welled up in him like lust. 'Well let me point out, Harriet, that there is a limit to my tolerance of that clan! I have warned you, and we have agreed. After that overcrowded and noisy party at Trenwith you may feel a greater degree of amity for the Poldarks in general. Let it not go too far! There can never be any form of toleration, let alone friendship, between Ross Poldark and myself. And as for his wife . . .'

Harriet got up. 'It is of the utmost indifference to me who comes to your tedious little party. Forget my suggestion.'

'Where are you going?'

'To sit in a corner and acknowledge my place in this household.'

'What nonsense you do talk at times –'

'Possibly we both do.'

The door that Harriet had opened was pushed wider and Ursula Warleggan came in. She was in a primrose yellow velvet frock that in the three months since it had been made had tightened across the bust. Her dark hair was in twin pigtails with yellow bows, her feet in yellow moccasins. At fourteen and a half she was large for her age. Next September she was being sent to Mrs Hemple's school in Truro. George, at first, had been much against it; however, he had come to realize that if she did not go somewhere soon she would get out of hand. She had mastered every governess they had hired. George's pride in her was intense.

'Papa,' she said, directly addressing her father across Lady Harriet, 'what is the meaning of this, what it says here in the paper? "Even a shopkeeper can begin to be a banker, by accepting deposits and discounting bills of exchange. The one stip-stipulation he makes is that he need not return the deposits immediately." I do not understand. Can you please explain?'

Naturally nothing more for a while about the coming party, but at supper George said:

'I have been thinking of your suggestion that we should invite Jeremy Poldark. I will raise no objection if it will please you.'

'*Please* me?' said Harriet, who was not in a good mood. 'For blood and hounds, I care nothing either way! I had forgot all about it.'

George uneasily sipped his hare soup. 'Well, it is also a matter of indifference to me. But I thought you wished him to come.'

'This is your party. Pray suit yourself.'

The soup was finished and taken away. A saddle of spring lamb was brought in, with two chickens and an array of vegetables and sauces.

'How long is Jeremy Poldark staying? Or is he home for good?'

'About ten days. His regiment is billeted in Brussels.'

'Some young men enjoy themselves.'

'Some young men get killed.'

'Not now,' said George. 'He was – fortunate in the time of his enlistment.'

Supper proceeded.

'In fact,' said George, 'we should all have been prepared for peace far more than we really were. As you know, I hazarded large sums of money in 1810 and 1811 expecting, preparing for peace then – a negotiated peace; as it certainly would have been at that time, had the Prince Regent not betrayed the political party he had belonged to for the *whole* of his adult life. When peace did not come I lost something like half my fortune.'

Harriet looked round to see that all the servants were temporarily out of the room. 'All to get me,' she said harshly. 'Good God, I have been a constant source of expense to you, even before we were wed!'

'Never mind about that,' George said testily. 'What I am saying is that, had I had the financial backing and stability to hold on to all my purchases then, I should be a much richer man today than I am. Even six months ago, had I read the signs of Napoleon's imminent collapse aright, I could have recouped most of my losses by buying the same sort of textile and engineering firms all over again. Or even possibly by buying in the metal markets . . . I must confess to you that it scarcely crossed my mind to do so. Having suffered such losses once . . .'

'A burnt child.'

'What?'

'Dreads the fire,' said Harriet.

'Ah, well, there is an old wives' saying for almost any situation.'

'I am indeed an old wife,' said Harriet. 'Thank you for the compliment. But in any event, though you may not be nearly as rich as you were before you met me, first, because of your unwise speculation, second, because I cost so much to keep; yet you are in a sound financial position, are you not?'

'Well, yes.'

'So does it matter a tinker's curse that we are not twice as wealthy? If we have an income of X guineas a year and it costs us X guineas a year to live, does it matter that our income is not 2X guineas a year?'

'With the children growing up there will be increasing costs,' said George defensively.

'Such, no doubt, as all these damned arrangements, whatever they may be, with John Trevanion. Oh, pray do not tell me, I am not anxious to know. Well, I shall be happy to see Valentine settled – so long as it does not mean my economizing on the style we maintain and the hunters I keep . . .'

She broke off as a manservant and two maids re-entered the room with the second course. Thereafter there was silence for quite a while on subjects which mattered. Harriet of course had not the least objection to discussing anything in front of the servants; she had been brought up to believe that as human beings they did not count. But she had soon observed that George was abnormally sensitive about such things. If one of the servants was ill, it was another matter; she was far more likely to have concern for the welfare of the sick person than George was; almost as much so as if one of her horses was ailing.

Towards the end of the meal George said: 'So I shall invite Jeremy Poldark?'

'If it pleases you.'

'It pleases me to please you, Harriet. It cannot make any difference to the outcome.'

'What outcome?' asked Harriet.

'Oh . . . the outcome of a pleasant evening.'

II

Jeremy told his mother of the invitation as soon as he received it.

'And shall you go?' asked Demelza.

'I think so. If you will permit it.'

'I permit it! You are being very gracious.'

'Well . . . my stay here will be all too short. One day I have promised to spend with Clowance and Stephen. One day I shall see Goldsworthy Gurney. This will take a third – or the half of a day. I can ride back of course the same evening. If I leave them at midnight . . .'

'Do as you fancy,' said Demelza. 'Your ten days will fly anyhow.'

'Dear Mother, do I try you hard?'

'All sons do.'

'And daughters?'

'And daughters.'

They were standing on the bluff of cliff just below Wheal Leisure. Jeremy had wanted to inspect the small whym engine which drew the kibbles of ore out of the earth and, though it had been installed last year, he had never seemed to find the suitable time when his mother was free as well, to take her over and show her how it worked, detail by detail. This he had now just done.

Demelza drew a deep breath. Even though one lived by the sea all the time, there were periods during a hard winter when one lived just within the near neighbourhood of one's house, more indoors than out, and forgot – or overlooked – the pleasure of breathing salt air. The distant sea was turning over in a big way this morning, chewing the sand like a coffee grinder, biding its time to come in and rush at its eternal enemy, the cliffs.

She said: 'I pray it will work out well for her.'

'Clowance? Yes. I think we've all done the right thing.'

'What do you mean, Jeremy?'

'Nobody can pretend it's an ideal match, but this time she has gone into it with her eyes open. You and father also behaved as I hope I shall have the wit to behave if I ever have a daughter and see her in such a difficulty. Never afterwards in all her life will she be able to say, "if *they* hadn't stepped in" or "if *they* had advised me different". That's what I mean.'

Demelza inclined her head. 'I only hope he also knows her faults.'

'Her faults?'

'Well, they may rate as faults in a marriage, though many would call them virtues. She is so very clear-sighted, Jeremy, sometimes I tremble for myself . . . And, until recently, she has hardly known what compromise means. I only hope and pray she – when the first passion wears off – she will not be so clear-sighted about Stephen, and willing to go on making the sort of compromise she has done in marrying him.'

Jeremy put his arm round his mother's shoulders. 'You married Father for love. Isn't that so?'

'Oh, *yes*.'

'Then when did the first passion wear off and you begin to observe his faults?'

Demelza laughed. 'We're talking close home now, Jeremy, but, since you ask me, I suppose twould be true to say that it never *has* worn off – or not yet anyway.'

'That, from close observation of the objects under review, is what I thought. So when *did* you begin to observe his faults?'

'Well, he hasn't any really *bad* ones! And those he has – they are part of him and therefore mean nothing to me.'

'Which is why you do not bicker?'

'I suppose. There is a way that you come to love a person when blemishes are part of him and therefore don't count for much in the whole picture.'

'If you could find the recipe for that and could put it on sale like a tincture or a bolus, you would make a fortune! . . . But tell me, Mother mine, if you have achieved a rare kind of union with Father, why do you suppose that your elder son and daughter, being of the same blood, should not be able to make an equal success of *their* marriages?'

'I hope to believe it. I pray it may be so.'

'So do I,' he said. 'So do I. Stephen had a rough start in life. It could hardly have been rougher. Maybe marriage to Clowance will set him up.' After a moment he added: 'Ben, of course, is greatly upset.'

'. . . I saw him in the distance on Monday but I think he tried to avoid me.'

'He's asked for a week's leave. He says it's while I am home, but in the ordinary way he would *never* take time off. It isn't in his nature.'

'I'm very sorry for him, Jeremy. We're all that sorry for him. But it was Clowance's choice. What could anybody do?'

Jeremy cocked an eye – or more properly an ear – back at the larger engine whose suck and beat he had thought hesitated for a moment in sympathy. But it was a false alarm. Girls were working in the washing sheds. The water gushed continuously from the main adit at the foot of the cliffs.

'There is another reason why I think I shall go to the Warleggans,' Jeremy said. 'Cuby may be there.'

He said it so openly and so lightly that for a moment Demelza was deceived and supposed him over it.

'Have you been writing to her?'

'No.'

'Valentine . . .'

'Should not be home, it being term time, but I would not put it past him to take French leave. Perhaps he will be there to announce their engagement.'

'But if you believe this even to be likely, why do you wish to meet her again?'

'I have a fancy,' said Jeremy. He did not, or could not, explain to his mother that he was sleeping with a Belgian girl in Brussels and felt the stronger to resist Cuby for it.

'A fancy for someone else?' Demelza asked.

He laughed. 'Dear mother, you should not ask these things! It makes me suspect you of second sight.'

'Maybe I have a sort of second sight where my children are concerned. For instance, I know you have had a special unhappiness, an unease, since January of last year. Is this explained because of what you have told me of Cuby and Valentine? It was then that you learned of it, wasn't it?'

'Yes. Oh yes. That and other things. I rather fancy I lost my sense of proportion. That's all I can say, even to you.'

She waited but nothing more came; so she turned to lead the way down the cliff path. He insisted on trying to help her, though she was as sure footed as he. At the bottom she jumped into his arms, and he regarded her gravely for a second or two before he released her.

She said: 'Shall you stay in the Army?'

'God forbid. There are so many things that offend me. It is a brutal life, for all its comradeship. The floggings sicken me.'

'Are they frequent?'

'In my regiment, no, thank God. The Fifty-second,

though I did not know it when I joined them, was one of the elite regiments trained as part of the Light Brigade by Sir John Moore. But in many of the other regiments flogging is as common an event as sunrise. The very bones of their back are laid bare! It is brutalizing and outrageous.'

Demelza shivered.

He said: 'You are cold?'

'Yes. With what you tell me. So how long shall you stay away from Nampara?'

They began to plough their way across the soft sand towards the house.

'Perhaps until some murky cobwebs have been blown out of my mind.'

'And the steam engines?'

'As I said, I shall see Gurney. There are movements afoot in the north of England. When I am free again I shall go up to Darlington, where an experimental railway is operating.'

'Where is Darlington?'

'I haven't the least idea! Except that it is in the far north. Anyway, I cannot go there so long as I remain in the army. And out of decency I must stay in the army for another six months.'

'What has decency got to do with it? Would they say you could not if you asked to leave?'

'No, I don't think so. Now that peace has come there will be many an old soldier begging in the streets before long.'

Chapter Six

I

On the Sunday about mid-day Sir Unwin Trevaunance arrived at Cardew. He was not expected and had not been invited. That was Unwin's way. Since he sold his residence in Cornwall to the Popes he had considered it natural that he should be put up by any of his friends he cared to call on, whether it was Chenhalls in Bodmin, or Sir Christopher Hawkins at Trewithen, or the de Dunstanvilles at Tehidy, or George at Cardew.

He had spent last night with Michael Chenhalls and would like to stop two or three days at Cardew, he bluntly said. This would cover the period of the card party but it could not be helped. How does one say no to a fellow MP of roughly the same political views, when one has a huge house with so many unused bedrooms?

He was not backward in declaring his business in Cornwall.

'I've really come to take a last look at this widow. You know, Selina Pope. This mine we were projecting, West Wheal Plenty, as we were thinking of calling it. Near Place House. The one old Clement Pope was objecting to.'

'You missed your chance of buying those surplus materials from Wheal Spinster,' said George. 'We sold them at knock down prices to the people at Tolgus. Too bad.'

Unwin, a man now approaching sixty, had only become more gaunt with the years. He thrust a hand through his long grey hair.

'Michael Chenhalls has been blowing hot and cold over this venture for best part of two years. The original assays were highly favourable, but then they can be deceptive, don't you know. You say Wheal Plenty was high grade ore and then ran poor, I remember?'

'Not exactly ran *poor*,' said George. 'But some of the lodes were thinning, and the ground was hard and wet. My advisers felt that the best ore had been raised, and with the price of copper falling it simply did not appear a financial proposition spending more money on exploration.'

'Well, that was Chenhalls' view last year, and we more or less abandoned the idea of trying to open a new mine on the Popes' land in the face of their opposition. Our lawyers advised us that if the Popes were really litigious they might contest rights of way and other matters in the courts. All things considered, we decided the scheme wasn't worth the candle.'

'And then?'

Unwin narrowed his brows. 'Then Clement Pope died! So we thought – or I thought – let us see if the hounds are chiming different now! First we must flush out the pretty widow and find if she is intent on staying, and then we must discover if she is as much against the proposition, especially if we were to offer her a small percentage of any profits we raised.'

'I saw her last October,' said George. 'She was then in deepest black but was not, I thought, the picture of sorrow.'

'Ah, no. Damned handsome woman, but not out of the top drawer. I expect that's how that skrimshanked old fellow got her. Well, I made inquiries six months or more ago through a Truro lawyer called Trembath. Took over Pearce's practice. Know him?'

'Very well,' said George.

'Trustworthy?'

'Oh, yes.'

'Well, her reply came through another lawyer, Barrington something –'

'Burdett.'

'Yes. To say that she had no intention of leaving the property and that she was as opposed as ever to the idea of a mine being opened on her land. What was more – and here came the surprise, dammit – she said she would like to purchase the mineral rights herself so that she need never be exposed to a similar threat in the future!'

'Ah,' said George, and hunched his shoulders. 'Tell me, did your brother never attempt any exploratory workings on his land himself – nor permit any venturers to try?'

'John was funny about things like that. He felt his property was not for such affrays. He liked his cattle and his sheep and his rolling fields. Didn't want 'em disturbed with industry. Oddly enough the one time he did try anything was when he took on smelting copper for the Carnmore Copper Co. back in, when was it?; it disfigured the hillside and lost him a lot of money. Ross Poldark burned his fingers on that.'

'So did I, in the end,' said George. 'Copper needs three times the fuel that tin does; it was never practical in Cornwall.'

'Well, that taught John a lesson, if he hadn't learned it before. His cove had been disfigured, and to no purpose . . . His real money was all upcounty, y'know.'

'I am wondering what made you and Chenhalls become interested in this project years after you had sold the property to the Popes.'

Unwin shrugged. 'Chenhalls had two prospecting engineers, made a survey of the way the tin and copper lodes were running all the way from Redruth and St Day. They worked it out that there could be profitable outcrops at Trevaunance. God knows, there are – or were – mines enough at St Ann's, next door.'

'D'you think Mrs Pope knows this?'

'Ah,' said Unwin. 'That is what I wish to find out. Is she spending money really to ensure privacy or, as soon as the sale has gone through, does she intend to start some mining venture herself?'

'For a woman,' said George, 'it seems very improbable. Especially for a woman who is not Cornish and understands nothing about mining.'

'That is, unless she is being advised.'

'Who would advise her?'

'I don't know. Anyone around. The Poldarks, f'instance. The Ross Poldarks, I mean. They are only a few miles away. I have heard that she has been rather thick with their son.'

'Well,' said George spitefully. 'Their son will be here on Tuesday. Perhaps you had better ask him yourself.'

Trevaunance looked at his host, and then broke into a laugh. 'That I shall not do. I shall go and see the lady myself. I fancy I understand women pretty well. I shall lay a few traps in my conversation and see if she falls into 'em.'

II

The card and supper party was to begin on Tuesday at six. The coach which was to bring Mr Trembath and Mr Rose from Liskeard was due at the Norway Inn at about seven p.m. on the Monday, and George had arranged that a small chaise should be waiting there to convey the two lawyers to Cardew.

He preferred that Mr Rose should be established in the house the day before the party began, because he did not want it to appear to Harriet that the identification, if it occurred, had been staged expressly by him. He was sensitive to her opinions, and if the outcome of all this was that someone, a friend, or at least a guest in the house, should go to the gallows – or be transported for twenty years – he did not want her, with her ambiguous views about the value of money, to hold him wholly responsible.

In his heart perhaps he knew that she would suppose this to be in some part a contrivance; but he could deny it with a greater show of sincerity if Rose were to be there as their guest for three or four days and be there on business to do with the estate.

So he was frustrated and annoyed when, about seven-thirty on the Monday evening, an empty chaise clopped up to the house and Nankivell, the groom, handed George a note which had been passed to him by the coachman on the stage coach.

Sir, (it said.)
  I regret to inform you that Mr Rose is suffering from a severe headache, which his apothecary tells him is due to a gouty condition of the cerebrum. Mr Rose is

spending the day in bed and is taking Wessel's Jesuit Drops, which he swears always set him to rights within twelve hours, so he is sure to be well recovered by tomorrow.

I am well aware, sir, of the importance you attach to his being at Cardew not later than Tuesday evening, and so is he. He has invited me to spend the night at his house, and this I have accepted, since this way I can be sure he does not default tomorrow. Indeed, I believe there is little fear of this, for he knows the fees you are offering him, and his conversation seldom strays long from the subject of the failure of banks, the emoluments he is owed, and the importance of money.

I have the honour to be, sir,
Your humble & obedt. servant,
Hector Trembath.

George swore under his breath, scrumpled the note, and put it into his fob pocket as he went up the steps to tell Harriet their other guest had been delayed.

It mattered little, he realized. He had thought to keep Mr Rose upstairs tomorrow on some pretext or other until all his guests had arrived and the party was in full swing; if he came down in such a way the effect would be greater; it seemed to promise a sound dramatic scene.

Well, now he would come bumbling up the steps in his black hat and travelling cloak when they were already assembled. If Harriet took some eccentric view that George should have arranged the denunciation with greater discretion, she would have to lump it. Even she could hardly countenance the robbery of bank money from a stage coach or assert with any degree of sincerity that it should go unpunished.

Tuesday, the thirty-first of May, was another beautiful day. Stephen and Clowance spent all afternoon aboard the *Lady Clowance*, which had come in with the morning tide, and Stephen told Andrew of his invitation for that evening. The vessel had brought a mixed cargo from Plymouth, and would be unloaded tomorrow when the drays were available. It was a thoroughly happy afternoon; they were all in high spirits; and it was four-thirty before they reluctantly ferried themselves to the quayside and walked home. Andrew said he would dash to see his mother; they were not to wait if he was late, he would follow in his own good time.

It was a plain little house, with sash windows and small square rooms, and very few of them; but Clowance did not compare it with the spacious, straggling Nampara. She thought it better than the Gatehouse, which they had been promised before, and the view was more exciting. One could see the end of Penryn Creek, and from the bedroom windows almost all the shipping as it came and went. Whether she would be lonely or unoccupied if Stephen went to sea she had hardly considered, but she was near enough to the Blameys, and there were plenty of small things she could do to improve the house provided she had the enterprise to do them. She had never handled a paint brush in her life, except to make genteel pictures of roses on canvas when she was at school, and carpentry was a closed book. But to an enterprising girl all things were possible.

The only tiny fly in the amber was the acid, grey-haired widow who owned the property and lived in the other half. She smiled too much and bowed too often to be sincere.

Changing was a longer process than it should have been, for Stephen could not yet see her in her underclothes without demanding to take advantage of it; so it was almost six-thirty when they clattered breathlessly up the drive to the front door of Cardew. By then most of the other guests had arrived, and shortly after them came Andrew, and then Jeremy.

Very properly, Jeremy was in what Harriet called his regimentals: a tight scarlet jacket with dull gilt epaulettes, collar and cuffs, brass buttons down both fronts of the jacket, a diagonal belt with '52' on it, and tight navy trousers fastening with a belt under the black shoes. Harriet had also said, what a uniform will do for a man! and it could never have been more true than of Jeremy. Perhaps in coming to Cardew in the hope of seeing Cuby he was not unaware of this.

If so, his reward was immediate. Cuby's face changed at

the sight of him, and as soon as they had a moment together she said:

'But Jeremy, how handsome you look!'

'It's the conventional resort of the slighted lover,' Jeremy said. 'At one time one used to do the Grand Tour, but Napoleon has made that impossible.'

'No longer! . . . But I heard you had gone . . . I am so glad at least that the danger is over.'

'There is always America.'

'You would not go out there?'

He did not reply but looked at her covertly, tried to think of Lisa, to compare them.

'How is Augustus?'

'In London. He has this post in the Treasury; but I believe it is almost a sinecure.'

'When are you coming to take tea with me in Truro?'

'Did I ever say I would?'

'I shall be home only until next Monday.'

'Where do you go back to?'

'Brussels.'

'What are people like there? Are they friendly to us?'

'Not noticeably. Nor are they unfriendly. Just dour. They are glad to see the back of the French but not sure they welcome the English or the Germans or the Russians.'

'And the ladies?'

Jeremy smiled at her. 'What game are you playing tonight?'

She looked startled. 'Game? Oh, you mean . . .' She looked at him doubtfully. 'You mean card game?'

'What else?'

'I don't mind. I have no preference.'

'Nor I. I have a slight preference to sit next to you, that is all.'

'I'm not lucky at cards. And I'm terrified of losing money!'

'Unlike your brother, there.'

'*Yes*. Perhaps it is because of him!'

'There's a Faro board on that table. This one looks as if it may be *Vingt-et-un*.'

'Let's sit here, then. I've never played Faro and I remember at *Vingt-et-un* one may be timid in one's bids!'

The party divided up cheerfully. Stephen took Clowance to the Faro table, promising he would teach her the rules. On her other side was Anthony Trefusis who swore he had never met her before and clearly enjoyed sitting next to her and patting her hand when an excuse arose. They drew at each table for banker; and Unwin Trevaunance, who had been over to Place House today but was very willing to join in the fun, drew one and Lord Devoran the other. The latter instantly disowned the responsibility of being banker and handed it to Lady Harriet, who laughed and took her seat. George had dropped hints all round about keeping the stakes low, on account of the young ladies present, so the games at each table began on an easy note.

George himself did not play, and invited John Trevanion to walk with him on the terrace outside, an offer which Trevanion had no excuse to refuse.

The time was already after seven, and George was concerned to keep the front of the house in view for when his last and most important guest arrived. Mr Rose should be escorted straight upstairs, where he could wash and change out of his travelling clothes if he so desired before descending to join the company. Supper was to be at nine, so he could come down about eight-thirty, before the tables broke up. This would be the perfect entrance.

'The church,' he said to John Trevanion, 'is still a matter for discussion. St Michael Caerhays is so *small*.'

'Yet it *is* the family church,' said the major. 'All my family, the girls of the family, have been married there, my parents, my wife are buried there; many of my ancestors for five or six hundred years.'

George said: 'I do not think this is an occasion for a small wedding.'

'Well, you know my finances better than I do, Warleggan. These things always cost a pretty penny.'

'I still don't feel it is excuse enough for something paltry. Valentine is my only son. I have many social connections. Lady Harriet's family must at least be invited. It is impossible to ask people to travel a distance to a wedding and then expect them to sit in the churchyard!'

'It has been done before now! What is the alternative?'

'St Mary's, Truro. I have a residence in the parish.'

John Trevanion made an irritable gesture. 'Your so-called Great House can hardly compare with Caerhays Castle for the reception afterwards!'

'Your castle,' said George with a reciprocal sneer, 'will hardly be flattered if you only have thirty or forty guests to receive.'

They turned about and paced back the way they had come. 'Oh, come, my good man,' said Trevanion, 'do we *have* more than sixty relatives and important friends betwixt us? Let sixty be invited to the church and another sixty to the reception after. Who cares a damn whether they witness the ceremony so long as the food and the wine be good after?'

George noticed a servant, an oldish man called Blencowe, busying himself furtively among the grooms and the horses. A portly, stooping little man who could read and write, he was the least ill-educated of George's servants and sometimes undertook errands with Tankard; he was one of the three George had instructed to be on the alert in case there was a denunciation and a sequel to the denunciation. The other two – strong young men – were posted inside the house. He took out his watch. Seven-thirty. The chaise should be here any time now so long as the coach was punctual. So long as a horse did not cast its shoe or the brakes burn out or there was some other stupid delay.

He hoped Mr Rose was not still unwell. Anyway he was sure that if Mr Hector Trembath valued his connection, nothing would stand in the way of his arriving with his guest in tow.

III

'What of your experiments with steam?' Cuby asked.

'What, *now*? They have been abandoned, of course. The

army does not encourage amateur scientists heating up water in boilers. They are interested only in *real* explosions!'

'. . . And that young man at Wadebridge; the one you had been visiting when we met in the music shop . . .'

'I saw him yesterday; but he has had little time to pursue his interests. Dr Avery, his partner, has died, and he has succeeded to the practice. And now he is just married – to a lady about ten years older than himself. No doubt he will begin his experiments again soon. I do not think he is the sort of man to allow love to ruin his life.'

'Surely you are not either!'

'Well, does it not depend when it is to happen?' Jeremy whispered. He picked up his second card.

'When what is to happen?' Cuby asked.

'I stand,' he said to the banker. 'You know what I am asking about,' he said to Cuby; 'your wedding to Valentine.'

She flushed. 'I suspect quite soon.'

Not much had altered. Affection for Lisa was no protection against the stab in the heart. 'You *suspect* so!'

'Well . . . yes . . . Do I take another?'

'*No*. Count your ace as eleven. So what is the month chosen for the happy event?'

'September or October, my brother thinks.'

The skin of her neck and arms was like toffee cream. You knew how it would taste.

'Thank God it will soon be over. You will be wed in glorious matrimony for the rest of your life to a man you do not love.'

'*Ssh!*' she said.

The banker drew twenty, and Jeremy pushed over his money. 'Miss Trevanion wins!' he called, and then *sotto voce*: 'as always.'

'And do you think *that* is winning?' she asked under her breath.

'Winning for your side, for your family, for your brother; as we have already agreed . . . Here, don't neglect your money!'

'I am not likely to, am I!'

'What better subjects than love and gambling? Lucky at cards, unlucky in love.'

At the next deal Cuby picked up a deuce and a three. She said: 'I'll wager you have no need to be unlucky in love in that *beautiful* uniform. I never saw my own brother in anything so fine.'

'Do you mean Augustus?'

'No, my other brother, George. The one who was killed at Bergen.'

Jeremy had picked up two queens. It seemed appropriate. 'I'll stand.'

Cuby whispered: 'What are the words if you want another card?'

'Hit me.'

'It sounds silly.'

'Miss Trevanion will take another card,' Jeremy said to the banker.

She was given an ace, which remained face up on the table. She looked at Jeremy. He nodded. She nodded. The fourth card was a five. The game went on. At the end of the round Cuby again picked up her winnings . . .

Outside the sun was just catching the pointed tree tops, sending arrows of light speeding over the front of the house. It was like Agincourt. George looked at his watch. Almost eight.

'I think we should go in,' said Trevanion sulkily, who had already paced too far for his own pleasure. 'There is a chill in the air, and I left off my velvet waistcoat yesterday.'

Pigeons were fluttering in the woods, moving from tree to tree before they settled for the night. They were multiplying too fast, George thought. At least *they* made excellent pies. What could have happened to the damned coach? The chaise had not returned, so presumably the coach had still not arrived at the Norway Inn.

'Have you settled on your own plans?' George said sharply.

'*My* plans?'

'For a year next September.'

'No – er – no. Certainly not. Not yet. I shall spend some

time in London visiting relatives. I have some residual property in Grampound, as you know. Something there could be enlarged for my use. Though I may not continue to live in Cornwall permanently.'

'Now that peace has come many new opportunities are opened up.'

Trevanion's lip curled. 'To travel? Only the rich can travel.'

'You have connections in high places.'

'A few. No doubt we shall see.'

The vexed question of Cuby's mother had still to be settled, but George did not feel he could be too insistent about that. Valentine was perfectly capable of ordering his house as he thought best, and of dealing with one widowed lady.

'It will soon be time for supper,' George said. 'You go in. I have some business to attend to.'

When the younger man had disappeared George went down the steps and crooked a finger at Blencowe. The man came trotting.

'Has Nankivell not returned?'

'No, sur. We been keeping watch.'

'The coach must have broken down, I suppose. One would not have thought it beyond Trembath's wit to hire a post-chaise if there was going to be a long delay.'

'No, sur. Maybe something's gone wrong betwixt post-'ouses.'

'That I too had thought of, Blencowe.'

'Yes, sur.'

George glowered at his servant and went in. Now that Trevanion had mentioned it, he too was growing chill.

The tables broke up at a quarter to nine, and supper was served soon after. Outside the long afterglow was fading, and indoors candles were lighted to illuminate the long table and the food and wine spread upon it. It had not been the sort of game the big gamblers liked. Anthony Trefusis would not have come had he known the stakes were going to be so low. But as a result, though no one was feeling too exultant at their gains, no one was feeling too set down by their losses, and this made for a more generally jolly supper table.

Stephen, who had won about eight guineas, was feeling quite above himself. His enjoyment of Clowance was in its very earliest stages, when every moment could be savoured. The money he had made from his last venture was warming his hands and earning credit at the bank; his abounding good health and vigour had at last got the better of the weaknesses of convalescence; and he was being entertained with his wife at the home of one of the richest and most influential men in the county. He was hungry and thirsty for the good things on the table and for all the good things life had to offer. There was nothing better than this moment, and every so often he squeezed Clowance's hand to tell her so.

'I been thinking,' he whispered.

'What?'

'You realize, being invited here when Valentine's not home – it means we're accepted in a new way. I expect it's me being married to you that's done it; but it's significant.'

'Well, it's better to be friendly.'

'Not just that. Clowance, I wonder if twould be fitting if I spoke to Sir George tonight – later on if the opportunity arises.'

'About what?'

'Business. I just opened this bank account with Carne's; but it would be little inconvenience to bank in Truro – at Warleggan & Willyams. I was wondering whether to transfer – to mention that I'd like to transfer.'

'Tonight? Oh, *no*, Stephen.'

'Why not?'

'Yours is a very small account so far. I think Sir George, fond though he is of money, would only wish to talk business at a party like this if it were really big business.'

'Mine may be big business someday.'

'When it is . . . But even then . . . Certainly not tonight.'

Stephen looked at her with a trace of annoyance, then his face cleared.

'Ye know these things better than I do, dear heart. I shall not go against your advice.'

George glanced at them from the end of the table; at her flowering fairness. So someone had got her at last. No longer the tempting maiden. Used goods. But she looked no different. The bloom was still just the same, the same candid innocence. Strange if it was *her* husband who was led away tonight. A worm of sexual malice moved in him. From the day he first saw her trespassing in his house, barefoot, carrying a sheaf of foxgloves, he had felt her physical attraction – a rare thing for him. As with Morwenna Chynoweth many years before, there would be extra pleasure in hurting someone he felt for in that way and knew was personally unattainable.

Someone was talking to him; it was Unwin Trevaunance, booming away about something, across Clemency Trevanion, whom Harriet had put next to him.

'What?' he said.

'You didn't ask how I got on with Selina Pope.'

'What? No, I didn't. Thought you might prefer to keep it to yourself.'

'Not at all. I never mind if my business is public property.'

How true and typical of him, George thought. 'You found the lady at home?'

'Oh, yes. Recently returned from London, but very *much* at home. She has grown an inch since Hubby died.'

There was a movement among the servants by the door, and George half started up. But it was not Blencowe with the pre-arranged signal. Three servants came in bearing the dishes of gulls' eggs which were to be served with a shrimp sauce as a first course.

Unwin said: 'I can tell you this, George, she knows nothing of mining but cares a great deal for her own dignity; and she thinks, like my benighted brother, only of preserving the amenities. It was this chap Barrington Burdett, this lawyer fellow, who put her up to the idea of making me an offer for the mining rights. He advised her, damn the fellow . . . Still, she's offering a fair price, and a bird in the hand etc. What's this wine? Was it run?'

'No, a new shipment from one of the Hanseatic towns.

The commercial world is going to be turned topsy-turvy with the opening of the Continental ports . . .'

'A cup of tea on Saturday?' suggested Jeremy.

'What?'

'At the Red Lion at four. Or take dinner with me there and tea right after. Clemency can come and sit between us so that I am not able to touch you.'

She began to eat one of the eggs, stopped and delicately licked a finger. 'I would have to ask Clemency.'

'The last meeting, then? The last before you marry. I shall certainly not return home again before Christmas. After Saturday your path will be unimpeded. I shall not even be a ghost at the feast. By the time I return it will all be over.'

'You will always be a ghost at the feast, Jeremy, and you know it!'

'No, no,' he said, 'I am thinking of taking a leaf out of my cousin Geoffrey Charles's book and bringing home some plump little Flemish girl for wife.'

She looked at him slantwise, through her lashes. 'Indeed.'

'They run to plumpness out there. Like little pouter pigeons. Some of 'em anyhow. A *few* are quite slender.'

'Better to marry a slender girl,' said Cuby. 'They can always plump up afterwards.'

'That's what I thought. But the one I have in mind, called Lisa Dupont, already tends to plumpness. Do you think she would be suitable for me?'

'*Any* woman, I imagine, would be suitable for you in your present mood!'

'There is a truth in that. But pray don't confuse the issue. I am only thinking of Lisa Dupont as a possible substitute for yourself when the time comes. Can you imagine what Cornish society will be like in a few years if we have such mingling of races? For take heart – or do I mean take warning? – we shall all have to meet and mix in the future, for the county is too small for us altogether to avoid each other. We can discuss this on Saturday.'

'On Saturday,' said Cuby, 'I shall certainly *not* be there!'

'Come, come. You cannot deprive a condemned man of his last happy hours.'

Jeremy could have been speaking little more than the actual truth if he had known what Sir George Warleggan had in store for him. As they were talking there was a further stirring at the door and George received at last the signal he expected. He excused himself abruptly from his neighbours and rose and went to the door, went out.

Hector Trembath was there, holding his black tricorn hat, looking flushed.

George's eyes went up the stairs. 'You're damnably late! What kept you? Is he already changing?'

'No, Sir George. I fear he is not here at all.'

'*What?* What in God's name do you mean?'

Trembath swallowed his bony Adam's apple. 'We *just* caught the coach this morning, sir. Mr Rose was still not at all well and complaining bitter of the gouty pain in his head – wishing even to delay another day, sir! – but I induced him, persuaded him, almost led him, linking arms, like. Once in the coach things seemed to be going better, and for a while we even had a lengthy conversation on legal matters . . .'

'Get on, get on!'

Nankivell was in the hall now, nervously fingering his crop. Three other servants were nearby.

'Then at Tresillian, just as we came in sight of the river, Mr Rose complained that the pain in his head could no longer be borne, the jogging of the coach, he said, had made it insupportable. The coach was stopped for near on half an hour. We lifted him out – a very big man, sir, very heavy, with heavily flushed face and white hair – we sent to a cottage for water – a man on the coach had brandy – he could not drink. After half an hour, since there was no help or apothecary near, we somehow got him back into the coach. The other two inside passengers said they would cling on outside to give the sick man more room – and so we came to Truro. There he was took out and carried up to a chamber. I did not know what to do, but felt it my duty to stay with him; a doctor or apothecary might bring him round and I might yet be able to persuade him to come on. Sir George, I intended to have sent you a message, but the coach, being much delayed, left without warning . . .'

'Yes, yes. Go on, go on. How is he now?'

'We were fortunate enough to find Dr Daniel Behenna at home – our most respected physician – *your* physician, if I remember, of *course*! By the time he arrived Mr Rose could not move his right side at all, and could not speak. He had talked so much all last evening and throughout the early part of the journey, that it was pitiful to behold him unable to utter a word, could only pluck now and then at his lip with his swollen left hand –'

'What did Behenna say?'

'That he had suffered an apoplexy of the brain, and he at once bled him by means of an insertion in the external jugular vein. I swear, Sir George, it made me quite faint to see the blood –'

'Spare us your feelings. How is he now?'

In spite of his nervousness, Mr Trembath would continue with his story.

'Dr Behenna stayed half an hour; and I did not know *what* to do then; for clearly there was no hope of carrying Mr Rose here tonight or of him being helpful to you in any way if he did so come. So I took the liberty of sending to my house for my own horse and having him brought to Pearce's Hotel . . .' Mr Trembath cleared his throat. 'However, before I took my leave – to hurry here with the bad news – the servant girl who had been put to watch over Mr Rose came rushing down to say there was a change in the patient. So I and the innkeeper went up with her. She was right. A grave change had come over Mr Rose. It took no more than two minutes to summon an apothecary who had just entered the inn for some refreshment, and the apothecary at once pronounced him dead.'

'Dead?'

'Yes, sir.'

'I see.'

After a moment George found he had in his hand the wineglass which he had brought from the dining room. It was his first impulse to smash it on the ground. Instead of that with a twist of his powerful fingers he snapped the glass off at its stem and handed the pieces to a staring footman.

He went in to rejoin the party.

IV

Stephen Carrington enjoyed the evening right to the end, always winning enough at the table to off-set Clowance's losses; in his element as he had been all evening, mixing in a higher level of society than he had ever done before, being accepted by them without apparent eye-raising comment on his voice or manners, married at last to the girl he had coveted from the day he saw her. He had never been in anything like this position before, never. His misdeeds, he felt, were behind him. The accidental stabbing of an able seaman was more than two years old, and the only person who had recognized him on that night was now his partner and close friend. The chance of his being identified by anyone else for that offence so late in the day seemed very small – though he would still steer clear of Plymouth for a while to be on the safe side.

As for his later adventure in the coach, that was a little nearer in time and a little more sensitive. But Stephen believed in riding his luck. It had all gone so well for him so far; and the money from that robbery had financed his maritime start in life. Many men, he felt, he *knew* in his bones, had turned a more or less dishonest penny to begin. He wouldn't be at all surprised if his sour-looking host had done much the same – only in Warleggan's case it probably consisted of cheating widows rather than the bolder and more risky form his had taken.

So Stephen, unaware of the mountainous body of Mr Arthur Williams Rose, at present being conveyed out of the back door of Pearce's Hotel on its way to the boneyard, held his head high and looked forward to the future with supreme confidence . . .

As for Jeremy, he too had wrung a sort of pleasure from the evening, though it was of an altogether more wry and perverse kind than Stephen's. He had in the end persuaded Cuby to take tea with him next Saturday, with Clemency. It was prolonging the agony, yet it appealed to Jeremy as a more suitable end than muttering together over a card table. So be it. He would return to Lisa with the confirmed knowledge that Cornwall held nothing for him any more. On his way home, riding over the dark moors, taking his time lest Colley should stumble and throw him, he presented a figure which even in the star-lit gloom of the early night was likely to deter footpads. Cut purses and the riff-raff of the mines did not attack soldiers.

Jeremy was no more aware than Stephen of the narrow margin by which he had escaped the risk of denunciation; but on his long ride he began to think of the practical problems of the money still left to him. When he had taken a substantial part of it to pay for his army outfit he had been aware that the damp of the cave was beginning to damage the notes. At the time he had done nothing, but now, on this leave, it seemed sensible to try to find some means of preserving the rest.

For an hour he thought about it and then came to a decision. The Gatehouse, from which they had galloped out on their foolhardy enterprise and to which a day and a half later they had returned, was still empty and part furnished, just as it had been when Clowance's and Stephen's engagement had been broken off. Jeremy, who knew the little house intimately, remembered a loose floorboard in the backroom at the top of the narrow stairs. It would certainly prise up and could be knocked back into place again. He also knew that in the kitchen was an old box iron. If you took out the part that went in the fire to be heated it left a substantial cavity which could well contain what was left of his money; and the notes would be safe from deterioration. He would make the transfer early on Thursday morning.

Jeremy had none of Stephen's ebullient belief in his own luck; nor had he his ability to throw off a sense of guilt. The robbery *seemed* to have succeeded, and one simply went on from there. Jeremy had felt less unbalanced about it since his impulsive confession to Geoffrey Charles. His cousin's laughter had put the adventure into perspective – so had his warning that they were not yet out of the wood, perhaps never could be altogether safe.

Maybe having done something like that it was not proper to be altogether safe. Perhaps his continuing in the Army created the equilibrium in his life that a sense of justice required.

Chapter Seven

I

In early June England was visited by the Heads of State of the collective Allies who had helped to defeat Napoleon. Alexander I, Tsar of all the Russias; Frederick William III, King of Prussia; the Chancellor of Austria, Prince Metternich; the Chancellor of Prussia, Prince Charles Augustus Hardenberg; Field Marshal von Blücher, and many minor princes, all reached England in the same naval vessel, but on approaching London by coach some of the more popular figures scattered and arrived privately, fearful of the enthusiasm of the undisciplined and unpoliced English crowds.

And enthusiasm there was in abundance; Blücher was mobbed, the Tsar could not issue from the hotel – where he decided to stay instead of the state apartments chosen for him – without being greeted and followed by cheering crowds. Great receptions were held: balls, dinners, operas. It would have been high noon for the Prince Regent had not the crowds greeted him with hisses and boos and reserved all their cheers for the foreigners. Canning was travelling in the north country and wrote to Ross. 'Peace,' he wrote, 'which is so welcome now it comes with honour, has in a few months wrought so many surprises that one stands aghast at one's lack of foresight and sagacity. It has indeed saved some of our industries, but it has created havoc in others. All merchantry is in the melting pot; Europe welcomes our exports with enthusiasm, but floods us with imports in return. Some of our fledgling industries, grown green and lush from lack of competition, are now cut down with cold winds which must grow keener every day. Even more so now we must press for the reforms which have been hitherto resisted.' But Canning was increasingly preoccupied with the failing health of young George, his eldest boy.

Another one in dubious health at this time was Dwight Enys who, greatly to Caroline's fury, had ventured once too often into the pestilence-ridden area of the Guernseys and picked up some fever of which he could not rid himself. It came on and went off and came on again, with depressing regularity. Dwight accepted a draught or two from his assistant, Clotworthy, but would not allow another physician near him. He went on a starvation diet and prescribed himself Peruvian bark and opium and continued with his work in the villages as usual.

So for the present, talk of the four of them going off for a few weeks to Paris was shelved. Dwight heard now that the Davy party, having survived the collapse of Napoleon, had left Paris for the Auvergne and were later bound for Florence. 'The autumn is the best time in Paris,' said Ross, with the authority of someone who had never been there. 'We'll go then.'

In the meantime the great Peninsular Army, forged by Moore and Wellington into one of the finest fighting forces there had ever been, marched to Bordeaux, parted tearfully from its Portuguese battalions, was reviewed for the last time by Wellington, and broke up for ever. The day after the review Major Geoffrey Charles Poldark went to see his commanding officer and told him that he was resigning his commission.

Colonel William Napier regarded him for a full half minute from under his eyebrows before he replied.

'Do I hear aright?'

'You do, sir.'

'On what grounds have you come to such a misguided decision?'

'The war is over, sir. I think it is time I returned to civilian life. I hope I shall be able to sell my commission.'

'You are a professional soldier, Poldark, not a time server.'

'The Army has been my life since I was sixteen. But I have recently married; my wife is expecting a child; I have a small estate in Cornwall that needs attention.'

'And you will have enough to live on?'

'Thanks to money that my wife will bring me, yes, sir.'

Napier got up and limped to the window of the cottage. He was a thin, pale young man who had himself recently married.

'War is not altogether over yet, Poldark. Perhaps war in one form or another never will be over for a country like ours with a colonial empire.'

'I presume we have no orders yet, sir?'

'We shall embark for Plymouth when transport is available. Thereafter . . .'

'I confess I have no stomach for this war in America,' said Geoffrey Charles. 'It is such a bad-tempered little squabble, with no real principle involved – and no issue, unless it is the future of Canada.'

Napier turned. 'How old are you, Poldark?'

'I shall be thirty this October.'

'I am by a year the younger. How many times have you been wounded?'

'Four.'

'I have been wounded seven. I am your senior at least in that.'

They smiled at each other.

'This of course will have to go before the Duke and the authorities in London.'

'Of course.'

'Who may not be pleased.'

'No, sir.'

'In the first flush of a happy marriage this course you are taking may seem very desirable. In a year – two years it may look different. Have you ever thought of doing precisely the opposite of what you are proposing?'

'What is that?'

'Stay on a few more years. Continue your distinguished service and then apply through the proper channels to purchase a brigade command.'

Geoffrey Charles looked up in surprise. 'You're too kind, sir. I had certainly considered that out of reach. But if I may say so, with due respect, I should have thought you are a far more likely person to do that than myself.'

The hot sunlight outside shone on Napier's pallid hand as he drew the curtain across.

'I could not *afford* it, my friend. My wife has little money of her own. In fact . . .'

'Sir?'

'No matter . . . Does this prospect appeal to you?'

'It appeals to my self-esteem. But until now, I have had barely enough money to subsist at all. Without an allowance from a much disliked step-father I could not have remained an officer. Therefore, though I will accept some of my wife's money to help to put my small estate in some sort of order, I cannot – could not – stomach the thought of using it to buy myself a higher rank in the Army. It would be – self-aggrandisement . . .'

'What if you asked your wife?'

'I could not, sir, for it would look as if I were turning it down for her sake.'

A bugle sounded outside.

'Very well, Poldark. I will pass on the request.'

'Thank you, sir.' Geoffrey Charles hesitated. 'You were about to say something just now. Is it too personal for my ears?'

'Yes, indeed it is! Nevertheless you may hear it. I was about to say that in fact I have somewhat similar thoughts to yourself – of leaving the Army soon. Like you, I have a young and pretty wife. Unlike you, who seem to have taken your wounds in your stride, I am stiff when I lie down of nights and need my orderly to help me up in the mornings. Sometimes I shake with the ague. My progress upwards in the Army, as I have told you, is limited by want of means. But that is all in the future. Who knows what the future holds for any of us?'

II

'Leave to speak, sir?'

It was Lieutenant Christopher Havergal. Geoffrey Charles had been surreptitiously opening and shutting his part-paralysed hand. The excessive courtesy – was it mock courtesy? – of the remark irritated him.

'Well?'

'There is a rumour about, sir, that you intend to resign your commission and leave the Army.'

'What is that to you?'

'Only the same as it is to the other junior officers, sir. And the men.'

'Why have the junior officers left it to one of the most junior among them to make this inquiry?'

'Because they think I have ...' Lieutenant Havergal paused, threw back his fair hair.

'Brass enough for anything?'

A little tweak showed at the corner of the mouth. 'Brass is another form of courage, sir. Isn't it? I hope I – we – have been misinformed.'

'Brass,' said Geoffrey Charles, 'is allied to that form of courage you showed when chasing the hare. It is not the sort most favoured by the Duke. Or indeed by the Army generally.'

'No, sir.'

'Incidentally, what brought you into the Army, Havergal?'

'Oh,' the young man shrugged. 'My father is a shipbuilder in Sunderland. He made unwise speculations, lost most of his – brass – begging your pardon, sir – and had to sell his house and his yards. I went to the Charterhouse, then was reading for the bar, but had a disagreement with my father and chose to buy myself an ensigncy instead. Stationed for a year on useless duties at Gibraltar, contrived a transfer almost too late for any of the fun. And here I am!'

'And where, if I may ask, did you pick up your Portuguese mistress?'

Havergal grinned. 'In Abrantes. She's a pleasant little thing and causes no trouble.'

'My wife is Spanish, you know.'

'Yes indeed, sir.' The young man added hastily: 'It is becoming quite the fashion: Captain Smith of the Rifles, for instance. His wife goes with him everywhere, sharing all the hardships . . .'

'Shall you marry yours?'

'Oh, no, sir. With me – with us – it isn't like that at all.'

Geoffrey Charles slowly unflexed his hand. 'Well, Havergal, you have asked me a question, so I shall answer it. Yes, I am resigning from the Army. It is for personal reasons which I don't propose to discuss; but I feel that our work in Europe is done, our future work, if there is some in America, is not for me; and I have, I believe, more constructive things to do with my life.'

'Well . . . there couldn't be a better answer than that, sir. I'll tell the others. And may I say that I am personally very sorry.'

'Thank you.'

Havergal coughed. 'And if there ever were a chance of us meeting later – in civilian life, I mean, I should welcome it.'

'Are you thinking of leaving the Army too?'

'No, no, sir. But it was just a thought.'

Geoffrey Charles looked down at his hand. 'Thank you, Havergal. I'll bear it in mind.'

III

On the day the Tsar and most of the princelings left England, the 23rd June, after a sojourn which had opened their eyes to many strange aspects of English life, Selina Pope rode over to call on the Poldarks.

She had never been to Nampara before; Demelza felt herself remiss in never having invited her; but most of the time it had been difficult, because Ross did not like Clement Pope, and since he died there had not seemed the right opportunity. So she came without invitation, riding Amboy with a groom in attendance. She did not bring her daughters.

Demelza thought, as she had thought at the Trenwith party, what a pretty woman she was. She could by now well have dispensed with her widow's weeds, but the discovery that black very much suited her might have been the reason why she had not.

She ventured to call, she said, because she happened to be passing near — a likely subterfuge — and Captain Poldark had been so kind as to offer his advice on matters to do with her estate when she had seen him last at the Trenwith party. Ross, Demelza said, was at Wheal Leisure, but should be home to dinner in about half an hour. If she, Mrs Pope, would care to stay and take pot luck she, Mrs Poldark, would be happy to entertain her. Until her guest called she had been trying to clear some of the litter out of Clowance's room; so she was in a green dimity frock with a paler green apron over it, and her hair, never the easiest to control, had come unlooped with stooping; her hands were dirty; and she knew Ross would arrive back from the mine in a thick woollen shirt, corduroy breeches and old riding boots; but it pleased her to feel that Selina Pope would be able to see them both in this condition and to judge for herself whether she wished to continue to know them.

Mrs Pope said she would be delighted to stay, if it were not putting them to inconvenience. A slightly awkward pause was filled by the arrival of Isabella-Rose holding Henry's hand and persuading him to walk upright. Until now trial and error had convinced Henry that he could get from one place to another more quickly on hands and knees, and he was protesting a little at this newer mode of locomotion.

Later Ross arrived looking grim, a cleft between his brows because of a complication at the mine; but he made an effort and smiled at Selina and said if they would give him time to wash . . .

At dinner they talked of children, of current events, of local affairs. Mrs Pope had recently been to London so she had seen some of the scenes of rejoicing for herself. The Tsar, it was said, adored dancing, particularly the waltz, but he had caused offence by picking only the young and pretty women and ignoring the elder and more important ones. He had also given offence by slighting the Prince Regent's mistress, the Marchioness of Hertford. Mrs Pope had actually seen Marshal Blücher coming out of a shop: he had at once been surrounded by applauding crowds; but an *old* man, with none of the splendid dignity of Wellington. Mrs Pope's daughters, who had been left behind for a few months with an aunt in Finsbury, had been quite enraptured of it all.

And had they heard from their son since he returned to Brussels? He had quite remarkable gifts. And had they seen dear Clowance since her wedding? And what did they purpose to do in August? August? said Ross, not hiding his puzzlement.

'Is it not,' said Selina, 'the centenary of the Hanoverian accession? George the First became King on August the first 1714. They are talking already of more celebrations to commemorate that.'

'I'm not sure,' said Ross ironically, 'whether it should not be commemorated as a disaster.'

Mrs Pope glanced at Demelza and smiled. 'I think your husband is a republican, Mrs Poldark. As my husband was.'

Ross disliked the thought of having had anything in common with Mr Clement Pope. 'In principle, perhaps. In practice I can't see any considerable advantage in having a president instead. Frederick the Great said that once the Americans had rid themselves of one king they would probably have to crown another to keep the country from splitting up.'

Selina nodded. 'A letter I had from a friend in Boston says if this war goes on there will be great pressures within the country to split up into – into loosely connected states, I think he said. Massachusetts is deeply opposed to the war.'

'Are you American?' asked Demelza.

'No. My parents went over there when I was a child. They lived in New York. I married from there and lived at Perth Amboy in New Jersey until my husband retired and we returned to England. He was originally from Kent. But, of course, living over there as we did, you make friends, see their point of view, you understand.'

'No country was ever founded on such noble principles,'

Ross said. 'It's something to have the principles even if one cannot live up to them. If your Boston legislators could but persuade the country to propose a peace, we should be shown up as the fools we were to provoke the conflict.'

I know who she looks like! Demelza thought. Every now and then she has a look of *Elizabeth*. I wonder if Ross has noticed it. I rather hope not!

'I came partly,' Selena said, 'to thank you for your advice at the Trenwith party, Captain Poldark.'

'Do you mean about the mining rights?'

'Yes. I had a visit from Sir Unwin Trevaunance a little while ago and I was able to convince him that a mere woman could be as determined as any man, so he has agreed to the purchase and the deed is being drawn up.'

'I did very little except confirm that the price you were offering was about right. You must have had advice before that.'

'Yes, I did. I think it was your son who advised me in the first place.'

There was a brief silence.

'At least now,' Selina said, 'I can keep my house in peace.' She stopped in confusion. 'Forgive me, I didn't mean in the least that the opening of mines was not – was not desirable in some – some circumstances.'

'In *our* circumstances, for instance,' Ross said pleasantly. 'I suppose it all depends on the degree of affluence one has. I think, had we had wealth we could draw upon from outside, my wife would have demanded there should be no piles of attle or red stream to disfigure our pretty valley. As it is, we welcome it because it provides us with some of the elegancies of life. Without it – and without Wheal Leisure on the cliff – we should be very little more than poor farmers.'

'But Captain Poldark, you are so famously well known about the county! *And* a member of parliament. *And* a banker, I believe!'

'Being the owner of mines,' said Ross. 'That is how I live, and that is how I came by the rest.'

'And now a member of a Commission in London, isn't it? Metals or something?'

'A Base Metals and Mining Commission,' agreed Ross. 'It is not of great importance. How did you learn of it?'

'Jeremy told me.'

Another silence. Ross said: 'I suppose it was a natural appointment. I live off the mines, as I have said. I never forget it. Or I try never to forget it. It maintains one's sense of proportion.'

When she had gone Demelza said: 'What a *strange* visit, Ross!'

'In what way?'

'Well . . . she seemed to assume a friendship which has never really existed between us. I am not saying that it shouldn't, for we are almost neighbours, but it *hasn't*. It never did between the Trevaunances and ourselves. We went to Place House – what? – three times in ten years. She seems to assume a sort of – sort of *relationship*.'

'I know.'

'You felt it?'

'In a way, yes. I don't dislike her, though. She has a charm and is learning fast. But d'you think – is it possible this fellowship she is feeling – claiming is something to do with her friendship with Jeremy?'

'I hope not.' Demelza went to shut a window, for the June day had turned cold. The light made a halo round her hair. 'Ross, what's the difference between a simile and a metaphor?'

'I have no idea.'

'Well, I am going to use one of them. My children to me are like streams . . . clear water running, shallow and clear enough to see to the bottom. Only Jeremy is different – sometimes he's too deep for me to understand. He lives a private life none of us can reach to. In spite of all his good humour and his fun, he is – not at peace.'

'Perhaps *I* never have been,' said Ross.

'It may come a little from you, Ross, but it isn't the same. Besides . . . you have been at peace – many times. I know that.'

'Yes, my love, I have. Mostly thanks to you . . . As for Jeremy – I don't know. Perhaps it's just growing up. He hasn't had anything *serious* with Selina Pope, has he? It never occurred to me until today.' Ross picked up a paper, read a few lines, put it down. 'Damn these young men and their young women! They all take it much too much to heart.'

'Now you're frowning the way you were when you came in to dinner. I wonder Mrs Pope did not take fright at the sight of you.'

'It will take more than one frown to frighten her away, I suspicion. Well, it was all on the same account, as you might say. A young man taking it all too much to heart – our godson.'

'*Ben?* Ben Carter? What has he done?'

'You mean what have *we* done allowing our daughter to marry Stephen Carrington! The men are complaining that Ben is half drunk when he comes in the mornings and drunker when he leaves at night.'

'But Ben never *drinks*. He has never touched liquor in his life!'

'He does now, it seems. And today he hasn't turned up at all. When I came in to dinner I'd just been in to Zacky, but they had seen nothing of him.'

Demelza sighed. 'Oh, dear . . .'

'Yes. Oh, dear.'

'How is Zacky?'

'Better. But not well enough to take his grandson's place underground.'

'I saw Mrs Zacky on Sunday. I thought she looked worried for something.'

'If you had only had four daughters of twenty,' Ross said, 'you would have been able to make four men happy instead of one, and he the least deserving of the lot.'

'Hush,' said Demelza. 'You remember we agreed never to say anything unkind about Stephen, even between ourselves. Let him prove himself.'

'All the same,' said Ross, 'it's a worry about Ben.'

Chapter Eight

Since Arthur Thomas was united with Edith Permewan in matrimony according to God's holy ordinance, things had not been the same at the Thomases' cottage. Art had been the home-maker, the tidy one, the one who saw to the food and occasionally brushed out the cottage. John was out two or three nights a week fishing, and when he was ashore and not asleep was off on his perennial pilgrimage to see 'Winky' Mitchell. The feckless Music slept three nights a week in the stables in Place House, and spent as little time as he could alone at home.

On Friday afternoons Music always had three hours off, when it was his custom to walk home, make himself a dish of tea, have a bite to eat, and feed the cats. Music liked cats – they didn't laugh at him – and his personal tally at the moment was five: a ginger, two scabby tabby toms, a thin black sleek female killer and a cuddly black and white. On his way home he stopped at the Nanfans, who had a cow, and bought a pennyworth of milk which he shared with the cats. For his part he cared nothing whether it was goat milk or cow milk he had in his tea, but the cats preferred cow milk so he really got it for them. They all sat on the table waiting for him until he joined them. They had a small pilchard each today, something of a treat, for they were really expected to feed themselves, which they did by catching mice and rats and rabbits and anything else that moved and was smaller than they were. Although John often had a bit of fish to spare, he didn't hold with the notion that cats should be fed by human beings, and it was only because he knew his brother would be out that Music had dared to buy the fish on the way.

The cats didn't have imaginative names. One of the

scabby tabby toms was called Tom, the other Tabby, the thin black sleek female killer was called Blackie, the ginger Ginger and the cuddly black and white Whitey. Blackie was so fond of hunting that Tom and Tabby were grown lazy: they would wait for Blackie to bring back enough for the three. They tended to form an exclusive club to which Ginger and Whitey did not belong. If they tried to belong they were soon taught different. Blackie's hunting skills were so well developed that she had twice stolen Jud Paynter's breakfast. After that for weeks Jud had kept a loaded musket by his bed, but Blackie had a keen sense of knowing where she was not wanted.

Music poured milk into five tin lids and distributed them around. He didn't have a saucer for his own cup because the last had broken at Christmas, but the cup had a handle and only one crack. They drank in silence except for the sounds of splashing from Whitey who was a noisy drinker. Then Music brought the pilchards and put one in each tin dish on top of the droplets of milk, and cut a slice of cold bacon for himself. He crumbled a hunk of bread into smaller pieces, and scattered some of it among the chickens on the floor. There was again a degree of silence.

It was a bare room: one wooden table, three wooden chairs, another table by the wall piled with sacks and smelly fishing tackle and a few tin plates; beside it was the fire, a few sticks just smouldering now from having boiled his kettle; a furze oven seldom used, a bucket half full of stale water; on a shelf above, the remains of a loaf, the piece of bacon, two onions, a cardboard box with potatoes, two more cups and a jug. Then the stairs, leading up to the one room with the three straw mattresses; outside a lean-to shed and a privy; beyond, the rough edges of the moor.

Music never had much conversation for his cats, but they understood each other. Occasionally he would stick out a long finger, usually for Whitey to rub his head against, sometimes to touch one of the others to establish contact. The thin black sleek female killer always growled if she was touched while eating, but Music paid no attention.

Wrapped in a piece of old newspaper was a sizable

bunch of asparagus he had got for Dr Enys. Once a week, if he could find something, he took a little present to Dr Enys, left it at the kitchen door for him. It was a way of saying thank you for his unpaid help over these last two years. He had given Music the confidence to try to walk on his heels, and it had been part successful. And he had tried lowering his voice when speaking, lowering it an octave or so. It had worked, but as usual it only provoked laughter from those who heard him. All the same, he was improving.

Dr Enys was none too proper himself, fever or the like had caught him; didn't do for a doctor to be slight, didn't do at all. It had crossed Music's mind more than once to go see Widow Crow, who was sure to be at the Midsummer Fair, and ask her for a potion; but even he could see how hard it might be to persuade Dr Enys to take any draught made up by a rival.

Music had not much idea of time, so his hours off tended to contract or extend according to what he found to fill them; but so long as he was back to lock up the stables before dark each night it was usually all right. Since Mr Pope died Mrs Pope had extended her staff to include four men – two young footmen to wait at table – another boy in the stables, and Saul Grieves to take charge. Grieves had been an ostler at the King's Head in Redruth and gave himself airs. He did not much like Music and often made jokes at his expense, but he grudgingly acknowledged Music's gift with horses.

It was a dismal day: skeins of misty rain drifted across the dripping countryside and the clouds were so low it was not possible to know how far the daylight still had to run. It was quite a walk to Killewarren so Music did not linger over his tea. He shooed the cats and the chickens out and shut the half door and slid the bolt. However, as the top half was never shut the cats could easily claw their way over and the chickens could flutter in again if they'd the mind.

Clutching his bundle of asparagus in its dirty newspaper, he went tiptoeing out of the village with his dancing walk, and had gone half a mile before he remembered to lower himself onto his heels. He passed the church and took the short cut over the stile towards Fernmore. As he neared the gates he saw two figures approaching. They had not come out of Fernmore but out of The Bounders' Arms a few hundred yards further down the lane. A woman was linking a man and supporting him.

It was Emma Hartnell and Ben Carter. Seeing Music, Ben straightened up and rubbed his free hand across his mouth.

'Av'noon,' said Music. 'Av'noon, Ben. Av'noon, Emma. Squibbly ole day, edn ee. Squibbly down, the rain d'come. Goin' far, are ee?'

'Not so far nor so fast as I should like!' said Emma, out of breath. She was wearing her scarlet cloak but was hatless, and the rain made a spider's dew of her hair.

'Reckon I can manage from here,' said Ben gruffly. 'Do you go back now.' He unlooped his arm. 'Thank you, Emma. I'll thank you to leave me go.'

He took a step or two but his knees were not supporting him and he would have fallen had Emma not caught him again and steadied him.

She laughed but without humour. 'Reckon Ben edn quite himself just now. Are ee, Ben? Never mind, my 'andsome. I'll fetch ee 'ome in due course.'

'Where be gwain?' Music asked.

'Never you mind,' said Ben.

'I best be gwain too,' said Music. 'I be gwain Dr Enys's, see. Got somethin' for 'im, see. I best be gwain too.'

He went past and they continued on their way. Music stopped and looked back. Emma was a big girl and Ben not a big man, but his dead weight, which came on her now and then, was near to pulling her over. Music had never seen Ben like this before and wondered if he had had an accident at the mine. He ran back.

'What's amiss?' he said. ''Ere, leave me, Emma. I'll take'n for ee. What's amiss, Ben? Took a fall, 'ave ee?'

'He nigh took a fall in my house, Music,' said Emma. 'Been here all day, haven't ee, Ben? It has been a sad and sorry day.'

With one holding each arm they began to walk him towards Sawle.

'Didn't know what to do,' said Emma, eventually. 'Ben's been here all day. Should've turned him out sooner, I suppose. Didn't like to, him being in a mood. In a mood, wasn't you, Ben. Ned's in to Truro. Ben come at eleven and stayed on. I got him a bite t'eat but he wouldn't touch'n. Just rum. One after another. Just rum.'

It occurred to Music for the first time what might be amiss with Ben. He started to laugh and then stopped. Ben was an important man. Underground captain of Wheal Leisure mine. *And* Katie's brother. It wasn't like him. Lots of folk got slewed; not Ben.

'Ned's in to Truro,' said Emma. 'Not be back afore ten. Went in on a wagon. I told him tis cheapness for cheapness sake. He should've took the pony.'

Ben said: 'Leave me bide, do ee. I can walk.'

Emma said to Music: 'I thought t'aid him just so far as the church, him being a thought unsteady, like; but so soon as we got out in the air his knees give way.'

Ben said: 'I don't want no help. You go back to your taproom, Emma.'

'Tis not my taproom I'm concerned for,' said Emma, 'tis Sammie and Beth. Never mind, they'll fare for theirselves this once. Now we're making progress.'

At Grambler Ben insisted they should go on the old path behind Grambler Mine, not wanting to be seen by all and sundry in such a state. It was specially humiliating that one of his helpers should be Music, the village buffoon; but at the mine Emma excused herself and accepted Music's assurance that he could manage. So she went running back towards The Bounders' Arms.

Ben's weakness was not quite the normal drunken kind. His head was clearly dazed with drink but every so often a sort of faintness would come over him and he would almost collapse. So every so often he sat on a wall or a hedge to gather his wits and his strength, while Music stood faithfully by.

The day was drawing in. Such sparse trees as there were leaned crookedly to landward, crouching from the expected lash. The stooping clouds moved faster than they seemed to have any reason to. All colour except the greyest of greens had gone from the countryside; it had a look of a leafy December.

There were few about in Sawle to watch the ill-assorted couple hob-nailing down the lane. Only one or two stared and called greetings, and Music answered cheerfully for them both. As they came to the shop Ben stopped and swayed and tried to straighten his kerchief.

He said: 'Tha's enough. I'm home now. Off ye go, young Music. An' thank ee.'

He swayed to the door of the shop and his knees buckled under him.

So Music ended by shoving open the door of the shop, which was temporarily unattended, and then hauling Ben inside and half carrying, half dragging him up the steep dark stairs to his bedroom above.

He had got him as far as the bed but not onto it when there was a rattle of footsteps and Katie appeared.

'What's to do? Music, what're ee doing here? Ben, where you been? Mother's been in a rare dido. Where d'ye find him, Music?'

So there was talk and explanation while they got Ben to bed. Music was never good at explanations, and the fact that it was Katie who was demanding them tied his tongue worse than usual; but truth wormed its way out. Ben hadn't eaten for a week, and the last few days had been the worse for drink as well. Jinny Carter was out now, taking advantage of Katie's visit to leave her care for the shop while she went to see *her* mother and father over at Mellin, to find out from them whether Ben was up at the mine or eating with them or what.

Ben snarled at his helpers, saying he was old enough to see for himself and if he cared to take a drink twas no one's business but his own, and to hell with them both.

Katie thumped her way downstairs to make a cup of strong milky tea and to set a pot on the fire to heat up some mutton broth. Music twice cracked his head on the beams before he learned caution, then fell to examining the organ Ben had built into one wall of the rafters. He was fascinated by this and badly wanted to pump it up and set his feet on the pedals; only Ben's baleful and ungrateful eye prevented him.

Katie came back, and after first snarling that it would make him sick Ben began to sip the tea and to keep it down. It was nearly dark outside.

Katie picked up a paper parcel and unrolled it. 'Dear life, what's this?'

''Tis 'sparragras,' smiled Music, who had somehow kept a hold of it all the time.

'Is it yourn?'

'Ais. Twere meant for Dr Enys, but then I seen Ben.'

'Where d'ye get it, Music?'

'Get what?'

'The 'sparagus.'

'Dunnaw.'

'Course you know. You must've picked it.'

'Well . . . out the garden.'

'What garden?'

'Garden at Place.'

'You mean ye took'n? Or did someone give'n to ee?'

'Dr Enys, he've gotten fever. I thought twas nice for he.'

'Ye mean ye *took* it? Stole it?'

A look of unease came across Music's long face. ''Tis 'ard to find somethin' to carry for Dr Enys. I thought twas nice for he.'

'Yes, but . . .' Katie looped back her hair and took the cup from Ben. 'Feeling better are ee?'

'If it d'please you to say yes,' muttered Ben, 'I'll say yes.'

'I'll go see for that mutton broth,' she said, and clattered downstairs again.

Music beamed. 'Reckon the mine be doing proper, eh? Proper job, that, proper job.'

Ben did not answer.

Music said: 'That's 'andsome organ, Ben. 'Andsome, 'andsome. How do it work?'

'Like any other organ,' said Ben.

'Ar.' Music angled his long body every way to suggest he

326

was about to sit down on the playing stool, but he received no encouragement.

'They d'say every man jack as works at Wheal Leisure 'll get a bonus come Michaelmas. Wish I could work at Wheal Leisure.'

'You're better off where you be,' said Ben. 'Horses you know 'bout. Copper and tin you don't.'

'Copper and tin, copper and tin,' said Music, and went on saying it because he liked the sound of it.

Katie reappeared with a steaming bowl. 'Drink this, Ben. This'll put a bit o' coal on the fire.'

'I think my fire's best doused and put out,' said Ben.

'Don't you get so sad for yerself! My dear life, a brother of mine talking like that!'

'Copper and tin,' chanted Music. 'Copper and tin.'

''Ere, Music,' said Katie in alarm. 'Aren't you promised back at dusk to see to the stables?'

Music peered out of the window. ''Tis dusk and dark, I see. Wind's moaning too. Shouldn't be astonished at more rain.'

'Aren't you promised back?'

'Ais. I didn't mind to remember.'

'Then off you go at once! Off quick! Else you'll be in dire trouble! That Grieves man . . .'

'Eh, well, maybe I'd best go.' Music looked around but did not pick up his parcel. 'I'd best be off, Ben.'

'Bye,' said Ben. 'And I've to thank you for yer 'elp.'

'Aw . . .' Overcome at being thanked, Music retreated from the room, knocking his head sideways on the door lintel.

Rubbing his head and muttering, he groped his way down to the empty shop, but before he could go out Katie came clattering down after him.

'Music. I want a word with you.'

'Ais, Katie?' He beamed.

'You stole that 'sparagus!'

'What?'

'You 'eard what I said!'

'Ais . . . Well, twas just standing there.'

327

'Standing where?'

'In the garden, like. Where it always be.'

'And no one told you you could pick'n?'

'No. I just thought . . .'

'So you *stole* it!'

'Twas not seeming like that.'

'But *twas*!'

Music continued to rub his head. 'Last week in me time off I went for the mushrooms. All down they fields where they belong to grow . . .'

'You wouldn't find 'em. Tis too early.'

'I searched and searched. Tis 'igh summer. I thought to find some.'

'Well you won't yet. But ye'll be in real grief if you steal things!'

'There was more there. More 'sparagus. Don't b'lieve Mrs be too fond of 'n. Oft times it d'go to seed and no one eaten of 'n.'

'That don't matter, Music.' She took his arm. 'What d'you think Dr Enys 'd say if he knowed you'd been stealing to give to him?'

Music hung his head.

'Well?'

'Don't know, Katie.'

'I do. E'd say, what, Music doing that? and 'im going church Sundays reg'lar! Him in choir too!'

Music did not speak. Under his shame was a burning pleasure that she cared enough.

'So afore you go, I want you promise me ye'll never steal again.'

'What?'

Katie repeated her sentence. 'Because if ye do and someone catches you, ye'll lose yer job and go jail. Understand?'

'Ais.'

'So do you promise?'

'I promise.'

'Faithful? Cross yer 'eart.'

'I promise,' Music said again. 'Cross me 'eart and spit to die.'

'There now, so be off with ee. And if Grieves be waiting tell 'im what ye've been about. 'Elping a man that's fallen down. Don't say he were drunk! Say 'e 'd fell down and say who twas. And say e's my brother, see. The underground cap'n of Wheal Leisure Mine! That's excuse 'nough, or I'll know the reason why!'

'Ais, Katie, I'll mind to tell 'im. An' Katie . . .'

'Yes?'

'That beer I gave ee to drink that time at Trenwith. Twas not on purpose. Twas not that way 'tall . . .'

'Aw, forget it, ye great lootal,' said Katie, and reached up – though she was so tall she hadn't far to reach – and kissed him. 'Now be off with ee, do.'

A little later as a waning moon lifted and lightened the clouds, a tall gawky long-necked figure could be seen skipping across the fields towards Trevaunance Cove. Sometimes he ran and sometimes he hopped, always on his toes, Dr Enys's instructions quite forgotten, and sometimes he gave a little chirrup at the top of his contra tenor voice, and then he would walk a few steps and leap high in the air and then again begin to run.

It seemed to Music Thomas just then that a new life had dawned for him. It did not occur to him to wonder why Katie should think she had so much influence with Saul Grieves.

Chapter Nine

I

A letter from Jeremy reporting his safe return, saying there were rumours that the regiment might be moved from Brussels to Antwerp. One from Geoffrey Charles telling of his decision to resign from the army and to join Amadora in Madrid. Whether they would then come home for the baby to be born in Cornwall he was not sure. Amadora, he knew, fancied staying in Madrid until afterwards, and he could well understand this feeling.

A letter from George Canning saying there might be a change in his plans. Lord Liverpool had offered him the Embassy in Portugal.

'He has promised to do everything in his power to raise the importance of this mission to something much above the ordinary, to make it a worthy task. The Portuguese Regent will shortly be returning from exile, and much tact and good will will be needed to ease the strains arising from his return. I confess I am sorely tempted – not for the pomp and circumstance but because my parliamentary career is in ruins, and George badly needs the sun. Even if I refuse this I feel I must take my son abroad somewhere. Compassion, like Charity, begins in one's own home.

'If I should agree to go, would you not come with us? I am certain I could persuade Liverpool, through Charles Ellis, to offer you some position which would justify your accompanying me. Perhaps for a six month period. Since you know Prince John, you would undoubtedly be *persona grata* with him and his family. Why do you not come and help to ease the situation; and bring your wife – whom I have never met but about whose beauty and charm I have heard so much?'

'Oh, no,' said Ross, when Demelza looked up from the

letter inquiringly. 'I would not go without you and I would not go with you.'

'But George Canning . . .'

'Is a dear friend. But I think that, having accompanied the Portuguese Royal Family in that Armada taking them to Rio six odd years ago, I have done my duty in their respect. Prince John has no mind of his own – or changes it as often as the wind. And when his mother was taken aboard ship to go to Brazil they had to fight with her.'

'Why, did she not want to go?'

'No, she is crazed – has been for years. It just happened she was in one of her violent moods.'

'Why,' said Demelza, 'why do so many kings – or queens – go insane? Or is it that there is an epidemic at the moment?'

'You might ask why do so many kings – who are brought up to rule – turn out to be incapable of ruling?'

Demelza returned the letter to Ross. 'If he goes, it will be left to you to argue for all the things you want . . . reform, help for the poor . . .'

'No, no – there are others far more ardent than Canning.'

'But are these "others" members of the government?'

He patted her hand. 'Not so. There are some who call themselves Radicals. I find much in common with their aims, for they want progress without revolution.'

'Shall you then become one of them?'

He smiled. 'I don't think I wish to become anything. In any case, my race is almost run –'

'Oh, Ross, do not be so silly! You are so fit and well, and by some standards you are still quite young!'

'Sorry, I meant really only in a parliamentary sense. I all but resigned at the last election, then stayed on to see the end of the war. Both the Falmouths have been patient with an eccentric like me, but I wouldn't expect the present Lord Falmouth's patience to stretch to accepting the views I might voice at any time now. Instead of peace bringing plenty it has brought poverty to many in England. Now no government has any excuse not to try to alleviate it. We cannot suppress for ever.'

'And do the Whigs think this also?'

'Some only.' Ross stuffed the letter in his pocket, got up. 'Have you seen Caroline today?'

'No, last eve. Dwight was better but still without appetite. Seriously, Ross.'

'Yes?'

'You have seemed more content – this last year or so you have seemed more content than I have known you – I mean for such a long period. It seems almost ever since Harry was born. Of course you have been to London twice, but you have come home more quickly.'

'Well, I have been little in Parliament. It was chiefly on this Mining Commission, as you know.'

'At least you have not become restless – not *seemed* restless. Do you think it will last?'

Ross laughed. 'Do you want it to last?'

'Yes, of course. Nothing could be nicer. But what you've just said – is it – d'you see it as the beginning of something new?'

Ross was some time in replying. 'No. I am not really a political animal. I could never attend great meetings and make speeches in favour of reform. If there were action of some sort . . .'

'Yes,' said Demelza, 'that is what I would be afraid of.'

He patted her hand again. 'I would try to keep it legal.'

'By the way,' said Demelza presently, 'those nice things Mr Canning said about me: "your wife about whose beauty and charm I have heard so much" – that is what they call blarney, I suppose?'

'Not necessarily.'

'I wonder how he could possibly have "heard so much".'

'I have no idea,' said Ross.

II

Valentine Warleggan returned that day. He had spent a few days in London with a friend, but George's annoyance at the delay was solved when he learned that the friend was titled.

George said nothing that night, but the following evening before supper he asked Valentine to come to his study to taste a new canary wine he had recently had shipped in. Valentine went along, thin and lean and bony and tall and slightly knocked in one knee but vigorous and handsome and sardonic with it.

He made an educated comment or two upon the wine, knowing this as only a preliminary to whatever it was George wanted to talk to him about.

And sure enough they had hardly finished the second glass before George said:

'I had hoped you would have returned for your vacation promptly this summer because I wanted to announce the engagement.'

'The engagement?' Valentine peered into his glass.

'*Your* engagement, of course. Your engagement to marry Miss Cuby Trevanion. I had thought we should give a small engagement party on Midsummer's Day, the 24th June, when this could be formally announced, with notices in the papers – including *The Times* – to follow. Unfortunately you have not given us time to arrange this now, so I suggest Sunday the 17th July.'

'Ah, yes,' said Valentine.

They sipped their wine in silence for a while.

'With Cuby's consent?' Valentine asked.

'Of course. It was all arranged, as you know, almost twelve months since; but John Trevanion has proved to be such an unreliable fellow, so unscrupulous when he gets his hands on money, that I have twice had to put the date off because I could not be sure he would adhere to his side of the bargain. Of course it would always be possible to invoke the law; but law-suits between the nearest relatives of a newly married couple are distasteful and create a bad impression when they get in the press; so I have bided my time and sought to make the agreement even more watertight. This has now been done, and nothing more *can* be done. I believe that out of very shame he will not make any serious attempt to evade the conditions of the marriage settlement . . . In any event the delay has been timely. You are now well past your twentieth birthday. Cuby is twenty-two. It has worked out very well.'

'Ah, yes,' said Valentine.

George turned the two guineas over in his fob pocket. 'The wedding can be in September. Early September I had thought, so that you can enjoy a full honeymoon before returning to Cambridge. I shall wish you to complete your studies at Cambridge; another year will do that, by which time John Trevanion has agreed to leave Caerhays Castle. You can then enter into residence without the encumbrance of an older brother-in-law.'

'Ah, yes,' said Valentine.

'The matter of your mother-in-law I will leave to your own good sense. Personally she strikes me as a sour creature. I suppose she is a disappointed woman – widowed too young. She is reticent, distant, self-contained; but I do not think she will be a serious obstacle to your convenience. If she were to be that I believe you could persuade her to leave.'

'Cuby is very attached to her family,' observed Valentine.

'True. But, once married, you will be the master of the house. As I say, I cannot see if you play your cards aright that you need be concerned about Mrs Bettesworth.'

'Ah,' said Valentine.

George was becoming a little restive at this lack of response but he said no more for the moment. Eventually Valentine said:

'I hear you had a card party while I was at college.'

George grunted. It was a very sore spot.

'The Trevanions came. It was then that I made final arrangements for the engagement announcement and the wedding date. Since then, when you did not arrive in time, I have had to write postponing the date of the engagement party.'

Valentine said suddenly: 'Do you think Cuby is *happy* about it?'

'Happy? What do you suppose? Women are always glad to marry; and she is doing very fine for herself; for as long as she lives she will be the chatelaine of Caerhays. She is extravagantly proud of her ancestry and of this castle: wed to a handsome and well-circumstanced young man, she will be realizing her dearest dreams!'

'As a point of interest, Father, how well-circumstanced *would* that be?'

George picked up the decanter and poured himself another half glass. He didn't offer his son any more. 'Well enough. I should see that you have an adequate allowance.'

'I have heard, sir, that you would expect me to supervise your new interests in the china clay industry.'

'Who told you that?'

'I forget. Did you not tell me yourself?'

'Certainly not . . . Well, you would not wish, I assume, to become nothing more than a country gentleman at twenty-one. Any responsibilities you undertook for me in eastern and south-eastern Cornwall would be paid for in a way that would supplement your normal income. You could be more affluent or less affluent according to your personal choice.'

'Ah, yes,' said Valentine, for the fourth time.

George said: 'It may also interest you to know that I am investing in the manganese production of north Cornwall. Indeed it seems likely that this market could come completely under our control. There are all sorts of interesting – indeed exciting – prospects for the future.'

'Ah, yes.' Valentine crossed and uncrossed his legs. 'Forgive me, father, if I seem to labour a point, but has Cuby ever said she is in love with me?'

The only sound for a few moments was the buzzing of a bluebottle against the window pane.

'What d'you mean?' his father said irritably. 'In *love*? Why should she say anything of the sort? In particular, why should she express any such sentiments to *me*? It is to *you* that she would address herself!'

'Well, she has not done so to me.'

'That in all likelihood is because you have not given her the opportunity! You have a somewhat cynical approach to life which must be vexatious to young ladies who have lived a sheltered existence. But what does all this matter? There is time enough yet for such exchanges. When next you meet you can very easily provoke the conversation into such a channel.'

'Time enough,' said Valentine, grasping quickly at the opening he had been looking for. 'Yes, that is what I was thinking, father. Time enough ... We surely have time enough to look on this engagement with a little more care. It has been hanging fire for more than a twelvemonth, and a little longer can do no harm. Being up at Cambridge I have had very little opportunity for conversing with Cuby. I should like to do so with a degree of gradualness. It would be more to the point to announce the engagement about Christmas and arrange a – a marriage for when I come down from Cambridge next year.'

George got up, stoppered the decanter and put it away in a glass cupboard. He locked the cupboard.

'That the matter has been hanging fire for twelve months is reason enough – and a very cogent reason – why it should be postponed no longer. It is all settled between Trevanion and myself. There can be no possible reason for further delay.'

Valentine said: 'You have not asked me if I love Cuby.'

George breathed out.

'Good God, why should I? She is a personable, intelligent, pretty girl! Young and healthy and well bred!' With a hint of boldness in his voice that could never have been there before his marriage to Harriet, he said: 'Many men would consider you a lucky dog. Why, if I were in your shoes I should not at all misfancy –'

'Oh, I fancy her well enough,' Valentine admitted. 'If she is untouched, as I suspect, I fancy deflowering her very much indeed. But then I fancy so many women. That's the fun of it. I'm not sure I wish to be tied to Cuby for life. Of course she is all the things you say, and I grant you that. I grant her that. But for marriage you want something more. I think it would be much better if we had six months longer to make sure.'

George looked at his sprawling son with an impatience that hid a growing anger.

'I do not agree that it would be better, Valentine. It has

been a long and difficult negotiation which further delay might well put out of joint. Once we break or stretch any condition, John Trevanion will feel free to do the same.' He made a great effort to be reasonable, conciliatory, even fraternal. 'It cannot have come as much of a surprise to you, my dear boy. You have known it all for over a year! You must have accustomed yourself to the prospect. As I have said, and as you have admitted, it cannot be too disagreeable a prospect. To be master of so fine an estate and so fine a woman at less than twenty-one years old! Do you appreciate how much *financially* it will cost me, this wedding? I am doing it for you, my only son, to set you up in this splendid style. The home that has been the Trevanion home for five hundred years will become yours. The Warleggan name, through you, may well become established there for another five hundred years to come! It is a great and inspiring thought! But the time for hesitation, for delay, is long over. You *must* accept my advice on this. The wedding must take place not later than September. I trust you will,' George swallowed, 'I trust you will excuse me for being adamant on the point. But I am. The choice is now only yours in the matter of a week or two one way or the other.'

Valentine climbed to his feet, rubbed a hand over his hair.

'Do you mind if I take another drink?'

George fumbled in his pocket, handed him the key. 'Help yourself.'

There was silence for a few minutes except for the squeak of the cupboard door, the clink of decanter on glass. Somewhere downstairs one of Harriet's dogs was barking: a great gruff sound, hollow and breathy and deep.

'Tell me, father. Tell me what you would do if I said no to your proposition?'

'What on earth do you mean, boy? Said *no*? You couldn't say no. This is decided!'

Valentine was sitting straight in his chair now, knees together, moving the glass slowly round in his fingers. 'But I surely have to be a willing party! Blood and bones, it is *my* life you are directing!'

337

'And I am directing it! Remember that! I am your father. You do as I say. There is no choice for you. You do as I *say*!'

Valentine gulped his canary.

'Ah, yes. I see. But if . . .'

'If nothing!'

Valentine filled his glass again.

'Don't make yourself *drunk*!' snapped George. 'That will do you no good.'

'On the contrary it may. Have you heard of Dutch courage, father? Perhaps I am seeking Dutch courage.'

George took several deep breaths to steady his temper. This show of reluctance on Valentine's part, he was convinced, simply grew out of perverseness and a desire to show off, to demonstrate his apparent independence. Valentine depended for his first and last penny on what his father gave him. He was unfitted for any form of work except the most menial, and his whole approach to life was so pleasure-loving that there was virtually no alternative but to obey. This streak of obstinacy, of sophistical wrong-headedness, of cynical rejection of homely virtues, was something George had long ago come to detest in his son. Normally one could make a deliberate effort and ignore the poses and the posturings. But why, over so important and so benevolent an issue as this, where an ordinary son would only, *could* only, accept and be enormously grateful, did he have to put on this show of reluctance, make this sardonic attempt at rejection? George was convinced that if he were now to say: 'Very well, Valentine, if that is your decision, the marriage is off, and I will cancel all my arrangements with Trevanion,' the one who would ultimately feel the bitterest disappointment at having his bluff called would be Valentine himself.

The trouble was George could not bring himself to call the bluff.

Perhaps Valentine's mind had been running along somewhat parallel lines for he said:

'What *would* you do if I said no, then?'

'Do you need such a detailed answer?'

The Dutch courage was working. 'Well, father, yes, I think I do. I suppose I might be permitted to return to Cambridge? . . .'

'I regret you would not.'

'Then I would continue to live here as a – as a sort of pensioner?'

'No, you would not,' said George.

'But I am your *son*,' said Valentine.

'Indeed. A son for whom I have the greatest affection and the greatest regard. For whom I have been striving to provide a noble and a settled future. As you must admit.'

'But does this mean so much to you – this arrangement – that if I wreck it you will attempt to wreck me?'

'I should not *attempt* to wreck you,' said George. 'But you cannot avoid the consequences of your own acts. And these consequences would be such that I should . . .' He paused.

'Disown me?'

'Come, Valentine, why are we talking like this? I do not know what has got into you to take this perverse and deeply objectionable line. It is all arranged. You have never before raised a single word against it –'

'I was not consulted!'

'But you *knew* of it and tacitly accepted it! This late objection does credit neither to your honour nor your common sense. Come, take another drink and let us go down to supper. Sleep on it. It will look different in the morning.'

Valentine got up and stood very still, the decanter firm in his hand.

'I do not think it will, father.'

George stared at his lean, patrician, dark eyed, narrow eyed, long nosed son.

'Just what does that mean?'

'It means that I will not marry Cuby Trevanion. Indeed cannot.'

'*Cannot?*' George spoke the word, his jaws opening widely as if about to bite on something. 'What in God's name are you talking about?'

'In God's name,' said Valentine. And then sardonically:

339

'Yes, I suppose it is in God's name, if you care to look on it that way. God has forbidden it . . . You see, father, I am already married.'

Chapter Ten

Ursula had been playing with her mine when she heard the raised voices. At first she thought it was someone calling her for supper; this sometimes happened in spite of her father's insistence that a servant should be sent up to her room if she did not respond to the gong.

Ursula spent a lot of time alone in her room; more than her step-mother thought healthy, but in spite of her stolid appearance she had a keen imagination and enjoyed little plays and stories that she made up to fit her models.

That, of course, of the mine was the most elaborate. Built by a man called Angove who had lost a leg in an accident at Wheal Spinster, it filled one side of her playroom, being seven feet long and three and a half high, and worked almost to scale and almost exactly like a real mine. Little miners made of tin picked in caverns and stooped in tunnels, with one side of the model cut away so that they could be moved at will. The engine worked, though so far only by turning a handle. Ingenious trays and catchpots had been built at floor level so that real water might be used without damage to the room. For this mine Ursula now had her own cost books and account books and lists of bargains struck by pairs of miners working on tribute. Recently Angove had been brought back to extend the workings round the corner of the room, with overhand stopes and whyms and adits and ladders and planks leading across shafts and genuine bits of ore, tin and copper, let into the tunnels here and there.

One rather errant game Ursula played, and was playing today, related to her mother's first husband. Some years ago Grandmother, who had now herself left them to join the angels, told her that her mother's first husband, father of that handsome soldier who had come to lunch here with his foreign wife, had met his death by going down a mine called Wheal Grace near Nampara. He had gone down on his own, not telling anybody, and started exploring in the old workings where nobody had ever been for years. He had tried to cross a plank over a shaft full of water, the plank had been rotten and he had fallen in. 'They found him,' old Grandmother Warleggan whispered, 'just too late by an hour. No more'n an hour. And d'you know what was in his hand? A rusty nail. He'd been clinging to it, holding himself up by it, till it came out of the wall!'

The story had made a great impression on Ursula, and she got a *frisson* out of replaying it. One of her little tin men was Francis Poldark. She walked him over to the mine, persuaded him to crawl down one of the narrow tunnels, brought him to the plank over the flooded shaft. She could not break the plank every time, so she had him slip and plunge into the water; then cling to the nail. That was the best part of it. In inky darkness and up to his neck in water, he clung to the nail. Then the rescue party started searching for him; but too late . . .

The raised voices were on this floor and coming from her father's study. She had never heard anything quite like this before. Twice to her knowledge since his marriage to Harriet there had been angry scenes, with both of them on the verge of shouting but it had never actually *happened*. Now it was happening. Ursula took more than an average girl's glee in trouble in the house so long as she was not concerned in it; so she slipped out of her room and along the passage to the door of her father's study.

Then she realized that this was not a quarrel involving her step-mother at all. The voices were both male, and she knew them both.

'. . . by God, sir, I shall put a stop to this!'

'To *what*? It has *happened*!'

'I shall see that it is annulled! You are not twenty-one! It is simply a form you have gone through to persuade some wretched girl –'

'No wretched girl, father. And it is *legal*. I made doubly sure of that!'

Something slipped and fell to the floor. Ursula skipped back expecting someone to come bursting out, but they did not. She did not much care for her brother, who was often supercilious at her expense, so this was a special pleasure to hear him being hauled over the coals for something; and something that sounded quite dreadful.

'And who is this girl?'

'Never mind that for the moment. The ceremony took place in St Benedict's —'

'*Where's that?*'

'Cambridge, father. It was performed by the Reverend Arthur Chisholm and was quite conventional and legal and public, and it took place on Wednesday, May the fourth last —'

'By God, this is *insufferable*! You knew *very well* what my plans were for you! By God, you shall not go unpunished for this! What got into you? — some insanity — some snivelling wench you'd got with child! I suppose her father and her brother —'

'She has *neither*! Nor is she with child. It was a perfectly deliberate choice on my part —'

'Deliberate in order to frustrate everything I had planned for you! *Wasn't* it! Tell me that! Wasn't it absolutely deliberate — an act on your part undertaken solely to bring down in ruins all the plans I had for you. Wasn't it! *Wasn't* it!'

'Only partly, my dear father. I confess I did not like to continue so wholly dependent on you as I have been until now. And, since you corner me, I have never much fancied being your lapdog. But my reasons for what I have done are altogether more complex than that — than a simple desire to thwart your arrangements and set them at naught. I can tell you . . . but I won't!'

'Tell me what you fancy! Explain to me *exactly* what I have bred, what simpering, scheming, sarcastic, good-for-nothing fop! What ungrateful, ungracious, greedy, drunken, malapert, lazy wastrel! From the moment I bred you you have accepted *everything* I have lavished on you with a smirk and a sneer. Never so much as a thank you! Never so much as a by-your-leave! *Everything* you have taken for granted as if by right. Well I will show you that it is not yours by right at all! I'll show you that, my boy; from now on! I'll show you!'

A glass shattered on the floor and Ursula again sprang away, but the quarrel was too absorbing to take her far.

Valentine's voice. It was cooler now but more bitter.

'And what have I received from you, dear father? For the first six or seven years of my life I remember nothing but harsh words and cold looks. Then after Mother died I became a sort of symbol to you, and that is what I have remained! The money you spent on me – on my clothes, my education, was really money you spent on self-aggrandisement. That you had a son who went to Eton was more your pleasure than mine. That he mixed with the sons of peers and had a baronet as his "fag", was something to talk about among your friends. That you fixed him up with a nice young virgin and a great house and just enough money to live on; it was all a part of the same pattern: the aggrandisement of Sir George Warleggan, the blacksmith's grandson!'

'You insolent *puppy*!' There was the thump of furniture and someone stumbling.

'Why do you take that as an insult, father? I am a blacksmith's *great* grandson. I cannot see that it *matters*. We all come from some humble beginnings, whether they be near or far. What I am complaining about is that you should be complaining about me! . . .'

'Leave the chair, damn you! . . . I shall not touch you again . . .'

'Had I married Cuby, your plans would have worked out well; but I'll lay a curse that you would have kept me on a short allowance, just so that I should continue to dance when you pulled the string. That was your intention, wasn't it! Blood and bones, I'll swear it was!'

'Well, I can promise you this: you'll dance to another tune from now on! You'll find a difference when you're a pauper! Most of your precious drinking and gaming friends will no longer wish to know you! And as for your lascivious habits, you'll find women's bodies less easy to come by when there is no gold in the hand!'

'One woman's body I have for quite a time now come by, and that is my wife's. I'm sure that a man of your moral attitudes would applaud our decision to make the union legal. Also, I am not in love with Cuby but I *am* in love with my wife. Indeed I worship the very ground she walks on!'

Ursula tittered, but not the man hearing it inside the room.

'I presume I do not know this paragon. Perhaps she has enough money to keep you as *her* pet lap dog. I trust so, for you will leave this house tomorrow with the clothes you stand up in and a couple of trunks to take your personal belongings. After that you will not receive a penny from me. You may go and rot in Hell!'

'Call it Hell if you like, father. In fact my wife has £30,000 in three per cents, so – although I hope to improve on that as time goes on – I do not suppose my life will alter for the worse in comfort or convenience. It will be very much better in one way for I shall enjoy the freedom of seeing nothing of you. You poisoned my mother's life with your insane suspicions and jealousies; and I am only happy and relieved that you will have no further opportunity to poison mine!'

The gong was being rung for supper. Quite out of the blue, Ursula suddenly wished it was *louder* so that it would stop them quarrelling. The most *terrible* things were now being said, and her father, whom she greatly admired, was getting the *worst* of it. Things were being said now that would never be forgotten, searing accusations, horrible insults, words that could never be unspoken. From taking a gleeful interest in a rumpus she had become very frightened. What was being said now was probably for ever. Her family life would not be the same again.

Silence had fallen inside the room. At least they were not fighting, as had seemed likely a couple of minutes ago.

Her father said: 'For saying those evil and ignorant things about my relationship with your mother I shall never forgive you. Pray leave this room and do not come in to supper. Leave the house as early as you can in the morning so that I shall have the least possible opportunity of seeing you again. Return to your woman in Cambridge and stay there. Cornwall is well rid of you.'

'I fear Cornwall is not rid of me,' said Valentine. 'I shall stay here. My wife has a house here. I could have wished to delay the announcement of our marriage by another six months, or so, but you have forced it into the open with your ill-considered pressure. My wife was Mrs Selina Pope. Now she is Mrs Selina Warleggan, and we shall live at Place House, barely fifteen miles distant from here. Before you have an opportunity for any more envenomed comments, she is thirty-two years of age, and I have two step-daughters. They are attractive young ladies and I shall do my best to marry them off in due course. Perhaps you will tell Harriet all this over supper, will you? I would like her to know the truth as soon as possible. I am sure she will be amused. But her amusement may possibly be more directed against you than against me . . .'

Ursula only just had time to flatten herself against the wall as Valentine swept out. She did not know if he saw her, but if he did he took no notice. His black hair fell across a darkening bruise on his forehead; his eyes glistened, his mouth was set, his nose hawk-like. He looked ten years older and, far from being fop-like or languorous, he looked a very dangerous young man.

Book Three

Chapter One

I

A cool and unkempt summer, with scarcely enough sun to ripen the hay or enough rain to lengthen the corn. May had expended the benevolence of the year.

The war in America was increasingly bitter, a victory for American forces near Niagara in July, and the capture of a British naval squadron on Lake Champlain in September, being sandwiched between the battle of Bladensberg which the British won and the burning of Washington in retaliation for the burning by the Americans of the capital of upper Canada a few months before. This reprisal was much deplored by the Prince Regent.

Geoffrey Charles's old regiment, the 43rd Monmouth-shires reached England on the 23rd July, were not disbanded like many of the others but given two months' leave. On the 10th October they embarked on transports to take part in the new conflict across the Atlantic.

American privateers were active off Bristol, capturing some ships and burning others and generally disrupting trade. *The Times* thundered against the iniquity and perfidy of the Americans. President Madison thundered against the iniquity and perfidy of those of his own countrymen who ran the British blockade in order to continue traffic with Britain.

It was suggested at the Congress of Ghent that the

Russians should mediate between the British and the Americans in an effort to end the war.

In France two attempts on King Louis the Eighteenth's life were frustrated, and in September the French introduced a budget in which an effort was made to establish a solid public credit against 'the robberies and gross deceptions of the previous Impostor'. The English flocked to Paris and were generally shocked by its run-down appearance.

In August came the centenary of the accession of the House of Hanover. Although a large part of the population of Great Britain saw nothing about the House of Hanover to admire, everyone seized on the opportunity for another junketing. Indeed, Ross sardonically observed that in Cornwall more celebrations were held to commemorate the perpetration of an unpopular monarchy than there had been over the liberation of Europe and the deposition of a fearsome enemy.

In Truro ornamental arches were erected all the way down Boscawen Street from Coinagehall to King Street, decorated with laurel, fir, oak and red flags. Under these arches two rows of tables 300 feet long were set up for a public open-air dinner with a band of musicians, and sides of beef, legs of mutton, mountains of vegetables and an alpine range of plum puddings. Tea and cakes were distributed to 1700 children, who later took part in a Furry Dance. Among the elders there was a mock Coronation of Louis the Eighteenth, and he was drawn in triumph through the streets on a dray.

There were fireworks and balls at Callington, and at Helston a dinner for 90 at the Angel Inn, followed by a distribution of 15 cwt of beef and mutton and a thousand 4 lb loaves to the poor. Processions, fireworks, dinner parties continued for a week. At United Mines, Chacewater, 1200 people sat down to dinner, and at Fowey, after the fireworks and bonfires, two boats on makeshift wheels were drawn through the streets, one containing musicians, the other a selection of the town beauties handsomely dressed and suitably garnished with flowers.

In London huge set pieces were arranged in the Royal

parks: fireworks, processions, brass bands; the celebrations went on for ten days with great drunkenness, much gambling and general immorality. In the end notices had to be posted in the parks to get the populace to move off.

The sensation of Valentine Warleggan's unexpected marriage swept mid Cornwall for a day or two; but people quickly accepted it. There was nothing particularly unusual about a young man marrying a woman twelve years older than himself, especially when the woman was a rich and pretty widow. That she was non-Cornish and did not come out of the top drawer were small matters, for Valentine's claim to breeding derived only from his mother's side. True he was still only an undergraduate, and he had already made for himself a reputation as a rake. Paul Kellow's comment that, 'I'll wager it'll not be long before he tumbles his step-daughters,' may have been echoed elsewhere. But Selina Warleggan, they felt, must have known what she was about and was by no means born yesterday. It was going to be a new ménage on the north coast at Trevaunance, and, if and when Geoffrey Charles returned, there would be two half-brothers with their new wives as resident neighbours. But on bad terms if their last meeting was anything to go by.

Some sympathy was felt for Cuby Trevanion, for she had missed a good match, and, although the conditions of her marriage were not known outside a restricted circle, it was generally assumed that the linking of her family with the Warleggans would have put the Trevanions on their feet again. Major Trevanion had never been a popular figure, but the sisters were well liked.

The first meeting between Sir George and the major after Valentine's marriage was also the last. Shortly after it Major Trevanion left for London, officially to take part in the celebrations, unofficially to try to raise new money to keep him out of a debtor's court. At the same time Cuby and Clemency left for a prolonged stay with their great aunt Bettesworth, relative of the Trenegloses, at Callington.

The situation was embarrassing to begin with at Place House, since the marriage had been kept as much a secret there as anywhere. Valentine arrived unexpectedly for dinner on the Tuesday, nursing a bruise on his forehead. Selina went scarlet when she heard his news, but after dinner, having recovered her composure, she called together all her indoor servants and announced that two months ago in Cambridge she had married Mr Warleggan. They had kept it secret until Mr Warleggan had had an opportunity to inform his parents, which he had now done. Henceforward they had a new master in the house, and would of course take orders from him in exactly the way they had formerly taken orders from Mr Pope. Selina carefully avoided meeting the eye of her parlourmaid Katie Carter, who rather less than twelve months ago had surprised her in bed with Valentine Warleggan while her husband lay empurpled on the floor of the landing. Katie, on fire with embarrassment and sweating with anxiety, simply did not know where to look. She was afraid that she might now lose her job, since the dread secret was now cloaked with respectability; but she need not have been concerned. So long as she continued to be discreet the new Mrs Warleggan would give her no extra excuse to talk of the past.

When Music was told he put a great hand in front of his mouth to stifle a guffaw; then his eyes grew round with apprehension, rather as Katie's had. A young master might be none too tolerant of one who was slow to pick up new instructions. And Saul Grieves and all, ready to say or do anything to confuse him the more. He began to fear for his job, with more reason than Katie.

When the news reached Nampara it explained a good deal about Selina Pope's call on them. Even so, she could hardly claim a relationship – at least so far as the world knew. That Ross and Demelza suspected different was something they could never speak of even between themselves.

Ross said: 'He's the strangest young man. There seems no *harm* in him. Yet there was harm enough in his bringing that boy to confront Morwenna.'

'I was afraid for a time,' Demelza said, 'that he was going to become too fond of Clowance.'

'At least now he's free of George,' said Ross. 'It will be strange to have another –' he baulked at the word 'to have him so close: but he has bought his freedom with a marriage that he may find constraining in other ways. Of course not only Valentine is affected by this marriage . . .'

'I was thinking the same thing.'

'No doubt Miss Cuby will be seeking out some other rich young man to marry. It may not be so easy.'

'Someone will have to write and tell Jeremy,' Demelza said. 'I think perhaps you should, Ross.'

'Why me?'

'I think if I wrote it I would make it seem like I was giving him good news. You would be – more detached – as is proper. The fact that she is not going to marry Valentine does not mean she is not going to seek another rich man – as you have just said. In fact when she first refused Jeremy I do not think the Warleggans had come on the scene at all!'

Ross said: 'I would willingly not tell him until he came home again, since anything to do with her seems to upset him. But if we do not write someone else will. The last thing I want is to seem to be withholding it.'

II

The following week Stephen Carrington rode into Truro and asked to see Sir George Warleggan. George saw him in the upper chamber above the bank. Stephen was wearing a buff nankeen jacket he had recently had made for him in Falmouth, dove grey breeches and well polished riding boots. His hair had been trimmed and brushed and was tied with a piece of black ribbon into a short cue. Although never quite at home in fine clothes, he looked handsome. Even so short a period of marriage had given him a new stability.

Stephen said he had come to see Sir George about opening an account with his bank. It was, he said, more convenient to keep his money at Carne's in Falmouth and to deal with them; but in view of Sir George's gesture of friendship in inviting Clowance and himself to that party at Cardew he felt it would be opportune and timely if he moved his account to Warleggan & Willyams. To have a friend as a banker was a rare privilege that he would very much appreciate, and he hoped that in the years to come the business he would bring to the bank would be of value to them too.

George sat for a long moment on the other side of the desk, fingering his pen. What confounded impertinence, he thought, what typical impertinence from this braggart sailor that when thinking of opening a pettifogging account he should ask to see the *owner* of the bank. Not content with a clerk, not content even with Lander, the chief clerk, he had to request an interview with Sir George Warleggan. As if he were a substantial landowner proposing some big accommodation. As if he were the chief shareholder in some industrial tramway with a proposal for a company flotation. As if . . .

Stephen's confidence was becoming threadbare with the long silence. Clowance of course had said, *don't* call. If you *have* to approach him, if you really feel you *must*, then write to him.

'What is the nature of your account?' The words when they came were more mildly spoken than George intended. At the very last moment he had had second thoughts.

'Oh, small to begin, Sir George. I am trying to run a few vessels, mainly in the coastal trade and with Ireland and France. So that most of me money is tied up. At the moment I have two small vessels, one built special, the other bought as a prize – fishing boats really, but adapted for carrying cargo. And I have hopes of buying a third when the right opportunity comes along. Me account, what I shall have to deposit next week, will be £300, but I shall hope to more than double that before the month be out.'

Through the window behind him George looked out at a mule-drawn cart unloading several glistening blocks of tin for the coinage, which would take place on Thursday of this week. These great blocks, weighing 300 lbs each, would be unguarded until the controller and receiver arrived to determine by assay if they were of a sufficient quality to receive the stamp of the Duchy arms. It was fortunate, George thought, that most of his own mines raised copper, over which this cumbersome and tiresome law did not operate. But the tin coinages were very useful to his bank, obliging as they did the tin mines to borrow money to tide them over from one quarterly coinage to the next.

He said: 'What shall you ship?'

'Anything that's going. We run – we ran the blockade last summer carrying pilchards to Italy, but twill not be the same this year with all the ports open – not the same profit, I mean. I've a promised cargo of moor-stone for Morlaix and shall bring salt back – that's for the *Chasse Marée*. But I'll quote for anything: clay, bark, corn; or bring iron from Wales or timber from Norway. There's cargoes enough at the right price. All I need is more carrying capacity. The lads who've crewed with me are keen to go again. There's much to be done.'

'Much to be ventured?'

'Aye.' Stephen caught George's look and added: 'But legal. There's no cause to break the law when there's so much chance for honest trading.'

Damned hypocrite, thought George. But was he not also a young man who could be used?

'Do you have more purchases in mind?'

'Purchases?'

'Of vessels. French prizes will soon dry up now.'

'Aye. That's true. But . . . there's a fine American brig, called *Adolphus*, lying in Falmouth at the moment. She was captured by a British frigate, the *Lyre*, condemned as a prize and brought in. She's been lying in the Roads two weeks now while her cargo's sold: 70 odd bales of deerskins, 50 of bear, 30 bales of cotton, 100 odd barrels of potash, a deal of logwood. The stuff's been going cheap; I would have bought more if I'd had the money, like.'

'Does the brig appeal to you?'

'Oh, she's handsome! Built in Baltimore. They're always fine boats from there. Seventy-two feet long, they say, by twenty-three in breadth. I suppose she'd displace about 150 tons. Very good rake to her; she'll travel fast through the water.'

'But you are not going to bid for her?'

'I shall go to the auction; but she'll be way above my means.'

'What would she be likely to fetch?'

'Oh . . . tis difficult to say. But she's in prime condition – less than two years old.'

'A thousand pounds?'

'More than that. She's been well advertised.'

'Ah,' said George, and got up from his desk. He noticed that Stephen did not get up as well. He noticed that Stephen did not call him, sir. He strolled over to the further window, not because he wanted to move but because he wanted to think. Fortunately Cary was in bed today: he had left off his winter vests and caught a chill.

'Have you tried to raise accommodation money from Carne's?'

'What for?'

'To enable you to bid for this ship?'

Stephen was genuinely startled. 'No. It is not likely they'd aid me, for I have no security to offer.'

'You own the other vessels?'

'Yes.'

'Would they not be security?'

'I suppose. I'm not well used to the ways of finance.'

'Commerce and enterprise build on credit. Without it much of industry would shut down.'

'Aye.' Stephen got up now, for George was talking behind him. 'I've Andrew Blamey as me second man, but I'm taking no nonsense from him: he's got to toe *my* line. Then there's Bert Blount, who's a first-class seaman: learned his trade the hard way, would navigate anywhere; two or three others you could give a bit of authority to. Course you have to see what they make of it; but I reckon it is a – what do they call it? – nucleus.' He was pleased with the word; it sounded important, learned, and he repeated it. 'Nucleus. Three vessels or four wouldn't be beyond me capacity to manage.'

'Including the *Adolphus*?'

'Oh, she'd be the *queen*!'

'King perhaps with such a name.'

354

Stephen laughed heartily. After a hesitant beginning this meeting was now going better than he had dared to hope. But he was still not sure of himself. Sir George had a fearsome reputation.

'I'm obliged to ye, Sir George, for giving me so much of your time. Can I take it, then –'

'Have you books?'

'Books?'

'Ledgers. Showing the profitability of your trade.'

'No. Till now I've been well content to keep all such details in me head.'

'Good enough to begin, but a mistake to continue. Could you produce them?'

'Well, there's little to produce so far. The outlay, the profits, the sharing of the profits. I could keep books if twas considered necessary to – to –'

'If my bank advanced you two thousand pounds to buy the *Adolphus*, it would be essential that ledgers be kept and that we should have access to them from time to time.'

Stephen took a deep breath. 'For that, Sir George, I'd be more'n willing to do whatever you say!'

Rain was trickling down the windows now. It was a humid day, with a sky as heavy as a soup tureen. The office was quieter and cooler with the windows and doors tight shut.

George said: 'When is to be the auction?'

'Monday week.'

'We have a little time to draw up an agreement. The conditions will simply be the normal banking conditions on which such a loan can be made. You should have time to study them, and you should be free to accept or reject them as you think best for your own interests. Perhaps you could call in tomorrow and see Mr Lander. He will have the details.'

'Thank you, Sir George,' said Stephen, shaking hands. 'Thank you, Sir George.' And went out walking on air.

After he had left George went back to his desk and made some notes on the interview. Not that he needed them, but it was a matter of principle. Then he left the room and went into the private part of the house, where once so much had gone on and now so little went on. Elizabeth had lived here almost all the time and only paid the occasional visit to Trenwith – to see her parents – or to Cardew – to see his. With no parental complications, Harriet spent nine-tenths of her time at Cardew, and only came reluctantly to Truro where, unlike Elizabeth, she had few friends. So often the only person in residence was himself, for about three days of the week, and old Cary, who hardly used more than two rooms in all. The full staff was of course kept on for the occasions when George entertained business friends, and the house would be a little more frequently used in September when Ursula began school. Valentine of course would never be allowed to darken its doors again.

Very silent now, and the odour musty and stale. Smells wafted up from the river; there had not been sufficient wind recently to carry them away. Oh for the days of Elizabeth . . .

Sometimes he fancied he saw her still, heard her; she had a particular step, like no one else's. Doors creaked, floorboards as if some weight had passed over them. It was a long time now; she was long since bones and dust; like his father and mother and hers . . . as he would be soon . . . Morbid thoughts for a heavy afternoon. Must ignore them – brush them away. Cobwebs in the mind . . .

Valentine's extraordinary marriage and the bitter quarrel following had deeply seared George. Ever since, he had been of raw and uncertain temper. To the frustration and anger of knowing of the failure of all his plans for Valentine's future was added the knowledge that he had lost his son. For a time his anger had diguised the fact, but in the night he knew it to be true. He had, of course, never really loved Valentine in the way he loved Ursula – not at least since Aunt Agatha had poured her poisonous lies into his ears – but since Elizabeth's death he had fully accepted Valentine as his true son. He had lavished, if not great affection, then many material benefits upon him. But possibly even by the age of six damage had been done from which their relationship had not recovered. As Valentine grew up he seemed to grow into another Geoffrey Charles – deeply attached to his mother's memory, and, in thought or by implication, resenting his father. So that once or twice the old worms of doubt had stirred in George.

Now he allowed them a freer reign; though he found himself doubly uncomfortable in doing so, knowing that he was breaking the vow he had made when Elizabeth, having given birth to a second premature child, had unexpectedly died. He had sworn he would never doubt again, and whatever the provocation he must try to keep that oath.

He thought of the young man he had just shown out of his office, and wondered if he could explain to anybody his motives for helping Carrington. They were so contrary, so complex, even running counter to each other, like pleas of not guilty in a court of law. (I wasn't present at the scene of the crime, but if I *was* present I didn't do it.) How list his motives; how explain them without sophistry even to himself?

Firstly, Valentine's defection had left a larger void than he could have foreseen. That reluctantly one had to admit. The loss of his only son – the only person left to carry on the Warleggan name – lost not in war, not from accident or disease, but by *marriage* – was a near mortal blow. Of course at some far future date the rift might be partly healed. But not for a very long time. Too many things had been said which could never be unsaid. And George's anger did not diminish, it grew every time he thought of it. The deliberate duplicity, the cold hostility infuriated him. And it had humiliated him in front of other people. Harriet had not laughed but he had thought he detected amusement in her eyes. Humiliation was something he could never endure.

Well, what had this to do with Stephen? Superficially nothing. But injured pride can sometimes find strange objects to assuage it. Stephen for Valentine? Of course not. But a sort of gap was there and could be filled. Nor was it impossible that Valentine, observing things from afar, would be irritated to see Stephen receiving favours that might have been his.

Secondly, Stephen had married a Poldark, and it might

also anger the Nampara Poldarks to see their son-in-law working with and for their old enemy.

Thirdly, Stephen's wife was Clowance Poldark. George had never touched her, except three times to shake hands, and never expected to do more; but in the event of something coming of this, he would certainly see more of her; might even see more of her than her own family.

Fourthly, if Stephen became difficult, egotistic, tried to push in ways George opposed, or attempted to interfere in matters that did not concern him, it would be not unagreeable to be able to bankrupt him at will.

Fifthly, George's other great disappointment of the summer – Mr Rose's death – had left him no less determined to keep the coach robbery in mind; and perversely, because nothing could be proved, he felt an increased conviction that Stephen Carrington had been a part of it. There was something swaggering and blustering about the sailor which fitted well with such an audacious robbery. *And* there had been a naval lieutenant taking part in it. Was it not typical of him to play such a role? Perhaps there never *could* be proof now. But a closer association, particularly where it involved money, might still provide evidence, for or against.

On the whole George did not regret his generosity to the young man.

III

And the young man, when he returned home, was full of his success. He told it all to Clowance over hot scones which she had baked for his return.

He ended: 'So you see I was *right*, wasn't I, him inviting us that night *was* a sign that he wished to be a friend! I'm glad I went to see him now, Clowance, I'm glad I went and didn't just write; twould not 've been the same. By God, it really means I shall be a shipowner! Tis hard to credit. In just the twelvemonth. Three vessels, if not more! We'll call it the Carrington Line!'

Clowance said: 'Watch tomorrow, won't you Stephen?

Read very carefully whatever agreement he puts before you. Don't think I'm not excited for you – for us –; but you see, though I have never disliked him personally, he has this reputation in Cornwall, always for getting his pound of flesh.'

Stephen stared at her. 'Maybe it's a sort of reputation to be proud of! Pound of flesh has a nasty meaning but it may cover no more than being a good business man and expecting others to be the same. There's too much laziness and slovenliness in the world. Maybe it's just that George Warleggan has no time for neither; and if that's so I could scarce blame him. Oh, I know your mother and father think harshly of him – and Jeremy too I believe – but the most of that was no business matter at all. Twas to do with your father and Elizabeth, George's wife, and your mother and many little quarrels over the years. That is not business, that is – well, jealousy and dislike and personal feuds which have naught to do either with you or with me. Why, if I had to choose . . .' He broke off.

'If you had to choose?'

He had been about to say that he would rather be a wealthy merchant and banker like George Warleggan than a small landowner and mine owner like Ross Poldark; but he had the good sense to stop in time.

'If I had to choose I'd rather be thought a hard man in business sooner than a soft.'

'But *fair*. Looking at other people as human beings not as cogs. My father says that is George's wrong way.'

Stephen spread a large pat of butter on his scone, then watched it begin to melt before he took a bite.

'I don't think you'd get far in the sailing world if you did that. I know it is only human beings banding together as crews that can make it work . . . But you got to be hard, because that's the way the world is and that's the way the sea is . . . All the same – all the same, if you have a rich banker as a friend you don't have to do everything the way he does. So long as you turn in the profit, that's all that counts.'

'D'you prefer these to the usual splits?' Clowance asked.

'What?'

'I thought it would make a change.'

'Yes . . . yes, I reckon I do. They're sweeter. But then I like everything you cook, you know that.'

She said: 'I'm taking care for the time when you will be harder to please, when the glow has gone.'

'Why should the glow ever go? It is not like you to be misanthropical.'

She smiled. Her eyes were thoughtful.

'I suppose it is always a mistake to take one's parents' view of another person. Handsome is as handsome does . . . After the first meeting I had with Sir George – when I admit I was trespassing and I think I gave him somewhat of a shock, when he was rude and snarly – after that he has always been coldly polite, with a look as if he'd like to like me but mustn't. Once or twice I've surprised looks that I wasn't supposed to see. I don't think he's as cold as he pretends . . . Certainly I do not dislike him. It is only what one hears. And not just from my parents. He is known for his ruthlessness in business. And is really *feared* for it. There are small business men up and down the county who have gone to the wall because of him. And if a man loses his work and says harsh things about the way he has lost it, then he'll find no more work in Cornwall – *anywhere*; because the Warleggans say not.'

Stephen fingered a few crumbs from his missing eye tooth. 'Where d'you learn all this if not from your parents?'

'Stephen,' she said, 'I'm twenty years of age and have spent *all* my life in Cornwall. Even living a *sheltered* life, one hears a great deal about the important people of the county.'

After a few moments he said a bit sulkily: 'And you do not trust me to be able to accept help from this man without becoming ruled by him?'

'No, I didn't say that. But I said, be careful.'

'Oh,' said Stephen, well aware that the ice he was treading on was far thinner than Clowance knew. 'I'll be that sure enough.'

Chapter Two

I

After the long bout of drunkenness Ben Carter shook himself out of the deathly mood that had gripped him, and went for a tramp along the cliffs. It was months since he had come this way. From Sawle Combe you could climb left towards Trevaunance and St Ann's, skirting Trenwith land and crossing behind Place House, a track which had been a right of way for centuries and which even the new owners, the Popes, had not objected to so long as you were discreet in your passage. Or you could climb right along the even wilder cliffs, above Seal Hole Cave and in sight of the Queen Rock until you came down into Nampara Cove. Ben chose the latter.

He had not shown up at Wheal Leisure for nine days and knew his absence simply could go on no longer. It was not fair to the Poldarks to leave them without news of him except such as the neighbours brought. He had to confront them. It was possible, even likely, that they had already decided to discharge him – to promote young Mark Daniel or someone like that to take his place. No mine could operate in the care of an underground mining captain who absented himself without so much as a by-your-leave for more than a week and who had been observed drunk on duty before that.

But the Poldarks being who they were, and him being their godson, it was quite possible that they would still be willing to take him back, *if* he was willing to go. He had to decide on this walk whether – if the opportunity was open – he was willing to go.

A loner all his life, a man who preferred his own company to anyone else's – or *almost* anyone else's – he had been quite content to follow his own eccentric ways, building, developing, improving his organ, living at home making just enough money in his one-man excavations to pay his mother for his keep and caring nothing for any more, he had been persuaded by Jeremy – over-persuaded, perhaps – to take an interest in the opening of Wheal Leisure, and then a responsible position there. It was possible that without him the old Trevorgie workings, which were now the most profitable part of the mine, would never have been discovered. He had become involved in its progress, its success. Along with that had come a closer association with Clowance than he had ever had before, and the following tragedy – to him – of her marriage to Stephen Carrington.

Now he yearned for a return to the lonely, carefree, un-responsible life he had known of old; when he was his own master, if yet master of so little. What he had been wondering during the last two days, while he was coming out of his soaking drunkenness, was whether that carefree life could in truth ever be recalled? He had to confess he had not disliked his time at Wheal Leisure; although it was against his deepest principles that any man should be 'managed' by any other or be given orders or generally supervised – just as he could not accept such a bondage for himself. But he had worked within such a system and had not been unhappy so working. Could you turn the clock back?

It was a fine afternoon with a few curvatures of cloud building up their white colonnades of cumulus. The tide was full in, licking white round all the rocks and brimming a scintillant blue to the very edges of the land. There was no sand left in the world. Fine veils of mist hung in the air above the rocks. A breeze rose and fell, errant, uncertain of direction.

Ben came to the declivity above Kellow's Ladder. He couldn't remember when he had last been down: one year, two years? That time he and Jeremy and Paul went to Ireland. It had been a bit of a crazy venture, without as much chance of profit as if they had gone to Brittany, but Paul had set his mind on it. They had come back laden with whiskey, illegally distilled of course. The *Enid* was an old-style down-at-heel lugger which had never been as good a sailor as *Nampara Girl*, but she had served her purpose at the time. The Kellows were not really seafaring folk or they would never have left their vessel in that cove all through the winter. Sooner or later a gale would do its destructive work. Anyway, though it was romantic to have your own little natural quay with its personal access, the approach was so inconvenient and sometimes even perilous that it was hardly worth the trouble.

Ben peered at the ladder, tested a rung or two and then went down, climbing with the practised ease of a miner. More than half way down was an opening to a low tunnel driven horizontally by some long-dead prospector in search of tin. No one alive remembered even the perpendicular shaft being driven, so it was easy to speculate, hard to be sure.

Ben went on down, picking his way among the half broken rungs, until he came out into the daylight of the cove. It was awash now, the curving rock of the natural quay half submerged, a few ribs of the sunken *Enid* still straddling the upper boulders where one strident storm had thrown them out of the reach of normal seas. A couple of herring gulls sidled their way along a flinty ridge, eyeing him with suspicion but not alarm. Spray damped his face.

The simple fact of the matter was that he couldn't go *on* behaving like this. After his fight with Stephen he had resigned his position, and only some weeks later had allowed himself to be persuaded back. Now for this to happen a second time was inexcusable from a Poldark point of view. The only course was to waste no further time pottering round desolate cliffs but to go direct to Captain Poldark and have it out: tell him that quite plainly he had discovered himself unfit for the regular responsibility of routine work, and apologize for the personal mistake he had made in ever supposing that he would be. *No* mention of Clowance. Above all, there must be no mention of Clowance.

Ben picked up a big stone and flung it into the water; it

disappeared with a plop that was inaudible among the grunts and rushings of the sea. He turned and began to mount the ladder.

Just near the lateral tunnel a rung of the ladder snapped under his foot and he bruised his knee. Rubbing this he looked at the floor of the tunnel and saw scuffings on the rock and part of a footprint on the muddy sand at the entrance. These surely were recent marks – not older than the rain of a couple of weeks ago – and he wondered who else had been down here and for what purpose. Some lonely miner like himself picking around to see what he could find? Some village girl doing away with an unwanted child? He swung himself off the ladder and into the tunnel.

The light was dim here at the best of times, and he had brought no candle; but he crouched in the entrance for a couple of minutes with his eyes closed and then turned to crawl in.

As far as he remembered from the old days, the tunnel did not go in far, but he did not venture all the way in case someone had dug a pit. If some man had begun prospecting again . . .

But he did perceive what looked like a sheet of tarpaulin and some sacks about ten feet in on the left hand side lying against the wall of rock. The entire pile was too flat and deflated to be able to contain anything like a foetus or the corpse of a new-born child; so he went across and picked the first sack up and shook it out and found it empty. He saw they were actually small flour bags, to contain probably about 20 lbs of flour, such as were used sometimes at Jonas's Mill, but there was no sign of flour inside them. Outside they were cobwebbed and dank.

He took up the second one and shook it, and there was a tinkle on the rocks. Ben groped about and found a ring and a metal thing which might have been a seal. He put these to one side and took up the third bag, being more careful now. His hand came on a few flimsy pieces of paper and he drew them out. Nothing else. The paper, though thin, crackled and was of good quality.

He took the sheets, which were of different size and

condition, to the cave entrance and screwed up his eyes to read through the damp stains. One said: 'Idless. No 24. 15 Oct, 1812. Recd of Thomas Jolly. Black Tin 4 cwt. 2 qrs. 19 lbs. Which I promise to deliver to him or order next Truro Coinage . . .' Another paper read: 'This is the Last Will and Testament of me Thomas Trenerry of Maker in the County of Cornwall.' A third seemed to be a bill: 'Item – one ebony snuff box; Item . . .' The last began: 'Received the sum of Thirty-Five Pounds'.

Ben hesitated and then thrust the documents back in the sack. They were none of his business. Whoever put them there would presumably come back for them – unless, as was more probable, they had been thrown away as out of date.

He picked up the ring and the engraved metal disc with the raised knob. He thought of putting these back too, but changed his mind and slipped them in his pocket to examine more closely when he reached the daylight. It was unlikely they were of value, but after the discovery of the Roman coin in the old Trevorgie workings you never knew what might turn up.

II

Demelza had been bathing on the beach with Isabella-Rose when Ben arrived. She was wearing an ankle-length scarlet cloak to hide her flimsy costume, and a towel worn turban-like about her hair. Bella was in pink frills – the only member of the family ever to wear a conventional costume: this not out of modesty but out of vanity; she thought the flounces suited her, and she was probably right. Ben was at the door, and Betsy Maria Martin, his cousin, had just opened it to him. He flushed at the sight of Demelza.

'Oh, beg pardon, I come . . . well, I come to see Cap'n Poldark.'

'He's not in, Ben. He's gone to Truro on business.'

This was a set-back. Ben shuffled his feet. 'Oh, I . . . Well, then . . .'

'Come in.' Demelza kept her expression and her voice pleasant but neutral. 'Have you been to the mine?'

'Not yet, ma'am. I thought – me being absent for a while – I'd best first see Cap'n Poldark.'

'Yes, of course . . . Go in, Bella, and make sure your hair is dry. Get a warm towel from Jane – there'll be one in the kitchen.'

Bella shot in ahead of them at great speed, falling over Farquhar, who was bounding out to meet them. Among the cries and the confusion Ben somehow found himself in the parlour. Demelza smiled at him.

'Are you coming better?'

'Better? . . .' Ben frowned. 'If it can be so called. Tis *time* I were better! Thank you. But I come to see – to see Captain Poldark and –'

'And I will not do? Well, he'll be in in the morning, Ben.'

'Well, tis not so much as you will not *do*, mistress. I wouldn't be so rude as to say any such thing! But seeing as Cap'n Poldark d'employ me, and me being off without so much as a by-your-leave, tis very necessary I shall see him about the future.'

Demelza took the towel off her head and shook out her hair. It was already drying.

'Have you seen your grandfather?'

'No . . . Least, not this week. Not for some time.'

'He's been worried for you. We all have. Are you in a hurry?'

'What, me? No, ma'am. What've *I* got to do?'

'Then will you stay till I change? I have damp things underneath and I shall not be more than a few minutes.'

'Of course.'

'Sit down.'

Ben did not obey but stood staring bleakly out of the window until she returned. She was in a plain blue sleeveless dimity frock, but with a small apron of Nottingham lace that gave it a touch of style. Ben, who remembered her from his earliest days, thought she had scarcely changed. She still looked like Clowance's sister.

'When are you coming back to the mine?'

He rubbed a hand across his pointed beard. 'I been walking the cliffs this afternoon, besting how to order my life from now on. I resigned once from Leisure – after that quarrel with Carrington. Now . . . now that he's wed to . . .' The name must not be spoken. 'Now that he's wed I been absent again. I came to see Cap'n Poldark. I got to come to some choice 'bout the mine and he's got to come to some choice 'bout me. Do he still want me back, and, if so, do I want to be back?'

Demelza picked up two rattle toys that Henry had discarded before he took his afternoon sleep.

'Ben, may I speak plain?'

'Please, ma'am. Tis your privilege.'

'Well, it is not common sense to pretend we don't know why you have been away – that it has all been because of Clowance's marriage.'

Ben winced. The name was out. 'Yes, mistress, I suppose.'

Demelza said: 'I know of your feeling for Clowance and I know of your feeling for Stephen. One is love and one is – the opposite . . . So tis very hard for you to see these two people wed, and us rejoicing and blessing them and happy for them, and you left out in the cold. No doubt you'd 've felt more reconciled if Clowance had consented to marry Lord Edward Fitzmaurice, who proposed marriage to her in Bath. Or even if she had married Mr Tom Guildford, who asked her to marry him when he last called here. Perhaps *I* would have felt happier too, perhaps Captain Poldark would, not just because they were wealthier or titled but because they *seemed* to be better *characters*, more obviously honourable and straightforward and of a respectable reputation . . . Stephen has none of these.'

She paused and pulled at her damp hair, which straightened under the impatient tug of her fingers and then at once sprang back into its delicate curl.

'Stephen has none of these. But we are not quite the normal family, Ben. Perhaps it is my fault. No – it is the fault of the both of us – Ross's just so much as mine. We believe in allowing our children freedom of choice. Even now I do not know whether this is a good thing. Perhaps I should have *instructed* my elder daughter to marry the brother of a marquis. But I did not. Perhaps we should have *forbidden* her to have any dealings with an unknown man who was washed up on our beach, and who soon proved himself to be – unreliable. Perhaps this is all due to our *weakness*. Our weaknesses. But – because we believe children should have the freedom of choice – Clowance was allowed to choose for herself. If she had chosen you we should not have put obstacles in her way. But she did *not*. She chose Stephen. Three times she had long absences from him and still she came back to him . . . So there is another thing to think, Ben. And that is, do we trust Clowance's judgement? Love is blind, they say, and lovers cannot see. But sometimes lovers see further and deeper than the rest of us: they see beyond the things in a man's nature that put other folk off, to a better and a deeper character. Who knows? I do not. I pray that someday, and not far off, it will be proved Clowance has seen better than the rest of us. Until then we must just – hope . . . and try to be tolerant.'

Ben stared down at a large splodge of muddy sand on the carpet.

'I think I brought that in, Mrs Poldark. I been down Kellow's Ladder. My boots . . .'

'It does not matter.'

He hesitated and looked at her and then out of the window. 'Thank you for telling me what you've just told me. Tis comforting to know that I wasn't – that nobody was ruled out. And tis comforting, in a way, that you and Cap'n Poldark also have your doubts. Maybe in time when some of the hurt have gone I shall be able to hope wi' you that Clowance has chose right after all. Any way, thank you for what you've said.'

'Why don't you go and see your Grandfather now? He will be pleased to see you.'

'Maybe he'll be pleased, but I doubt he'll show it. I reckon he'll be tearing mad. For letting of you down, see.'

'I'm glad I've seen you first then,' said Demelza. 'I think you've made up your mind, haven't you?'

'What way?'

'To come back.'

Ben screwed up his eyes. 'Tis hard to tell. It depend a lot if Cap'n Poldark d'think the way of you.'

Demelza said: 'I think Captain Poldark will be half way between me and Zacky. He badly wants to be able to *rely* on his underground captain, especially now Jeremy's gone.'

'Yes, I see that.'

'In a few weeks he will be going to Westminster. He will want to leave Zacky in charge, and you, if you stay, will have to be Zacky's eyes and ears. Ross would not take kindly to you being absent then!'

'If I d'stay, he'll have no cause to fear on that!'

'Well then I think he will want you to stay.'

'Thank you, Mistress. Well, I'd best be going now, then. But if tis all the same to you I'll not go to the mine till I've had word wi' Cap'n Poldark. I don't think twould be proper.'

They walked to the door. Ben said:

'Oh, I said I been Kellow's Ladder. I seem always to be finding things! What with Roman coins and the like!' He showed her the ring and the metal seal stamp.

Demelza took them. 'You say you found them in Kellow's Ladder? But I thought . . .'

'Twas but a down shaft? Quite right. But there be a side tunnel half way down. I seen some footmarks – recent footmarks, so I went in. There were these three little sacks. One was empty, second had these in, the third some old papers, legal papers or the like, and a few copper coins. I left 'em there. They seemed no business o' mine. Maybe twas no business o' mine to bring these away.'

Demelza studied the seal. It had some sort of spider-like creature embossed, and it looked as if it was made of silver lead.

'Sacks, you say? What sort of sacks, Ben?'

'Oh, just like flour sacks. But small ones. Like Miller Jonas sometimes d'use.'

'They weren't marked Jonas, were they?'

'No, no marking. Except a marking in red ink – like red ink. One sack was marked S. And another one J. And the third was P. or B. The ink'd run.'

'I see.' She put her free hand up to rub her heart, which was thumping. 'Can I keep this seal, Ben, just for the time being? I'd like to show it to Captain Poldark. I'll leave you have it back later.'

'You can keep 'em both for good, ma'am. They don't b'long to me.'

Demelza studied the ring. It was a thick ring and looked as if it had had a jewel – or two jewels – at some time; there was the remains of a raised piece with broken claws. She tried it on and it fitted her middle finger.

'Findings are keepings,' she said. 'I think it is yours to do what you will with, Ben. It is a woman's ring. Maybe your mother would like it.' She handed it back.

III

A week ago she had had a letter from Dr Goldsworthy Gurney. He had explained in somewhat unnecessary detail his friendship with Jeremy and then told her of Jeremy's visit to him while he had been on leave. He went on:

Mr Jeremy Poldark kindly offered me all his drawings and designs made for use in an experimental horseless carriage, and before he first left to join his regiment he brought over a portfolio of these. But when he last called he said there were still two drawings which had been made by Mr Richard Trevithick last year and which he had forgotten to bring. He said he would send them, but in his short leave he must have forgotten to do so. They are marked, according to your son: 'Sketches front and side of recoil engine and boiler, November 1812.' If it is at all possible I should greatly esteem a sight of these.

Should you wish to write first and obtain your son's permission, I will of course fully understand the delay. But it so happens that my wife will be staying with her parents all of next week, and I am hoping during her absence to visit my uncle at St Erth, and from there to go to Hayle; and it would advantage me to have had an opportunity to study the drawings before then.

Believe me, my dear Mrs Poldark,
Your humble and obedient servant,
Goldsworthy Gurney.

On reading this Demelza had gone in search of the plans. In the closet under the window, Demelza knew, Jeremy kept almost all his papers, and for a young man not notable for his tidiness about the house, these were usually in excellent order. She had soon found the drawings referred to, but not before she had picked up and read a press cutting from the *Royal Cornwall Gazette*, eighteen months old, reporting a daring robbery of a stage coach during its journey from Plymouth to Truro. It was a very odd thing, Demelza had thought at the time, for Jeremy to keep. Far removed in subject from all the other cuttings, which exclusively dealt with the development of steam carriages and high-pressure steam.

IV

Ross was late getting home. Daylight had long since fled and the lights were out in the house. Only Matthew Mark Martin was waiting to take his horse and lead it to the stables.

'Is your mistress abed?'

'I don't rightly know, sur. I believe she've gone.'

'Well don't wait up after you have seen to him. I supped in Truro.'

'Thank ee, sur.'

Ross went in, hung up his cloak and hat. A candle was burning on the bannister post of the stairs. There was a faint light from the parlour and he went in. One candle had been left burning, so that he might light the others from it if he wished. He did not wish. He was sleepy enough. He had ridden in this morning, and more than six hours in the saddle had tired him.

He was about to blow out the candle when something stirred in the chair by the fireplace.

'Demelza!' he said. 'You should not have waited. I said I should be late, and you know how early Henry is abroad in the mornings.'

'Oh,' she said, and stretched her arms, but did not rise. 'I just thor I'd –' She blew out a breath. 'I just thought I'd wait a little while.'

He picked up the candle and took it closer to her. She blinked and held up a hand to her eyes.

'Take it away . . . Too . . . too bright.'

'Demelza, are you not *well*?' He turned and lit another candle, spilling grease in his haste. The second candle seemed an age in adding anything to the light of the first. He went down on one knee to peer at her.

'Go away,' she said. 'Stop staring.'

He took her by the shoulders. 'Tell me.'

Her breath was liquorous.

'Ross, I thought – I dreamed . . .'

'By God! You're drunk!' he exclaimed in surprise, and released her shoulders. She fell back in the chair. '*Aren't* you?'

'Coursh I'm not. Just took a glass of port . . .'

'My God,' he said again. 'What has got into you? You – you're *drunk* Demelza!'

As the light of the second candle at last grew he saw the empty port bottle in the hearth, and beside it a broken glass.

'You stupid slut! How long has this been going on?'

'Whassat? Going on? Nothing's been going on. I just – just felt some sad, and I just took a drink to cheer me up, and then and then . . .'

In exasperation he turned to light the other candles, while she protested she couldn't stand it. He looked into her eyes, which tonight were lacking focus. The impulse came to him to hit her. To check himself he picked up the gloves he had let fall, put them on a table beside a newspaper, knelt to poke the fire. But it was as far gone as Demelza.

She whispered: 'Do you believe in God, Ross?'

He said: 'What's *wrong* with you? What has happened?

Has something happened? Are the children all right?'

'The children?' She hiccupped. 'Pardon. The children. I've been wondering.'

'Wondering *what*?'

'What're we here for, Ross? Who put us here? Eh? Why do we marry and have children and grow old and go to our graves? Wha's at the end of it? Do you b'lieve we go to Heaven? Do you believe Julia is in Heaven? What is she doing there? Is she perched on a cloud chirruping like a bird? Has she grown any bigger since she died? She should be a fine girl of twenty-something now. I – I . . .' She blinked at him . . . 'I believe you blame me, don't you, always have, for going to help Francis and Elizabeth when they had the – the morbid sore throat. You've always blamed me for – for going to help them and catching it and giving it to Julia . . . What if I had died too? Maybe I ought to have died too. If I had died too, should I be perched on a – on a cloud with Julia chirruping like a bird?'

'Stop talking such damned nonsense! Tell me about the children – are they well? Is Harry well?'

'Yes. Yes. He is learning to walk and what is the good of that? He's only growing up to . . . There's nothing for you to worry about.'

'So what are *you* worrying about? When did this begin? Did the children see you like this?'

'No, no. Bella had been tiresome so I sent her to bed early . . . Ross, maybe I *am* talking damned nonsense, but I do not believe if I had died all those years ago I would – I would be perched on a cloud chirruping like a bird. I believe I would be buried in the ground, mouldering to dust – like Elizabeth, like Francis, like old Agatha. I do not believe it matters what age we are when we die – we all become ageless – not chirruping on clouds but silent, with our mouths full of attle and sand. And what is it all for? That's what I wanna know. What is it all *for*? . . .' She took a deep shuddering breath. 'Oh, Judas, can I have another drink?'

'*No.*'

'Why not?'

'Have you eaten?'

'Could not fancy supper. Lost my appetite.'

'Why have you got drunk?'

'Not drunk.'

'Yes, you are.'

'Give me another drink.'

'No.'

She said: 'Are we good parents, Ross? I sometimes wonder. Are we too easy, too easy-going, too *sloppy*. No discipline, no example, come as you please, go as you please. That's us. Maybe the old way is best. The strap and the birch and the slipper. Stand in a corner, lock you in your room without supper.' She swallowed hard, and coughed. 'Maybe children really love you *better* that way, look up to you, respect you, listen to what you say. Animals – they're animals really, are they not. Animals never mind a beating so long as they know what they've done wrong and where they stand.'

'Shut up and tell me what has gone *wrong*!'

'Nothing's gone wrong. Everything is handsome handsome.' She sighed again, even more tremulously. 'I just felt sad. Nasty dreams.'

'You do not have dreams in the daytime, woman.'

She smiled crookedly at him.

'*I* do.'

'Are you going to take to the bottle seriously?' he asked. 'If so I shall throw you out.'

They stared at each other for several long seconds. Tears came to her eyes and began to trickle down her cheeks. 'Just felt – sad.'

Ross got up again, went to the window, frowned out. No one had even bothered to draw the curtains. He knew his inability to stand Demelza's tears, so had turned away from them to try to maintain his anger and his concern. Her partiality for port was a known joke in the family, and even Jeremy teased her about whether it was four or five glasses she had had. But always – or almost always – she had known when to stop. And on other rare occasions when she had taken too much it had been at celebratory parties where nobody minded in the least.

This was different. This drinking on one's own after the children had gone to bed ... A change which turned a mildly comic weakness into a risk of something else. And yet ... why today? Had it been going on unknown to him for some time and this the first time it had got out of hand? When he was home he was not infrequently near to her during the day; he could not remember catching any whiff of spirits. In spite of all her denials, was she concealing something from him, something that had happened today, which had driven her to this excess? It seemed far more likely.

He turned, intent on questioning her again. She was sitting there, having lost her handkerchief, trying to dry her eyes on her sleeves.

'Demelza,' he said.

'Yes, Ross?'

'I'm going to help you to bed.'

She blinked at him owlishly. 'No, you're not. I – can find my own way.'

'You can't.'

'I don't wan *any* help from anyone who's going to throw me out.'

'That we will talk about in the morning.'

'I don't wan *any* help from someone who's –'

'Come along now.'

'I don't wan *any* help. Not from you, Ross. Nor anyone, anyone else. I can stand up for myself ...'

'We'll see about that in the morning.'

Chapter Three

I

In fact it was very early morning when they spoke again. When he had got her upstairs she had immediately fallen into a heavy stertorous sleep and he expected her to be unconscious until Henry roused her; but, waking himself about six when dawn had just broken, he turned cautiously on his side to find her sitting up in bed, hands behind her head, knuckles on the bed rail.

'You're awake early,' he said.

She looked at him but did not speak. Her brows were in a corrugated line.

'Have you a headache?' he found himself saying.

'Yes.'

'Well, I suppose it's not to be wondered at.'

'No, it isn't, is it.'

'What got into you?'

'One thing led to another. I *did* have a terrible dream.'

'When?'

'The night before last. It stayed with me, oppressing me all day.'

'That hardly seems reason enough.'

'No?'

The swallows were flying to and fro across the window, up to their exercises before they took off for their long trek to Africa.

She said: 'Did you mean what you said last night?'

'What was that?'

'That if I took to drink you would turn me out?'

'How could I? We have made our lives together. We are part of each other. I come *home* to you. This house now belongs to you just as much as it does to me. And our family. How *could* I?'

She slid a little further down the bed. One hand came from behind her head and lay on the sheet.

He said: 'All the same, there is one thing I cannot stand, and that is a drunken woman. It may be hypocrisy on my part to make such a distinction, since at times I have drunk much myself, and we are both accustomed to drunkenness among some of our friends. But it still remains a fact. A drunken woman turns my stomach. I suppose at heart I still think of women as having too much taste and restraint and charm. Drunkenness contradicts these – these beliefs.'

'I know, Ross.'

'Will it happen again?'

'I don't know.'

There was silence for a while. There was no further sleep in either of them.

He said: 'What was the dream?'

'Oh, that . . .'

'Yes, that.'

'Well, Ross, I dreamt that you and I were both dead. Lying on this bed together, beside each other. Or almost dead, not quite.'

'How do you mean?'

'We were lying beside each other – almost dead – but holding hands. Your right hand. My left. And I knew that so long as we continued to hold hands we should not die – should not *quite* die, *just* stay alive. And I thought: who will get tired first – him or me? Will I let go first and let him die, just because my hand is clammy and I want to turn over and I am tired of holding on? Or will he? Will he get tired first and let me die? It's only a matter of time. It's . . . only . . . a matter of time.'

II

When she had stopped crying and had sniffed a few more times into the bedclothes she said: 'What a fool I am! When you are young you can afford to be sentimental; no longer when you are getting old.'

'Did nothing else happen yesterday to upset you?'

'Nothing.' She volunteered more brightly: 'It was so lovely and warm I took Bella bathing. The sea was all bubbly as if you had dropped soda in it. We had a lovely time. Oh . . . and I forgot to tell you. Ben turned up.'

'Ben?'

Glad of being able to change the subject, she told him of the visit, though not the whole of it.

Ross concentrated on this new matter with some difficulty. He had a stone in his chest from the night's events, and it was hard to see other problems in their proper prospective. Eventually he said:

'However much Ben may feel, however upset and grieved he may be, I cannot have an underground captain I cannot rely on. Although Zacky is about again, it is really on Ben – or on Ben's replacement – that we shall depend for the smooth working of the mine, with Jeremy and myself both gone.'

'He knows that,' said Demelza. 'I believe that if he feels any further grief over Clowance he will show it by an excess of work rather than by neglecting the mine.'

'Always before he was a conscientious man.'

'I believe he will be so again.'

'We'll see how he comes up today. Time is getting short if I am to find a replacement.'

She moved incautiously. 'Ooh, my head!'

'Why do you not sleep in this morning? Everyone is used to your occasional days of megrim.'

'But this isn't one of them, Ross. No, I will take a powder when it is time to get up.'

He said again: 'That was the strangest dream. It is on you I depend for my cheer and comfort, not for such gloomy and despondent thoughts.'

'Perhaps I am changing; perhaps life is changing me.'

She was better for her powder and went about the early morning normally enough, though they were guarded towards each other. But just before breakfast she took the piece of silver lead out of her pocket.

'What is this, Ross? This seal? Do you know it?'

He took it from her and frowned at it, suspecting that again she was diverting or trying to divert his attention. 'Yes,' he agreed reluctantly. 'It is a scorpion. It is the seal of Warleggan's Bank. Where did you come by it?'

'I picked it up on the road. Near Pally's Shop.'

'I suppose one of his men must have dropped it going to Wheal Spinster. Though why ... Did you go that far yesterday?' he asked suspiciously. 'I thought you took Bella bathing.'

'Oh, I did that too.'

He eyed her, noting the unusual pallor of her face, different from the healthy pallor of normal times. (She never had much colour but the glow was underneath.)

'I have to make arrangements to see Francis de Dunstanville at Tehidy this morning. I want more details about the quality of the tin at present being mined at Dolcoath and Cook's Kitchen. But it is two weeks before I go to London. I can send John over with my apologies and suggest another day.'

'Why should you? Because Ben is coming?'

'No, of course not; I shall not leave till ten. I was thinking it better, if you are not well.'

'I'm well now, thank you.'

'Well enough?'

'Well enough.'

'But depressed.'

'Not depressed enough to greet you as I did last night, if that is what you are thinking.'

'I did not say I was thinking that.'

'You may lock up the port if you wish,' she said stiffly. 'I believe there is a key on my ring that you may have.'

'I trust I shall never have to do that.'

'Then go today. There is no reason at all for you to change your plans. What time will you be home?'

'Oh, about seven.'

Bella and Harry had already eaten so they had a quiet and mainly silent breakfast. Towards the end of the meal Demelza said:

'I have been thinking about Jeremy.'

'Do you ever stop?'

'No. I have been wondering how much it cost us to fit him out in all those regimentals.'

'Little enough,' said Ross. 'I bought him a few things, but he produced quite an amount of money of his own. I was surprised and pleased with him. I suppose he saved up what little we gave him – and then Wheal Leisure produced a dividend just in time.'

'And since?'

'He has come on me for nothing since; so I imagine he must have managed for the first few months on his pay. Now there are fatter dividends from the mine, he should have no particular problem.'

'You didn't think to ask how he was going to manage?'

'No, I didn't wish to interfere. Why – are you worrying about him? Did you have some private letter from him yesterday?'

'*Nothing!* I've heard nothing from him! It was just an idle question.'

'Well, I believe he has a fancy to arrange his own life. Jeremy, you know, however much we love him, is rather the dark horse. Not long ago we were talking: you said so yourself.'

'Yes . . . I know I did.'

Jane Gimlett came in. 'If you please, sur, Ben Carter is outside.'

'Tell him I will see him in a moment.' Ross got up. 'Are you sure you don't need me here today?'

'Quite sure.'

He hesitated a moment more. 'I suppose it could have been nothing *I* had done to cause you to behave as you did yesterday?'

'Of course not.'

'Yet you are stiff towards me.'

Demelza said: 'Only because I am stiff towards myself.'

After Ross had gone Demelza spent a quiet morning, nursing her headache and her queasiness, and making preparations for the afternoon. Although not at her best today, some things could not be allowed to wait.

Even getting away seemed a major task, for she had to surround it with so many excuses. She knew this was one of her weaknesses: she never seemed able to make a majestic pronouncement simply that she was 'going out'. (She remembered an occasion when Jeremy was eight and she had put on her cloak and Jeremy had said, 'Where are you going, Mama?' To which she had replied, 'Nowhere.' Instantly he had said, 'Can *I* come?')

Eventually this afternoon Bella was dispatched and Henry 'seen to', and some cider-pressing that she had agreed to superintend postponed until the following day. She went upstairs and, the weather still being warm, she put on a cool linen blouse with short sleeves, and a linen skirt which wrapped around and was secured by five big bone buttons. Under the skirt she pulled on Clowance's shabby blue barragan trousers which Clowance had been too ashamed to take with her into her married life. These could be rolled up to the knee and prevented from unrolling by means of pieces of ribbon elastic. She put on thin lisle stockings and a well-worn pair of leather-laced boots which would not slip easily.

Then she took up a small bag, put in it two candles, a tinder box, a pair of scissors, a twenty-foot length of rope. She had no certain use for the rope, but she thought it appropriate to carry it, just in case.

Even now she had to shake off one member of the family, and the one most difficult to reason with: Farquhar.

Farquhar was the family's dog, and most particularly Isabella-Rose's; but like most animals he had a habit of attaching himself to Demelza. So he did today, and was constantly ordered to go home, only to be observed a few minutes later following at a distance crawling on his belly. Demelza was painfully reminded of that other day and that other dog which had been so much a part of her life and was now long gone. There had been an occasion when she had walked this way one Christmas long ago and Harry Harry, the Warleggan gamekeeper, had shot Garrick in the ear . . .

This of course was not so long a walk. Kellow's Ladder came even before Sawle Cove.

She had passed it many times but never investigated it. The Ladder was something she knew the boys had used – and Charlie Kellow also had used before he became so fat and boozy – and she had, without personal examination, assumed it to be about as safe and as unsafe as any other cliff climb in the neighbourhood. If you bred young children and lived in the neighbourhood of fearsome cliffs and a treacherous sea you just had to close your mind to the dangers and accept the fact that young people grew accustomed to their environment – otherwise you would never have a peaceful hour.

To get to the ladder you climbed or slid down a narrow path running diagonally across the face of the cliff, which here was not sheer but inclined inwards and upwards towards the land. This cliff face was tufted with grass and thrift and heather and the occasional stunted gorse bush, and was populated and punctuated by rabbits and rabbit holes. Then you picked your way further downwards among an outcrop of granite boulders. By this time you had dropped about 150 feet, and here you came on a platform slanting at about thirty degrees towards the sea, largely grass covered, but part of it stone-walled with the ruins of a mine-working. From here it was about another fifty feet, slithering among boulders until you saw a V-cleft in the precipice face and at the bottom of the V was the hole and the ladder. Demelza reached it, lonely and breathless, and peered down the hole at the sand sixty feet below.

As she looked the sand was covered by the sea, and then uncovered again. The tide was later today.

It was not nearly so good a day as when Ben had come. There had been an uncertain, watery sun all morning, and streaky clouds had gathered to make a birch-broom sky. It looked as if autumn was on its way. But you could not be certain: in this peninsula of land thrust out into the Atlantic you could never be sure even of the bad weather.

The hole – or shaft – was about eight feet across. She had hoped it might be sloping but it was not. The ladder, which at first she could hardly see, was nailed to the side with large-headed iron nails, and to her dismay was not quite continuous; that is to say it ended at one place and began a few inches lower to the right and then six more rungs down it moved to the left again. She guessed it was because the people who put it there – had it been the Kellows? – had found in places that the nails would simply not go into the rock and had had to adjust their ladder accordingly.

She knelt for a minute or two staring down: she could see only one rung actually missing – otherwise they looked sound. Anyway they had borne Ben's weight.

She wondered at her own breathlessness and dizziness. Was it just vertigo and loneliness? How much *had* she drunk last night? Certainly far more than Ross guessed. Her head still throbbed. But she *had* to be alone on this mission, however iron-bound and looming the landscape. The gulls of course had soon seen her and were crying overhead. Otherwise nothing stirred.

She unbuttoned her skirt and unwrapped it and laid it beside the hole. She put a heavy stone on it so that it should not blow away. She tied the cloth bag round her shoulder in such a way that it would not flap or fall forward at an inconvenient moment. She edged her way to the rim of the hole and got her foot far enough down to rest on the first rung. It seemed willing to take her weight. Slowly she manoeuvred herself round, clutching at tufts of grass for support until she was facing the wall of the adit. She transferred her hands to the ladder sides, took a second step down and then a third.

The rock wall was greasy with Saturday's rain; this hole must serve as drainage for a large area of sloping land. The rungs too were slippery. Should she have taken off her boots and come down in bare feet?

She reached the broken rung. She tested it with her toe and a piece of the rotten wood broke off and fell down and landed in the wet sand with a plop. As she would, if she fell. It was not too long a stretch to the next rung; thank Heaven they were only about a foot apart. She stretched down and found it. As she transferred her weight to it it gave an ominous crack. Gripping hard to the sides of the ladder, she moved quickly to the one below. It held her without complaint.

How *far* had Ben said was the side tunnel? Had he said at all? Awkward if she missed it.

Step followed step until she was half way. The circle of daylight at the top was by now scarcely larger than a full moon; that at the bottom was growing ever greater. The sea covered the sand again; bubbles and froth, swirling, bottle-green vomit veined with white. Something fell on her hair, wriggled down her shoulder and was gone.

She saw the tunnel. Another thing Ben had not mentioned was that it was not immediately adjacent to the ladder: you had to make a three-foot stride. Not much for a man. Not much for an agile woman. But an agile woman suffering from the effects of drink, with more than a trace of natural vertigo, and entirely on her own, tends to become more nervous at each step. Her foot slipped on the edge as she fell gasping into the mouth of the tunnel.

Her hands were shaking so much that she could not light the tinder. She sat back against the edge of the tunnel taking breaths to steady herself. Water was dripping here, as if the land were bleeding. Wherever there was water and a sufficiency of light some sort of vegetation grew, whether it was moss or grass or tiny ferns. You could not stop life, could you?

Except by death.

There were splendid colours in the rock here: mottled browns and veins of green and russet streaks and speckled greys, with dashes of ochre and yellow; no wonder they had opened this tunnel.

She began to feel sick. It was all imagination, she told herself. What was she doing with imagination, let alone a queasy stomach, who had been a starving brat not above picking up and eating a half-chewed and rancid bone off the rubbish heap where someone who could afford to be more particular had thrown it? Thirty years ago. Thirty years of genteel living had so weakened her digestive juices, thirty years of happiness and sorrow and love and childbearing and work and play and breathing the genteel air of Nampara had so developed her sensibilities and her imagination, that because of one mere night drinking port she was about to be sick, and because of loneliness and vertigo she was trembling scared of attempting to climb the ladder again.

What if she did find herself incapable of returning up the slippery crumbling ladder? Would anybody ever find her? It would be dark when Ross got home. No one would have any idea of where she had gone. Perhaps tomorrow they would scour the cliffs, see the skirt . . .

She was sick, and after a few minutes wiped her mouth distastefully on her sleeve and began to feel better. Shutting her mind to her situation she tried the flint again. This time the tinder lighted, and from it the two candles caught. The cave grew around her, dripping here and there, flickering yellow.

It was easy to see the sacks, with a sheet of tarpaulin beside them which presumably had been used to protect them from the damp. The first sack was marked 'S' and was empty. So was the one marked 'J'. The third one, 'P' or 'B' had the documents in.

She took them out, read what was on them. Then she took a candle back to the opening of the cave and one by one set fire to the documents, holding them by a corner until they were properly alight and allowing them to burn on the edge before brushing the ashes over into the sea. These all burned, she took up a sack and lit that. It caused a lot more smoke, and the channel of the breeze blew much of it back into the tunnel and made her cough. She went on with the second sack. This was damper and took a long time to lose its identity and its ink initial. Eventually she was satisfied that nothing recognizable remained and she thrust it over the edge like its fellow. And presently the third sack followed in the same way.

The few coins that Ben had mentioned were scattered on the

floor. Among the pennies were to twopenny pieces, which were already becoming rare. She hesitated over these but presently threw them down the shaft.

All that remained was the piece of tarpaulin. Plain black, dirty and cobwebbed, it was unidentifiable, unrecognizable in any way; but it might as well go the way of the rest. As she pulled it forward something clinked and she saw a piece of silver, part fallen down a shallow cleft. She picked it up.

It was a silver cup, very small, but nicely fashioned, with two handles. Not more than two and a half inches high. Like a toy. But prettily made. She rubbed the tarnished side of it and could see some inscription but could not make it out. Perhaps a foreign language. She dragged the tarpaulin to the edge and tipped it over. At first it caught in some errant draught, but after flapping for a few seconds it collapsed and slowly descended to the waiting sea.

The cup was in her hand. Dangerous to keep? Perhaps. But hard just to jettison. She hesitated and then put it into the bag she had brought. It could be looked at again.

A further circuit of the cave showed nothing more. She snuffed out one candle, then the other, waited until the tallow had cooled before she put them away. She strapped the bag back upon her shoulder. Then she looked out at the ladder. It was a long way away.

The first step was the worst: three feet to get your foot on the rung. It was much easier coming down because you could hold firmly to the ladder side while you groped for the tunnel entrance. But in reverse, what did you hold on to? There wasn't a convenient outspur of the rock that you could clutch. All the rock was smooth and straight and hard and damp.

She sat down for a minute or two to try to stop her knees shaking and to work this out. She thought, if I think of falling I shall never face it. I shall be here, still crouched here, a trembling, half-frozen, half-starved, pitiable wretch when (if) they find the skirt tomorrow, or the next day. Or perhaps even the next. She could find moisture in the cave but no food. Could you eat fern?

She remembered Cousin Francis going out that rainy

September afternoon so many years ago, and never coming back. He had gone down Wheal Grace on his own and slipped and fallen. Only fallen a little way compared to what she would fall here. But he had fallen into water – and he could not swim. *She* could swim, after a fashion, but the water at the bottom of this shaft was not deep enough to break her fall. The distance was probably less than thirty feet. Well, it would be soon over. She would likely break her back and that would be the end of it.

She again began to take breaths to steady herself. She had decided she must not think of falling and since then had thought of nothing else! Well, what were the choices? If she tried to climb and failed she was certainly dead. If she tried to climb and succeeded she returned to Nampara as if nothing had happened; no one would ever know she had been down here. That was the whole object of the mission. If she stayed where she was, the chances were that she would be found alive, eventually, though one knew not when. Also, she would then be asked to explain what in Heaven's name had got into her, going down an old adit with treacherous steps, on her own and unaided. If she refused to give the true explanation – as she must – then she would, rightly, be regarded by Ross as a mental case.

Illogically it was the dislike of this that stirred her to make a move. She unhitched her bag again and took out the rope. There was no use for it. There was no way in which she could attach it to the ladder. The rungs were too close to the wall of the adit, and if by any remote piece of luck she was able to sling the rope through a rung and retrieve the other end, an improbable feat in itself, she would be more likely to find it an encumbrance round her waist. She could see herself slowly but helplessly sliding down the rope into the sea.

Did that matter? Could she not, when in the sea at the bottom, or somewhere on the way down, grasp the rungs and begin a normal climb?

She thought: This is *not* an adit over the sea. This is *not* a cave from which I have to step to death or safety. This is a step in our back yard, where the calves are fed. Three feet?

Dear life, I could jump *four*. Why should I miss the rungs? Why should I fail to grasp the ladder sides? In any case I don't have to *jump* – I only have to stretch. *And* balance at the same time. It's really only standing on the edge and letting yourself gradually fall. If your foot misses, your hand should hold. If your hand misses there's another hand close behind. Judas God, what are you *made* of? Are you one of those elegant, simpering, pampered maidens at Bowood, who have never known the sort of exercise you take every day, who have never ridden a horse astride or fought with the waves on Hendrawna Beach or scrubbed a floor or fed pigs or milked cows or brewed ale? Come, come, my dear, take a grip on yourself.

So she carefully re-wound the rope around her forearm and repacked it, carefully re-fixed her bag, carefully stepped to the very edge of the adit, below which the sea, bottle-green and vomit-stained with white, swirled backwards and forwards, covering and uncovering the sand like a magician at a fair; and she took a breath, the deepest breath of all, and looked at the ladder only three feet away, and stretched out her leg and could not reach and *could not* reach until she began to fall, and then put out her foot an extra six inches, and clawed with her hands against the slippery rock face, and her foot jarred and held and almost slipped, and her hands, like helpless prisoners in some failed prison escape, slid and clutched and slid and clutched, and then one hand felt something more secure than the rock face, and held on to it. And then she swung, toe only just holding, hand only just holding, while the thirty-foot drop became three thousand feet and the earth swung and the adit swung, toppling her further and further into the gaping, sucking hole. And then her other hand clutched, just in time as her foot slipped off the rung. And she held, kicking desperately for twenty seconds, bruising her knees and her toes; a panic-stricken groping until her foot found a rung again, and her other foot found the rung above it; and, with an immense effort of will, she unloosed her hands from the ladder side and, panting, trembling, shuddering with every breath, she went up, rung by rung; to the break in the ladder and the missing step, and changed her grip, and blindly, dizzily, reached the top. And crawled out and lay on the rubble near the hole gasping like a newly landed fish but knowing she was safe after all.

Chapter Four

I

Ross left for London late in October, and, the sea routes being no longer hazardous, he sailed from Falmouth in a tin ship. But as usual, it seemed to him, when he was aboard the trip was a foul one, and they did not drop anchor in the Pool of London until the 11th of November. There was much to be said for Jeremy's steam carriages, he thought.

He found London returning to normal after the famous junketings he had shunned, and Parliament, whose opening he had now missed, preoccupied with matters which, while certainly of moment, did not in his view embrace some of the more pressing issues of the day. The Houses had expressed their deep regret at the continuing 'indisposition' of His Majesty King George the Third; there had been discussion on the disbanding of the militia; a vote of credit had been passed necessary for the services of the year 1814; provision made for the household of Princess Charlotte; long speeches on the thorny matter of the Prince Regent's debts; complaints had even been aired that Parliament had been recalled too early.

And of course that corner of the world where war still raged attracted some attention, and was concerned with the unjust demands of the executive government of America, with the condition of the British army in Canada and its indifferent leadership, with the necessity of negotiating from strength not weakness. One member, speaking of the burning of Washington, referred to the army and its commanders as Goths and Vandals. This was sharply rejected by the Chancellor of the Exchequer, who stated that when we witnessed the utmost malice on the part of the Americans we were justified by the laws of God and man in executing a strict retaliation.

All very important indeed; but where was the debating time given to the condition of the starving poor of England? Even the Earl of Darnley, who had made an impassioned speech demanding that the rest of the world should follow England's example in abolishing the slave trade, had not dropped a word about conditions in the North of England – and the Midlands and the West.

Ross was in time for the meeting of his committee, and made some use of his position to explain the basic needs of the tin and copper producers. On the second Thursday he was in London he accepted an invitation to supper at a house in St James's Street, Buckingham Gate.

This had no connection with metals, but perhaps rather too direct a connection with the matter of his own sympathies. His host was an elderly landed gentleman called Major Cartwright, whom Ross had known on and off for fifteen years; but only as it were on nodding acquaintance, and of course by reputation. Cartwright had been one of the stormy petrels of England for as long as most people could remember. Long long ago, at the outbreak of the American war, when offered a high position in the Army under Howe, he had rejected it and shortly afterwards brought out a pamphlet entitled 'American Independence the Glory and Interest of Great Britain'. A major in the Nottinghamshire Militia for seventeen years, he had been cashiered for celebrating the fall of the Bastille. He had begun the first Corresponding Society which had been the forerunner of the many others that had become the revolutionary nightmare of successive British governments.

When Ross had taken Gwyllym Wardle's side in the House in 1809, in his attack on the principles of the rotten boroughs, Cartwright had written Ross a warm letter of congratulation. Ross had replied politely but had gone no further. The war was on, and though he had spoken his mind on Parliamentary reform it must all wait until the menace of Napoleon had been removed.

Cartwright was the brother of the clergyman who had invented something called a power loom which was revolutionizing production in the work places. This Cartwright,

John, was a tall thin straight old man with a smiling, open face and a plain brown wig concealing his white hair. He greeted Ross warmly and they went into a salon half full of men. Only two women were present and they quickly absented themselves. Ross sipped a very good Canary wine and munched a biscuit while being introduced to this guest and that.

Most he had not met before but some he knew by name. A youngish middle-aged man called Clifford, who wrote on legal matters and was making a name for himself as an advanced radical. Henry Hunt, of about the same age, known for his size and his bombast and his inflammatory speeches. A very young man with a broad Lancashire accent whom Ross took to; Samuel Bamford, he said his name was. Beside him was Henry Brougham, the radical lawyer who had helped to found the *Edinburgh Review* – temporarily without a seat in the House. Samuel Whitbread, the brewer's son and sworn pacifist, was there, but he looked ill-at-ease.

But the guest of honour, if there was such a thing tonight, was a 40-odd-year-old mill owner and reformer called Robert Owen. Uneducated and poor, he had, it seemed, been apprenticed to a draper at the age of ten, but by the time he was nineteen by some alchemy of his own had come to have the management of a mill in Manchester employing 500 people. Since then he had become the philanthropist owner of the New Lanark Mills on the Clyde where amazing experiments had been carried out in welfare, child education and profit sharing. His recent book, *A New View of Society*, had created a big impression last year. Ross had read it during the summer, so was able to congratulate its author when they met.

The evening was a pleasant one, and after they had supped and brandy was circulating Major Cartwright said, nodding towards Robert Owen:

'*A New View of Society*, eh, Poldark. Isn't it what we all seek?'

'It is what most of us here seek,' said Ross. 'I'm not sure you could answer for the country as a whole.'

'It depends how you define the country. Not, I agree, among the nobility. Not among gentry such as ourselves –'

'Nor among the mercantile classes, the bankers, the mill-owners, the trading folk . . . But of course I take your meaning.'

'It is an ideal I have been fighting for all my life.'

'I know. No one has done more.' Ross added: 'I have recently read your *Letters on a Reform of the Commons*. A very good piece of reasoning. I'm sure it will have due effect.'

'Due effect. Small effect, I fear.'

'Oh, I would not say that,' Ross began, and then stopped, aware that his host probably spoke only the truth.

Cartwright said: 'Someday a historian may write that reform in this country has been put back fifty years by the example of the French. Those who promote peaceful evolution in Britain are instantly suspected of contriving it by bloody revolution. There is a continuing impasse; a continuing misunderstanding not of ways but of means.'

'Now the war is over, Parliament will be much more susceptible to your ideas.'

'I hoped, sir, you would say *our* ideas!'

'Very well. Let us say that.'

Cartwright thumped one hand into the other. 'So much remains to be done! We particularly lack parliamentary help, people who can speak for us in the House, persuade, argue, advocate. Look at tonight! Apart from yourself the only member of the House here is Whitbread, who for all his splendid gifts is no longer well – and driven to distraction, I believe, about the Drury Lane Theatre. You may know I have stood for Parliament often but have never been elected. We, the forerunners, the Radicals, who want no other than to proceed by constitutional means, we are looked upon with suspicion and distrust, the breeders of discontent and sedition!'

Ross sipped his brandy. 'What you have advocated all your life, Major Cartwright, is not so very far from Tom Paine's "Rights". A vote for every man, pensions for the old, the secret ballot, annual Parliaments, and the rest . . . Is it? I am sure it is all good and will come in time; but the full programme, read on a single sheet of paper, does look alarming to the average Member. Do we not first of all want much more *practical* measures to alleviate distress *now*?'

'Such as what?'

'Well . . . a system of supervision of the working conditions in factories, a law forbidding the employment of children under a certain age, a law limiting the number of hours any one man, woman or child may work in a day, some amendment of the Poor Law which, while not removing the incentive to work, allows people in distress a minimum means of comfort and food?'

'And why do you suppose such measures would have a greater chance of Parliamentary support than those I advocate? Of course all these I would urge too and press for equally; but the need for a total change in the representation of the people is central to all the others!'

'Why do I think such measures would have a greater chance? Well, because, as you well know, a fair number of Whig gentlemen – you could name a dozen influential ones – and a fair smattering of Tories – have some compassion in their bowels, and know the hardships and the poverty, and would like it to be alleviated. The tragedy of the Enclosures has to be reversed somehow. But that is an *economic* change. What they fear to face is *political* change . . . It will come, of course, even if we do not see it. The whole system is out of date – has been rendered out of date by events elsewhere; but it will be a long haul . . . One sees all this in so influential a member as George Canning, who is greatly in favour of helping the poor – but not in favour of helping the poor to vote.'

'Oh, Canning, yes,' Cartwright said in a derogatory tone.

'Masters of the Commons are few. Any one of those few is invaluable to any cause.'

'In the event,' said Cartwright, 'he cannot help us from his rich and luxurious ambassadorial house in Lisbon . . .' He sighed. 'No, it is on men such as yourself we depend, Poldark. Men of integrity. Men of known stability. Men of proven patriotism.'

So it was out.

'You have my good will,' Ross said after a moment. 'That I can promise. And vote, of course, if it comes to a vote. I feel much more urgently for your cause now the war is won. But I believe I am too old to be of great practical use to you. At fifty-four . . .'

'I am seventy-four, Captain Poldark.'

Ross half smiled. '*Touché*. What I meant is that at heart I am a Westcountryman who feels he has already been a member of parliament too long and is looking forward to retirement. I do not really like the atmosphere of Westminster, but while the war was in progress . . . The war was my cause. It seems to me too late to take up another cause, however sincerely I may support it.'

'However sincerely. I take some comfort from that.'

'Oh, have no doubts of my support. My regret is that it may not be of the extent you are seeking.'

'Have you ever met Cobbett?'

'No.'

'I think you should. He is a great man.'

'I have no doubt of it.'

'You may have read his recent article on the rotten boroughs.'

'No. But, Major Cartwright, I have to remind you that I sit for one of the rotten boroughs myself.'

'But that does not mean you support the system! You have said so!'

'Certainly I do not. But there are — courtesies to be observed. Lord Falmouth is my patron. He and his father before him have always treated me with particular consideration and tolerance. Within reason I have felt free to take up what attitudes I chose, and when I made my speech in the House in support of Wardle, it did not occur to me that I had any duty to write to my patron and explain. But a solitary speech is one matter. An open campaign against some principle to which the Falmouths are committed is another.'

'Such as the abolition of the pocket boroughs?'

'Yes.'

'You should resign and contest an open seat, as Canning

did at Liverpool. Of course even that sort of election is inadequate and corrupt; but at least you would have no master to serve.'

Ross never very much liked being told what he should do, but he smiled easily and said: 'You perceive the difficulties in my case. My instinct – and perhaps it is a lazy one – tells me enough is enough. To embrace your good cause would mean going against that instinct to the extent of a total re-assessment of what I am to do with the rest of my life. Beginning with a determination to try to return to Parliament, where I have never had the greatest success, and to fight for an open seat on policies which would almost certainly result in my defeat. I don't see it as a practical proposition.'

Cartwright sighed again. 'In good causes, Poldark, it is sometimes only the impractical that succeeds. Determination to do a good thing is all.'

They argued more or less amicably for another five minutes, and then the mixture changed and Ross was first with Samuel Bamford and after that with Robert Owen again. The party broke up about one o'clock, and, the night being fine, Ross walked down to Westminster steps and took a boat to the Adelphi and his George Street lodgings. There had been no conclusion to the discussion, no product of it all, no promises asked for, no undertakings given. But clearly Major Cartwright was disappointed with Ross's response.

Ross was not happy about it himself. He was irritated for not having perceived more clearly where the visit was likely to lead. He should have had the mental honesty to work it out beforehand and to have made his choice then. Go to the party with a willingness to do something definite for the group, or not go.

Yet he was also irritated with Cartwright. Surely one could accept an invitation to a casual evening supper to show one's approbation of Radical aims, without expecting to be *recruited*.

Of course the true Radicals, those represented tonight and their colleagues, were, as they said, desperately short of parliamentary support. Their proposals were too advanced for reformers like Wilberforce, who saw them as extremists. The name of Poldark, though meaning nothing to the masses, would be a valuable recruitment.

And he *did* support them. Though aware that some of the programme was too idealistic, he acknowledged the justice of it all. And if any abstract word meant anything to so essentially a practical man as himself, it was the word justice. Was he not therefore letting himself down when he turned away such a straightforward request for help with an evasive answer?

Yet the obstacle to his speaking for them in Parliament was genuine and could not be evaded. To resign and to seek re-election elsewhere would need a dedication he was sure he did not possess. Nor was it in his nature, as he had said to Demelza, to attend big rallies making speeches, nor was it among his talents to be persuasive in print. His sole use in such a cause was as a member of the House.

He got into bed and blew out the candle and for a while lay unsleeping, watching the light from the passing cart or flickering torch: they made bizarre patterns of wolves and bats on his ceiling. It was one occasion when he needed to talk to Demelza. Not necessarily to seek her advice but to use her as a sounding board, arguing his own case with his own conscience. Not that Demelza's advice would have not been worth having. Or that it would have been predictable.

He began to wonder about her and to worry about *her*, just for a change. In the days before he left she had seemed subdued, but there had been no hint of her again taking too much to drink. A sort of tacit understanding had grown up – a glance at the bottle, a couple of glasses but no more. When he left he had begun to mention it but she had put her finger to his lips and said: 'Don't say it,' so he had not said it. He hoped she would be all right on her own every night, both Jeremy and Clowance gone, only the younger children and the servants for company.

One day he had noticed several nasty scratches on her hands and she seemed to have sore knees, but she said she had slipped on the rocks coming back from Wheal Leisure.

She had also found an interesting small silver cup on the beach, which had cleaned up very nicely. Sometimes these days she seemed to prefer taking walks on her own instead of with the children.

Who would ever have supposed that the unsubtle starving child he had brought home from Redruth Fair should become such a complicated woman?

Anything anyway so long as she did not take to drink . . .

It was hours before he got to sleep, and then he dreamed of drowning miners.

II

Another meeting of a very different kind took place on the following Monday. A letter was delivered by hand.

Fife House. 24 November.

Dear Captain Poldark,

I understand that you are in London, and should consider it a favour if you could call upon me this afternoon at Downing Street about 4 p.m. If that should not be suitable perhaps you could name a time on Wednesday, a day on which I am likely to be free.

Believe me to be, etc.,

Liverpool.

The messenger was waiting. Ross wrote an acceptance saying he would attend upon the Prime Minister at four, which he did with an open mind, not having the least idea what to expect when he arrived.

Robert Banks Jenkinson, second Earl of Liverpool, was some years younger than Ross, slight of build turning to stoutness, unpretentious, amiable, astute, economical of movement and speech. Two and a half years ago, when Perceval was murdered, Liverpool had taken over as head of a temporary administration which gradually had come to have an aura of permanence. Overshadowed by and squeezed between his more brilliant colleagues, particularly Castlereagh and Canning, he had somehow so far preserved a balance pleasing to the Prince Regent and not altogether displeasing to the country. He had happened to be at the helm when Britain achieved victory in its endless war, and even now with that great pressure gone there was no obvious movement gathering to unseat him.

He said: 'Sit down, Poldark; it's good of you to come at such short notice. I had not heard until Friday that you were in Westminster, and as I gather the Committee will complete its hearings this week I thought to have a word with you before you went home.'

'The last meeting is on Thursday,' said Ross. 'I shall hope to leave on Friday morning.'

'Just so.' Lord Liverpool pulled a bell. 'I often take tea at this time of day. It is a habit I have caught from my wife. But I have a good brandy or a more than passable canary if you'd prefer it.'

'Thank you, my lord. I am content with tea.'

The servant silently came and as silently went.

'Have you heard from George Canning recently?'

'No, sir, not since he left.'

'There are reports of severe storms in the Bay. I think his ship is due in Lisbon this week, but I shall await with some anxiety for news of his safety.'

It was a long room with tall sash windows, and they sat at one end of it looking out over the Horse Guards Parade.

'Were you here for the opening of Parliament?'

'No, I came by sea and was embayed for several days in the Solent.'

'Whitbread made a fierce attack on Canning's appointment in the debate on the Address. Suggested it was merely an expensive and pointless emolument we had created for him. He was answered, of course; Charles Ellis made a sincere and moving reply. But since then *The Morning Chronicle* has taken up the cry.'

'I didn't know.'

'In fact Canning's task will be a formidable one in Lisbon. Relations between ourselves and the Council of Regency have never been at a lower ebb. And even when the Regent returns Canning will have to walk a knife-edge of tact and diplomacy.'

Tea came in. The servant poured it out. Ross was offered milk and sugar, both of which he refused.

When they were alone again Lord Liverpool said: 'You know of course Canning and I were at Christchurch together. We have been friends ever since. Though with many ups and downs. He is a brilliant fellow.'

'So I think, Prime Minister.'

'Sometimes too clever for his own good. I often think he is his own worst enemy.'

The last light of day was fading from the sky. Ross had often noted the shortness of the twilight in London compared to Cornwall. People were shouting outside, their voices hollow in the accumulating dusk.

Lord Liverpool said: 'I did not offer him Lisbon as a sinecure. He was glad to go for his son's sake, and also I believe it will do him no harm – no political harm – to be away from the House for a year or so. Castlereagh will have a freer hand in Vienna, and Canning will come back refreshed.'

'No doubt.'

'You have been one of his closest associates, Poldark. He holds a high opinion of you. You were one of his "group", were you not? Sincere and believing friends who could be relied upon to support him in the House: Leveson-Gower, Huskisson, Boringdon . . . you know their names. Some of them even refused opportunities of preferment out of loyalty for him.'

'I don't think I did that.'

'No . . . Of course you sought none. But it does not remove the condition of – what? – obligation? Perhaps not so much; but loyalty need not be weighed: it is enough in itself.'

'Loyalty on my part,' said Ross, 'was simply a matter of conviction. His views and mine on many subjects were close.'

'Yes . . .' Liverpool blinked and sipped his tea. He was

known as 'Old Jenky' to his rivals and a few friends, or sometimes 'Blinking Jenky' because of an affection of his right eyelid which caused it to flutter. 'Before Canning went, he and I talked long on this subject. In going to Lisbon, in leaving the House – at least for a year or so – he was aware that he was leaving his friends. Many of them would miss him.'

'I do.'

'And he felt that it was his duty and his pleasure to take some regard for their future. I agreed with him. We came to an amicable understanding. As a result of it I have recently offered William Huskisson the position of First Commissioner of Woods and Forests. Leveson-Gower has accepted a viscountcy. Boringdon will become an earl. These peerages will be granted in the New Year. I have not entirely decided yet about Bourne . . . There are, as you will no doubt know, many trials and hazards in the path of a Prime Minister of England; but one of its rewards is that he can dispense patronage where it seems to him it should be good to dispense it. He can reward good, honest, loyal service; and that is what I have done in these cases.'

After a pause Ross said: 'I am glad to know it.'

Lord Liverpool stirred his tea. 'I have it in my mind to offer you a baronetcy, Captain Poldark.'

The servant came in again and refilled their cups. He also lit six extra candles on the mantelpiece. He was going to draw the curtains but the Prime Minister stopped him. Presently they were alone again.

Ross said: 'You are very kind, my lord. More than kind. But I seek no reward for following my own inclinations. I was an admirer of Pitt. Since he died I have become an admirer of Canning. These loyalties if that is what you would call them – have cost me nothing. It is not fitting to be rewarded merely for following one's own inclinations.'

Liverpool smiled. 'Oh, come, Poldark, that is not all there is to it. While it is true that your name came before me because you are Canning's friend, it is not *all* you have been, is it. Three missions abroad on behalf of the government, and another one with tacit government approval. You have more than once found yourself in situations of personal danger in the course of those missions. Whether they were following your own inclinations or not, they were all of value to the country. Is it not therefore suitable that your country should see fit to reward you?'

Ross nodded his head. 'I am greatly obliged for the thought, my lord.'

Silence fell. A bell rang in the house. Liverpool rose to his feet and went to the window. A light fog was creeping up from the river, resisting the lights.

'If you wish to take time to consider it, you may do so. Give me your answer before you leave London.'

'Thank you, my lord, but I don't need time. It is a very gracious offer and I am fully sensible to the honour you do me. If I refuse, it is not out of a sense of ingratitude.'

'But you do refuse?'

'Yes.'

'I will not ask why.'

'It would be hard to explain, sir. Partly it is a feeling that service to one's country should not be directly related to some later award. Partly it is a feeling that the Poldarks and the Poldark name have been so long rooted in Western Cornwall that they need no title to distinguish them from their neighbours.'

His Lordship smiled thinly. 'This kind of pride is something I have come upon before, particularly in the shires where some men of ancient name consider a title vulgar. I think it is an old-fashioned concept, but naturally I respect it.'

'Thank you. And thank you for the thought.'

Ross was prepared to rise and leave, but the Prime Minister seemed in no hurry to end the interview. Back at his desk he picked up a pen, ran his finger along the quill, put his empty tea cup back on the silver tray.

'The situation in the world is far from the peaceable one I had hoped for by now. After the splendid celebrations of the summer one had looked forward to a winter of reconciliation; but so far there is little sign of it.'

'Well, in a sense, we are still at war.'

'Oh, yes, but a puny, trivial war – which should be terminated at the earliest possible moment. We want nothing from our ex-colonies except a peace honourable to both sides. Negotiations are going on alongside hostilities, but no one knows how long the negotiations will take. Clearly America can afford to be much less aggressive now that France has collapsed ... But it was not of that I was thinking so much as the situation in Europe, which still remains potentially explosive.'

'In France?'

'In France.'

Ross said: 'I suppose the return of so many dispossessed aristocrats demanding their possessions must have put a strain on King Louis.'

'On everyone. Of course it is an internal problem that time will heal, if time is allowed. France, you know, Poldark, has never been treated as a conquered nation. Napoleon has been treated as a conquered *tyrant*; but from the moment peace was signed the nation as such has been given every assistance and consideration to help it to its feet again, and every encouragement to take its place in the comity of Europe. The unrest within its own borders at present makes its contribution unsatisfactory and unreliable.'

Ross nodded.

Liverpool said: 'As the goodwill attending on the return of Louis has evaporated before the constant problems he has to face, so the British have become deeply unpopular. There have been threats against the life of Wellington, and unpleasant scenes. Realize that in the House of Peers, the ancient nobles of France number but thirty; the remaining hundred and forty are marshals and generals and the like ennobled by Buonaparte. Realize that the army has been recently swelled by the return of one hundred and fifty thousand prisoners of war, from England, Russia and Prussia, most of them ardent to avenge the dishonour and hardship of their captivity. Realize that the princes of the blood royal have been declared colonels and generals by the King, and many other superior posts have been filled by the emigrant nobility, so that the flower of Napoleon's fine army of veterans is subject to the command of old men past the age of service or by young men who have never known it. After the calm early months of Louis' reign, all these discontents and many more have surfaced. And much of the blame – most unfairly – has focused on the British and particularly on their Ambassador. This week I have come to the reluctant conclusion that Wellington must be recalled – for his own safety.'

'He will not like that.'

'There are two principal risks: one, that the dissident army may stage a coup and take him prisoner as a hostage; the other, that he may be murdered. Last week I received a message from our most trusted secret agent in Paris.' Lord Liverpool moved some papers and took out a thin sheet of parchment. 'The message reads: "Unless Duke of Wellington is instantly recalled from France he will be privately assassinated; a plot is now forming to complete the horrid deed."'

Ross eased his aching ankle but did not speak.

'I have twice *suggested* to Wellington that he should leave Paris,' the Prime Minister said, 'but he was never a man to shun danger, and each time he has said he does not wish to. Now I have made it an order. He will leave next month. I have appointed him Commander-in-Chief of the British forces in America.'

'Indeed.'

'We badly lack a man of his genius out there. We have many daring officers but courage – against equal courage – is not enough. Wellington alone has the tactical and strategic grasp to bring the war to a speedy conclusion.'

'By defeating the Americans?'

'By winning a conclusive battle and then making a magnanimous peace. That is all we want.'

'And France?'

'I am glad you see the drift of my remarks. Do you know Lord Fitzroy Somerset?'

'Yes.'

'Well?'

'Moderately so. We met last at Bussaco. But before that in

Cornwall when he was a boy. His mother is a Boscawen. They stayed at Tregothnan.'

'Oh . . . I see. Do you find him a likeable young man?'

'Oh, yes. After Bussaco he was more than helpful in toning down Wellington's impatience at my being there.'

Lord Liverpool smiled and blinked. 'Did you know that Wellington wrote to his brother, the Foreign Secretary, complaining angrily of your visit? What was the difference, he asked, between a "neutral observer" and a "government spy"?'

'I thought this sometimes myself. But you do me more than justice in supposing I see the drift of your remarks.'

'Ah, well. I was about to add, as I am sure you know, that Fitzroy Somerset has been Wellington's aide at the British Embassy in Paris. It is my intention to leave him in sole charge when Wellington leaves.'

'He is young.'

'He is very young, of course, for such a post, though he will have the support of Sir Charles Bagot, who is a few years his senior in age. It will be a testing appointment. Fitzroy Somerset has more than proved himself in battle; it will remain to be seen if he can prove himself equal in diplomacy.'

'I wish him well.'

Lord Liverpool reached forward and snuffed one of the desk candles which was smoking.

'From here forwards perhaps you will have no difficulty in following the purpose of my remarks. It is my intention, it is my Cabinet's intention, to watch events very closely in France over the next few months. It may be that events will stabilize themselves, that the removal of Wellington, who has been, I fear, distinctly arrogant – a living symbol of the conquering armies – will take away one of the main causes of French hostility; it may be that the good sense of the average Frenchman – who has seen so much distress and devastation over the last twenty years – will help him to draw back from any form of civil war, that by the spring the worst discontent will be over and we can settle down to an era of genuine peace.'

'I trust so.'

'But if it does *not*, if discontent in the army generally continues to grow, it is in my mind to send a special envoy to Paris, a man of some experience both in government and in military matters who would report daily direct to me on anything he saw, so that we should not be caught unawares by any revolt, whether it was Buonapartist or on behalf of one of the other royal pretenders. He would be closely attached to the Embassy, and able to draw on them for any assistance he needed but his real mission would be kept secret. For that reason it would have to be a man of some eminence but one not internationally known, a name not known to the French, for instance, a man who could be visiting Paris – and France generally – and combining a holiday, perhaps with his wife and family, with a lively interest in his old gallant adversaries, the French Army.'

Ross saw exactly where it was all pointed now.

Chapter Five

I

Stephen was away for two weeks at the end of November, having sailed with the *Chasse Marée* as far as Bristol. Left much on her own, Clowance accepted an invitation to ride over and dine with Mr and Mrs Valentine Warleggan.

A brooding, gloomy day, mercifully dry and without appreciable wind, but sunless and lifeless. This being only her second visit to the north coast since she was married, Clowance had hoped for brilliance of sky and mountainous seas. (Living in an estuary seemed scarcely to be by the sea at all.) But when she dismounted at the front door of Place House it was as if someone had drawn a grey screen across the view, leaving no lineal mark to distinguish the horizon.

Valentine came instantly out, ran down the steps to meet her.

'Cousin Clowance, my only little cousin. You rode over alone? You should not! We would have sent a groom.' He helped her down and kissed her as if she was the first woman he had seen for a month. Selina Warleggan was smiling from the doorway.

The young women greeted each other, kissing warily; a new life had begun for them both since they last met.

In a flurry of idle conversation they went in, Clowance was helped off with her cloak, her new frock much admired; two blondes together, Selina the more ashen, certainly the more willowy, yet perceptibly the older against Clowance's abounding youth.

'What are you doing *home* so early?' Clowance asked. 'Surely it is not yet time. Or have you given up your studies?'

'On the contrary. In spite of the fascination of my life here I returned promptly to Cambridge, and took Selina with me, of course. My studies were at least as diligent as usual until she tired of the Cambridge air, whereupon I decided that my father was grievous ill and we left two weeks before the end of term.'

'I trust he is not!'

'Alas, no. But –'

'Val, you must not say such things!' exclaimed Selina. 'The time for bitterness is over. What harm has he ever done you? Serious!'

Valentine rubbed his nose. 'I suppose the greatest harm is that he ever sired me. And yet –'

'My dearest, I hold him in the highest favour for that! Just because –'

'Wait until you have been wed to me for a year or two.' Valentine looked Selina assessingly up and down. 'Or twenty year or two. Come to consider it, I think I shall be able to bear you for a long time.'

Selina coloured becomingly. 'We are talking in the presence of another newlywed. How is dear Stephen? It was quite by chance Valentine heard he was away, and thought to ask you over. What do you do with yourself while he is away? And does he prosper? I understand he owns several vessels now and will soon be looked on as a big ship-owner.'

'Scarcely *that*,' said Clowance, smiling, 'but he prospers. So far.'

Over dinner Clowance let out inadvertently that they had been seeing something of Sir George and Lady Harriet, and then that Sir George had financed Stephen's latest purchase, of the *Adolphus*.

Valentine said: 'My father is a useful man to have on board – always so long as you steer in the direction he considers appropriate. Once get at cross with him and he'll have you on the rocks in no time.'

'Well, thank you,' said Clowance drily.

'Oh, it may not come to that, little cousin! Though I feel some responsibility in having introduced them to each other. Never mind, I believe Stephen to be a man of determined character, and that will stand him in good stead . . . And how is that rapscallion Andrew Blamey behaving himself?'

'Very well so far. He lacks your influence . . .' Clowance paused, anxious not to say more in front of Selina.

Valentine laughed. 'You see, Selina, my influence is always bad! What have I been telling you? Live with me and I will corrupt you in no time!'

Selina lowered her eyes and smiled as if to herself privately, nurturing what had been said, her own feelings, her assessment of Valentine's feelings, her own secret conclusions.

It was not in Clowance's character to see deeply below the surface of an enjoyable first visit to Place House; she took people as they came, reacting with the natural warmth of her own uncomplex nature. But being entertained by this ill-assorted pair stirred her curiosity and her observancy beyond its usual limits.

She had first seen Mrs Pope as the slim, secretive, blonde young wife of the ailing old man, and then later as the pretty, nearly-demure widow in becoming black. Once or twice, chiefly at Geoffrey Charles's party, she had come out of her shell; but even at such times she had seemed on her guard, a little unable to relax her dignity in case someone took advantage of her. Jeremy had told Clowance that Mrs Pope had had an eye for him, and clearly she had not been above a flirtation here and there. When her 'flirtation' had begun with Valentine Clowance had no idea – perhaps even as early as the Enys's dinner party in July of three years ago – before Mr Clement Pope was even ill: she remembered them sitting all together at the dinner table, and Valentine had asked her who his other neighbour was before he spoke to Mrs Pope. Thereafter that evening, Clowance remembered, he had had no attention for anyone else.

'My charming step-daughters,' Valentine said taking Clowance by the arm as they left the dining room, 'are with a Mrs Osworth in Finsbury. We visited them on the way to Cambridge and again on the way home. Mrs Osworth is a well-connected widow who will do her best to further their education and their entry into society. But I have been telling Selina, once I am free of Cambridge, that we would do well to take a house in London for a season to see them properly launched. And for that purpose I shall have no hesitation in calling in my step-mother's connections. Let it be said that I hope never to have to exchange another word with my father as long as he lives; but Lady Harriet is another matter. I fancy Lady Harriet – decorously, of course, in her case – but still I fancy her; and would feel sorry for her at the outlandish marriage she has made, were it *possible* to feel sorry for Lady Harriet. Happily it is not. She is far too strong, too much mistress of her own soul to allow one terrible mistake to jeopardize it. So I shall solicit her assistance on behalf of Letitia and Maud. And although no doubt she will call scorn on me for having such petty ambitions for them, I believe secretly she will be amused to help.'

'My dearest,' said Selina, 'you are so kind to take this interest in my step-daughters. Is he not so, Clowance? For they are nothing to him.'

They took tea in the drawing room and asked after Jeremy. He was still quartered near Brussels, Clowance said. She had heard from him about a week ago. (But when he wrote he had not heard of Valentine's marriage.) Amadora Poldark, if they did not know it, was expecting a baby next month. As soon as possible after it Geoffrey Charles was to bring his family to England again. Did they know he had resigned from the army? Although he was not quite free of it, being retained on half pay. Which would not come amiss, Geoffrey Charles said, since money was not easy to transfer from Spain to England at the moment, and in any case the less he had to depend on Amadora the better he was pleased.

Cuby was not mentioned. Clowance did not utter the name, for she did not know to what extent if any Selina had been informed of Sir George's plans for his son.

Valentine, of course, was less tactful. 'Tom Guildford will be in Cornwall for Christmas. Naturally he was heart-broken at the news.'

'I wrote to him,' Clowance said shortly.

'I know. He told me so . . . D'you know, he said a very strange thing. A very strange thing indeed, Clowance. He said: "I'll wait for her." Just that. "I'll wait for her."'

He had said the same in a letter to Clowance.

'He was joking.'

'I suppose. He's a queer character, old Tom. You don't bottom him easily . . .' Valentine helped himself to a biscuit. 'I often think it a pity charming young women cannot be three or four people – multiply themselves, as it were. I hear Lord Edward Fitzmaurice is still unmarried.'

'Is he?'

'Yes, he is, dear Cousin. You'd have made a good wife for him. And a good wife for old Tom. And I'm sure Stephen is happy. But only one of 'em can have you!'

'And what about charming young men?' Clowance asked.

'Ah, yes, well that is sometimes true too. Though a little different in some respects.'

'Yes, do tell us, Valentine,' said his wife, her wisteria blue eyes narrowing. 'If you were able to have three wives, who else would you choose?'

'My dear,' said Valentine coolly. 'I should go around the country looking for two more Selinas.'

When Clowance left, which she did at four, they insisted on their head groom, Grieves, riding with her to Nampara, where she was to spend the night.

They walked with the two horses a little way, since Valentine said he had had no exercise that day and he liked the time before the fall of night. Arms linked, they watched their visitor and her escort going off, waved, stood a while until the horses had disappeared round the corner into the evening mists.

Valentine said: 'I like little Clowance.'

'I noticed.'

'But a virtuous girl. Having married Stephen Carrington, she will feel herself bound to him through thick and thin, and never look elsewhere.'

'Isn't that the purpose of marriage?'

'There are exceptions. Can you walk with me a little further?'

'Down that old slope?'

'Down that old slope.'

'It will soon be dark.'

He held out his hands. 'Trust me.'

She laughed. 'Oh, that I shall never do!'

'A very proper approach. But you may be surprised.'

'Nicely?'

'Who knows?'

'Very well, then.' She gave him her hand.

He helped her down a few feet and then drew her closer to him and began to kiss her.

She wriggled, but without conviction. 'Not here.'

His lank dark hair was falling over his brow. 'I often think it strange that this is all now legal. No more listening for the old man in the other room.'

She shivered. 'Don't speak of it.'

'I speak of it to make the contrast. Don't tell me you liked it better when it was forbidden.'

'Of course not! Valentine, it is wicked of you to suggest it.'

'Pleasure thrives on wickedness.' He released her, took her hand again, and they slid and stumbled down to a plateau of ground which had been cleared of gorse bushes.

Valentine said: 'This is the site that first enticed Unwin Trevaunance and Michael Chenhalls.'

'I know. When Sir Unwin called in the summer we walked out this far.'

'We are well rid of him . . . D'you know, your eyes are like a cat's in the half dark, Selina. They close like a cat's. Yet they see everything. Unloose your hair.'

'Dearest, there are servants!'

'What is it to them?'

'Source for gossip. Guess what I seen Mistress do last night!'

'Far more likely to gossip about what master may do at any moment if you continue to look like that.'

'How shall I look? Cold? Austere?'

'I disbelieve you could!'

There was a pause. Out at sea the lights of a half dozen fishing boats winked.

Valentine said: 'Would you like me to tell you something?'

'Please do.'

'That evening at Cardew. D'you know when I told my father of our marriage and we quarrelled, I said to him that I worshipped the very ground you walked on.'

Selina leaned against him. 'Oh, Valentine, you are so kind.'

'But I meant it. It was the truth!'

'Of course I believe you. However unworthy I may feel –'

'The *literal* truth,' he said.

There was another pause. Selina pushed back a strand of her hair.

'I don't think I conject what you mean, Valentine.'

'The literal truth. This is the ground I worship that you are walking on now.'

She brushed some dust and fragments of heather from the hem of her skirt. Her voice was smaller, a little colder. 'Is this some sort of jest? A joke? Yes, I see it is a joke. That is *funny* Valentine.'

'Funny but utterly and precisely exact. I could not have spoken more clearly what was in my mind.'

'That? . . .'

'That I worship the ground you are walking on! Do you not understand? Or covet it, if you prefer the word. The early assays that Chenhalls had taken were over-optimistic, but later ones have shown a real basis for a new enterprise. We should do well.'

She was very still against him. After a while she said: 'Sometimes before you have shown sarcasm, cynicism. I have always persuaded myself that it would not be turned upon me. Why now?'

He stroked her hair but she moved her head away. He said: 'It is not turned upon you, my kitten. It is turned upon life.'

'That I still don't understand. Are you trying to inform me that you have married me for my money, for the house and land I own?'

He thought it over, eyes fixed on the fishing boats. 'I

married you for *yourself* – and for everything you possess – and for the ground you walk on. There is mining blood in me and I cannot disown it. Nor do I wish to. That letter I was writing this morning, was to friends I have who may be able to advance me the development money. I think I can convince them.' The statement was plain and unemphatic, not governed or affected by friendship or emotion.

Suddenly, bitterly she burst out: 'Why bother? My money is now yours. I am now no longer the rich widow but the unimportant wife!'

'Thank you, but I have my pride and prefer to try for my own fortune. However, I shall call on you for much. Money, true, to live on. Indulgence. Your body, which I covet most of all at this moment . . . If there is cynicism in me, Selina, you must bear with it . . . just as you will bear my love. Just as you will have to bear my infidelities.'

She turned to look at him incredulously, doubting what she had just heard, but she could only discern his sharp profile. Because of some trick of the light it was as if his eyes were dark sockets under the ledge of his brows, empty of life and expression. It had suddenly happened, this change of mood, a matter-of-factness, a coldness, which seemed only the reverse side of all the charm, all the ardour. The coin had turned. She swung angrily round to climb up the way she had come, but he caught her. She hit him across the face, but it stung only a moment as he gripped her arms.

'Do not do that, Selina, for I need you.'

'You're hurting me!'

'Not very much. Besides, we are bound together in holy matrimony, are we not, and that bond will hurt us both much, much more from time to time. Can we not be honest about it?'

'Honest!' she exclaimed. 'What honour is there in what you've just said?'

'I did not say honour, but honesty, my little pussy cat. Or candour, if you prefer it . . .'

'The candour of a brute! Why are you doing this to me? Why are you saying this *now*?'

'No reason. Just that it had to be said sometime. And one

thing led to another . . . I have been faithful to you for five months, Selina. Truly. Genuinely. Is that not a great deal? But I cannot be faithful indefinitely, for it is not in my nature. There are too many pretty women in the world. I simply cannot resist them. Nor shall I try . . . Many wives – most wives – find this out in time. Look around you. But look at their husbands, who do not have the honesty – or candour – that I have but behave just the same in the end.'

'Let me go!'

'Not yet. For I have now said all that will be disagreeable to your self-esteem. Now let me say that if I stray from you – when I stray from you – it will always, I think, be to return. There is something in you –'

'I may not be here to greet you!'

'There is something in you that I do not find in any other woman –'

'So far!'

'So far. And believe me, that has been quite far. I have not wasted my youth –'

'I do not want to hear any more of your reminiscences! Do you enjoy insulting me?'

He tried to kiss her again but she averted her face.

'For me,' he said, 'women are a game. A game I greatly relish. But still – just that. You, my little Selina, are not a game; you are a reality. Whenever I come to you it is to someone *real*, a touchstone – and a wife that I cherish: perhaps I should say that! – I lose myself in you as in no other woman. Marriage to you has been a consummation. We belong to each other. Have you realized that? If another man touched you I should kill him.'

'My God!' she exploded. 'You are telling me *that*; at the same time you are demanding all the freedom in the world for yourself!'

'I am indeed. I am indeed. I am indeed.' Although she had not relaxed, his grip slackened and he took her in his arms. 'You have to believe all this. You have to understand all this. For it is going to be the very essence of our relationship.'

'Who says so?'

'I say so. And I am your husband. And you must obey me. You promised to in the marriage service.'

'That is nonsense!'

'Far from it. You promised it, and you must keep your promise.'

'I shall not!'

'Yes, you shall. As my only beloved wife. On whom I am shortly going to exercise every husbandly privilege and right. Be still now. Be still.'

She still struggled, but not with all her strength. She knew what he meant and she knew what he was promising, and although she was fierce and hurt, she found it hard to resist that promise. She thought: I will never forgive him for the cynicism and brutality of what he has just said. If he behaves in that way I shall break his head when he comes crawling home! She thought: I *hate* him. But he desires me. All right, I desire him. In the morning it will be different. In the morning I will have this out; in the morning I will show him he is not such a master as he thinks; I shall be cold and distant; he must be taught that he is *not* the owner and controller of everything. I, I, Selina, am the mistress of my own body. I can deprive him, deny him, taunt him, control him. If he *really* desires me as he says he does, then *I* am the mistress. He cannot take me against my will, and my will is at least as strong as his! Place House will still belong to me.

But for the moment lust was too strong. She knew it for what it was and despised it with the relish of a woman who had never known what sensuality was until Valentine took her. So for the moment she was quiet in his arms.

Mistaking her quiescence – or reading it correctly – he said:

'This mine will need considerable exploration before we can be sure of everything. I hope – I very much hope that we can arrange the workings so that they run away from the house down the valley, so that little of our view from the house looking north will be spoiled. I think it may be a very important working once it is launched.'

She did not speak, licking her lips, licking her psychic wounds.

Valentine said: 'I have thought about a name. Perhaps it is premature with scarcely a sod yet turned. However I have thought about a name.'

She still did not speak.

'Wheal Elizabeth,' he said.

Selina peered at him. 'After your mother?'

'Just so.'

II

Clowance thought Demelza had gone thin again, but put it down to the monthly megrim. Good to be home among all the friendly faces, sleep in her own bed, listen to Isabella-Rose bubbling like a hoarse nightingale, see young Harry's fat little pudding-basin of a face crack into a beaming smile at sight of her, ride across the beach at break-neck pace, have long talks with her mother by the fireside. She asked a number of intimate questions about her own body and sex life which Demelza tried to answer. She stayed three days.

Demelza asked her few questions in return; she felt the need above all not to pry. But that scarcely mattered. Whatever else married life had done to Clowance, it had not changed her frankness. She said she was more in love with Stephen than ever. In spite of his upbringing and his harsh life, there was no physical coarseness in him, she said. They talked a lot, she said, sometimes had arguments, but he seemed to want to learn of things she knew and he did not. She found they could learn from each other. When he went away she was desperately bored, and couldn't wait for his return. As he was likely to travel in his boats from time to time she felt she must find something to do. Of course, if a child came, that might alter her views, but so far there was no child on the way. She saw a lot of Aunt Verity and they had become closer friends than ever before. (Demelza felt an unaccustomed twinge of jealousy that of the three women she held most dear, two were enjoying each other's company and she could not be with them.)

Verity had promised to come over last month, Demelza

said, with her step-son, the ever-popular James and his wife and child, who were now living in Portsmouth. But young Alan had gone down with measles so they could not come where other children were. It had been a big disappointment for everyone.

And what of Papa? Clowance asked. When would he be home? Probably next week. The Committee was holding its last meeting on Thursday and he had promised to leave immediately after. All would be home for Christmas, so she and Stephen must spend at least three days with them. It would be a lovely party time: the first Christmas of peace – or nearly peace.

'All?' said Clowance. 'Do you mean Jeremy as well?'

'I heard from him yesterday. He says he has applied for leave and there is so little for the battalion to do at the moment, that he has a fair hope of getting it.'

'Thank goodness he's not been sent to America,' said Clowance, and then at the shadow on her mother's face wished she had not. She went on: 'Does he know about Valentine's marriage?'

'I told him. In his reply he simply says "What a shock about Valentine!" and nothing more.'

'No mention of Cuby?'

Demelza shook her head. 'No.'

'Perhaps he is "over" her.'

'I don't know, Clowance. I used to think I understood my children. Now I don't believe I understand Jeremy any more.'

Clowance admired the little silver cup on the sideboard in the dining room and asked where it had come from. Demelza gave her usual explanation. They examined it together and read the motto. Presumably the cup had been washed up from some shipwreck. Talking of ships, Demelza said, she hoped Stephen was going to prosper. Had he had to *borrow* the money for his first two vessels?

'No, an uncle in Bristol died, left him quite a lot of money. He had the *Clowance* built at Drake's shipyard, and the other was a French prize he picked up cheap at St Ives. It was lucky because it was just enough to start him off. Then he sailed as you know to Italy with pilchards and brought — another cargo — back.'

'I thought his mother was very poor.'

'Well, so she was. But he has lost touch with her. When last he heard she was on the stage. This uncle was his father's brother. Stephen says he kept an inn at Clifton. He met him years ago when he first went to Bristol; but of course he never expected any money.'

'No,' said Demelza. ''Twas indeed fortunate.'

'You know that Stephen has *now* borrowed money — from Warleggan's Bank — to buy the *Adolphus*? Everybody has been warning us of the risks we are taking!'

'If it is just business it may be well enough. Many hundreds of people bank at Warleggan's Bank and come to no hurt. And Sir George has always been of a favourable disposition towards you.'

'To me? Well, yes, I believe he has.' Clowance stretched out and patted Farquhar, who was leaning against her skirt. 'I must see the Kellows before I leave. Is it true that Daisy is now encouraging Horrie Treneglos?'

'I thought Horrie was fixed up with Angela Nankivell. Certainly it would please his parents more.'

'I'm sorry for Daisy. She does not seem quite to settle on anyone. Of course I blame Jeremy partly for that.'

Demelza said: 'Does anyone still use Kellow's Ladder? I was walking along the cliffs last week and looked down. I believe part of the ladder has become dangerous.'

'I don't think it has been used since the Kellows' lugger was broken up in the storm. That must be nearly three years ago.'

'I didn't attempt to go down,' said Demelza falsely.

'I should think not! What an idea! You would be crazy to consider it. We walked that way when Geoffrey Charles was home — he and Amadora and Jeremy and I; and I wanted to show it to Amadora, and Jeremy would not let me go *near* it.'

'When I next see Paul,' said Demelza. 'I will ask him . . . Have they not been better off recently?'

'Who, the Kellows?'

'Yes. There has not been so much talk of bankruptcy.'

Chapter Six

I

On the assumption that the weather could not be adverse always, Ross came home again by sea; and this time four days of fine December weather and a helpful wind brought him into Par, and he hired a post horse and was home before Demelza was expecting him.

Ross could not help but think of the changes: ten years ago it would have been Jeremy and Clowance hot-footing it to greet him, to swing in his arms, to prattle and crow and search his pockets for presents; now they were both gone; instead it was Isabella-Rose with bulbous Henry falling round his feet, and not Garrick barking but the far handsomer though never-so-much-loved Farquhar; and Demelza. She was the one constant, apparently unchanging; taken for granted but instantly needed; sometimes an irritant and an anxiety, yet without her the other welcomes would have been hollow; for better or worse everything in his life operated against the background of her continuing existence.

Because of what had happened before he left, he looked at her assessingly over the children. At first she returned his inquiring glance without apparent comprehension; then when he had made his meaning unmistakable she shook her head at him coldly.

'Really?' he said.

'Count the bottles if you wish.'

'What bottles?' Bella asked instantly.

'Spice bottles,' said Ross, 'that I promised your mother and quite forgot, daring to have no thoughts for anything but what I must bring my noisy, noisy daughter.'

'And what have you brought her?'

'You wait until Christmas Day, my girl.'

'Oh, Papa!'

That night, when even Bella had been persuaded to retire, they exchanged news and again he hinted at the subject.

Demelza said stiffly: 'I have been – very well.'

'Not feeling too morbid?'

'Morbid at times. But well enough.'

'Why were you so morbid that night when it happened?'

'Do not ask me.'

'I am only anxious –'

'Do not mention it again – else I shall take offence.'

'Very well,' said Ross.

There was a moment's mutinous silence. Then she said: 'After all, if I want to get drunk I shall!'

'Of course.'

'You cannot stop me, Ross.'

'No, I am aware of that.'

'So allow me please to stop myself!'

'Of course,' he said again.

'Until then . . .'

'Until then,' said Ross, 'the subject is taboo.'

Later still when her irritation had been assuaged she lay against his arm in bed, and they gossiped more companionably together. Even then it was a while before he told her of Lord Liverpool's suggestion.

'And what did you say?'

'That I would consider it.'

'You seriously think you might go?'

'It depends on you.'

'Now, Ross, you must not –'

'Seriously. I would not consider going on my own without you and the children.'

Her hand smoothed the sheet, drawing it more closely about them. 'But I know no French. I still think of France as an enemy.'

'I know. Nor is my French good.'

'Then why did he suggest *you* should go?'

'It seems he knows as much about me as I know of myself! That I spoke a little French as a boy, lost it almost entirely, but then when I was in Paris those months with Dwight in

1802 I made an effort and began to understand it again and to speak more freely. Liverpool said that for the purposes for which I should go, an *apparent* lack of the language might be an advantage.'

'It sounds as if he wants you to be a spy!'

'I made much the same comment. He replied that he had an ample network of spies without the need to add to them. He says he wants an observer, particularly a person of some modest eminence who could visit the French army and be received by them and might gain their confidence, and so report back to him on their current feelings of loyalty to the King.'

'Could it be dangerous?'

'I raised that point also, in the matter of you and the children. He said he supposed he could not promise that my mission would be entirely without any risk, however small; but he deemed it trifling. There would be no point in trying to assassinate some ordinary English member of parliament, as he drily put it; and we are not at war with France; if I fell into a quarrel with someone and fought a duel he could not of course guarantee my safety. (His Lordship has a long memory, you see.) But as for you and the children – he saw you at no greater risk than if you were in London. The Duchess of Wellington will be staying on in Paris while the Duke is in America. Liverpool was at pains to point out that the English are highly unpopular in the French press and with certain sections of the populace; but in so far as society and the King are concerned they are welcomed and fêted everywhere.'

She plucked at the sheet now with a hint of nervousness in her fingers. 'Then you *are* of a mind to take it?'

'As I have said, only if you would like to go. And then only if it was definitely offered me – which is not yet.'

'I don't quite –'

'Liverpool was but sounding me out. After Wellington leaves, the situation may simmer down, the discontent may find its own level; there may be no need for any such mission.'

'But if there is?'

'Well, there you are . . . He sees me as a suitable man to send. Apart from Fitzroy Somerset, the other main officer at the British Embassy is also quite young. A man of my age, even though of inferior rank, would he believes be valuable all round.'

She moved against his arm.

'Your nose is cold,' he said.

'Healthy . . . Did I ever meet Lord Fitzroy Somerset?'

'Oh, yes. As a boy, I think once, when Mrs Gower was down. But more recently at the christening party for George-Henry, not much more than three years ago. The young lieutenant.'

'But of course. Fair hair; fresh skin; rather short; good looking.'

'That's the man. One of the scions of the Boscawen family with whom you did *not* fall in love.'

'Oh, Ross, that is cruel! Even as a joke.'

'I am sorry. It never was a joke. And I had no right to say it.'

He kissed her ear, which was all he could reach. After a minute she said: 'But he is *very* young.'

'Twenty-five or six by now, I suppose. At Bussaco he was already aide de camp to Wellington and a captain. I believe he was made a lieutenant-colonel before the war ended.'

'I don't think I should be happy going into that sort of society.'

'You've said that so often, and you've always been a success.'

'But this is worse than ever – where most of them do not even speak the same language!'

'You managed very well with de Sombreuil and de Maresi.'

'Well, I could not understand scarcely a word that the Count de Maresi said, except that he wanted me to go to bed with him.'

'Yes,' said Ross, 'that's the same in any language. Or, at least intelligible . . . That's a nice bit,' he remarked, stroking her inner thigh.

'Ross, you must not do that if you want me to go to sleep!'

'Well, if I may not do it, who may do it? I ask you. There are few privileges a husband has. The Comte de Maresi was not allowed to do it. Sir Hugh Bodrugan was not allowed to do it. John Treneglos has never been allowed to do it. But if a husband may not do it . . .'

'Very well,' she said, 'if that's the way you want it, so do I.'

II

So it was not until the early morning that he told her of his other offer, the one he had turned down.

'My dear Judas God!' she said. 'Ross! What a *thing*! He meant it? Not half meant it? Not a quarter meant it? He really *did*?'

'Oh, yes.'

After a minute or so she turned over to face him. 'What exactly would it mean?'

'I would have had to become a Sir. Like George. Only better than George because I should have put Bart. after my name. Which means that it would go on.'

'How "go on"?'

'Well, when I died Jeremy would have it, and when he died his son would have it.'

'For *ever*?'

'Well, until there wasn't a son. These things die out in time.'

'And me? What would I have become?'

'Lady Poldark, of course.'

'That would have been *impossible*! I *couldn't* have been!'

'Why not?'

'I'm a miner's daughter. I was dragged up any way and strapped every time he could catch me.'

'Nobody knows that, and it wouldn't have the slightest effect if they did. Anyway you have been saved the risk.'

'You turned it down utterly?'

'Yes.'

'Coh,' she said, 'it has made me come out in a sweat! Feel me. No, not *there* again! My forehead will do.'

'Yes,' he said. 'I see by how much you are relieved to have escaped the peril.'

'Well, for myself, yes ... Was this because of your friendship with Mr Canning?'

'Liverpool says it is chiefly for services rendered – those tin-pot missions I have been on. But I suspect that, but for Canning, they would have been conveniently forgot.'

'Well, at least you would not have had to *buy* your knighthood, like George.'

A low late dawn was bringing the daylight by stealth, with as little change from moment to moment as the hand movement of a clock. But very soon Isabella-Rose would be stirring; you would hear her knocking about in her room as soon as she was awake. She usually roused Henry, who otherwise would sleep till nine.

'I'd have died,' she said.

'Would you, indeed.'

'It wouldn't have been an embarrassment exactly, it wouldn't have been laughter ... except maybe laughter at *myself*. But some folk are just not born to – to – to – to ...'

'Go on.'

'Well, to carry a Lady in front of their name!'

'You were born to carry whatever you set your mind to carry. But I'm glad I have pleased you.'

'Of course it would have suited you. Sir Ross. Yes, that would have suited you handsomely.'

'As Liverpool said, some men of ancient name consider a title vulgar. That is exactly my feeling.'

'He seems content with his!'

'He inherited it. Though his father began as a Mr Jenkinson. But, to be fair, he was simply attempting in his own good-mannered way to provide a more acceptable reason for my refusal.'

Someone had let Farquhar out. He had gone racing onto the beach and was barking at the seagulls. One of their cocks was crowing, answering another in Mellin. All the world was coming awake.

After a while Demelza stirred and sat up.

'Judas, it fills me with ignoble thoughts, Ross.'

'Tell me them.'

'I hardly dare.'

'There has never been a time when you have hardly dared.'

'Well, I hardly dare because it might seem as if I regretted your decision to refuse – which is not true, for whatever you personally feel is right, is right for me too.'

'Go on.'

'. . . It would not even have been just the pride of knowing that all your good work had been noted – and appreciated – and justly rewarded . . .'

'What would it have been, then?'

'It would have been . . .' She rubbed her eyes, clearing them of sleep. 'I suppose you could say there are two things I'm a little sorry about. Don't think I'm complaining to you! You did *right*, I know . . . But it would really have been gratifying to have gone one rung up the ladder above George.'

'You are quite correct,' he said, 'to consider that an ignoble thought.'

'The other,' she said. 'The other is less dislikeable – at least in a mother. It would have been for Jeremy. It would have been good – warming to feel that he would have had it after you.'

'Let him earn his own distinctions.'

'Yes, I agree. But you see what I mean. His son – his son's son – would all bear the honour that was given to *you*; they would all know what a great and good man their grandfather – great-grandfather – was.'

'And how deluded they would be!'

'Not at all! You cannot – should not – be mock-humble to me, Ross.'

'Well, regarded in any sort of perspective, it is not mock-humble at all. I have married and raised a family, and owned a mine or two, occupied a rotten parliamentary borough for a decade and a half and gone on a few missions that others could have done as well. There is nothing exceeding great

426

and good about that. It would have been different, perhaps, if I had been Wilberforce with his dedication to the abolition of the slave trade, or even Cobbett with his – his equal dedication to universal suffrage and parliamentary reform.' He scratched his nose and stared out at the coming day. 'I'm not sure I recognize goodness when I see it, m'dear, but I know greatness.'

There was a long silence, and she lay back again, stretching her legs. 'What shall you do today?'

'Today? First, go over the cost books with Zacky. I presume all is well?'

'With Leisure – oh, yes. Wheal Grace you know . . .'

'Is Ben come good now?'

'It was a thought difficult when Clowance was over, but they met twice and the awkwardness passed.'

'After I've seen Zacky I've promised to take Bella a ride across the beach.'

'Put her off if it's raining. I have never known anyone get so thoroughly wet as she does. Sometimes when she comes in she might have been in the sea!'

'Perhaps she has. I wouldn't put it past her. Demelza . . .'

She looked at him but did not speak, observing his strong bony face in the pallid light.

'While I was in London I had another proposition.' He told her of his visit to Major Cartwright's, of the men he had met there. She let out a slow breath. He finished:

'But if I had devoted my life to *them* and to their cause, I might feel a little more persuaded of my right to some king's honour.'

'If you had devoted your life to them and to their cause,' said Demelza, 'a King's honour is the one thing you would *not* have got!'

Ross smiled grimly. 'Very true. Perhaps I did not realize how true until this time.'

'Why?'

'I told you, didn't I, that Lord Liverpool seemed well informed about me. He was too well informed, for he knew about my visit to Major Cartwright, that it was a supper party with many of the best known "agitators" there.'

'However did he know that?'

'He hinted to me that he thought it would be "unfortunate" if I allowed my sympathy for their aims to lead me into active co-operation with them. I told him warmly that I very much resented being followed in this way. He said on the contrary, I had not been followed; it was Cartwright and his group who were "watched", and usually the Government arranged for an "observer" to be present at their parties, just "to keep their activities in view." '

'But that's spying!' said Demelza. 'That's like being at *war*. But with one's own people. I did not know it could go on in England!'

'Oh, it does.'

'But *are* they dangerous? And if so, who are they dangerous to?'

'Liverpool gives me the impression of being a well balanced man, but he has a phobia about revolution.'

'What does phobia mean?'

'A fear. A morbid aversion. He told me – I didn't know before – that he was in Paris in 1789 and actually witnessed the storming of the Bastille. He also lost a number of friends in the Terror . . . And then, of course, it is not so long since his predecessor was assassinated in the House of Commons. That cannot often be absent from his mind, night or day. Bellingham, as far as I know, had no connection with any agitators, but the death of Perceval gave great delight to the mobs in the Midlands and the North . . . Therefore harmless groups of reformers now get spied on and run the risk of imprisonment.'

'And if you joined them you would run that risk?'

'Perhaps. It is an interesting speculation. They are all free at present – technically free . . . I did not, as you will suppose, take kindly to Liverpool's advice. The very fact of being warned off something gives one a greater incentive for joining it.'

Demelza's mind picked a wary way through the pitfalls of the situation. The last thing she wished to do was to copy Lord Liverpool's mistake.

'I see you have had a very interesting trip.'

'Stimulating, certainly.'

'Shall you discuss it with Dwight?'

'Some of it. But first I am discussing it with you.'

'Thank you, Ross.'

'Now do not be mock-modest in your turn. There is no one so important as you, and I shall be much influenced by your feelings. Now have we time for another sleep?'

'No, my lover. Bella will be singing any moment.'

'God's my life, what are we to do with her?'

'Just let her sing. She's young. Tis lovely, I think.'

'Not at six o'clock in the morning.'

'It is much past that. You forget it is December.'

He put his hand out to reach his watch but she stayed him. He rubbed his nose against her arm.

She said: 'Yours is cold too . . . Ross, we must discuss all this very seriously. How long before we have to make up our minds?'

'I expect France will settle down and that will make up our minds for us. In any event, I have agreed to wait on Lord Liverpool in early February with my reply. So we have weeks before any decision has to be reached. Let us enjoy Christmas first.'

Chapter Seven

I

A few days later, a terrible storm struck England and lasted nine days without a break. *The British Queen*, a packet boat, was lost on the Goodwin Sands with sixteen drowned, another nine died in a wreck off Folkestone, a brig and a galliot were torn to pieces at Dunkirk. The city of Bristol came to a standstill with five feet of snow in the streets, Dartmoor became a waste land of isolated farmers and dying sheep. Mail coaches were overturned and children froze to death.

Cornwall suffered with the rest, and there was the usual rash of small wrecks around the coast, though nothing to approach the tragedy of the previous January when the *Queen* transport came to shelter from a south-easterly gale in Falmouth, parted her cables, was dashed upon Trefusis Point, to sink in twenty minutes with a loss of more than 200 lives. Indeed this December the entire West Indian fleet of near 300 sail was able to make the protection of Falmouth in time and rode out the succession of heavy gales with insignificant damage. The *Chasse Marée*, carrying timber and granite for the new harbour at Porthleven, was embayed and eventually ran aground at Mullion and nearly became a wreck; only the desperate efforts of her crew saved her.

So Christmas came and with unwelcome speed was gone. Those who could enjoyed it. The newly married Warleggans gave a party and were themselves entertained, at Nampara and at Killewarren. Only Trenwith was dark. The newly married Poldarks were to have spent several days at Nampara, but even though the weather relented, Stephen pleaded work on the *Chasse Marée*, and sent his wife in company with the Blameys for the celebrations.

Jeremy too was absent. Demelza had hoped against hope that he would turn up on Christmas Eve just as he had done for the wedding. For her it was the one thing missing.

Yet he did come, and in the most timely way possible, on New Year's Eve, and with the best possible news.

After the paroxysms of the middle of the month, the weather had fallen into a fit of idle good behaviour, with an easterly breeze, cloudless skies, and a globular sun like a Chinese lantern appearing and disappearing through the winter mists. The sea lumbered and thundered unceasingly on the hard beach, throwing up its wild heads but no longer amounting to much when the tide came in.

Ross was walking back from Wheal Leisure when he saw a figure dismounting at the door and at once recognized the black cloak, the red tunic, the lanky shape. Jeremy saw him at much the same time and instead of knocking at the door vaulted the enclosing wall of Demelza's garden and ran to meet his father. They clasped each other, putting cheek to cheek.

'*Wel*-come. So you have come to bring in the New Year! You're looking *well*, boy. Flanders must suit you!'

'Not so much as coming *home*! Or the news I bring! Have you *heard* it, Father? Have you heard it?'

'No? What news? What has happened?'

'Peace with America!'

'What!'

'It is in the paper I bought in Truro! They signed the preliminary treaty on Christmas Eve! It waits to be ratified but that is surely only a formality!'

'By the Lord, that is – is *good*!' Ross took his son by the shoulders again. 'Of course peace was only a matter of time, for we have little to dispute over; but men and governments are so pig-headed, I had feared perhaps another twelve months. And once pride and prestige are engaged . . .'

'I know . . . Incidentally the next war we engage in *must* be in Brittany, for the journey home this time was outrageous. Half my leave has gone!'

'We must tell your mother. Instantly. I believe she is at Caroline's.'

'And the children?'

'Bella is walking with Mrs Kemp and pushing Harry. I don't know which way they went but they are liable to explode upon us at any moment.'

Jeremy took his father's arm. 'Let us go to Killewarren. It will only take you a moment, won't it, to saddle a nag?'

'Less than a moment.' Ross turned and ran round to the stables.

So soon they were off up the valley, leaving Jeremy's pack dumped in the hall as notice that he had arrived. And they found Demelza and Caroline playing with a new pug puppy Caroline had just bought called Horace the Third. The women squeaked with delight, and Jeremy hugged them both, and apologized for his bristly chin but he had been in such haste to get home he had not paused to shave.

'Half my leave has *gone!*' he complained again. 'We were in Ostend a *week* waiting for the gales — one week *wasted* and —'

'Does it matter with the news you've brought?' Ross said. 'Where is Dwight? We must tell him as soon as possible.'

'I must be back by the seventeenth and no excuses —'

'It does not *matter* now,' said Demelza, hugging him.

'Sophie and Meliora are brave, I hope?'

'Brave and well,' said Caroline, smiling.

'Brave and well as we all shall be now!'

He looks different, thought Demelza. Or may be it is just that *I* think he looks different now. But he has filled out, grown stronger in the shoulder and the thigh, more of a soldier, with that long hair, more like his father; yet totally *different* from his father. Ross would never have . . . Ross's nature is less oblique, less devious — is it *my* family that has brought this complexity to Jeremy? God knows I was not aware of it; but then there was Joshua Poldark. Thank God the last final war is over. Now if he stays in the army for a while . . . But perhaps he will come home. He *must* come home.

They arranged a party for that evening, to celebrate the peace and to let in the New Year. Could anything be more fitting? In six hours they did celebrate it, in Nampara library, with Bella singing her songs and Demelza playing her piano, leading them all in communal singing. All the indoor staff were invited to join in: John and Jane Gimlett, Mrs Kemp, Betsy Maria Martin and the rest. The evening did not break up until 3 a.m. when Dwight, much recovered over the autumn but pleading an early rise, dragged Caroline and his sleepy daughters away. Even then talk and jollity went on in the family until the crisp, half frosty dawn of January the first, 1815 was not far away.

II

Jeremy slept late, as he was entitled to after his arduous journey, and when he came down at eleven all the others had gone about their business. In the dining room he ate a plate of porridge, two eggs and some cold ham, part of a rabbit pie; with a pint of small beer. The newspaper he had brought with him had been much read by the others and he opened its two sheets at the centre page, where the leading article was to be found.

It was headed 'Peace' and ran,

> The sword being now unanimously sheathed, we may reasonably look forward without complaining to a considerable diminution of our burdens. We have borne much and we have suffered much in the way of privation – our struggles have been long and our exertions unremitting. The result has been happy, and we therefore confidently hope that in a short time our shoulders will be eased from a considerable part of the weight beneath which we have bent so long, and that a series of years of Peace and Plenty will repay the unexampled expenditures of the last astonishing contests.
>
> 'The Name of the Lord is a strong Tower,' and to that we have fled, and there we have been safe.

A slightly less elevated and more cynical note was struck by the actual news item which began: 'To the disappointment of some, the gratification of many, and the surprise of all, a provisional treaty of peace with America was signed at Ghent on Christmas Eve.'

Jeremy was about to turn over to the back page when his eye caught something on the sideboard. He got up, picked it up, stared at it, twisted it round, read the inscription.

As he was about to put it back, Demelza came in.

'Morning, my lover. I trust you slept well. Jane has been looking after you?'

He kissed her. He had flushed at being found holding the piece of silver, and he looked closely into her eyes as if seeking the answer to a mystery. He did not find it. Demelza could be as disingenuous as anyone when she chose, and her eyes were as clear as undisturbed pools.

He said: 'I slept well. By God, it is good to be back; I wonder I ever left.'

'I wonder too.'

'Perhaps I was trying to escape from myself, and you can't ever do that, can you.'

'I have never tried . . . But we are being too serious! A Happy New Year to you again!'

'Thank you, Mama. It should be.' He flipped the newspaper. 'And shall be. You have lost weight since I was last home.'

'It is nothing. I'm brave. We have a lot to tell you. And a lot to listen to – I hope!'

'Well, a soldier's life is not one of great variation – except when he is fighting – and they have kept me out of that! But I will try.' He looked down at the little cup he was holding. 'What is this? Is it new?'

'I found it,' Demelza said.

'Where?'

'On the beach.'

'Do you mean – just loose, lying there?'

'No, it was in a small sack.'

'At the tide mark?'

'Thereabouts.'

He turned it round again. 'I wonder how it came there.'

She did not speak. A cow was lowing behind the stables.

'Was it like this?' he asked.

'Like what?'

'Well – bright and shiny.'

'No, I cleaned it up.'

'It's pretty. This inscription. *Amor gignit amorem.* Do you know what it means?'

'*Love creates love*, I believe. It is a – a loving cup, they say.'

'Who says?'

'Oh, only your father and Uncle Dwight.'

'Have you shown it to anyone else?'

'Who is there to show it to?'

Jeremy nodded.

'It is very small. I thought a loving cup was bigger.'

'I have never seen one before.'

'Is it silver?'

'Oh, yes. The mark underneath will tell you where it was made and when.'

He put the cup back on the sideboard. The flush was still in his face, would not go.

'Mother . . .'

'Yes?'

'Someday, sometime – not now – perhaps when we are both a few years older – I would like to talk to you.'

She smiled at him. 'Don't leave it too late.'

III

Jeremy spent almost all the first day at Wheal Leisure. The engine was working satisfactorily, all parts shiny and well-tended, but the engine house could do with a thorough clean out: there was too much greasy deposit on the non-working parts, and too much coal dust in crevices of wall and floor. Of course, steam engines of their nature were not clean to work; but one should make an effort. He said nothing at the moment, being occupied with other thoughts as well as the welfare of engines.

Ben Carter went over the mine with him, and he greeted

the miners and chatted to them as he went by. The producing levels were mainly on the 30 fathom, 45, and a new 80, all of which were yielding well. The 30 – that which led to and consisted of the old Trevorgie workings – was still the most profitable, but the 80, which had only been begun in June, was already into high-grade copper ore.

In the afternoon Jeremy went for a walk on his own along the cliffs. In the early evening he called on the Kellows at Fernmore. At first there were the family greetings, during which Daisy was noticeably and understandably cool; but later Paul walked back with him in the total blackness of a cloudy moonless December night.

Jeremy said: 'When were you last down Kellow's Ladder?'

'Oh . . . it must be six or seven weeks ago.'

'And what did you find?'

'How d'you mean, find?'

'Well, was it the same as when you were there before?'

'Yes, I think so. Why?'

'I went down this afternoon. The entire cave has been cleaned out.'

'Cleaned out? Do you mean the sacks?'

'Everything. The sacks, the tarpaulin. Everything has gone.'

'Well, there was nothing of value left, was there. Perhaps Stephen has been.'

'Nothing of *value*. But what *was* left? What was there when you were there last?'

'Well, you took everything belonging to you in May – you told me. I cleared mine in September. Stephen long before that. When I was there last there were just the sacks and a few papers –'

'*Papers*? What sort?'

'Oh, a few deeds, a tin cheque or two, letters of credit. Nothing of any importance. I had them in my sack and thought to burn them.'

'But you did not?'

'No. Sorry. After all they were worthless.'

'And the loving cup?'

436

'What?'

'You remember, the silver cup.'

'Oh, yes. Did Stephen have it, or was it yours?'

'We never decided. But it was taken to the cave, wasn't it?'

'Yes . . . Oh, yes, I'm sure of that.'

'Well, it has now turned up on the sideboard in our dining room.'

'What?' Paul stopped and tried to see his companion's face. 'How in God's name ? . . .'

'Quite so.'

'How did it come there?'

'My mother says she *found* it on the beach. In a sack. At high water mark.'

They stumbled on a few steps further.

Paul said: 'Well, it could have happened. Some drunken old tramp . . . perhaps he dropped it. Perhaps he fell down the ladder as well.'

'Maybe he gave it to my mother and told her where he found it.'

'Does it matter? She could never know, never guess.'

'I am never sure with my mother, what she can guess. She has a sixth sense.'

Paul said: 'She would have to have twelve senses to connect a little silver cup found on a beach – or in a cave – with a robbery that took place two years ago – and *then* connect it with us.'

'Yes . . . yes, I suppose so.'

'You don't sound totally convinced.'

'No . . . I wish you had burned those papers.'

Someone passed them quite close by in the dark and said 'Good night,' in a high-pitched voice. They responded because it was the tradition, a means of recognition in the dark, a satisfaction of curiosity.

'Who was that?' Jeremy asked.

'Music Thomas. I wonder why he's abroad. They say he pines for some girl who won't have him, and I'm not surprised. Jeremy . . .'

'Yes?'

'Talking of pining. You know Daisy still has this great taking for you.'

'I suppose.'

'If you ever had a thought to speak, it would be a kindness to speak this time, while you are on leave. You would make her very happy.'

'Yes, I suppose I would.'

'You have, you know, in the past given her much reason to hope.'

'Yes,' said Jeremy, and said no more.

They reached the battered pine trees and the chapel, and the remains of Wheal Maiden. The chapel, for once, was dark.

Paul said: 'I have reason to suppose that Daisy, even at this late stage when you have done so much to affront her, would still look favourably —'

'Paul,' Jeremy said, 'do you remember our talking once and your saying you almost envied me the ability to feel as deeply as I did? I remember you said that to you most things happened, as it were, behind a fine sheet of glass. You observed them, took a degree of pleasure or displeasure from them but seldom — or even never — became entirely engaged.'

'Yes, yes, it is true. But —'

'Well, it is not true of me. It was not true of my impulses that led to the coach robbery. It is not true of my impulses now. Were I to marry Daisy I would no doubt attempt to make her a good husband. But, wretchedly, I should not succeed. If I have trifled with her feelings, then I am bitterly to blame. But it were better to be blamed for the smaller rather than the greater wrong. Daisy is very attractive. *I* find her very attractive. There is nothing wanting in her face, her personality, her body, nothing that I do not admire, nothing that I could not easily desire. But married to her *I* should be behind the glass screen, for I do not love her and could not *bring* myself to love her. It would be a splendid solution, to wed the sister of an old friend. It would suit us all so well. But it would be a hollow and desperate mistake.'

Whatever he might have betrayed to Paul, Jeremy said nothing to his mother or father during the next few days. On the Tuesday he left at dawn and rode over to Wheal Abraham at Crowan and was gone all the daylight hours observing Wolff's new double cylinder engine in action. Thursday he spent at Porthleven where the new harbour was being built. The *Chasse Marée* had been refloated and was back in Penryn, so he did not see Stephen and Clowance until the Friday. He did not call on Valentine. He did not call on Goldsworthy Gurney.

On Saturday the seventh a sea fog came down, and Jeremy spent the morning with his father, first going over every level of Wheal Grace, and then in the counting house examining the cost books and discussing whether there was any way out of a closure of a spent mine. They came to the conclusion there was not, and it simply remained to decide how best it might be effected, how gradually, how many of the men working there could possibly be re-employed at Wheal Leisure, whether any new venture might be attempted in the neighbourhood to absorb the rest.

They walked home together, father and son, in sympathetic accord; there had never been a greater friendliness between them.

It was that accord, with his tall soldier son walking beside him, and perhaps something in the lonely, misty day, that brought Ross to the impulse of broaching the so far forbidden subject.

'I notice you have not yet been to see Valentine.'

'No . . .'

'Shall you go?'

'I don't think so. My leave is so short.'

Ross transferred the cost book to his other arm.

'Valentine's marriage has clearly put all George's plans for him out of joint.'

'Yes, I am sure.'

'So will have clearly upset Cuby's as well. Whatever happens she will never now become a Warleggan.'

Jeremy's face was stiff. 'As you say.'

'Do you still wish her to become a Poldark?'

They walked on a few yards.

'My dear Father, what a question! There is little greater prospect of it just because of this. She is determined – and always has been – to marry a rich man. I shall never be that – not to the extent she requires. So there is no more to be said.'

'Jeremy, answer me something.'

'If I can.'

'Do you still love her?'

The younger man shrugged his shoulders irritably. 'Love – hate – I no longer know what it is!'

'But you have found no other like her?'

'I have never had her.'

'You know what I mean.'

Jeremy said: 'How the seagulls cry! They seem never able to resist a fog.'

'My mother – your grandmother – always used to say they were the souls of drowned seamen crying for what they had lost.'

'You seldom speak of my grandmother.'

'How can I? I have few memories. She died so young.'

'Was she beautiful?'

'I *think* so. But it is so long ago. There isn't even a miniature. That is the terrible thing. She is so completely gone.'

'Where did she come from?'

'From St Allen. The Vennors were small landowners. Just off the road from Truro to Bodmin are a number of pleasant small manor houses, hidden away. Theirs was one. But your grandmother was an only child, and I know of no relatives except a cousin, Claude Vennor, who lives at Saltash.'

After a moment Jeremy said: 'Cuby isn't beautiful.'

'Do you think not?' said Ross judicially. 'Perhaps not. But I was greatly struck with her elegance and charm at the Trenwith party.'

'Were you?' Jeremy was pleased. 'Yes, well.' They walked

on again. 'On the whole I think it is better to talk about the past, don't you?'

'No,' said Ross. 'The present is what concerns us.'

They would soon be home. They had left the last of the washing floors behind. The low wall of Demelza's garden was just ahead.

'Very well,' said Jeremy violently, 'if you want me to *talk* about it! . . . My feeling for Cuby — it is — not a voluntary emotion. I cannot shut it off, the way you can shut off steam from an engine. But I have a young woman in Brussels. I shall have other young women. They — help, even if they do not remove the — the sore place.'

'And Cuby cares for you?'

'Oh, that I doubt! How *can* she?'

'But she has given you the impression that she cares. Has she not? Quite often.'

'Oh, yes. Quite often.' Jeremy frowned angrily into the mist. He was not enjoying this, and wondered at his father's lack of perception in forcing it into the open. 'I think she *likes* me. She gives me the impression that what I feel is not unreturned. But rationally she knows I am no good to her, so she — she discards the rest.'

'That I find quite difficult to believe,' said Ross.

'Why — in God's name?'

'Why in anyone's name? Because it is not a feminine reaction! All right — her heart is governed by her head. But perhaps you have not tried hard enough to institute a contrary process.'

Jeremy stopped. 'What the blazes do you *know* about it? In any case, what do you *mean*?'

Ross stopped also. His blue-grey eyes were almost hidden by their heavy lids. He stared at the swirling mist.

'I mean, why don't you take her?'

Jeremy swallowed. 'What in hell do you mean?'

'Just what I say. Go over and take her. She owes allegiance to no one now. She cannot have found some new suitor yet. Ride over to Caerhays. She belongs to you more than to anyone else.'

'Are you — *joking*?'

441

'No. I was never more serious.'

There was a long pause. Jeremy said: 'This is the nineteenth century.'

'I know. But people change little whatever century they live in. If you are in any way in awe of the castle, I can assure you it is not built to stand the siege of even one determined man. Its walls are thin. So, you may find, are Cuby's defences.'

Jeremy let out a breath. 'God Almighty, I did not *believe*! ... My dear Father, I do not know whether to laugh or cry!'

'Leave either until you have made the attempt. Would you like me to come with you? I can engage John Trevanion and his servants in a degree of intense conversation – or, if necessary, threat.'

Jeremy thought: God! My father is still living in the dark ages of twenty or thirty years ago when he used to go over and confront George Warleggan, and if necessary fight with him on the stairs of the Red Lion Inn or throw him, or be thrown, through the window of Trenwith! He thinks people can still behave in this way! As a young man he was lawless, and a soldier . . .

Well, Jeremy thought, he was *never* so lawless as I have been; and I too am a soldier! Perhaps he is not so far wrong after all. Perhaps it is I who am making the wrong assumptions!

He said stiffly: 'I am sorry to have been so much away from you both on this short leave.'

Ross accepted the rebuff. 'No matter. There will be others. And there is less risk of your being sent to the Americas.'

'You have not heard from Geoffrey Charles yet?'

'About their baby? No.'

'Goldsworthy Gurney's wife is expecting a child this month. That is why I have not been to see him. I imagine even he will abate his preoccupations with strong steam for a few weeks.'

Ross laughed. 'Would you?'

Jeremy's mind roamed at large over the question; and

over the people he knew; and over the enormities of life. 'It depends, who the mother was.'

'Yes . . . just so. For you it is Cuby or nothing, isn't it.'

'Maybe.' The young man spat it out.

They reached the gate leading into Demelza's garden.

Ross said: 'My advice embarrasses you.'

Jeremy snorted. '*Yes* . . . well, not exactly.'

'Forget it.'

'That I shall certainly not do!'

'It was well meant.'

'Oh, I'm sure, Father.'

'And sincerely meant, for what that is worth. Only you can judge how it applies – if at all – to your situation.'

Chapter Eight

I

Two days later came a joyful letter from Geoffrey Charles. Amadora was confined of a little girl, and both were well. They had decided to call her Juana. 'In Cornwall,' Geoffrey Charles added, 'this will probably become Joanna, but no matter, who cares?' They had made no plans yet for returning to England; it was early days. In the meantime how glad he was to have become a half-pay officer and to be with his wife at this happy time. He sent his warmest love and best Christmas wishes to all.

It was nearly time for Jeremy to return. His parents had of course discussed with him the proposition put to Ross while he was in London.

Jeremy had said: 'I don't see why you should *not* go. You were promising yourselves a visit to Paris last summer with the Enyses. Of course it would be different.'

'Very different,' said Demelza. 'I might see nothing of your father. I cannot imagine myself very happy in an apartment in a strange city where no one speaks my language, and Bella would be at a loose end. To say nothing of Harry.'

'Have you mentioned it to Bella?'

'Heavens, no! You know she would want to go anywhere!'

'And you do not, Mother? It is rather a change of character for you.'

'I did not say I would not wish to go,' said Demelza. 'But it would be different from a holiday.'

Ross squeezed her shoulder. 'I think you can set your mind at rest. Since Liverpool spoke to me circumstances have so changed that I doubt if the offer will go any further.'

'What circumstances? You mean –'

'Peace with America. There will be simply no point at all in sending Wellington to take command of a returning army, so the chances are he will remain in Paris. In that case I should not be welcome, even if it were still thought necessary to send some officer to establish a relationship with the French army.'

Jeremy smiled. 'His Grace does not get on with you?'

'I doubt if there is anything very personal in it. But he does not take to having people about him who come on unspecified missions.'

'What do the Enyses say?'

'If we leave earlier they will join us at Easter. If we do not, they suggest we all then go for a few weeks together.'

'I wish I could join you too.'

'Ah, that would be something like!' Demelza said.

'Unfortunately,' Ross said, 'there have been no British troops in Paris since last spring. We have to exert any moral authority we have from Brussels.'

'Still, perhaps I could arrange another leave. It would be considerably closer than coming home to Nampara.'

Later when Jeremy was alone with his mother he said: 'Do you think he wants to go?'

'I'm sure he will go if he is asked. It suits his nature to travel on some mission, and then come back to Cornwall. But for several years now he has not seemed to hanker after adventure so much as he did.'

'You do not want to go, Mother?'

'Oh, I would dearly like it for a short while, I'm sure. To go with Dwight and Caroline at Easter would be *perfect*. But if it were for a long time I think I should grow homesick – for all this.'

Jeremy looked around. 'As I am at times.'

'Well, you need not be.'

He sighed. 'No.'

'When you are born in a place – at least a place like this – it is very hard to leave it for long. Not that I ever minded leaving where *I* was born. Nor ever wanted to see it again.'

Demelza was darning a hole in the heel of one of young

445

Henry's socks. She was wearing a light green lacy frock, drawn in at the waist and ruched at the neck; it was one of Jeremy's favourites. He looked down at her fingers on the needle and wondered why it was that his mother, who had so many talents, had never mastered more than the simplest sewing.

She looked up at him suddenly and smiled. 'This leave, then, you are not to see Cuby?'

He turned to poke the fire.

'You know what Father suggested?'

'Yes! At least, he gave me an idea!'

Jeremy knelt and threw on some wood. In a district with practically no natural timber, these were split fragments of old pit props. He watched them flicker and begin to sputter and burn.

Demelza said: 'Of course it isn't possible.'

'What is not?'

'What your father suggests. You cannot just "help yourself" to a woman. Even your father . . .' Demelza paused, aware that Ross in fact had once done just that. She pricked her finger. 'I mean, you cannot take a woman against her consent. You can go and *ask*. You can go and *demand*. But – unless you are a – a drunken brigand, it is her decision at the end of it.'

Jeremy said: 'I think Father was suggesting a half-way stage.'

'Yes, maybe he was.'

Jeremy straightened up and sat back in his chair. Demelza sucked her finger.

'Anyway,' said Jeremy. 'I shall take his advice.'

'*What*?'

'It must be unusual for a son to take his father's advice – especially in such matters! – isn't it? I'd guess so. But I have been considering it carefully for the last few days, and it seems to me it is not unsound.'

'D'you mean . . .' In alarm Demelza got no further. 'I don't think you should –'

'No, I don't think I should. But there is much to be said for the half-way stage . . . I am answering your question,

446

Mother. You asked me if I should be seeing Cuby on this leave. The answer is probably yes.'

These are very peculiar conversations I am having with my son, Demelza thought. I never imagined, when I bore him, that time would pass, that so much time *could* pass, so that one day I should be sitting in front of a crackling fire on a grey January day twenty-three years later and talking in this fashion with him about a woman with whom he is in love. He is a *man*. And a very strange man. He is older, several years older, than I was then. Now it is *his* life, *his* future, *his* love, his fate in more ways than one . . .

'Have you pricked your finger?'

'Yes. It is nothing.'

'Take my handkerchief.'

'No, thank you. It is very little . . . So . . .'

'Cuby is at home,' Jeremy said. 'That much I know. I shall leave for Belgium on Thursday – which is only one day earlier than I would have had to leave in any event. I shall take Colley, and borrow one of the ponies, if I may. Whatever comes, I shall leave them at the White Hart in Launceston with money enough to have them sent home. That way, if the weather is favourable and other things unfavourable I shall be in Brussels from my leave a day or so early.'

'And if the weather is *un*favourable?'

Jeremy cocked an eyebrow. 'Or other things favourable? Then I shall be late . . . But be sure of one thing: I will write you from London. Telling you of what has occurred.'

Sparks fell out on the hearth and Jeremy knelt again to brush them up. He does not look so different now, Demelza thought; the same boy; people don't change that much; they only change in their relationship to each other.

On impulse she said: 'Do you want me to look after the loving cup for you?'

He looked up sharply. 'What? What do you mean?'

'I just thought – you had taken a special interest in it.'

'Did I? No, I don't think so.' He had flushed.

'Perhaps it will bring you luck.'

'Bad luck?'

'I didn't mean that.'

'Do what you please with it! You found it! It's yours, not mine.'

'Yes, of course. I just thought it was – pretty.'

After a moment, he said: 'I did not mean to snap. I have – other things on my mind.'

They sat quietly staring into the fire. She had stopped sewing.

'Do you want me to tell your father? About Cuby, I mean.'

'What? Well, certainly. I shall say something too. I owe him that. But one thing – did you know? – he offered to come to Caerhays with me.'

'No, I didn't! Do you mean –'

'I shall tell him no, of course. With appreciation and thanks. There would be no man better than he I would choose to have with me in the ordinary tight corner. But this is a – peculiar tight corner of my own choosing, my own making. And, if I may vary the metaphor, this time I shall sink or swim alone . . .'

II

He left at noon on Thursday the twelfth. Demelza, his lips still warming her cheek, watched him go.

'Did he tell you what he intended to try to do?'

'No,' Ross said. 'Perhaps it were better I had not spoken. It is so hard to advise other people.'

'Is Major Trevanion a hot-tempered man?'

'Yes. But not a ready fighter, I would judge.'

'What servants do they have?'

'Three oldish men, Jeremy said, who attended on the family. A number of maids. Some outside staff.'

'Far too much for one young man.'

'If I know Jeremy he will not seek violence if it can be avoided. It all depends really, does it not, on the girl. As you warned him, my ideas of forcible seizure are quite out-dated.'

'Oh, Ross, I did not say that! All I said was that in the end it all hinged on her.'

'Which is what I have just said, so we agree. I am simply of the opinion that some girls don't know their own minds too well, and a little aggression can often help them to decide.'

'I knew my own mind before you did.'

'Well, that was different.'

'But,' Demelza said, 'does Cuby give you the impression of a girl who cannot make up her mind?'

'No.'

'No. That is what I fear.'

'It is certainly something to be feared. But perhaps we underestimated Jeremy.'

'That,' said Demelza, 'is something I shall never do again.'

III

Jeremy had dinner in Truro, and remounted soon after dark. He rode cautiously thereafter, first on the turnpike road and then down the narrow rutted tracks towards the south coast. He did not want any plans he had to be encumbered by a horse that had gone lame through stepping in some unseen ditch or hole. Even so he was at Caerhays much too early. A new moon hung over the house, which looked splendidly medieval and romantic silhouetted against the cobalt blue of the sea. Lights were glimmering in a number of rooms.

Because of his excursions with Cuby, he knew a way into the grounds without having to pass the lodge gates, and presently he reined in behind the house and dismounted and made Colley and Hollyhock comfortable, and settled to wait. Just ahead of him was all the paraphernalia of building; but nothing so far as he could perceive had been recently done. The same overturned wheelbarrows, the same spades, the same hods, the same ladders, the same mound of bricks and stones and window frames and heaps of sand and piles of gravel. Now less than ever would Major Trevanion be able to pay his workforce.

The moon went down, silver-stitching the sea, glowing a few moments behind the trees on the headland like a prima donna reluctant to leave. Then a less shadowed dark set in, while stars, previously unregarded, began to take the stage.

He knew which was Cuby's bedroom; it had been lit until half an hour ago – so also had Clemency's; now they were dark; the family was at supper. It was very much a gamble as to when he went in, but he knew they were not a family who kept late hours, nor one that had the traditional big meal before retiring. A roast duck or two, canary wine, a dish of apple tart and cream, cheese. It could not last more than an hour. After that Mrs Bettesworth usually went quickly to bed; the two girls might play a game of draughts or chess. John Trevanion would doze or read the latest racing news over his port. Most of the servants, except those engaged in serving the meal, would be in their own quarters. There was likely to be little activity upstairs.

He peered at his watch to check the time, pocketed it, patted the two horses, stepped lightly towards the house.

Caerhays Castle was built with a flat roof behind its handsome castellations. He had been up there once with the girls, until John Trevanion came after them calling them down for fear they might damage the delicate roofing. Jeremy groped around for the longest ladder, gradually reared it against the wall of the house. It would reach Cuby's bedroom window easily, but that was not what he wanted. It went up well beyond, but he could not see whether it actually reached to the turreted stonework. He blamed himself for not risking this much while the moon was up. Well, it was too late now, and only trial and error would answer the question.

He put the ladder as close to the castle wall as he could, to give it its greatest length, and wedged it by building a pile of bricks around the base. Then he began to climb.

It was a shaky ladder, and the thought crossed his mind that it had been lying here so long some of the rungs might have become rotten; all the same he went up it with few of the vapours his mother had suffered climbing another ladder not so long ago.

It did not quite reach, but the distance was only a matter of a couple of feet, and he could grasp the stonework with both hands. He sprang from the top rung, got his hands well gripped about the stone, tensed his arms and put a leg over. As he did this his other leg slipped and he pulled himself to safety and peered down, observing that though the ladder had not fallen it was now askew. A descent that way would not be desirable.

He listened. Only an owl broke the stillness, screeching in the wood hollows in the mild winter night. He tiptoed across the roof, careful to kick nothing, came to the trapdoor, grasped the handle and lifted. It came up. No one expected burglars from above.

He went down into the loft room. The greatest danger when he entered the house proper were Trixie and Truff, Trevanion's two spaniels. The servants might be sleepy and wanting to go to bed, but let those dogs hear one unfamiliar footstep or smell one unfamiliar smell and they would raise Cain.

It was darker in the house, so the risk of kicking something over was far greater. But time was on his side, he could afford to proceed at a snail's pace, feeling each inch with finger tips before he moved. Patience was all.

It took him several minutes to reach the door. He supposed it could have been locked but it was not. It opened with a damnable groan. Now it was slightly less dark: the crack let in the faintest of lights which by comparison was welcome; some candle on the stairs, no doubt, left to light the Trevanions to bed.

Another six inches of groaning; the gap was wide enough and he slipped through. One of his buttons caught on the door edge and made an unwelcome clack. He shut the door, which did not complain at being moved back into place.

Although he had had no reason to memorize the plan of the house, he knew with certainty that to get to Cuby's bedroom you simply went along this corridor, turned left and her room was on the right.

451

Floorboards in a new house should not creak, but some of these already did. By stepping close to the wall he avoided most of them. He had reached the end of the corridor when he heard quick footsteps coming towards him. He shrank back against the wall: there was nowhere to hide.

A woman's voice said in an undertone: 'Well, tis all very fine fur you, James, but maybe I don't see it that way 'tall, see?'

'Ar,' said a man. 'I reckon I can get ee to see it my way in next to no time.'

The girl giggled. 'Leave me be, you great oaf!'

A maid came up carrying a candle: the light spilled everywhere. A footman Jeremy had not seen before followed her. At the very entrance to the corridor in which Jeremy tried to shrink, they turned right towards the other bedrooms. They should have seen him but they had no eyes except for each other. Jeremy retreated to the door of the loft room, almost panicked into retreating into it, but decided to brazen it out. There were, as far as he knew, no bedrooms in use in this corridor; in all probability the maid had gone into Mrs Bettesworth's room or Cuby's room, for some ordinary purpose such as to make up the fire, and would be unlikely to come up here.

Unless they sought privacy . . .

He waited and counted. By the time he reached a hundred the voices were audible again. They were coming this way. Then they turned and went down the stairs. A door closed and the voices ceased.

So he could not yet altogether rule out the staff.

He proceeded inch by inch to the end of the corridor. The faint light did indeed come from a lantern in the hall. He turned sharp left and made for the bedrooms that he knew. And there he stopped, for his memory had played him false. There were three doors, well spaced out. He knew it was not the last, but he had no idea which of the other two to choose. The third, he felt certain, was Clemency's. But did not Mrs Bettesworth occupy the largest room, which was in between?

He chose the first door. It opened easily but almost before

452

he got in he stumbled over something: a slipper or a book. He clung to the door, waiting for someone to discover him. Nothing happened. He bent and picked up what he had stumbled over: it was a shoe. And it was not Cuby's.

He backed out. There were voices downstairs again, and he thought it was Major Trevanion. Light was spreading up from an open door.

He tried the second door, and he had hardly entered before he knew the room was Cuby's. The scent she used; a gown lying on the bed, indistinguishable as to colour but unmistakable as to wearer. Caution slipping, he made his way by finger tip from bed to wardrobe to dressing table to — yes, to alcove. He had remembered that aright. And there was a curtain across it.

He stumbled in, tramping on another pair of shoes, a fallen frock hanger. The curtain rattled on its rings and then was still.

He was still. All he had to do now was to wait.

Chapter Nine

Yesterday, Cuby and Clemency had been out all day with the Tregony Hunt. After early fog, when the going had been wet and almost blind, they had drawn a fox near Creed and had had a fine run for over an hour before losing him in one of the upper reaches of the Fal. Nobody seemed to mind, and, the weather turning sunny, they had gone on to find another fox, and had killed about three in the afternoon. It had been a glorious day in the open air and both girls had come home tired and muddy and glowing with content.

Today they had been occupied with other things, small things, house and parochial things, which in their way were the perfect foil to yesterday's excitements. They had walked with John's little boys on Porthluney Beach, and Cuby had returned home to write letters, one to her brother, one to her aunt. At dinner they had entertained the Rev. C. T. Kempe, rector of the parish of St Michael Caerhays, with which were joined the parishes of St Dennis and St Stephen-in-Brannel. Mr Kempe, a second cousin, was a cheerful outgoing man who seemed so certain of his future in the afterlife that he neglected his dress and his circumstances in this. After dinner they had strolled back to the rectory with him to look in again at his great pig, Alexander, which he was convinced was the largest in the world. It measured, he claimed, nine feet from snout to tail-tip, stood four feet high and weighed over 600 lbs. It had already won him prizes, but it was now become so fat it could not get to its feet unaided. Then they walked on together, sick visiting with Mr Kempe in the scattered cottages.

Returning at six they had found horses at the door and that their friends Captain and Mrs Octavius Temple from Carvossa had called in on their way home from staying with Lady Whitworth near Mevagissey. So it was a pleasant and jolly tea time, and seven o'clock before they left.

A happy, comfortable day. A happy, comfortable way of life, country-house life at its best, unexpectedly made more easy for the time being by the surprisingly good sale of Trevanion's last remaining unencumbered farm near Grampound. Like Restronguet, sold earlier, this had belonged to the family since Bosworth Field, and it was the property Trevanion had intended to retreat to and live in under the terms of the marriage settlement, if that had come to pass. The proceeds of the sale would not last for ever, but just in time it had taken the most pressing creditors off their backs. Sufficient unto the day . . .

After Valentine's defection Cuby had accepted the fact that she would not marry now – at least for some considerable time. There was no suitable man, young or otherwise, on the horizon. About a month ago her brother had brought up the name of a rich lawyer from Torbay who had recently lost his wife and might be lacking in companionship; but Cuby had not encouraged the idea that he should be invited to spend a week at Caerhays. John had not pressed. He was very fond of his younger sister and liked to have her at home. The arrangement with Warleggan was about as much as he could stomach. He had been driven into it; but now that it had fallen through he did not feel he could harry her into some new match purely for the money that match would bring. The disappointment at Valentine's defection was at first profound: disappointment and panic, for he knew how his creditors would pounce; but the sale of the farm had removed the axe from his neck. So, making a virtue of necessity, he had expressed his own relief that he would now never be related by marriage to Smelter George.

Cuby lived from day to day and enjoyed each one as it passed. Tomorrow there would be hunting again . . .

Sometimes she thought she would perhaps *never* marry now. She had never of course loved Valentine, and she knew she had been wrong – flirtatious and silly – to encourage Jeremy as much as she had. For she knew she had never really loved him either. In a perverse way she had enjoyed his attentions, been flattered by his ardour. Conceit had been at the bottom of it, she realized with self-critical

455

contempt, not really attraction. She blamed herself and was glad that it was over.

She looked after John's two little sons, worked samplers with her mother or with Clemency, superintended plantings in the gardens, watching the new shrubs growing up under the protection of the tall trees, the brilliant cold sea between the low black rocks, the gentle sloping of green and russet cliff. She had taken up the piano again. She had children here, John's children; why did she ever need any of her own?

She sometimes thought she would never come to care for anyone in the way that men expected her to care. Particularly in the way Jeremy had expected her to care. He had seemed to demand so much, of which she had never at any time been capable. Was she cold? Frigid, even, as they called it nowadays. Perhaps. The fact that she was attractive to men did not necessarily make them attractive to her. Her affections were of the stabler and staider kind. Love of family, love of comfort, love of home. She wanted no more.

Her brother was in very good spirits at supper. Offering Mr Kempe snuff at dinner – a habit he never personally indulged in – John had flipped open the top of the silver snuff-box and found it entirely empty, except for eight guineas which he had put there in October and completely forgotten. It had set him in a good temper for the rest of the day.

This evening he began to discuss London, and his younger brother Augustus's letters, and the temptations open to a young man of good name but no property. He spoke of these temptations with disapproval, but with a hint of envy in his voice, Cuby thought, as if he would once again like to be subject to them himself. All the games of chance they played at Crockford's for high stakes: *Jeu d'Enfer*, Faro, Blind Hookey, *Vingt-et-un*, and, of course, Whist. He had personally been there when a man called Leary played whist without a break from Monday night to Wednesday morning, and then only broke off because he had to go to a funeral. It was on that occasion that the Duke of Wexford had lost £20,000.

How difficult it was to get into the Argyle Rooms: some said you were easier in Debrett's than past those gilded doors! How the courtesans flaunted themselves; it was known that the most exclusive of them paid £200 a season for a front box at Covent Garden, as a shop-window for their own allurements.

Dinner at the Thatched House in St James's Street, he remarked wistfully, smacking his lips, where Mr Willis presided in an apron stitched with gold thread! Then down to the St James's Coffee House; as an ex-Dragoon Guardsman he was welcomed; the little Coffee House had become almost a private club for the Guards; trouble was you could not keep all the undesirables out; sometimes the fashionable bullies would force their way in; then there were fights.

His mother said reprovingly: 'Those days are well past, John. And I am sure Augustus will not consider such dissipations appropriate to his small salary. Indeed he knows well that we cannot ever help him even with the smallest debt.'

'I remember "Soapy" Wargrave,' said John, taking a gulp of port. 'My senior officer at the time. Very rich man who *impoverished* himself at the tables. Almost broke! Then he had a great run of luck – won a fraction of his losses back. He was beginning to learn his lesson by this time, so he went *immediately* out and spent *all* his winnings on presents: jewellery and wearing apparel for his mistresses, so that, he said, "those rascals in the salon stand no chance of winning it back again!"'

'I'm afraid that is not a very moral story, John,' said Clemency, smiling.

'Fraid he was not a very moral man. When we were stationed at Windsor he took up with one of the ladies in waiting to the Queen, Lady Eleanor Blair – quite a passionate affair, I believe; but when we returned to the Portman Street barracks it cooled off – at least on his side. She was very angry, very tight about it, I gather, sent him a letter demanding the return of the lock of hair she had given him. D'you know what Wargrave did – terrible thing, I think. He sent his orderly up to Windsor with a packet containing more than a dozen locks of hair of all colours – fair, dark, auburn – and invited her to pick out her own!'

Both the girls laughed. John helped himself to more port. A thin disapproving smile crossed Mrs Bettesworth's lips.

She said: 'From such elegancies as those, John, it will no doubt seem quite demeaning of me to mention mere domestic details, but I will do so before Carter returns. He *must* have new livery soon. As Harrison must, and Coad and the rest. The men's coats are becoming quite threadbare.'

'Let 'em make do,' said John. 'At least they are *paid* now, which is an improvement on recent times. Get Mrs Saunders to put two maids to repairing the coats.'

'Coad's does not even fit him,' said Cuby.

'Well, he is a bigger man than Trethewy. And of course younger. He is the one most likely to split the seams!'

'We cannot get new coats for him without getting them for the others.'

'I am not sure that I like Coad,' said Clemency. 'He is a little intrusive.'

'*He*'ll settle down,' said John, stretching his legs. 'Not been trained properly, that's all. What can you expect, getting a man from the Hicks.'

Supper ended. John Trevanion retired to his study to smoke a cigar. Mrs Bettesworth took up her needlework, but after a few minutes set it down again and said:

'Dear me, I do get so sleepy these days. I wake so early, that is the trouble. I wake before dawn and lie watching the day break. There is nothing I can *do* at that time except wait for the house to wake. But because of that – as a consequence – I am sleepy in the evening before it is proper time.'

Clemency exchanged a private smile with Cuby: they heard this speech almost every night. Whether it was true or not they could not say, but it did not convince the more with repetition.

After they had kissed their mother good night Clemency suggested a game of chess; but with the prospect of an early rise for the hunt tomorrow Cuby demurred. They played one game of backgammon, and then Clemency decided to stay down and read for a while, so Cuby kissed her and went in to put her lips to John's brow as he sat in a wreath of idle smoke turning over a news sheet devoted to racing.

So then to bed. She lit a candle at the lantern in the hall and went up with it, shielding the flame from draughts with her cupped hand. Past her mother's room and into her own. She began to light the six other candles.

She agreed with Clemency about Coad. He had come only in November, with a good reference from the Hicks of Truro, but instead of settling down in the right way, as John predicted he would, he seemed to her to be settling down in the wrong way, so that, as he became more familiar with his surroundings, he became more familiar with the people *in* those surroundings; or tried to. She knew that the older maids did not like him, and thought that one or two of the younger maids found him too pushing for their own good. Particularly Ellen Smith, who was a nice girl but could not resist the sight of a man. So long as it merely remained at the state of ogling and giggles no one would come to any harm. But how long would it remain so innocent? Not long, if Coad had his way.

As she lit the sixth candle the curtain rail rattled and a soldier stepped out.

She screamed, loud and clear.

'Ssh!' he said.

She put her knuckles to her mouth when she saw who the soldier was.

'*Jeremy!*'

'Ssh!' he said again.

They stared at each other.

She was wearing an old but attractive frock of indigo velvet, with muslin sleeves at the upper arm and tighter transparent muslin to the wrists.

'*Jeremy!*' she whispered again.

'I have come to see you,' he said. 'I have come to take you away.'

'What are you *talking* about?'

'No matter for the moment. Will anyone have heard?'

'I don't think so.'

They listened. The house was silent. One of the dogs was

barking, but it was far away. Jeremy took a deep breath to speak again but Cuby held up her hand.

There was a tap at the door.

'*Yes?*'

There was another tap and then the handle turned and Mrs Bettesworth came in.

'Did I hear you cry out, Cuby?'

Although seconds only had passed, Jeremy had slid back behind the curtains of the bed.

Cuby passed a hand over her eyes. 'Yes, Mama, I'm *sorry* . . . When – when I came in the room I was thinking of Coad; and the air – the air created by my closing the door made the curtains move. For a moment I thought there was someone in my room!'

'Oh.' Her mother hesitated. 'I see. So you are all right? There is nothing amiss?'

'Thank you, Mama, nothing.'

'You are quite sure?'

'Quite sure. Good night again.'

'Good night.' Mrs Bettesworth took her time about withdrawing.

Cuby stared at the long-fingered hand that came to hold the curtain, the scarlet sleeve with the gilt cuff, the slowly emerging figure of the young man who for more than three years had loved her devotedly. Lank hair, but curling at the ends and dark, worn long and a little untidy – somehow it was *like* a soldier's hair –; fresh complexion, strong nose, blue-grey eyes with heavy lids, clever mouth, small cleft in the chin. Looking at her. Staring at her. Feasting his eyes on her. She *didn't* love him and never had. Hadn't she realized that only these last few weeks, when she had had time to pause, to reflect, to decide her own life?

'Jeremy, my heart near stopped! . . .'

'I'm *sorry*, there was no other way of breaking my presence to you.'

'I still don't understand – *anything*.'

There was a pause.

'You're very pale,' he said.

'I – haven't yet recovered . . . The shock . . .'

'Sit down. Is this water?'

'Yes, but I don't want it.' Neither did she sit down.

He came slowly into the room. 'Are we likely to be disturbed again?'

'*Why?*'

'Because I want to talk to you.'

'Clemency might come. But it's unlikely.'

'Will anyone hear our voices?'

'Not if we keep them down.'

Somehow, to her indignation, she found herself a part of his conspiratorial web.

'How did you get in?'

'A ladder to the roof.'

'Have you been here long?'

'An hour perhaps. And an hour or so outside.'

His eyes were heavy on hers. He had grown up so much this last year; his face was set with resolution.

He said: 'Who was this Coad you spoke of?'

'A footman. I had to invent something to explain to my mother.'

'Not a future husband, then?'

'No . . .'

'Just as well. For I am your future husband.'

'Oh, Jeremy, please be sensible.'

'I have been sensible – as you call it – too long. I consider it being *in*sensible, what I have been until now.'

After a moment she said: '*Why* did you come?'

'I've told you.'

'Well, you must go immediately! It is not right for you to be here in this way!'

'But you cannot get rid of me before I choose to go. That opportunity passed when your mother came in. Now they will know that you lied about my being here.'

'You are not being very chivalrous.'

'All's fair in love.' He came near enough to put a hand very lightly on her arm. 'Look, my dear. I shall never touch you without your consent, understand that. But I want to talk to you. We have all night. Pray do sit down and listen to what I have to say.'

With the first glint of a troubled smile she said: 'Where is your horse?'

'Tethered behind the house. Near the builders' workings.'

'He will get restive.'

'Not for a while. And it is not horse, Cuby, it is horses.'

He caught the flicker of her hazel eyes as she turned to look behind her. She took a chair, sat down.

'Very well. I will listen. But have we not said it all before?'

He perched on the bed, one boot, highly polished but with a few splashes of new mud adhering, slowly swinging with a nonchalance he did not feel.

He said: 'I have come for you. To take you away. I have money enough for us to live on. The mine we opened is paying higher dividends and should make me moderate independent. I am going back tonight to rejoin my regiment in Brussels. If you come with me we shall ride only to Launceston tonight and stay at the White Hart.'

'*Come* with you? Jeremy, I am very, very sorry. Have I not *tried* to explain *often* and *often* –'

'Yes, but then Valentine was about –'

'And before. I have *tried* to explain . . .'

He took her hand, turned it over, palm up, held it quietly. It lay there like a not-quite-tame animal which any moment might spring away.

He said: 'I want to marry you. I – I want you to become a part of me – each to become a part of the other . . . I want to claim the honour of knowing your body intimately – and your mind and your heart. Cuby, I want to take you into the world and to live with you always, to – to experience everything that the world offers, in *your* company – to talk to you, to listen to you, to face with you all the dangers and the sweets . . . the pains and the pleasures, the – the exhilaration, and the joys of being young – of challenge and fulfilment and happiness.' He stopped, short of more words with which to break down her defences. She sat head down, but listening.

He said sombrely: 'I know I can marry someone else. I know you can. But it would be for us both a retreat into a half life, never breathing deep, never feeling all there is to feel, passing one's days without the ultimate and – and vital flavour . . .'

'Why are you so *sure* of all this – for me as well as for yourself?'

'It is *in* me to be sure,' he said, stroking her palm. 'Come away with me now. As I said, we'll spend the night in Launceston – as cousins or whatever you like to give the journey the necessary respectability. We'll take the London coach tomorrow, be married in London, then travel straight to Brussels. It may not all be easy, comfortable, safe – in the way that perhaps living here is easy, comfortable, safe; but it will be everything else I can make it for your pleasure and happiness. My beloved, will you come?'

The spaniel was barking again in the easy, comfortable, safe depths of the house. She sat in the easy, safe, comfort of her bedroom with a red-jacketed young soldier stroking her palm. This room she had only occupied since the new castle was built, but most of the furniture she had known all her young life. She was sitting in one of the green velvet bedroom chairs in which fifteen years ago she had sat to have her first hunting boot laced up by the maid. In the frame of the faded gilt mirror showing damp spots over the mantelshelf were stuck little mementoes she had collected from time to time: a ball programme, a tie-pin which had belonged to her father, a sprig of rosemary from a picnic, a crayon drawing Clemency had made of her. An embroidery workbasket with pieces of silk slipping out of the lid was on another chair; in front of it slippers and a pair of kid gloves. The curtains of the bed were of heavy yellow brocade, the window curtains of a similar material but faded with the sun. Her room. *Her* privacy. Invaded by a rather formidable young soldier.

'Will you come?' he said.

Even if she loved him, which she did not, his proposition was beyond the impractical, bordering on the insane. How to break it to him gently, deflate once again the vain and pitiful hope so that he would go quietly, leave her and go, not too badly hurt, return to his regiment able and willing to lead and enjoy a life without her? It was such a pity, for, had circumstances been different, he would have made her a better husband than Valentine, and she would have made him a better wife. It was a pity that she was not the sort of girl he imagined her to be. Nor ever had been, nor ever conceivably could be. He imagined her warm, gentle, yielding; but she was cold, hard, firm. Family meant far more than any love-sick young man. *Far* more. John and Augustus and Clemency and the little boys, and Mama, and the great splendid castle, and the wonderful vistas, and the noble woods and the gentle cliffs and the ever changing yet unchangeable sea. She was a Trevanion of Caerhays and that was all. And that was enough. More than enough.

For the first time in several minutes she looked up at him, and he was watching her. Something stirred, crawled, came to life within her. Of course it had not been entirely absent in the past, but it should not come up now. *Must* not come up now. Suddenly, as if aware of the danger, caution, common sense, calculation started screaming at her. She put her free hand up to her mouth.

'Will you come?' he asked again.

'Yes, please,' she said.

Chapter Ten

I

Letter from Ensign Jeremy Poldark, Gravesend. Dated 19 January, 1815.

My dearest Father and Mother,

The briefest note and in haste – belated but as promised – to give you my News. It is to say that Cuby *agreed to come with me*, and we were married by special licence at the church of St Clement in the Strand last Tuesday, the seventeenth. I should by rights have obtained the permission of my commanding officer, but it would have meant delaying until we reached Brussels, and I felt that could not be.

We are here now waiting for suitable transport, which is promised us in a vessel leaving on the noon tide tomorrow. I expect now to have exceeded my leave by about a week, but I don't in the least care. I don't care about Anything any more. I am just the *happiest* of men!

I cannot thank you both enough for all your help and forbearance and *advice* over this very long period in which I have been in travail. By the mercy of God, no actual *force* was necessary when I called on Cuby, for force, at least of that sort, does not seem to be in my nature. It took a deep – and deeply felt – persuasion, and then . . . and then I felt like Joshua before the Walls of Jericho! We stole away hurriedly, she seeing none of her family but leaving letters to explain; we spent that night in Bodmin and caught the mail coach at Launceston. London late on Monday. I trust Colley and Hollyhock are safe back with you: I tipped the ostler an extra guinea so that he should deal gently with them and not ride them too hard. You know what these lads are.

Cuby left Caerhays with the contents only of two saddlebags, so the one day in London while we were waiting for the licence we spent in a number of shops trying to fit her out in a way more suitable for a junior officer's wife. I must say that she was very Careful as to the amount I spent on her, and that nothing at all should be unduly extravagant. I do not know what sort of housewife she will make, but the impression is that she will not lead me unnecessarily into debt! Perhaps her brother's example is too fresh.

My dear Father and Mother, *no man* is happier, or could be, than I am at this moment! But I so much regret that it has had to be this sort of wedding – a wedding in flight, almost – that I have had no opportunity of bringing Cuby to meet you and to seek *your* approval of her. How thankful I am that at least she came to Geoffrey Charles's party and that you were able to see here there, and she you.

Instead of all the happy preambles to a son's wedding, of an occasion for *family* rejoicing, there has had to be this hole-in-corner elopement. I can only hope and trust that we shall both be able to make it up to you in the future, when my next leave comes or when I resign my commission. I think the latter must be brought nearer by this Event.

I imagine you will see or hear nothing from the Trevanions. Cuby has told them what is necessary; if they should inquire, pray tell them all you can. She is writing to Clemency from here. Flurries of snow are blowing against our windows as we sit at this writing desk together; I hope it will take off before tomorrow, for the crossing can be unpleasant. Tell Clowance and Stephen, of course, and when you write to Geoffrey Charles please inform him too.

I hear there was a terrible battle in America, at a place called New Orleans, with heavy British casualties, two weeks *after* peace was signed. What an appalling waste on both sides! Geoffrey Charles was well out of it.

Mother, you asked if I wanted the loving cup. I said no, rather edgily, I believe: that it was yours and was of no importance to me. I am not a superstitious person but somehow I felt at the time – as I said then – that if it brought me any luck at all it would be bad luck. Instead I have had the most wonderful luck in the world. So may be I should change my mind and consider it an omen of good fortune after all. And, if I still may, I will have it. Can you keep it for me? *Do not* leave it on the sideboard but put it in a drawer in my bedroom, and I will collect it when next I am home. Or when we first make a home of our own.

I hope you will go to France, if only for a holiday. A lieutenant I was talking to this morning says Paris is an experience not to be missed. There are many musical performances available for visitors who do not understand the language, and Bella might well profit from listening to those who can sing in tune. *Please* do not show her this!

We are called for dinner, so I must stop. This is not such a short letter after all. Cuby joins me in sending love to you both. Is that correct? It will be correct for the future, for henceforward my only beloved wife will I trust share *everything* with me. We are man and wife, joyously united. But for this first letter after our wedding perhaps I should continue just this last time to say *I* send my love to you both, and thank you again for your love, your forbearance and your trust.
Jeremy.

II

When he had finished Jeremy sealed the letter and put down the wax, looked across at his wife whose head was still bent over her letter, dark hair hiding her face. She was wearing one of the two frocks she had allowed him to buy her: of fine beige wool with long full sleeves and scarlet collar and cuffs, drawn in at the waist with a knotted cord. At that moment, as if conscious of his gaze, she glanced up at him and smiled, pushed her hair back with two elegant fingers. Beautiful and young. His heart and stomach turned over at the sight of her.

'Have you finished?' she asked.

'Yes.'

'Then I'll finish too. I can seal it later. Have you told them all you can?'

'All I can. Yes. All I can.'

As they went down the stairs he thought of what he had written to his mother and father, and of all that necessarily must remain unwritten. So many of the essential details which could never be related to anyone. How could he even begin to explain everything that had happened already?

'What I can,' he said again. 'What I can.'

III

They had left Caerhays that night about eleven, by which time the house had been quiet no more than half an hour. Cuby had scribbled a note to her brother, one to her mother, a third to Clemency. She had not shown Jeremy what she had written, and he had not asked. He had stood there like a man of stone, watching her pack a small valise, turning his back while she changed into a riding habit, then helping her to gather a few more things together in a second bag. He had kissed her just once, but was afraid at this stage to do anything, anything good or bad which might conceivably affect her sudden choice.

They had stolen down the front stairs but then through the kitchens to the back. The dogs had not barked any more. Once on the horses, they had picked their way up the dark miry lane towards the road which led to St Austell. It was plain by now that Launceston was out of the question, and it would have been more sensible to stop in St Austell, but Jeremy had his own reasons for a distaste for doing so, so they pressed on as far as Bodmin. He had made the excuse to Cuby, which was not an unreasonable one, that if John

Trevanion discovered her absence in time he might follow them that far.

It had been two in the morning before they reached Jewell's Hotel, formerly the old King's Arms, and it had meant hammering on the door and rousing half the house before they were reluctantly admitted. Jeremy knew John Jewell, but that could not be helped. Indeed it had had its advantages, for once Jewell's sleep-laden eyes had widened at the sight of Jeremy's companion, he asked no questions and rapidly had two separate bedrooms prepared. As rapidly they occupied them. It was as if, the decision having been made, they had said all that had to be said, and they must somehow try to sleep and wait for the morning.

So they tossed and turned in their soft feather beds until, as requested, Jewell woke them at dawn. They breakfasted together, still hardly speaking, but looking a lot at each other. Glints and glances and occasional cautious smiles and just the business of eating and repacking their valises and taking the long ride across the moors for Launceston. They took dinner at the White Hart, left their horses to be returned and caught the afternoon eastward-bound Royal Mail Coach which reached Exeter at ten at night. A very long day. Saddle-sore and coach-jolted, they had slept deeply and were only just abroad in time for a hasty breakfast and a resumed journey.

The fourth night had spelled a change. They had spent it at Marlborough, where they had arrived earlier than on the other stages of the journey. London would be reached next day, but very late.

In the last few stages Cuby had become quietly sombre again, mainly watching the tall-treed leafless countryside as it jolted past, exchanging the occasional word but never making or encouraging conversation either with Jeremy or the other passengers, sometimes dozing, sometimes, it seemed, meditating as if lost far away in a distant country of her own, eating her food and drinking her wine dutifully, seldom meeting Jeremy's eye but then when she did so glancing quickly away. He speculated much on what was going on in her mind but, still uncertain how he had at last persuaded her to come away with him, afraid to probe. Was she thinking of the hunting she had missed? Or some church duty? Or a problem of the estate? Was she wondering what her brother would say and do? Was she regretting the way she had deserted her family? Was she yearning for Clemency's warm friendship? He did not know.

For much of the time, instead of being lovers fleeing to marry, they might well have been cousins or brother and sister travelling mutely on some set purpose partly removed from themselves.

Yet there was also a sense of flight. Jeremy had scarcely felt more on edge even after the coach robbery. Though he now carried notes and coins deriving from that time, he was not now fleeing from any pursuit by the law but from pursuit by what Cuby called 'logics of the mind'. And he feared these more. Common sense, family ties, family obligation were behind them in Cornwall exercising a gravitational pull. The further and more quickly he bore her away, the safer he would be.

What if she just said to him when she got to London, 'I am sorry, Jeremy, I have changed my mind.'?

The weather had been kind so far, and only a few flakes of snow had drifted in the wind as they left Bath. The innkeeper at Marlborough asked if they would like fires in their bedrooms, and Cuby accepted for hers. There had only been two travelling with them inside the coach, which was a six-seater, and these two, an elderly couple, were at another and distant table in the dining room. It was not a favourable month for travel, and the inn was half empty.

They ate a brace of tench and then a roasted shoulder of mutton with caper sauce. Rhenish wine but not sweet. A plum pudding to follow, which Cuby refused.

'You are not hungry?' Jeremy asked.

'I have eaten *well*. I don't eat so much as this at home. Fortunately, or I should become fat!'

'I know you have never been a big eater.'

'Oh, I *enjoy* my food. Just not so much of it. It is different for you, who are a man and so tall.'

'The food here at least is better than last night.'

470

'What time do we reach London tomorrow?'

'Late, I think. Even if all goes well.'

'Should it not go well?'

'One always fears that a wheel might break or a horse go lame or . . .' He did not go into his private fears.

She pushed her hair back from her forehead. 'What plans do you have, Jeremy? You have not told me them.'

'This coach stops at the Crown & Anchor. In Fleet Street, I think. I hear it is adequate and I thought we could stay there for a night or so, to save the trouble of seeking another inn so late.'

'And then?'

'I shall make the most urgent inquiries about obtaining a special licence. I believe for an officer it can be got in twenty-four hours.'

She said: 'You had not made all these arrangements on the way down, then, assuming I should be with you on the way back?'

'I assumed *nothing*! Good God! Even my hope was barely alive.'

'It did not seem so when you invaded my bedroom on Thursday. You seemed so – *purposeful*.'

He half smiled. 'I sought to take you, if not by force, then perhaps by force of moral argument.'

'I assure you your moral argument had no effect on me at all!'

'What did have, then?'

She picked up a crumb of bread from her plate, rolled it between her fingers. 'Just you.'

He said: 'My love. My Cuby. My dearest Cuby.'

Her black eyebrows were knitted over the startling hazel eyes.

'Jeremy, I have been thinking a lot.'

'I was afraid so. I noticed it.'

'You must not joke.'

'God knows it is no joke to me, when I fear your thoughts!'

'Why should you fear my thoughts?'

'Why not, when all through they have been the enemy of

my hopes, the stumbling block to all my attempts to love you?'

She seemed touched by this. 'Perhaps you are right. Perhaps I have always been too – material, too steady-headed for my own good. But I do not think you need fear my thoughts any more. After all, have I not come with you on this – this adventure, this *crazy* adventure, which no level-headed person could decently justify? Am I not mad, running away with you like a romantic schoolgirl when, had I chosen to become engaged to marry you and done so in due course, my family could hardly have stopped me! It is – this adventure is really without rhyme or reason!'

'That is what I am afraid you will still decide.'

She looked sulky for a moment. 'I have been thinking over my life on this long journey, especially my life during the last three years since I met you. Perhaps all the jogging and jolting has helped me to concentrate! I have been thinking of how we first met. It – it seems to me that from the moment we met, when I shielded you from the attention of the gaugers, you never had – any doubts.'

'About you? No. Never any doubts.'

'Perhaps I should not have had.'

'You had so many other claims on you – on your loyalty and your love.'

She frowned across the low room with its smoky lanterns hanging from blackened beams, the brasswork flickering in the light of the open fire, a parrot clawing its way round a cage.

'You knew I was fully prepared to marry Valentine Warleggan.'

'I knew.'

'Clearly it injured your feelings for me!'

'It injured them a great deal, but it did not change them.'

'And you knew even before I met Valentine that I was expecting to marry money and therefore could not marry you.'

'Yes.'

'Do you remember I said to you once that I could not marry for preference and go away somewhere to some other part of the country and watch from afar as the house and the lands were sold and the Trevanions vanished from a countryside which had known them for centuries?'

'You said that, yes.'

'Is that not precisely what I am doing now?'

'I think so. I trust it will not happen to your house and lands that way, but I pray you keep to the same mind.'

'Do not pray so, for you need not. I cannot explain it to my reasonable self, except in one quite unreasonable way. Which is that I think I must love you, Jeremy. Even though I thought I did not!'

He slowly pushed his plate away.

'Finish your pudding,' she said.

'I cannot now! Do you think anyone would mind if I shouted aloud?'

'I should.' She put her hand out and touched his. 'But, Jeremy, how could it be otherwise? How else could you have drawn me after you in this – this escapade, against all the logics that my brain put up? And if I love you – as it seems you love me – then I have treated you very ill – have I not? – all this time, pretending to myself and to you that it was only some petty little attraction between us that would fade if ignored . . .'

'Does it matter now, my dearest Cuby, that we are at last together? Does anything *else* matter at *all*?'

'It does to me.' The crescents round her mouth moved into a half smile. 'I am sorry if I seem – analytical. Believe me, it is not as bad as that. But all this jolting . . . I think . . .' He had seldom seen her so hesitant. 'I think I need to show you some proof of my – of my love. Perhaps even proof, if you want it, that I am not going to change my mind. You see, I seem never to have had faith in you, never done anything, never given you any *trust* or *confidence* or *belief*.'

The waiter came and asked them if they would take tea. Cuby shook her head. Jeremy shook his head.

When he had gone, bearing away plates, Jeremy said:

'I need no proof but the proof of your being here, and your promise that you will stay. What else do you suggest?'

The candles flickered in her breath as she said: 'I don't think now I can suggest it.'

'Pray do.'

She raised her head and looked at him, face colouring. 'I think I would like you to take me as your wife tonight.'

He looked back at her, swallowed, looked again.

She said: 'Pray do not *stare*.'

He said: '*Because* we are not yet married?'

'*Before* we are married, yes. Do you understand what I mean?'

There was a lot of noise and laughter from the next room, where the tapsters were busy. But there was no sound in this room for what seemed a long time.

Jeremy said: 'I have no words.'

'Say no if you think no.'

'I have no words except to say yes. No words to tell you what I feel.'

Cuby said: 'Dear Jeremy, remember, I am only of the same *stuff* as you; I am mortal, flesh and blood, ordinary, and – untutored.'

'My love . . .'

'Other women you have known . . .'

'No woman was ever like you. No woman ever will be.'

The innkeeper came across, rubbing his hands on his green apron. Had the lady and gentleman supped to their satisfaction? Was there anything more the lady and gentleman required? Because of the early start in the morning, hot water would brought up at 6.30 a.m. Would that be satisfactory?

Everything was satisfactory, said Jeremy. He had, he said, never had greater cause for satisfaction. The innkeeper went away looking faintly surprised.

Cuby said: 'I cannot explain to you why this seems right to me –'

'I can explain why it seems right to *me*. But do I need to? Dearest Cuby.' And then: 'Has this been in your mind all day? Is this why you asked for a fire to be lighted in your room?'

'I did *not* ask for a fire to be lighted! I did not *refuse* one!'

474

'And this is why?'

She bit her lip. 'Pray do not ask me any more questions.'

He said: 'It is hard not to when the answers are so beautiful and fine.'

IV

In the night she touched him, and he instantly awoke.

'Jeremy, if I wish to keep my reputation for another day it is time you left.'

'Have we slept long?'

'I don't know. But there is a faint light behind the curtains. Whether it is moonlight . . .'

'No. It must be dawn.' He struggled to get out of bed, kissed her bare shoulder. That stopped him for a while. He began to sip at her skin as if it were some pale liquid to be savoured.

'My love,' he said. 'Did I – I hope I did not hurt you.'

'No. But little. Nothing.'

The fire was out. A solitary candle still guttered, half an hour from its end. The dusty green velvet curtains of the bed half hid her as he began hurriedly to dress, to collect what he need not put on. Buttons clinked, leather creaked.

She watched him with big grave eyes, her black hair feathering the pillow.

A cock crew. He came back to the bed.

'We are liable to be roused any moment.'

'I know.'

He kissed her. 'I wish I knew the Song of Solomon.'

She suddenly smiled, all her face radiant. 'We'll read it together.'

'Tonight?'

'Tonight.'

'And Jeremy,' she said.

'Yes?' He was at the door.

'I trust you still wish to marry me.'

Chapter Eleven

Ross and Demelza read their son's letter standing in the doorway of Nampara in the late January sunshine.

'He is *happy*,' she said. 'Is that not wonderful? I am so *very* delighted!'

'Thank God it came good for him,' Ross said. 'If it had not it would have ruined his life.'

'And your advice was right!'

'He did not take it.'

'Enough. He took it enough.'

'So now we have our two eldest children wed. *We* should be happy.'

'Are we not?'

'Yes, in this respect we measure our content by theirs. God, I envy Jeremy!'

'For what?'

He took her arm. 'For being at the beginning of it all.'

She sighed. 'I know.'

'Are you — better about Jeremy now?' he asked after a moment.

'Better? In what way?' She was startled at his perception.

'You have been depressed about him, haven't you? Worried in some way.'

'Yes, Ross, I've been worried in some way.'

'And this news helps?'

'It helps a lot!'

'But not altogether? There's something else?'

'Perhaps there need not be now. Perhaps there never will need to be.'

'You don't wish to tell me what it is?'

'No, Ross. I could not. It is too — too queasy.'

'Something to do with your instinct perhaps?'

'Yes, perhaps. Feelings I had.'

'No longer have.'

'I have forgotten them! All I think now is how wonderful it is that they have come together!'

'Amen.' He squeezed her arm. 'I think we're specially lucky, aren't we, lucky in having two younger children to be coming along in their place.'

'That's true.'

'You're very thin.'

'I am not at all thin, Ross. Even at your age, you cannot wish for a fudgy-faced wife.'

'Even at my age I do not wish you to be fading away.'

'I am *not* fading away. Believe me.'

'We must buy some scales ... You really liked her, Demelza?'

''Tis hard to say too much on so short an acquaintance, but I thought she had great spirit. We — seemed to understand each other.'

'So I noticed. On the whole I agree. She has great spirit and charm. I cannot quite forgive her for being so mercenary. But I suppose — according to one's standards — one could see a certain spirit and nobility even in that.'

Demelza put the letter in her pocket and looked over her garden.

'Those *winds* last month. They were so vindictive. Look at our wallflowers! Although we've done our best with them they'll never be right now.'

'It's the penalty of living where we do. After all, there are compensations.'

'And the hollyhocks were a *calamity* last year. I wondered whether to give them a miss, try perhaps columbines, just for a change.'

'You haven't sown any seed, have you? They're biennials, you know.'

'I do know. But Caroline has some spare plants.'

'Well, as you say, it would be a change. But it wouldn't be quite like you not to have a few hollyhocks, would it.'

'Oh, well.'

She ventured out into the garden but soon drew back into the shelter of the porch again.

'Is it not wonderful this news! Where will they live? I mean when Jeremy comes out of the army.'

'Heavens, I have no idea. You're jumping ahead. We might enlarge the Gatehouse.'

'Enlarge it?'

'Double it in size. It is very small. Perhaps some of the miners who are going to be out of work when Grace closes could be employed in this way. We could give this to Jeremy and Cuby as a wedding present.'

'A lovely idea! Do you think Clowance would mind?'

'Mind? Why?'

'Well, we offered it to her and Stephen just as it was.'

'I'm sure she would not. Clowance is our daughter, and one expects her husband to provide for her. This is the other way round. But it would never be meant as an indication of any different regard.'

Demelza gave a little skip of pleasure. 'Are we *wealthy* again, Ross?'

'We would be if we closed Wheal Grace. But I cannot do that except little by little, a level at a time, giving men a chance to find other work, or make adjustments to their lives, possibly take more on at Leisure. That way we lose a part of our profits, but are still better off than for some while.'

'Rebuilding the Gatehouse will cost much.'

'We can take our time. I doubt if Jeremy will come out of the army for another twelvemonth, and I suspect Cuby will stay with him wherever he goes.'

'Could I spend more on my garden?'

'Of course. What do you want to do?'

'First raise the wall at least another three feet. Did you see that walled garden at Place House?'

'No.'

'Selina took us out there after dinner. They are in just as exposed a position as we are, but the peach trees growing on the walls! And these new things, these hydrangeas, that I thought would only live indoors!'

'Three feet you shall have. Though we'll have to match the stone so that it won't show. Anything else?'

'You're teasing me!'

'Not at all.'

'Then I would like a proper music teacher for Isabella-Rose. Don't laugh, for she has some sort of overwelling music in her if only it can be harnessed and trained.'

'She should go away to school, my love. Just for a year or two. She's twelve and a half, and already far too bright for Mrs Kemp.'

Demelza pulled at a curl in her hair, twisting it round her finger and then releasing it. 'I was feared you might say that.'

'Is it not true?'

'I do not know if I can spare her just yet.'

'Well, soon perhaps. I think it would do her good.'

'Clowance ran away.'

'Only twice. And was no worse for it.'

The wind was sneaking round the corner, and Demelza turned to go in. As Ross opened the door she said: 'Had you some school in mind?'

'Mrs Hemple's in Truro has a very good reputation. And being near St Mary's Church they hear some good singing. Take part in it too, I believe, at times.'

They went in.

Demelza kicked off her shoes and put them under a chair, sat on the chair and thoughtfully pulled on one slipper and then the other.

She said: 'Can good come out of evil, Ross?'

'What? . . . Of course. And the other way round. More often, I fear, the other way round. Why do you ask?'

'And can you profit, truly profit from some wrongful act . . . I mean, can happiness, do you think, come about when maybe you – you haven't quite done what you ought to – or where what you have done might be expected to spoil it?'

Ross stood with his hand on the latch of the dining-room door. 'I don't know, my dear. Who knows what is deserved? But why do you ask me this now? It's not easy to answer theoretical questions, and it's not quite like you to ask them.'

'It was just thoughts passing through my head.'

Ross grunted and opened the door, passed inside, turned and saw Demelza at the door watching him.

He said: 'What did Jeremy mean about the loving cup?'

Demelza hesitated. 'Oh, nothing in particular, I believe. He seemed to take a fancy to it when he was here, and I offered it to him but he refused.'

'And now he wants it?'

'Yes.'

'I wonder why. How is it in any way connected with him?'

'I think he came to look on it as some sort of an omen.'

'Not like him really. I mean . . .'

Demelza thought a moment. Trouble again crossed her brow and then passed. She said: 'Well, is it not suitable? A loving cup to bring two people together?'